"Granted is like Come True's hotter, more experienced brother. This genie sequel has everything we loved from book one, with sparkly new adventures, uneasy alliances, enemies-to-friends, quirky characters and all the banter. You'll laugh, you'll scream. You'll want to throw your book against the wall, and you'll be counting down the days until the next installment of this amazing series is here!"

—H.R. Truelove
Author of Alter

"A spectacular sequel to Come True! Granted is filled with the snarky, sexy, and swoon-worthy characters you've come to love (and love to hate). Brindi Quinn has done a fabulous job on delivering an intriguing story filled with charm and complexity, while balancing humor with heart."

—Nicole Northwood
Author of In Flames

"Brindi Quinn is a genie genius! [. . .] If you're a fan of Come True, like I am, this next installment won't leave you disappointed. It's such a fun action-packed story that will make your mouth drop. [. . .] These characters are hard not to fall in love with, and the balance between the sarcastic banter and those deep raw moments make waiting for the next book very difficult."

—Adina Chiles
Author of Secrets of a Rose

"This book, y'all!!! What a freaking roller coaster. If you wished for multiple hot AF genies to thirst over, it was definitely Granted. [. . .] Everything in this book was done right. [. . .] It's a must read for fans of romcom, fantasy and paranormal romance—it has a bit of everything."

—Stephanie E. Donohue
Author of Windsong

"What's better than one sexy genie? Two of course! This book gave me All. The. Feels. And my poor heart didn't know what to do as I read. I loved all the sass, banter, humor, and tension. What a fantastic continuation of this series. You won't want to miss this one. Trust me."

—Whitney L. Spradling
Author of Of Flames and Curses

"A super fun sequel that had me addicted from page one! This had all that I expected after reading book 1! Quirk, swoon, twists, a very cool world, and lovely dialogue! [. . .] I'm already anxious to read the next book!"

—Candace Robinson
Author of Tin

Granted

A BOMB-ASS GENIE UNIVERSE

Efatall the Moondropper Realm

Célesteen the Celestial Realm

Makaya the Djinn Realm

Auearyon the Fairy Realm

Earth the Human Realm

Aphrotica the Nymph Realm

Hannethis the Greenie Realm

Wragaros the Zombie Realm

Bluvespea the Mermaid Realm

Drecconata the Vampire Realm

Dhiant the Reaper Realm

Nedril the Goblin Realm

Granted

A BOMB-ASS GENIE SEQUEL

Come True Book Two

BRINDI QUINN

Granted
Copyright © 2022 by Brindi Quinn
Second Edition, 2024

Evermore

Published by Evermore, an imprint of Never & Ever Publishing | @neverandeverbooks
Edited by Meg Dailey | @thedaileyeditor
Cover artwork by Em Ryn Art | @emryn_art
Cover typography by Victoria Cooper Art
Bottle graphic by Dinah Draws | @dinahdraws
Map by Centaur Maps | @centaurmaps
Interior formatting by Brindi Quinn via Vellum

This is a work of fiction. Names, characters, brands, trademarks, places, and incidents either are the products of the author's imagination or are used fictitiously. Any resemblance to actual events, locales, organizations, or persons, living or dead, is entirely coincidental and beyond the intent of either the author or the publisher.

All rights reserved, which includes the right to reproduce this book or portions thereof in any form whatsoever except as provided by U.S. Copyright Law.

Original publication date: December 14, 2022
Illustrated Paperback ISBN: 978-1-949222-64-7
Standard Paperback ISBN: 978-1-949222-82-1
Special Edition Hardcover ISBN: 978-1-958673-29-4
Standard Hardcover ISBN: 978-1-949222-65-4

Contents

A BOMB-ASS GENIE PROLOGUE

1. Momsicle — 3
2. Uninvited — 19
3. A Little Luck — 39

A BOMB-ASS GENIE SEQUEL

4. Faux Leather — 59
5. The Black City — 69
6. Magical Seed — 77
7. Evangeline Tower — 87
8. A Large Fucking Bird — 97
9. The Rellies — 109
10. The Other Side — 123
11. The Experienced Brother — 139
12. The Cruel Brother — 153
13. Prisms — 169
14. The Golden Brother — 181
15. What Happened in the Hall — 189
16. Ambush — 207
17. Cartoon Sheets — 225
18. The Truth about Arrik — 245
19. Very Lucky — 255
20. Smoky Little Swish — 267
21. That Rainbow Bitch — 277
22. That Green-Eyed Bitch — 289
23. Always and For— — 303
24. Lace and Ink — 317

A BOMB-ASS GENIE EPILOGUE

25. Up All Night — 337

Acknowledgments	343
About Brindi Quinn	345
Paranormal & Dystopian Romance Books by Brindi Quinn	347
Epic Fantasy Romance Books by Brindi Quinn	348
Young Adult Romance Books by Brindi Quinn	349

This book contains sexual content and drug use inappropriate for a younger audience. This book also contains a hearty dose of F-bombs and other adult language that may be offensive to some readers. Triggers include: swearing, body image issues, implied (non-graphic) animal cruelty, infertility, fantasy racism, drinking, smoking, and fantasy violence.

Granted is Book 2 in the Come True series and a direct continuation of the story. Do not be swayed by the tatted hottie on the cover. This book should not be read first.

To my MTP tribe and all your fucking numnums, love buttons, and corn. Thank you for giving me a safe space to be my weird self. I love you guys!

A Bomb-Ass Genie
Prologue

CHAPTER 1
Momsicle

An ambrosia-scented breeze compels the curtains to dance and coil, whispering of the great big magical world beyond these narrow windows. Am I the only one who wants to run and fling myself over that fancy fucking balcony? Not because I want to end myself—I know my genie would save me anyway—I just want to feel it, the freedom of leaping into clear blue skies over rows of obedient flowers, if only for a moment.

"How do I look?" the genie who would save me asks from the opposite side of the room, where he stands before a heavy mirror in a carved golden frame stuck to the wall by either magic or cement.

The answer to a question like that from a mouth like his is always: *Fine as hell.*

"Meh, you'll do."

He leers because we aren't untethered yet, and he can feel my body's reaction to him. "Come on, *Master*. Can't spare a little *flattery* for one day? You know I'm nervous as shit. I don't do well with parents."

Genie boy is nervous. Because he wants to prove himself by gaining the approval of someone he's vastly overestimating. It's cute to see him struggle. Maybe he's right about me being a sadist.

For the occasion, he's wearing a preppy little sweater over a navy button up and the world's whitest sneakers. Quite chic for a boy who prefers gray sweatpants and nothing else.

I set my hands to his shoulders the way wise fathers do on wedding days. "You look like a laird, Vel."

Gaze blue enough to cause frostbite in summer, he reveals the grin he's been brewing.

"But I'm really not very sympathetic," I tell him, brushing away nonexistent dust. "After the way I met your dad. It may have been the most mortifying moment of my entire life."

"Do you mean nearly passing out from downing that hookah, or that whole 'him using you to draw out my heart's desire' thing?"

"*All of it.*"

And I haven't gotten a chance to regain any of the face I lost, either. Daddy Djinn has been sending his bow-tied butler to do his bidding all week.

All week. Velis and I haven't even been a couple two weeks yet.

Explains all the sex.

"Stop it," he says, unbuttoning a collar criminally restricting his tantalizing neck. "Stop distracting me with those desires you've got *writhing* around in there. If we do all that, we'll be late."

Whatever. He's initiated two of any three encounters over the past few days anyway. And that last one, when he popped in to visit me in the shower, wasting countless souls on needless teleportation—

I raise a brow at him, conjuring up vivid imagery of the steam and sweat and those water droplets sliding down his hot, hot abs.

His brow, on the other hand, gives out like a man on the verge of failing a test. "I could freeze time," he mutters, bartering with himself, abstracted by the thought of us boning. "It's hard, but I could freeze it."

No, we're not wasting those poor influencers' sacrifices just because we're horny.

"Come on," I say with a laugh. "My mom's homemade bread

will satisfy urges you didn't even know you had. We'll save whatever's *writhing* in me for dessert."

He resembles a deflated balloon as I abandon him to move through the inviting curtains and out onto the veranda overlooking the magical djinn gardens stretching over the backyard of a magical djinn manor. I take hold of the smooth stone banister doing its best to keep me from the great beyond and let the wind finally have its way with my hair.

Yup. Strange but true. This is life.

And finally. Finally, finally, after a year of self-inflicted isolation for a crime I didn't commit, I'm going home to hug my mother, and to introduce her to my . . .

Boyfriend? Genie?

Velis. I'm going to introduce her to my Velis.

From behind, my Velis slips both arms around my waist and sets his chin to my shoulder, enjoying the beauty I see in the fantasy landscape. He's quiet, his breathing content. These moments are my favorite. The moments when he holds me and silently tries to convince himself I'm real.

"Humans get sad when there's no sun, right?" he murmurs like it's a secret.

"Some do," I say. "Why?"

He squeezes me closer. "It feels good to be in your light, Master."

He's too charming for his own good.

My lips graze his chin as I twist to seek out his face. "There is one thing, Vel. One thing you might consider changing about your appearance." I pause to make sure my delivery is right. "What if you went with your natural hair?"

He pulls away to inspect me. "You want me to look like a nymph when I meet your mom?"

"I want you to look like whatever you want to look like when you meet my mom."

He stares, puncturing me with wide-blown pupils, as if working to understand what I like about him. And then he smooths one hand through the dusky blue roots to drive them blond. I had suspected that was what he would pick if given the choice. I've come to learn he feels a little naughty wearing his hair that way since he wasn't allowed to for so long.

"I really fucking love you." Every pore of him, every tastebud on his tongue, imparts the weight, the truth, the hurt of a statement like that. "I swear to Maka, I'm going to make all your wishes come true, Dolly Jones. Every desire you've got in there, I'm going to fulfill." He closes in on me, his shadow intent on devouring mine, the rest of him no longer caring about the consequences of giving in to love and lust.

I put my hands to his chest to create a wall between us. "Let's just start with meeting my mom, Romeo."

"Who the fuck is Romeo?"

It's so hard to tell whether he's being cute or serious. I've begun to assume it's the former.

A slight tug at his mouth betrays it's the former.

Knew it.

He steals me to his chest and blips us away, smirking the entire way, to a place far less grandiose than the fantasyland manor we've been shacking up in all week.

A simple rambler on the bend of a cul-de-sac with aged oak trees that rain down their weight in acorns each fall. It's like they do so just to piss off my mom. And me, by association. Mom used to make me vacuum them up with a shop vac.

It's all even less impressive than I remember. The peeling paint and the cracked driveway. I wait for Velis to realize how modest it is, expect him to ask if all these houses are part of a larger complex. Surely my mom's house is smaller than the stables where they keep his family's unicorns or whatever. Only—

"It's just how it looks in your desires," he says with glimmering affection as he scans the tree limb where my tire swing used to hang and the doghouse that's been here since we moved in, even though we've never owned a dog. The sky smells like earliest summer, the grass its most refreshing shade of green. "I can just picture the different versions of you scrounging around in the dirt here," he adds with a chuckle.

That's... it? No teasing?

"C-come on." I take his arm to pull him after me, stopping at the base of the steps to gift him a quick but intentional kiss. He absorbs it like he wants more but is unsure what he's done to deserve it. He always processes these situations like he really is an alien taking records of Earth, like he's learning the way a human brain works and liking what he sees.

He analyzes me like he wants to pick me apart.

I lead him up the cement steps where I'd spend my summers sketching the neighbors in all their Midwesterner glory. Nothing more inviting than a slab of hot concrete on the ass. I used to sit out here like a Gila monster, bathing in the sun and popping frozen grapes into my mouth, thinking I was hot shit in my braces and ugly bangs.

Hot, because a teenage alien was into me.

Whenever I think of him that way, it makes my stomach flutter like I'm twelve.

I ring the bell twice and wait. Mom will be a minute. She's probably scrambling to make sure everything looks presentable.

It's weird we didn't arrive in a car, right?

We'll tell her we took a Lyft from the airport.

But... it IS weird we didn't bring a bag.

"Can you conjure a suitcase, quick?" I whisper at Velis.

A dart of darkness hits him. "Is that a *wish*?"

He'll take any opportunity he can get.

"I wish you'd fabricate a suitcase, *doll*."

His body shivers, and his eyes light up as a large duffle materializes over his shoulder. "Thank you, Mast—" He stops himself as the front door to my childhood home swings open to reveal the hobbit residing in this hovel: a squat, hyper woman with curly hair and a love for yard sales.

"Lizzy!" Mom pushes Velis out of the way to tackle me with all the love she's stored up over the last year plus.

"*Lizzy?*" repeats the slighted genie with laser focus.

"My middle name is Elizabeth," I spurt, blue-faced between squeezes. "She calls me Lizzy sometimes."

"*Interesting.*"

I don't like when he *purrs* like that—like he's locking the information away for future leverage.

"Mom!" I scold, wriggling out of arms that pull and nuzzle to make up for a year of absence. "Knock it off and come meet Velis!"

She doesn't smell . . . boozy. That's good. She's had some issues with that since Dad died. Never anything violent or unruly —just, I've had to tuck her in passed out on the back porch more times than I can count. We don't need Velis seeing that side of her.

Mom releases me but doesn't stray far, looking around me toward where waits a hot, sun-kissed creature who seems to seep pheromones from his oil-less pores.

I prepared her for this, told her he was a babe, but apparently, I wasn't convincing enough over the phone.

"*That's* Velis?" she says rather rudely before raking him over in search of some obvious flaw. "*That's* your boyfriend?"

Velis perks forward, as if he's been waiting for an opening. "Fiancé, actually," he says, eyeing up my mother with hunger for approval while he extends a hand.

Fiancé? I mean, I guess, technically, I did agree to become his human bride. But we haven't really talked about that since the day I got 'low' off hookah in his dad's drawing room.

Mom lets Velis's hand go untaken as she sizes him up, flashing suspicious eyes from me to Vel and then back to me before landing calloused gardener's hands on my shoulders. "Dolly Elizabeth Jones, are you *pregnant?*"

"What?!" I hop away from her. "NO. Why the hell would you think that?" I glance down at my squishy middle.

"*This* guy wants to marry you?" She says it like Velis isn't even there.

Ugh. I let my head fall to hide my face in strands of dark hair. "I know, Mom. I warned you he was . . . that he looks like that."

Velis's head pokes into the scene: "Looks like what?"

No, we aren't starting that up again. I shoo him away.

"I'm not pregnant, Mom, and this isn't a joke. Velis is my boyf —m-my . . . He's . . ." I waffle through it, to Velis's unreadable observation. *"We like each other."* I flare my eyes and flex my jaw to prod her into civil nicety.

"Oh. OH!" Mom finally realizes her rudeness and accepts Velis's offered hand minutes too late. "I'm Marcy. You'll have to forgive me—this is all a little out of character for my daughter. You are, of course, welcome here, Velis."

A spark of excitement zings across Velis as he raises the back of my mother's hand to his perfect mouth and tips his head forward darkly. "I've been *dying* to meet you, Mrs. Jones."

Woah. *I* didn't get an introduction like that.

Mom isn't prepared for it either. She blinks at him, freckles displayed over flushed cheeks. Yes, Mom. I know the genie is attractive. Yes, Mom, I know he's a charmer.

She slips away from him as tactfully as she can and then props the door open with her backside to usher us in. "I hope you two are hungry. Supper's in the oven."

The smell of it hits me as we cross the threshold—some casserole or another, with cheese and hidden vegetables and crumbly bits on top. It isn't strong enough, though, to mask the true scent of this place.

We may not be fancy, and I may never have lived in one of the swanky developments on the other side of town where they hand out the good candy on Halloween, but our house always, always smelled good. The scent of baked potpourri will marinate into my clothes and hair, tagging along long after we leave.

My mom is a bit of an organized clutterer, and our house is a dragon's nest of the things that remind her of the people and places she loves. The version Velis created for me back in my apartment was an older one. Mom's since upgraded the couch and swapped out some of the wall hangings. Velis doesn't note the differences as he takes my elbow and tugs me close enough to drown out the scent of childhood with the smell of boyish manhood.

Our arrows touching means I'm like a monster in heat around his chemicals polluting the air.

Not the time.

"What is it?" I ask, hushed so that my suspicious mother won't hear.

His response is delayed. "Is it . . . weird if I call her 'Mom'?"

Maybe the last thing I'd expected, but when I size him up, I find he's asking in earnest. Oh. That's so . . . cute. Is it because he no longer has a mom of his own? Or is he just trying to get in good with mine?

"It's weird, right?" he says, doubting himself when I don't answer right away.

It is weird, and my mom will definitely think it's weird, but . . .

"Call her whatever you want, Vel."

After, he shines.

Adorable.

"I'm going to give Vel the tour quick, okay, Mom? Are we staying in my old room?"

One final time, my mother probes the space between us, looking for a punchline that doesn't exist. "Sheets are clean, Lizzy. I put extra toilet paper in the bathroom down there."

I scurry away, Velis in tow, to give my mother a chance to process. I did tell her I was bringing home a new boyfriend. I did not tell her I was engaged to a hunky mythical being. Damage control will be necessary once we get a minute alone.

The genie in question is poking at shelves and craning his neck to see around furniture like he's at an amusement park. Can this really be all that interesting to him? He's been in lots of human dwellings over the past few months. I'm sure this one's somewhere near the bottom.

As we descend the carpeted steps into the depths below, the temperature steadily drops, offering up a new aroma of laundry and earth. I always liked sleeping down here, cool and cave-like—though I was never a fan of the centipedes competing for dominion over the space.

My bedroom is off the far end of the family room and opposite a room housing boxes of Christmas decorations and lonely second-hand workout equipment my mom has never used. It would be a workout itself clearing off that treadmill.

Velis casts eyes to the sofa that's seen a hundred sleepovers and the rug that's endured hours of shitty dance routines stolen from online videos. He drums his fingertips along the trim of the bathroom door as we pass like it's marble in a museum.

Why is he so *invested* in everything? He had to have known I'd come from a place like this. He's seen it in my heart, so what's he collecting all that data for?

"This is the place that made you," he muses, turning to show me the fondness covering his face. "I can smell you in the walls here, Dolly."

I swallow the girlishness bubbling in my throat and draw him after me, to a destination that feels like a pandora's box of memories.

My mecca.

I flip the switch long disconnected from the center bulb. Instead, stringed lights border the ceiling to cast humble glow over walls coated in my favorite sketches. Books too good to let go but not cherished enough to bring with me to college are settled neatly in shelves I've had forever, the old wood covered in stickers of my favorite bands. My bed is only a full, so we'll have to snuggle closer than usual tonight, and because of my thing about beds, it's set slightly away from the wall, without a headboard and with sheets frequently laundered.

It isn't much, but Velis is right. It's like my scent is in the walls here.

Velis sets down the duffle and begins to meander without a word, skimming over sketches from various eras of my life. Meanwhile, I'm scanning my room in search of embarrassing artifacts I may have left behind. I wasn't a cool teenager. I likely have a retainer or a diary out in the open and ripe to be picked by someone who needs no ammunition. I stash a framed photo of me and a high school ex into the top drawer of my dresser. Why I thought a tacky prom photo worthy of being framed is beyond my current self.

Evidence hidden, I scrounge over the rest of the dresser in

search of blackmail fodder, but I've misplaced my focus, and I realize it the moment Velis says:

"Wait—is this ME?"

Oh shit. I forgot about *that* sketch. Conveniently at eye level with my bed so that I could fantasize about his random school appearances before falling asleep.

"It's not you," I lie.

"This is definitely me." Velis rips the paper from the wall and holds it to the light. "This is the outfit I was wearing when I hopped back in time. But . . . what are these things poking out of my head?"

Oh hell.

"Babe?"

My hands find my face to distort my voice: "Antennae."

Velis cocks his head. "Like what bugs have?"

Face still buried, I fight the truth about to reveal itself. "Like what aliens have."

I can hear the evil in his voice, low, as he simpers, "Dolly, Dolly, Dolly." The creak of weight on springs notifies that he's settled onto my mattress. "So then, when you lived in this room, did you ever think I would be sitting on your bed?"

My skin sears with hell's heat as I relive the crush I had on him in another life. No, I never thought he'd be sitting on my bed. No, I never thought we would do the things we've done together.

I lift my face to tell him off and am met with a demanding hand around my waist that easily tosses me onto the bed with magical precision.

"Did you ever dream I'd be on top of you, thinking about the way the inside of your mouth tastes?" He gives me the fullest extent of his seduction as he looms over me, bathed in shadows broken only by the sky-blue gleam of his eyes.

"Fuck you."

His mouth twitches. "Now? You sure?"

I should wish a double chin to sprout. Maybe even a third.

"Mean," he coos. "Why are you always so mean to me, Master?"

Because being around him floods me with aggression. I want to dig my nails into his back. We are most certainly going to end up fucking in my childhood bed, and there's got to be at least some level of depravity in that, right?

His hold is strong enough that it makes me feel smaller and weaker than I am. It's not like I want to be weak. I'll never *become* weak. But . . . am I allowed to find this hot? After what I've been through, I feel like something of a hypocrite to admit how exciting it is to be in a compromising position when the one in control is him.

Because he has my trust.

"I love it, Dolly." The front he's putting up gradually begins to recede into something gentler as he watches my defensiveness melt. "I love seeing this dorky side of you. It's not a turn-off, if that's what you're worried about."

I am helpless under his stare as it pins me down like a collected butterfly and searches the intricacy of my wings.

"It's weird having you here," I utter, reaching up to push at hair that spills out from behind his ear. "Like two worlds converging. I love it too."

It feels like it's pulling us closer, bonding us tighter, blending our lives. I want to feel his skin against mine, in the dark, hear him give up his power by whispering vulnerable things.

But because I know my anxious mother is one floor above us, likely toking on her secret stash of cigarettes she saves for when she needs them most, I force my desires elsewhere.

"Y . . . yeah," Velis says when he reads them. "Probably a good idea." He lowers his divine mouth to my forehead before rolling off me and offering a gentlemen's hand, which he swiftly uses to bring my knuckles to his mouth, like a prince. "Because you wanted one of these earlier," he adds with a wink.

Cheesy.

And I'm cheesy for being unable to stow the raiding grin it causes me.

When we return to the surface, the fan above the stove is running. I knew it. Mom snuck a quick one, and she doesn't want me to know it. She hurries to busy herself with tossing a salad as I finish out Velis's tour—the addition that leads to a porch and fire pit, the office, the guest room. There isn't all that much to see, but Velis takes it all in prudently, peering into doorways with one hand settled on my back.

It's surreal that he's here, and fuck if I'm not feeling *giddy* over it all. But my mom is over there stewing and fretting enough to make those wooden spoons assault our dinner salad with particular fervor.

"Hey, our cat Steve is out back if you want to go say hi," I tell Velis. "I should probably have a quick chat with my mom."

He takes the hint to make himself scarce as I set my attention on the timebomb ticking in our presence. My mother ignores me when I ask if she needs help with anything, instead watching Velis venture away through the window over the sink before spinning to me with judgmental hands on judgmental hips.

"What's going on, Lizzy? You aren't really getting married, are you? You mention nothing about this guy all year and now you expect me to believe you're MARRYING him?"

No, I didn't actually plan on telling her that bit.

Thanks, *Vel*.

I suck in a breath. "Look, the whole marriage thing is complicated, Mom. His . . . culture is kind of gung-ho, and my acceptance is tentative. I really do like this one, but we haven't been together that long, and you know I'd pull out of it if I started having doubts."

My mother, again watching Velis sniff out our cat in the back garden, is stuck on another detail. "Where is he from? Is he Brazilian?"

Brazilian?

"Y-yup, he's Brazilian, and you know they've got some weird customs there."

A lie. And I apologize to Brazilians everywhere.

My mom returns to the salad, slicing bleeding strawberries through the center with a paring knife she trusts enough to push against her thumb. "I can tell you like each other—he can barely keep his hands off you—and I can see why you'd become infatuated with him after what you went through with Jim, but I have serious reservations about the rest of it. I know you don't want to hear this first thing coming home, but I have to say it: be careful, Dolly. People don't let their true selves show this early on. You've got to dig away at them."

"He's a good guy, Mom. I know that much. And I'm always careful."

Except for, you know, all the times I haven't been.

"But I appreciate your concern, and I promise you I won't do anything stupid," I add.

Such as agreeing to depart for the land of nymphs to gain approval to become Velis's bride and lady to his magical estate.

Mom pokes the knife in my direction. *"Don't* get pregnant. I mean it, Lizzy. No grandbabies for at least another five years."

I'm not interested in spawning gremlins this early in the game. Maybe not ever.

"IF this marriage thing gets serious, you'll be the first to know, okay? I promise. For now, just think of him as my boyfriend. And I know he seems . . ." I turn up my palms, not willing to say *too hot for good intentions*. "But he's actually really sweet and encouraging. Just, try to get to know him a little bit, please?" I wait for her to break with the minutest nod. Good. I set a cheek to her shoulder and a hand around her side. "I missed you, Mom. It feels good to be home."

My mother accepts the gesture by leaning her head against mine, still watching Velis as he scoops up our cat and holds it out like he's presenting a newborn to the animal kingdom. "Next time, it had better not be a year, or so help me, Lizzy."

"I know. I was having a hard time for a while there. Velis actually helped get me out of it."

She doesn't like that. "You don't need a boy to solve your problems."

"I know. I don't need him; I just like having him around," I say.

Whatever other lectures my squat mother has for me are cut

short as the amber sky, previously clear, gives an unannounced crack on the horizon.

"Was that thunder?" Mom pushes over the sink to inspect the sky, paring knife clenched in her fist. "It isn't supposed to rain all week."

Whether or not it was supposed to, a minute later, a sheet of water drops, and our house suddenly finds itself in the center of a storm for which there was no buildup.

"Velis!" I run to the porch and throw open the screen, hoping he has the sense not to magically dry himself off along the way. Suspiciously fast, as if he's *teleported*, he appears at the base of the steps, soaking wet and clutching an angry Steve, who claws out of his grasp and makes a leap for the safety of the house.

I pull in Velis, who's laughing over his misfortune, and whisper, "NO magic." And then over my shoulder, "Mom, grab a towel!"

"I don't think your cat likes me," he says, leaning his head forward to let the water roll off his hair while moist air too warm for spring bursts into the house from the push of the storm.

Weird.

"Did you do that?" I search him as I latch the door.

"What, decide to friggen' drench myself before my first dinner with your mom? Tempting, but no."

The floor gives a squeak as my mother rushes over, arms full of our fanciest towels. She's distracted, skimming her weather app for confirmation that there was zero chance of precipitation. Defiant, the sky announces more intentions with another spank of thunder.

Velis doesn't seem to be worried, but—isn't this a little suspicious?

Maybe I'm just being paranoid because it's my first time bringing home a GENIE.

"Why don't you get him a shower quick?" Mom suggests, giving up on her app, which has nothing but empty promises of sunshine. "I'll finish supper."

Velis IS sort of sticky. Which he could fix with a snap, but a normal, *human* boyfriend who had spent all day on a plane and in a car and then got caught in a muggy storm would likely hop in the shower before dinner.

"Come on, Vel." I take him once more into the depths of our basement, where his wet turns quickly to chill.

"It's cold," he whines, "hug me."

He means to share his wetness, but as I've said before, I'm *slipperier* than he is. I slide out of his path and push him gently into the bathroom.

"Be that way," he says darkly. "I'm patient, Master. I'll get you later."

Flirt.

"Hey," I redirect, putting out feelers, "you don't think that storm was . . . magical or anything, do you? It just seemed to come on abnormally fast."

He shrugs. "It precipitates one-hundred-twelve out of three-hundred-sixty-five days in this region."

He looked that up?!

He puts a steady hand atop my head, dropping his playfulness for something sturdier because he knows I need reassurance. "No one knows we're here but my father and Evaris. We're fine, and if we aren't fine, I'll protect us. Enjoy your time with your mom."

I trust him. I feel safe with him. I'm overreacting.

"Help yourself to a fresh towel. I'll throw that one in the laundry." I wait to steal a glimpse of his shirt being removed before closing the door to seal him inside a sauna of steam and lilac-scented air freshener.

It's cute, the way he's playing along. And it was sweet of him to insist we carve time out of his busy laird-in-training schedule to spend a night here. Being home is grounding. My roots are here, and it feels good to water them.

With Velis's wet towel bundled in my arms, I ignore the sound of my mom clanking around upstairs and make my way to the darkest corner of the basement. Even as an adult, the laundry room is my least favorite place in the house. There's nothing outright wrong with it, but it's unfinished, and there's something eerie about being able to see inside the bones of a building—a perfect exit strategy for anything scurrying between the walls.

The worst part is the light. An ominous bulb commanded by a string, so you have to get halfway in before you can see whatever monsters might be lurking. I tap open my phone's screen to do a quick flash of the area, making sure no new obstacles have appeared in the last year. It's a clean shot. The smooth cement guides my bare feet that are at the mercy of those damned centipedes as I creep a path I've crept many times before.

I've always feared the monsters in the shadows.

Never has one caught me.

Until now.

There's a muffled yell—my own—as a large hand with defined fingers takes my neck and pushes me against a naked two-by-four.

Before I can comprehend what's happening, and with the cadence of blood rushing in my ears, the monster snaps, and the ominous bulb kicks awake. The laundry room is washed in forced light, revealing the person holding my neck.

A person who bears his tattooed chest like it's a mural in an art gallery.

CHAPTER 2
Uninvited

"ARRIK?"

The tattooed triplet stares down at me through chilling blue eyes, never deigning to tip his face, plushy mouth slightly ajar with cool indifference. His midnight blue hair is that same rebellious style, slicked back through the middle, shaved at the sides. A cleaned popsicle stick dangles over his bottom lip, bobbing when he speaks. "Hello, *kitten.*" He slides his thumb down my throat, as if rubbing the ridges of a percussion instrument, before releasing me.

Because that's what every woman wants—to have her fucking *esophagus* stroked.

I rub at my neck to wipe away his fingerprints, fury resting on my tongue. "What the hell are you doing here?!"

"I'm here to human-nap you," he responds, all shruggy and with that crispy voice sounding like he was out all night shouting at trains.

"*Excuse me?*"

He scans our surroundings, lacking interest, through eyes that refuse to make effort. "That's the plan, at least. Human-nap Vel's girl, make the new LIW relinquish his title."

LIW? LIW . . .

Laird-in-waiting. Got it.

I fold my arms. "You're going to kidnap me? Seriously? You know what that makes you?"

A specific set of adjectives comes to mind.

"Yeah, yeah." He fans a lazy hand at me. "Cool your shit. I haven't decided yet. I just agreed to make those two shut up. Beck and Jeb are pissed as fuck. You're lucky I'm the only one who knows where you are."

I glare sharply enough to stab his chest. "How *did* you know where we were? We only told Daddy Djinn and that butler dude, Evaris."

The popsicle stick drops low as Arrik's mouth falls open. "*That's* what you're calling our father?"

Oops.

One side of his top lip pops with dry amusement. Then he tosses his hands behind his neck and begins pacing through the small space like he's been invited. "I know where you are, *Dolly Jones*, because I put a tracker on your soul the last time you were cuddled up on my lap." He pauses to ingest my fuming annoyance. "What? I wasn't lying when I said I had to touch you to read your wishes. I just left out the parts you didn't need to know. Can't blame me for taking an opportunity like that."

Goddamned genies are all the same.

"*Take it off*," I demand.

"Crawl into my lap again."

Not going to happen.

He opens his arms to invite me in anyway.

And that's when I notice—

"*Hey*."

"Huh?" He drops his arms and follows my line of sight. "Oh."

"Your tattoos . . . changed?" I force him into the light to reveal the curve of his shoulder. Where there was once an anchor now lives the open mouth of an angry snake about to strike. His popsicle stick follows me as I look him over for further alterations, finding that much of his left sleeve has changed, though it still bears the same distinct style as before. Dark outlines. Sharp edges. "So then, is this"—I circle my hand in front of him—"all magic?"

"Not all of it. I just like leaving room for creative allowance." He sizes me up like he's weighing my worth. "I'm sure *you* understand."

I'm not sure why I would understand that.

"Your art," he says. "You were good, even as a kid. I was surprised."

Meaning—

"You snooped in my childhood bedroom?"

GODDAMNED GENIES ARE ALL THE SAME!

"I'm an artist too." He touches his finger to his neck, and an inked noose transforms into a blooming rose.

Okay, that's pretty cool, but I'm not about to go throwing out compliments.

"Thanks? Look, Arrik, what is this? Do you want me to call for Velis so that you two can duke it out?"

He doesn't take the bait, instead playing with the stick in his mouth, swiveling it with his tongue and chewing at the end. "You need to be more careful," he says. "I conjured that storm as a distraction, but I didn't expect you to actually leave his side. Our father forbade us from interfering with you—said we'd lose our inheritance if we tried—but those guys are losing their fucking minds. Beckham's straight-up become obsessed with you, and Jeb's . . . well, he's Jeb. Not smart to stray from the estate, and if you're going to leave it, don't separate yourself from the guy who can do magic, yeah?" He stops to flick me on the nose. "That's just stupid."

He shoots me a sidelong glance before sniffing and shifting it away.

Hold on.

"You didn't come here to kidnap me," I say slowly, "you came to *warn* me. You're trying to help Vel!"

"Tch. I don't give a shit about him." His apathetic gaze passes over my features. "Are you really going to become lady of our estate? That's something you want?"

"I . . ." Not a question I can answer just yet, so I decide on something else I know to be true. "I love Velis."

"That's not what I asked. If you want to be with him, it means becoming lady of the estate. They're a package deal now that he's the new LIW."

Obviously, I know that. I'm the one that helped him get there. But . . . getting married, becoming his *lady* . . . It's just a lot to process. And it's only been a week. For now, I'm just trying to soak up as much time with him as possible.

"Why do you care?" I deflect.

"I *care* because if you decide it isn't what you want, there are other djinn who would entertain you. No pressure. No titles. And not just for a hookup either."

Wait. *Wait*. I eye up his exposed biceps with new suspicion.

"Arrik, did you come all this way here to ask me out?"

"Ah, *no*." He spits the popsicle stick into the corner wastebin with inhuman accuracy. "I came to human-nap you."

"Good, because like I said, I'm in love with your brother."

"I'm not looking for love, sweetheart."

Okay, but he just said—

"Don't get the wrong idea." His frosty eyes are suddenly even colder. "Humans are leisure equipment to us. You're no different. I was talking about wishes."

"Well, fuck you too."

In a flash, his fingers have found the pulse of my throat. "You know what? Maybe I will human-nap you, Dolly Jones. Maybe I'll feed you to the *wolves*. I'm offering you a lifeline, and you don't even—"

"You have five seconds to release my neck," I challenge. "I'm not above ball shots. In fact, they're my favorite kind of shots. I have metal plates implanted in my knees."

I don't. That would be ridiculous.

Yet I stare him down with as much deadly intent as I can muster.

"Heh." He breaks into a grin and releases my neck. "Sorry. I'm not used to being turned down. And I can't figure out what that little shit has that the rest of us don't. It's frustrating."

Humility, manners, a conscience . . .

The sound of running water persists. Vel likely doesn't know the typical length of a human shower—*because he's constantly interrupting mine*—and is hanging out in there until an acceptable amount of time has passed. Meanwhile, Arrik stands before me, grin still unholstered, giving me eyes that are somehow bored and suggestive at the same time.

Okay, but could he not, though?

I'm not the kind of girl to stray. I would never cheat, especially after living a life where I thought I had. And I sure as hell wouldn't pursue one brother while dating another.

That doesn't mean I can just pretend Arrik isn't hot. He's the hottest one of them all, aside from Velis, dangerous and conceited and interesting. The kind of person that has stolen *many* virginities and probably made it worth it.

"You should go, Arrik. Thank you for warning us about your brothers. Vel deserves this more than either of them, and I know you know it. Why not consider joining our side for real? Help him for real?"

"How about I 'help' him under the condition that if this all gets to be too much and you need an out, you shoot me a text?"

"You guys don't have phones."

"You know what I mean."

Yeeeah, if I need an 'out,' it won't be through Arrik's bedroom. But before I can tell him so—

"D-Dolly?! Who the heck is this now?"

Oh no. That voice. I know that voice, and it definitely doesn't belong in the vicinity of Arrik Reilhander!

I twirl around to find the voice's owner standing in the doorway, holding the towel we used to clean off the floor from Velis's rainwater, looking all petite and vulnerable with her pretty little eyelashes and that wavy mop of hair. The single bulb casts long, eerie shadows to either side of her.

A slow, anarchic smile slides across Arrik's mouth as he locks eyes with my hobbit-like mother and settles his bare arm around my shoulder. "I'm their third."

"DOLLY ELIZABETH JONES!"

"N-no, Mom! He's kidding! This is Velis's brother." I buck the unwelcome limb off.

"Well, how'd he get in? And why are you hiding him in the basement? And why does he look like *that*?"

Yes, Arrik's appearance is far more offensive than Vel's. Velis may be disgustingly attractive, but Arrik looks like he was designed to rip daughters from their mothers' very bosoms.

"On second thought, you know what might be more fun than playing nice with you?" Arrik rumbles under his breath, slipping around me with evil intent. "How about I make your mother my master and find out *her* darkest desires."

"No, Arrik!" I dive between them. "You are NOT going to bang my mother. And if you try it, I'll never forgive you! VELIS! VEL, come out here NOW!"

"D–Dolly?! What are you—?" Mom's hand is to her chest, her cheeks heated behind her freckles, and she's looking at me like I've lost my mind.

Uh-oh. This situation is no longer salvageable.

"Geez." Arrik puts a hand to his hip. "I was kidding. I would never do that. Well, not to your mother, at least. I do like the older ones. No training wheels required with them."

Gross. Oh, and also CREEPY.

And oops, he was joking? Well, it's too late because I've already called for Velis, who appears on cue, releasing driblets of water and clutching a fresh white towel around his waist. He nearly slides into my confused mother standing in the entryway.

The uninvited one among us bends over to me like we're friends. "Hey, what's with Goldilocks's hair?"

Velis spews invisible daggers. "*Arrik.*" And then he does something stupid.

"No, Velis! NO MAGIC!"

Too late. With a magician's flick, Velis conjures a genie-blue bolt of energy from his palm that he sends directly at Arrik's nipple-pierced chest, earning a shriek from poor Marcy Jones.

Arrik hops out of the way of the bolt with more agility than I've ever seen him spare before twisting his hand in the air over his head and summoning dark markings in the style of his own tattoos that crawl over the floor beneath Velis's feet. With a shout, Velis leaps into the air, grabbing hold of a spare beam as the ground beneath him sizzles and pops.

And through it all, that towel has slipped dangerously low on his waist.

"ARRIK, enough!" I scold. "Velis, put on some clothes!"

"M-magic?" Staring hard at the ink settling into the cold floor, Mom looks probably about as stupefied as I did the first time I witnessed Velis using magic in my apartment. She blinks to combat the absurdity of the situation, like a robot that can't compute. Blink. Blink. Blink.

So that's where I get it from.

I run to comfort her. "Mom! Th-they're—He's—"

"Don't bother," Arrik says, lazing over and putting a finger to my mother's temple, causing her eyes to flutter and her knees to buckle. He catches her as she begins to fall, scoops her up as though she weighs nothing, and makes his way to the stairs, stopping to elbow towel-clad Velis along the way. "She won't remember any of it. She'll think I arrived with you and have been here the whole time."

"What?" says Velis, glower far from shy. "You aren't staying! Bring her back so that I can make her forget about you!"

"I can stay, or I can go tell our other brothers where you are," Arrik counters. "Choice is yours."

Velis shows his teeth. "Why, Arrik? What could you possibly want here? You've already lost the contest—"

"I want to try Master's mother's cooking."

I'm no longer Arrik's master.

A string of insults and profanities follows Arrik up the stairs. "Cocksucking, literal mother-fucking—Argh! I'll take care of this, Dolly." Velis snaps his fingers to clothe himself. "I'll make sure he leaves, and then I'll cast the house in a protective barrier so that he can't return. I should have done that before."

"Actually, I think he came to warn us about Jeb and Beckham. I think he's kind of . . . figuring out what side he's on? It wouldn't be so bad to have him as an ally, would it?"

"Arrik is a dick. There's no way he'd ever help me. What he's after here is YOU because he knows it would hurt me. Even if he pretends to help, it's just the long game with him. Trust me, I've dealt with him my whole life."

Well, I've always thought people could change.

But it's not my business.

"Okay," I say. "You know best, so it's your call on this one. I'll help you get rid of him."

But the carpeted stairs, worn from being slid down atop sleeping bags through my youth, take us to an unexpected sight. A tattoo-less Arrik sits properly alongside my mother at the table, dressed in a . . . *polo shirt?* A pastel yellow one.

How unnatural.

Almost scary.

Velis, in sweats and a plain T-shirt, looks far underdressed. He casts me a scowl of knowing.

Okay, maybe he was right.

Arrik leans forward, drink in hand, *schmoozing* my mother with a disarming smile akin to something Beckham would wear. On second glance, he does have one small tattoo left. The one stamped at the high corner of his cheekbone. A smoky little swish. It almost resembles an S.

"I told Vel just to change into his pajamas, Mom. Hope that's okay."

"Pajamas?" mutters Velis, glancing down at his favorite outfit.

"Sure, sure." Mom waves us over. Whatever Arrik did to her, it seems to have melted all her anxieties away. "I'm just happy I finally get to meet your boyfriend after all this time. You've only been dating, what, a year? And what a treat that you decided to bring Arrik along. You never mentioned that the brother who introduced you two was so charismatic."

Heat.

Dangerous heat stewed from boiling fury leaks off Velis over Arrik's manipulation of the narrative.

Well, at least he solved the overnight fiancé problem for us. Arrik must not have a master right now. It seems he can use the 'big magic' on anything he wants.

I take Velis's hand to calm his rage and pull him to the table, where Mom's laid out a good midwestern 'supper' for us. A casserole with rice and cheese and something green. Pickles from the farmer's market. A steamy pile of corn. And you can be damned sure there's a pie lurking somewhere around here.

"Too bad Arrik can't stay the night," I fake pout. "He has that *thing* in the morning." I conjure my most spiteful expression from behind my mom's shoulder.

"Oh, didn't I tell you?" fancy Arrik croons, knuckle to his cheek. "My *thing* got canceled."

He taps his glass against my mother's, which is filled with something clear and carbonated. He got her a drink?! I was hoping we could avoid that.

Vel's free hand is white knuckled and shaking. Shoot. He was so excited to meet my mom, so excited to have this night together in my past before pressing on into our future.

Enough of this. Whatever it takes to get Arrik to leave, Vel can just wipe Mom's memory after, and we can start over. I clutch the collar of my own shirt and bend forward, ready to let Arrik have it, when—

"Hey." Vel's fist is no longer balled, his posture no longer wrathful. His hand has claimed the space between my shoulder blades. "You don't need to feel that way," he says, controlled. "I wanted this for you, not me. If we retaliate, he'll just push back harder. It's not worth it. He can share tonight because I get you forever."

When I redirect my gaze, I find that his has turned soft, compelling a wave of tingles to run down my spine. I've seen him be rash, hardheaded, puckish—but the more he sinks into this relationship, the more he's becoming . . . mature, stable, understanding.

I love him. So much.

And it feels like it's rapidly becoming deeper.

Maybe me being his former master means Arrik can still feel my emotions. The salad bowl jumps as he shoots from his chair, hands pressed into the aged wood, leaning over his plate to inspect us. "Hmph." He wilts back into his chair and returns his efforts to wooing my mother, keeping one eye on us the entire time.

Fine, we'll just ignore him. Until he decides to quit toeing the line and join Team Velis for real.

With a shit-eating grin, I dig a wooden spoon into Mom's sticky casserole and plop a helping onto unnaturally prim Arrik's plate. "Eat up, *bro*."

He eyes the slop with disappointment that neither Vel nor I caused a scene. Or maybe he's simply questioning the gooey contents of his plate. It's better than it looks.

I tell Velis so when it's his turn to be dished up.

By the sound of those giggles, Mom's a bit buzzed. Better than her thinking I'm pregnant or that Velis is some viper after my money, I guess. Arrik spends the meal flirting with her while trying to bait Velis with comments that go over my mother's head. But Velis stands his ground, responding cleverly or deflecting, keeping one hand on my thigh beneath the table to show me his calm.

I reward him by sliding my fingers over his and dragging them up his knuckles, rubbing his thumbnail or playing with the pads of his fingertips until he takes my hand firmly and bobs a noticeable swallow.

Hot.

The pie that was hiding on top of the refrigerator boasts blackberries from the garden and crust made with my grandmother's recipe. Arrik may not have been taking the meal too seriously, but even he stops to pay homage to the pie.

Yeah, I know it's good.

I don't know how many times Arrik has magically topped off

my mother throughout the night, but even if she meant to drink one glass, it's clear she's had more. Dick. Forcing others to become inebriated isn't doing much to help his case. Lest we forget, he did the same to me back in that nightclub.

"Mom? Why don't you go lie down? Let us clean up, okay?"

Velis stands to help her up. "Good meal, M . . . Mrs. Jones. Thank you."

Shame. He can't bring himself to call her 'Mom' in front of Arrik.

The culprit sits quietly, face hard to read as he plays with a toothpick in the corner of his mouth and watches us like we're a spectator sport.

"I like this one, Lizzy." Feeling warmer than usual, my mom pats Velis's firm chest. "Polite, cute. He'd make a good son-in-law." She offers a hug that Velis eagerly takes, Arrik be damned. "You're welcome for supper anytime, Velis. Take care of my girl."

Oh my. Quite endearing to see him looking so happy over a human mother's approval. He hugs her like he's missed her.

"You, on the other hand—" Mom tips her face over her shoulder at Arrik, cunning like a middle-aged fox. "You're a troublemaker, aren't you? Watch out for this one, Lizzy."

She can see through him?!

Of course she can. Mom's shrewd, especially when it comes to me.

Mouths pulling at the corner, Velis and I escort my mother to her room, where I tuck her in, and after, Vel moves his hand over her door to create a magical barrier to seal off entry from the unpredictable djinn waiting in the kitchen.

We return to find said djinn's appearance back to normal—shirtless, tatted, the toothpick transformed into a blunt that smells like . . . apricot?

"Are you done here?" Velis asks, unamused.

"Done?" Arrik rasps, joint bobbling. That goddamned eyebrow of his cocks when he feels my eyes on his body. No, I'm not checking you out, *Arrik*. I'm merely looking for new tattoos. He shakes the ice in his empty glass. "Beck and Jeb are planning to ambush you when you go to the nymph realm. Thought you might like to know."

"How do you know we're going to the nymph realm?" counters Velis.

"Besides you just confirming it? Beck's in good with one of the maids who overheard Evaris talking about it. They don't know when you're leaving, but they're relying on me to tell them when you do, seeing as how I placed a tracker on your human's soul last week."

News to Velis, and his distrust is strong. He crosses his arms. "You think I'm stupid enough to believe anything you say, Arrik?"

"Don't. Or do. It's up to you." Arrik releases a dragon's breath of apricot smoke at the ceiling. "I have to tell them when you leave. They'll get suspicious if I don't. But I can give you a couple days' head start if you want." He takes note of Velis's unwavering skepticism, adding: "Not keen to see how those two take out their revenge on your human. They can't do much at the estate, but in a foreign realm? Wouldn't be hard to cover up the disappearance of one little girl."

"They can't go to the nymph realm," Velis argues. "It's restricted."

"No realm is restricted if you don't care about consequences, *little brother*."

"Beckham wouldn't."

He still believes that? After that shaking rage Beckham displayed when we stole his contest winnings?

"I think he would," comes my two cents. "I know I only spent so many minutes with him, but I could feel it, Vel. He's manipulative and nasty. I actually fear him the most of the three."

"She's right," says Arrik. "He was the one that sent us after you in the first place. His plan was for me and Jeb to corner you into a position where you'd be forced to reach out to him for help. Sorry."

He doesn't *sound* sorry.

Velis scowls at the back door like it was responsible for the betrayal. "Why are you telling me this? You've never liked me."

"And I probably never will, but three against one's getting a little old, don't you think? And now you've got something shiny. I don't want to see it fall into the wrong hands." He eyes me, the *shiny thing*, over.

"You're trying to impress Dolly," Velis concludes.

"Mmm, why would I care about impressing one midrange human? I can have any human I want."

"Except this one," Vel charges. "And this one's awesome."

Well, shucks.

"Okay, okay." I step forward. "I'm right here." And I won't stand for being talked about like an object. "Whatever Arrik's motives, I believe him, and I think we should take his help. From what your dad said, the nymphean pilgrimage is going to be difficult on its own. We don't need your brothers after us too. But, Arrik, how do we know you aren't going to flip flop?"

He flicks a clump of ash into his leftover corn as smoky haze surrounds him like a feather boa. "Wish it."

"I can't. I'm tethered to Velis."

"You can still present him with a wish," Velis says carefully as he tries to get a read on his brother. "And he can choose whether or not he wants to grant it. He just can't siphon you or become bonded to you in the process because you're already tethered to me."

Ugh. This whole system is hard for me to follow.

"Arrik, I wish that you would stay loyal to Velis," I say.

Arrik's eyes remain unignited. "Try again, kitten. Like I said, I don't give two shits about him."

Then—

"I wish that you would stay loyal to me?"

With that, Arrik's eyes blaze a flash of genie blue, and after, he takes another drag, exhaling smoke as he says, "There. Now I can't betray you even if I wanted to. I'll give you a two-day head start when the time comes. Fair? Now, where am I sleeping?"

"You're not staying," Velis says, as stormy as the sky outside.

"Yeah? And how will you explain that to Dolly's mother in the morning?"

"I won't. I'll erase you from her memory."

A woody click sounds from Arrik's tongue. "Not smart, little brother. You should be saving up as much soul balance as you can for this journey of yours. You really are a shit wish granter, you know that?"

"The couch," I tell him, pushing seething Velis away. "Downstairs. I'll get you a blanket. It's cold, and there are spiders. Enjoy."

Five minutes later, I've created the most half-assed nest I've ever offered any guest. Arrik and I wait alone in the thin darkness while Velis works to secure the perimeter up above.

"Do I get a goodnight kiss, Master?"

"I'm not your master, and I'd sooner sand off my own lips." I waft the air from my face. "And contain your smoke, okay? You're messing up the smell of home."

He pulls the joint into his mouth, and the next moment, it's magically gone.

Showoff.

I was hoping that after seeing his lodgings, he'd opt to dip out, but no. It seems he's committed. Why? There's a clear swarm of energy coming off him, like he himself was the storm that came rolling in.

I prefer to watch things . . . implode.

"Hey." He catches my wrist as I start to back away. "Are you still afraid of me?"

Afraid? Because he could feel my chest sprinting that time I sat on his lap. It wasn't fear then, and it isn't fear now.

"No, I'm not afraid of you."

"Does that mean you like me?"

Why is he so thirsty for my approval?!

I look past him to where Velis is coming down the stairs, having placed a barrier that will ensure no more uninvited guests break into my childhood home. "Yet to be determined. Helping Velis is a good start."

That's a satisfactory enough answer, apparently. He frees my wrist, and Velis and I leave him sitting on the edge of the couch, shirtless and musing.

"Dolly Jones. Get up."

The voice is close enough to have been spoken directly into my ear, startling enough to wake me from however deep a sleep I was just in.

I smack at my assailant, but they're already across the room, the dim of it all not dim enough to hide that painted body. "Arrik?! What are you doing in our room? And how'd you get in? Vel put a barrier around the—VEL?"

The lump beside me is not, in fact, a sexy genie but a sexless pillow.

If accusation could kill. "*What did you do with him?*"

"I did nothing with him. He's upstairs, fixing up your mother's memory. Didn't trust me to do it, apparently." He scans me over—my nasty hair, my nasty breath. "Get up. We need to go."

"Why?"

He sighs. "Because you were followed. Or I was. Hard to say."

"By whom?"

"*Whom?* Ha. Look at you, fancy."

"ARRIK, WHO FOLLOWED US HERE?"

He lifts his shoulders and releases a lazy 'I dunno' sort of grunt. "Lucky for you, one of us was smart enough to place a detection spell out in your yard. Spoiler: it wasn't Velis. There's something magical out there. I can't tell what it is, but I can tell it's strong. Who knows how long that amateur barrier your boyfriend placed will hold up. You didn't exactly pick the strongest of the Reilhander djinn to mate with."

I bolt from the covers. "Mom! We can't leave her here!"

"Which is why," Arrik adds, "Velis is up there convincing her she took a vacation to some place called the Salty Flats. He's gonna pop her there speedy-like and then come back for you."

"HE'S SENDING MY MOM TO BOLIVIA?!"

"Would you rather she stayed here?"

No, but—Bolivia? *Seriously?* We're going to undo that the minute we know she's safe.

"Do you have to smoke in here?" I swish Arrik's popcorn-scented fog out of my face.

"Yup." Hands to his waist, he leans backward to crack his back before moseying over to my wall of sketches, ripping one of a chonky creature from the wall titled *Clifford the Big Black Dragon*. "I'm keeping this," his blunt wags.

Whatever the hell for? But if I ask him, he's sure to pick something worse. I'm pretty sure there's at least one pony in the mix.

Fine. Vel's already stuffed that alien picture into some pocket or another anyway.

Arrik continues, "Vel and I went up to see if we could figure out what's out there, but no dice. Not without breaking the barrier. So he sent me down to wake you up while he works over your mom."

According to Arrik.

"Is this a trick?" I accuse.

"Do you want it to be a trick?"

"Was anything you said since waking me true, Arrik? I wish you'd tell me."

"Again?" His mouth ticks. "Smart girl."

I'm not sure what he means by 'again.'

His eyes blaze blue as he absorbs the wish. "Everything I just told you is true. Except—" He contorts his mouth, fighting whatever the wish is about to make him confess. "My little brother's barrier wasn't amateur. It's actually pretty good." He scowls over his inability to hide the truth. "Fuckin' A."

Delightful. And speak of the devil.

Vel rushes into the room, hand outstretched like a sexy Peter Pan. "Dolly! We need to go. Do you need to grab anything?"

"No, but you didn't seriously send my mother to Bolivia, did y—" The last words I get out before Velis takes me in his arms and blips us into the darkness between realms.

The space is like ink. Empty nothingness that feels warmer and fuller than the last time I was here.

"Vel?" My voice muffles against him, my chest still racing

from being abruptly woken after a night that was nothing like we planned.

Vel's embrace doesn't budge. "Can we just . . . hang here a sec?"

He seems heavy, and because I can feel our bodies, it must mean he's using his magic to make us tangible. Because he wants to hold me, uninterrupted.

"Of course," I say.

He cradles me closer. "Your mom isn't in Bolivia. She's staying at your neighbor's dwelling with Steve the Cat. She believes your home has bugs in the beds that must be eradicated."

Thank god. Leave it to bedbugs to make a comeback.

I feel the muscle of Vel's back flex. "I'm sorry, Dolly."

"For what?"

"Something magical followed us. It was probably Jeb's bird. Your visit got cut short because of us. I know how much you desired to see her."

"It's okay." My voice ripples in the void. "You got to meet her."

"She's funny."

"Yeah."

"Sorry about my brother," he adds.

"It's not like you invited him there. And we managed to fend him off. He complimented your barrier spell, by the way, while you were upstairs. Said it was pretty good."

"Yeah, right."

"I wished the truth out of him."

"And he obeyed you?" The quiet seems to thicken as he pulls away to study me. "He likes you, Dolly."

"If he does, it's only because I'm with you."

Velis shakes his head. "I told you before, you're his type."

"You're my type," I counter.

A lie. Velis is nothing like anyone I've ever dated. 'My type' doesn't hold a candle to the being that is Velis Reilhander.

"Be careful. He knows the most about humans. And he's got the least to lose. I know you can take care of yourself, but you're kinda my heart's desire, so forgive me for being that guy."

The least to lose? Velis doesn't seem like he wants to elaborate on whatever that means.

"Psh. Do you think I'm the kind of girl to get mixed up with suspicious djinn?"

He drills me with crystalline focus. "Do I have to answer that?"

"I prefer aliens."

Rolled eyes and the cutest, smallest grin prelude the end of the darkness as our suite at the manor materializes.

No Arrik in sight. Just fluttering curtains and a magical breeze, far nicer than any human hotel I've been to.

"Let's get some sleep." Velis snaps to turn the room dark. "My father has me in meetings all day tomorrow."

Meaning I'll be spending the day alone. Again.

The trip to see my mom was a diversion. Truth is, Vel's been busy with LIW-esque things most days. And I, the now unemployed human bum, have been . . . bumming in a closed-off wing of the manor like a princess in a tower.

He reads my emotions. "I promise this is temporary. As soon as we leave on the pilgrimage, we'll have all the time in the world. I asked a couple of my friends to come check on you tomorrow. One of them's Caliko, the greenie we saw in the gardens the first time I took you here. You'll like him."

"Greenie?"

"I forget what they're called on Earth. Luck-rechauns?"

Luck. Green.

"That gardener guy was a *leprechaun*?!"

"Half," clarifies Vel. "Or a third?"

Visitors. It would be nice to have someone other than that stuffy butler stopping by while Vel's at work.

"Speaking of pilgrimage," Vel continues, "I should have good news for you soon. My father said he'd pull some strings. I'm ready to get the fuck out of here. A week back, and I'm already feeling suffocated."

Says the new lord of this suffocating manor.

"I know, right?" He smirks, feeding off my energy. "Sucks we can't just hop over there under the radar. I've already got a couple of strikes on my record with that unauthorized visit to the goblin world and screwing up the paperwork when I went back in time, so they're making me do this one by the book, especially with Aphrotica being a restricted realm. I promise it won't be like this when we get back, okay? My father's just trying to cram in as much laird shit as he can before we leave. Get a contingency plan in place now that the winner's been announced."

Translation: the genie is worried about me.

"I'm not the kind of needy sponge who misses you after a few hours away, Vel. You're hot, but you're not that hot." LIES. He is that hot. And his personality's that hot too. And now that my heart's desire has been unlocked, these days away from him feel excruciating.

"Guess I'll have to work to become that hot, then," he flirts back. Then he takes my wrist and pulls me into himself, dousing the room blue, and the next moment, we're cuddled up in bed. "I'll miss you too, Master."

In the darkness, once his breathing has settled, I let myself drop the charade he can already see through. It's easy to be stony with him. Being softer is so much harder. But it's always worth it.

"It sucks, Vel," I whisper, fingertips to the divots of his heated chest. "I miss you the moment you leave. I'm not used to pining over someone like this."

"It's okay," he whispers in response. "I feel it too. It's like the universe stretches the farther I am away from you. Being laird is my dream, but I've only got one ear on it, you know? I'm always thinking about rushing back here to be with you afterward."

I've seen his face when he comes bursting through that door.

"I'm going to make up for everything I've put you through, Dolly. I promise. Hang on a little bit longer, okay?"

My hum of agreement is lost to some nook of him. Vel's body is like a beacon pulling me out of a dense wood. I find it, I melt against it, and when I next open my eyes, it's gone.

This is what I get for falling in love.

CHAPTER 3
A Little Luck

WITH GOLDEN DAYLIGHT SURROUNDING ME, I push myself from a bed that feels like it's been enchanted to suck me in deeper. It gives a small rock against its supporting chains as I stand. Vel was right: a suspended bed does make for fun *endeavors*.

If I think about them hard enough, will he feel it? Even way over on the other side of the manor? Hopefully. Conjure up a little nasty to go with his morning briefing.

The coffee table at the center of the room holds a note and a single uncooked egg.

Made you breakfast.
—*Vel*

Smart-ass.

Determined to let the smell of home linger in my hair, I don't wash it when I wash the rest of me. I dribble shimmery water across the shimmery marble of the bath, unwilling to wear one of those fleecy robes Evaris keeps laying out for me every fucking day.

I've been branching out with my wardrobe. The leggings stay, but my shirt is olive green.

For my own safety, I'm not allowed to leave our quarters without Vel. At first, it was a nice vacation away from the job I no longer have. Vel conjured a shit ton of books for me, which I really don't feel like reading now, and a knockoff handheld gaming system that has a few well-known Earth platformers but with all the characters replaced by 16-bit genies. That occupied my time a good two hours on day one.

But since then, it's been a struggle to find things to do. I can have literally anything I want here, except the one person I want to spend time with, so I haven't wished for much. I haven't admitted it to Vel, but being here feels a little like being a background character in someone else's story, and that banister is looking more and more like prison bars the more time I spend here alone.

One more week. Or something. One-ish more week, and our permit will come through, and we can be off on an adventure of our own.

I pretend to faint onto what I assume is a fainting couch overrun with decorative pillows, and after, I stare into the ceiling, replaying last night's events. Vel's cool djinn magic. Arrik's shrouded motives. I can't believe he freaking showed up at my mom's house. I trust Vel's judgment, but I can't figure out why Arrik would grant a wish not to betray me if he really were playing a long game with us.

Confusing. I'm glad I don't have a brother.

FWOMP.

I stiffen where I lie, concealed by the mess of pillows, because that definitely sounded like someone falling onto the balcony of our suite. By the lack of groan, I'd guess it was a clean landing.

WHAT THE FUCK?

I thought there was a protective forcefield around this wing! Which one of the triplets would be crazy enough to jump from the roof?!

"Arrik, I swear to fucking Maka, if that's you again, I'm going to—"

"Milady Dolly?" A muffled voice I only semi-recognize pushes through the breezy curtains, followed by a mumbled, "Cripes, this is weird." There's a throat clearing, and then louder, "It's, eh, me. Caliko? Vel, er, the young laird, e-er, I mean, the laird-in-waiting said he'd let you know I was stopping by?"

OH. It's the *leprechaun*. Vel mentioned he'd be sending his friends to check in on me, but I hadn't expected an entrance like that. I gopher my head up over the rim of the couch, excited at the prospect of gleaning embarrassing stories about genie boy from his posse. "You can call him Vel, and you can call me Dolly," I say as the curtains blow away to reveal a full head of greenish hair and rose-kissed cheeks.

"And you can call me Cal," he says with an accent. Scottish? Irish? *Makayen?* "Sorry for the unannounced arrival. Meant to come in the proper way, but we ran into a spot of trouble on the way and had to improvise."

"'We'?" Vel did say 'friends,' but this is only one friend.

Cal stuffs his hands into his pockets. "Er, yeah. There were two of us, but Bellamy got held up."

"And you didn't?"

The corner of his mouth wiggles. "I'm a little lucky."

Caliko. The last time I saw him, he didn't see me. And the last time I saw him, he was coated in dirt. Today, he's clean and wears a sports jacket with the sleeves pushed up to the elbow and a deep boatneck tank underneath. His hair is short in the back, long and messy in the front. A bit of a baby face, with playful eyes and a little scruff.

"H-hey. Do you, uh, want me to leave? I can leave if you want," he says.

I stand from the protective barrier that is the fainting couch. "Leave?"

"Yeah, you look . . . mad."

No, I don't want him to leave. I saw the sparkle in his eyes the day he greeted his 'young laird' in the gardens. This one adores

Velis as much as I do, I am in desperate need of friends here, and, to be honest, I'm a little worried about the mental spiral I might dive into if left to my own devices.

I remind my mouth to smile. "I think that's just my default setting. Sorry, I'm used to intrusive djinn being able to read through it."

Cal throws a hand behind his neck. "Ugh. Tell me about it. I mean, I'm part genie too, but I don't have that set of skills, and it's like, sometimes you just want to feel a way without people probing around in you, you know? And the young laird—er, Vel's such a dern softie, he can't let it rest. Soon as he gets a sniff, it's all over. Boy's had me weepin' more times than I'd care to share."

This time, I don't need to remind my mouth to smile; it's reacting all on its own. Because finding someone to gossip about Velis with may be second best only to having the man himself. "You don't have to stay out on the balcony, Cal," I say, gesturing to my ritzy abode.

Cal pokes his head into the room, whistling. "Rumors were true, then. They really do have Vel's human locked away like a princess. That's one hell of an aversion spell they've got over your quarters. Won't let in anyone what ain't invited. They say it's to acclimatize you to our world slowly, but I surmise it's for other reasons—one by the name of Arrik, the other by the name of Beck."

I'm surprised he picked those two names. "Not Jeb?"

"Meh, Jebidirah's a pussiwinkle. Punched him right in the face when we was kids. Never came for me again. Can't say the same of the other two." He stops. "But don't let that get to you."

"Why would that get to me?"

"Huh. Wonder. Thought I sensed a spark of empathy, on account of the kinder bullying." He patter-pat-pats his hands on the edges of the doorframe. "But that'd be rare for me. And as to the invitation into yer quarters, milady—wouldn't you rather get outta here a mite? Vel says you've been feeling cooped."

Cooped is accurate, but—"I can't leave. I'm not supposed to."

"Aye, but you *can* leave, so long's it's with me."

I search him for grounds.

A second time, he grins in an absentminded way. "I'm a little lucky."

I'm not the biggest believer in luck.

"Sure, then," he responds, though I haven't said anything, then shoves past me into the suite, where he plops into a gold-rimmed armchair like a prince. "Take a trinket in one of your hands, but don't show me which."

I choose one of Vel's knock-off genie games, though I'm not sure it counts as a 'trinket.'

"It's in your right, ain't it? Again. Aye, see, now it's in your left. Left again. Right. Right."

"That was luck?" I question after he wins a dozen rounds.

"Blind, brainless luck. Done nothing to deserve it. Easiest superpower ever. Now, since I'm a halfer, I'm not strong enough to shield more'n two people at a time. But as I sit here, seems to be two of us, and one of them's my mate's girl who desperately needs a cure for her boredom. And I'm nothing if not boredom averse." He winks but does so in a way that says he's only half-confident in it.

Okay, he's a charming one.

"Do you have a girlfriend, Cal? Or maybe a boyfriend?"

"Naw, I'm not really the romanticizing type. Bit of a loner that way."

A tragedy for library girls everywhere.

"So what say you, milady? Let me share a bit of my luck with you, and we'll go explore the manor a beat? Got no direction in mind, mind ya. Always a bit thrilling to let luck lead. Lots of close calls I've had."

Fangirling with a cute leprechaun boy over my genie boyfriend while exploring a magical mansion-castle? Beats poking at my own pores in the mirror.

"There's only one catch." Cal scratches at his chin. "Need to kiss you, to get the luck to transfer. Closer to the mouth, the better it'll stick, but I'm not expecting that outta you. Cheek okay?

Chin'd work just as well." He brushes his fingers over his own lips, and they pulse with greenish energy to match his hair.

"What is with magic and kissing?"

"It's the intimacy what's important," he explains. "Magic loves intimacy. Harder to cast magic for the sake of a person you don't care about."

I offer him my cheek because he seems like one of the most harmless guys I've ever met and because the offer to get out of this room is just too tempting. My skin reacts to his peck with a static-electricity-like spark, and after, I feel the power he's just placed on me spreading warmly over my face and down my throat.

"A test," he says as he pulls away. "How many fingers I got behind my back?"

I take a stab in the dark. "Two?"

"Aye." He shows me. "Again, then."

"Five? Three. Now they're crossed. And that one's an obscene gesture where I come from."

"It's obscene here too. Good job, lady luck. You passed."

We exit into a cavernous hallway adorned with rich, swaggy décor and the smell of foreign flowers bunched together on showy little tables. "That's not necessary," Caliko instructs as I purposely try to mask the sound of my footsteps that wish to clap against the shined floors. "Trust me. If anyone finds us, it'll be a friend. You just tell me if you feel that luck of yours beginning to run out, and I'll re-juice you, yeah?"

I absorb his self-confidence, feeling rebellious with the warm glow of luck still throbbing in my veins. There were many occasions over the last few weeks I could have used a feeling like this.

"You'll have to forgive me if I speak outta place, milady. Don't have much experience with humans. Met a partial one once or twice but never a full one."

"You're good." To be honest, I'm much more likely to offend him than he is to offend me. I make small talk as we pass under a massive, framed portrait of Vel's mother with heavenly blue eyes and the same necklace she always wears in these things—a delicate silver strand with one red stone at the base of the neck. "Did you really punch Jeb once?"

"Swear it on my mum," says Cal.

It feels like my blooming smile is a sinister one. "Bet that was satisfying."

"You've no idea. Vel helped reduce my punishment with good ol' Evvy, too, so it was totally worth it."

Evvy? Oh, Evaris. The least nickname-worthy person I've ever met.

"So, you've lived here since you were a kid?" I ask.

"Sure have. Came with my mum when I was young, been workin' for the estate ever since. You might think it strange, someone kissed by luck working as a domestic, but my luck's well reduced on account of my blood. And Amoira and the triplets aside, I like it here. Laird Reilhander's always been good to me, as was our departed lady. Thought I'd have to leave 'til Vel won the contest. Like to think it was cuz I blew a little luck onto his vessel before he set off."

"Amoira?"

"Ah, haven't met that one yet, eh? Should stay that way if you've an ounce of luck. Monster woman she is. They say she's pretty, but I couldn't tell you one way or the other." He stops beside a *vahz* as tall as my shoulder and bursting with crisp blue flowers. "It's their mum. Jeb and those other cads' mum. That's Amoira."

My father left her shortly before he got with my mom, but she still waltzes around here like she owns the place. She's ... kind of a nightmare.

Vel doesn't talk about her much.

We come to an intersection of hallways with a mosaic glass ceiling glinting richly in the daylight. "Don't it feel like we should turn here?" asks Caliko.

He's right. My feet were already turning before I even realized it. It's like that hallway is drawing us in deeper.

"Does this power ever, like, lead you to treasure?" I ask as I follow the pull.

"Treasure?"

Rainbows? Pots of gold? No. Vel insists it's okay if I use the word 'genie,' but I should probably leave my other preconceptions behind in the human world. I'm not sure what kinds of cultural implications they might have. "Er, does it ever lead you anywhere interesting?" I correct.

Caliko spasms amusement. "Always."

We venture through the veins of the sprawling mansion, up a few sets of steps, down another, taking in the polish and gleam of a dwelling so fancy it doesn't feel real. I've caught glimpses of this place but never a glimpse so expansive. It's like our lucky feet are taking us on a tour.

"How many libraries does one household need?" I mutter.

"Right? And only one of 'ems used. Four kitchens. Countless washrooms. Totally excessive." Cal smiles fondly. "And all of it's set to be Vel's. Yours too, from what I hear."

That's . . .

I mean, I always intended to have more than my shitty apartment, but I definitely don't need all this. And for no other reason than because Vel's horny little arrow happens to be poking at mine.

Cal tips his head. "What's that, now? Guilt?" To himself, he contemplates, "Humans really are easier to read, aren't they? Easy enough for me, even." Then back to me: "Don't feel guilt, milady. From what Vel's said of you, we're all glad he'll have someone like you at his side when he inherits the estate."

Someone like me. "I'm sure you can tell I'm out of my element here."

"Don't much care." Caliko's gaze softens. "He's different since he got back, Vel is. Haven't gotten to see him much these last days, but from what I have seen, he's . . . Never seen him so content. Never. Like he's been holdin' his breath his whole life, and now he's finally gotten to let it out. Don't know you well, don't know what you had to do with his win, but I do know you're good for him. We all do. All of us who keep this place shiny. Means even more now we know who we're shining it for."

Oh. That's sweet.

Almost too sweet.

Tooth-achingly sweet.

I'm not sure how I feel about having people I don't even know so invested in my relationship. The weight of expectation is heavy. An end to our relationship seems to mean a great deal more under this massive roof than it did back under my shitty third-floor one. And while being near Vel is everything to me right now, I'm not one to be blinded by a honeymoon stage. People are capable of change.

For better or worse.

Cal stops to survey the hallway ahead of us. "Shite."

I glance around him. "What?"

He hesitates, slinging caution over the marble ahead. "Feels like we ought to keep going, doesn't it?"

It does. "Why, what's wrong?" I press.

Cal rubs at the back of his neck. "Vel's aside, the other young lairds' quarters are down that way."

"Wait—" The hallway ahead, which looks no different than any of the other many hallways we've perused, suddenly feels a bit darker than all the rest. "The triplets? Their bedrooms are down there?!"

"Mm. Though more than just a bed. Belongings too."

Bedroom. Not a common term here. Noted.

Cal's face squirms as he weighs the decision before us. "I mean, feels like we really, *really* ought to go that way. But . . . Vel'd be fine, me taking you out like this, but I'm not sure how he'd feel about me leading you straight into the wolves' den."

Not sure how I feel about him leading me there either.

"Does your luck ever lead you into danger?" I ask.

"Not directly. Near to it, but never directly." Cal's eyes graze over me. "Still feelin' warm, milady?"

I give him a nod.

"Your call," he says.

I'm . . . curious as to why luck would have us venture into this section of the manor. Maybe we'll catch some dirt on Beckham for use at a later time? Or maybe Cal's being set up to give Jeb another good punch. Or best of all, maybe Vel's on a break from meetings. Maybe luck's leading us to him. The thought of it is nothing short of *elating*.

Goddamned arrow.

I offer the leprechaun another nod and press past him, ears perked for signs of disturbance. But the corridor is deserted, like all the other corridors we've passed through today.

Caliko shrugs. "Thought to give us a scare, I guess. If we're to just pass through here, there were other ways we could have take—m-milady?!"

Fwomp!

The unmistakable sound of my ass hitting the ground. I've tripped. And by the looks of it, it was over my own damned feet.

"Guess my luck must be running out after—"

Fwomp!

I'm joined in my embarrassment by a greenish-haired leprechaun who has also just tripped over nothing.

Both of us lie on the ground in a small enclave between two doors—each door likely a gateway to a different Reilhander brother's lair.

"W-what the hell was that?" I roll to all fours to inspect the ground for invisible genie boobytraps, assuming that if there were invisible genie boobytraps anywhere in this mansion, it would be here—where the spawn of Satan reside.

Crouched, Cal holds up a finger, as if listening for something. Then he steadily begins backing farther into the enclave, motioning for me to join him, which feels exactly like what my body wants me to do anyway. Together, we waddle, and the moment our shoulders hit the slippery wall is the moment I feel my accelerated pulse begin to poke through the confident glow of luck. The silence has been broken by the determined clack of heeled shoes echoing down the hall in the direction we were just headed, while obnoxiously large bouts of flowers block us from view.

I pantomime at Cal—*Whose rooms are these?!*

He points with his thumb to the left, at the room we already passed, mouthing, *Jeb*. Then to the one we've yet to hit, *Arrik*. And still farther down: *Beck*.

By the sound of it, Beckham's room is where the shoes stop. But unless Arrik has some hidden kink—which, let's be honest, is not off the table—I can't imagine any of the triplets wearing shoes that sound like that.

The person fiddles with the handle of the door, and after, the voice that comes out definitely, *definitely* doesn't belong to one of the triplets. "Beckham? Beckham, darling?"

It's a woman, and though I can't see her, it's almost as if I can *hear* her beauty. The voice is angelic enough to paint a picture on its own. Like white flowers. Like lavish garments. Beside me, I feel Cal stiffen. He gathers my wrist in a tight clench, as though he's ready to tear me up and go running down the hallway at any moment.

Well, that's not reassuring!

"Beckham? Open up. I made the trip all the way over, the least you could do is say hello to your—"

A second door, the one immediately to our right, swings open. "He isn't here."

This time, I'm the one to paw at Cal. Because that rasp also paints a vivid picture of the body to which it belongs.

"*Arrik.*" It's the woman who has spoken again, but this time, the tone is something else: wrenchingly cold, and conjuring a very different image than it did just a sentence ago. "What are *you* doing here?"

"I live here," says Arrik disagreeably. "Same can't be said for you, can it? I'd appreciate if you'd stop yelling outside my door. I'm trying to sleep."

Sassy.

"Hmph. Where's your brother?"

"Fuck if I know. He and Jeb took off this morning."

"*Language*," hisses the woman. Several footsteps clack to close the space between them. And then they halt. "And why do you feel so guilty? What have you done now?"

"Tch. That's not m—" Arrik stops. "None of your business."

Oh shit. That's definitely ME she's feeling. Guilt? Kinda my thing. And right now, I'm feeling it because I'm listening in on a conversation that wasn't meant for me. A conversation that feels *tense*.

Cal shows no further signs of alarm, now wholly trusting in his luck to carry us through.

Another "Hmph," from the woman, once she's satisfied with what I assume is staring Arrik down. "Tell your brother to check his Ray. I need to speak with him."

"I'll get right on that," Arrik croaks.

The footsteps start away, then stop. "And Arrik?"

"What?"

"You're disgusting. Clean up your skin and wash the stink of human off you, and maybe your father will stop favoring that half-breed."

"Fuck off."

Whatever face she's wearing, the woman does, indeed, fuck off. Her stormy footsteps prelude Arrik's slamming of his door.

Woah. Drama. Dramarama that, for once, has nothing to do with me or Vel.

After, there's silence but for lucky Caliko bending forward and panting, "Phew! Close one, amiright?" By the way he's twinkling, he isn't upset about it.

Is he some sort of . . . luck *junkie*? Does he get a rush from the adrenaline of seeing his own luck carry him through?

"Cal,"—I stand and offer him a hand up—"who was that woman talking to Arrik?"

"That," he says as he accepts my hand and stands to join me, "was the she-devil of the manor, our ex-lady, Amoira."

She still waltzes around here like she owns the place.

Amoira. Mother to the unholy trio.

Then Arrik's own mother . . . calls him disgusting?

Also, I think you're kind of creepy and gross.

Oh.

"Woah, woah, woah, babe. Seriously. Stop."

"Huh?" I glance into concerned blues framed by a perfect golden face as strong, warm hands gather mine.

"If you keep that up, there won't be anything left to gnaw. Your thumbnail's almost gone." Velis slides the pad of his thumb against the jagged edge of my nail. "I could grow it out for you, but wouldn't you rather talk about whatever's bothering you? Your empathy is so thick right now that it's making me a little nauseous."

"Er, sorry."

His eyes taper shrewdly. "And now there's guilt. What is it?"

We sit together under a full lavender moon that bleeds to blue against the midnight sky, as friendly wind sways the long curtains behind us and imbues a slight chill into the glassy stone of the balcony. Are we basking? We might be basking. Basking in each other's presence after a day apart. Basking in the moon's light, which sets the distant fields shimmering as we sip on the human 'consumables' Vel conjured for us. The sky above is blotted with smudged stars, as if my vision is blurred. Vel's warmth and love radiate as he cuddles around me from behind.

"Dolly?" he presses. "What is it?"

It isn't anything I want to talk about, so I tip my chin to offer him my mouth.

His features give a small twinge of disapproval, but ultimately, he can't help accepting the offer and meeting my lips with his.

We've kissed more in the last week than I kissed James probably ever, yet every single time, I feel a shivery burst over my skin and a secret drop in my stomach. I'm usually the first one to open my mouth—he likes to know it's okay to progress—but he's always the one to meet my tongue, setting off the rapid thrum of my heart.

His fingertips glide beneath my loose shirt that flutters in the wind, feeling electrically charged the moment they meet the covered parts of me, like our destined attraction is securing itself through magic-infused touch, as I offer him my heat, my breath, and he pulls me into his lap by my exposed waist.

Kissing him out here feels forbidden. A human and the djinn laird's son. Bared to the open world, ripe for being caught.

"Dolly," Vel whispers, mouth moving to my neck, sucking at me with enough buried intent to make me grip his hair. "I'm going to lose this battle."

He's right. What started out as an admittedly unhealthy distraction technique has quickly turned into an unstoppable force. A quickening, throbbing, combustible force. I want him to take me right here. The way he did two nights ago. And the night before, covering my mouth to keep us from being found out.

"Yes," he mutters, feeling what I want, nuzzling at my jaw. "That."

There's no need to admit that the empathy I've been feeling all night is for the most problematic of his mortal enemies—problematic because it's the one who's taken an amicable interest in me.

Arrik.

But the problem with becoming more and more intimate with a genie is that it's getting harder and harder to hide things from him. Even thinking the name 'Arrik' makes Vel's hands pause their onslaught. "That emotion wasn't there yesterday, and there are only two people you've seen today. Me and Caliko. So unless it's for Caliko—"

I really need a codename. He's getting warmer.

"Wait—" Velis releases his hold on my breast. "It is? It's Caliko?"

The only way out of this now is by outright lying, which I'm not about to do.

"No, it's not Cal." I straighten my body off him, lamenting the damage my next statement will do to our momentum. "It's actually Arrik."

He leans away sharply. "You're joking. Dolly . . . you aren't joking?! That cloud of empathy that's been swirling around you all night is for *Arrik*?"

I let out a thin breath of reluctance and straighten my disheveled shirt. "This is why I didn't want to tell you. I'm not interested in fueling your feud with him, and I already told you it's your call since you obviously know him better, but . . . yes, it's for Arrik. I overheard something today when I was outside his room with Cal."

And now there's a dash of misgiving. "You guys went to the other side of the manor? Why?"

"I don't know. I think Cal's some kind of adrenaline junkie, but that's beside the point. While we were over there, I overheard Arrik." I gauge Vel's response and add, "With his mother."

Vel's reply is blunt: "Oh."

"So you know?"

"What, that she's the actual devil? Yes, I'm aware. Imagine being the kid of the woman her husband left her for."

I do imagine it.

And it causes Velis to grip his own chest. "G-geezus, Dolly! Your empathy's in overdrive! That was a joke. I'm fine. Arrik's fine. We're all *fine*."

I wait, listening for non-existent crickets.

He sighs, feeling the pull of the truth oath. "Are you really going to make me say it? Are you really going to make me say that I'm not fine? Because that's a shitload to dredge up, and I'd rather not start that conversation at sixty-seven in the aftermorning."

He knows I have no reference for what time of day it is here. That was an offer to stop this encroaching argument and divert to banter.

"Fine," I say, flinging my hand like I'm the one who has magic. "I revoke it. But you have to promise we can find time to talk about it soon." Nope. Let's try that again. "I mean . . . *if* you decide you want to talk about it, I'll listen, and I won't judge you for anything you did or didn't do to defend yourself when you were kids, okay?"

He's right. He shouldn't be forced into telling me.

Just as I shouldn't have been forced to tell him I was worried about Arrik.

His jaw falls. "I'm only just realizing how hypocritical that was."

You know, it's a lot easier to resolve conflict when your boyfriend can practically *read* your *thoughts* and is committed to making you feel good at all times.

"It's okay." I extend an offering of peace. "And to be totally honest, I'm not even sure I should be the one you talk to about it. The creep of codependence is strong." I stop because he laughs. "What's funny?"

"You open the door with basically an empath's dream, and then you immediately slam it shut. So atonement-arc Dolly." He leans forward as he reads me, softening. "Sweetheart. Of course I'm going to talk to you about it." The warmth of his thumb grazes over my cheekbone, and his crystalline gaze shifts from one of my eyes to the other. "Eventually, I'm going to admit to you that I'm not fine, and then I'm going to expect you to comfort the shit out of me. But . . . there's some truly fucked-up stuff, and I'm not about to tarnish your whole image of me in one night." He gives me honesty, followed by protective teasing. "I haven't tricked you into marrying me yet."

Sweetheart.

Has he ever called me 'sweetheart' before?

And why doesn't it feel cheesy when he says it?

"And about my brother—I get it, okay? I can *feel* it through you, so I know where you're coming from. But knowing the things he's done over the years? Not only to me but to my friends? My *girlfriends*? It's just hard to stomach the thought of you caring about him."

"I don't care about him," I say too quickly.

Velis waits.

"Much," I add.

Goddamned truth oath.

"Ha. You have no idea how badly I wish that were true." He allows a spark of humor to manifest before dulling it. "Listen, I know we've decided to stay tethered until we're back from our pilgrimage so that you can wish us out of trouble if things get dicey, as well as maintain free access to your world, but for me, it also means being in a relationship with someone who can't keep anything from me. But you are entitled to that. You shouldn't have to stifle your feelings just because I can feel them. It's just that your empathy is crazy distracting sometimes. It's a lot stronger than other humans I've been around."

I'm not sure why. I'm not all that sparkly of a person.

"Can I just wish for it to be less?" I ask.

"No, you don't want to start messing with that stuff. You need your empathy. Just promise me you'll be careful with my brother, okay? They're both dicks, but while Jeb is malicious, Arrik is *sneaky*. He'd do anything to make himself feel better about himself. Anything."

And again, we've left out Beckham.

If I had to guess, Vel's vision is clouded when it comes to all three of his brothers. But I know this isn't my call to make. And I know he'll do the same for me in the future. Compromise is different than submission, and I'm not interested in complicating things by befriending the bad-boy brother.

"Today was a fluke, Vel. I plan to keep my distance."

He studies the night wind playing at the ends of my hair. "I think I can help with that. What are your plans tomorrow?"

Pfft. He knows I have no *plans*. "Sleep until noon. Eat an egg. Masturbate. Eat another egg."

His eyes shine over my answer. "Shame. It sounds like you're all booked up."

"Why?" I bait. "Were you planning to take me somewhere?"

"Nowhere special," he says. "Just the nymph realm. But if your time's all taken up by scarfing eggs and wanking it—"

I laser focus in on him, waiting for the oath to enact.

It doesn't.

The slow dispersal of his dimples is a thing of beauty. "Aphrotica, Dolly. I'm taking you to Aphrotica. We leave first thing in the morning."

I do my best not to knock him over both physically and emotionally. "You got it? Velis, you got the permit?!"

He laughs. "My father crammed about three weeks' worth of paperwork into one to accommodate this, but yeah. I actually found out a little while ago, but I wanted it to be a surprise. For future reference, are surprises something you like, or . . . ?"

A cute genie wants to know if I like surprises.

I give him a full, disarmed smile that makes his throat dance. "I love them, Vel. I love surprises. And I can't wait to leave."

At last.

At last, at last.

Our adventure will begin.

A Bomb-Ass Genie Sequel

CHAPTER 4
Faux Leather

"Oh my god, Velis, what is *that*?"

The genie tips his head like the puppy he is. "You mean my riding uniform?"

Yes. His cute-ass leather uniform.

"Why do you need that? There's no real danger of crashing, is there? Doesn't your bike run on magic?"

"It does here, but I don't know how it's going to react in foreign realms. I might have to conserve." He tosses me a jacket made of leather. "Here's yours. I'm sure you'll feel right at home in it."

I nod to the suitcase strapped to the back of his sleek motorcycle-like vehicle. "Lucky my whip disassembles."

"Oo, which one did you bring?"

Pervert. With his stupid, cute, perverted smile. This is going to be one redundant journey if I can't get my desires in check.

"Ready, Master?" Still wearing that dirty smile, the genie extends a hand to help me onto his bike.

To me, it just looks like the electric version of a dirt bike, but according to Velis, the two-wheeled vehicles are called 'zippers' here. For once, we won't be teleporting.

Only registered wish granters are allowed to pop in and out of the human realm without restriction. Any other realm, or any other djinn, and they're supposed to cross at designated gates. Genie Customs, if you will. And the reason Vel got in trouble for his stint in the goblin realm when we were trying to throw off Jeb's bird.

Vel's neck is craned to get a look at me getting situated behind him.

"What?"

"That looks good on you."

He's referring to the fitted jacket I've just finished zipping to the neck. It does feel a bit sexy. Especially with the way he's eyeing me up like I'm the last tater tot in the basket. I glance down at my sleeves. "What kind of leather is this?"

"Pegasus."

Blink. Blink.

He winks. "Kidding. They're endangered. It's synthetic." He moves to adjust the chinstrap of my helmet, his eyes full of mischief and life, his fingers a little clumsy.

"So pegasuses—pegasi? They exist. As in, we could go see one?"

"Oh, Dolly Jones. I'm gonna show you so much shit." The last I see of his grin is amused and a little smug as he turns to face front. "Hold on tight."

I've never been on a bike before. A bicycle yes, but not a bike-bike. And I've definitely never been on a magical djinn bike before. I grip Velis with my thighs, wrap my arms around his middle, and wait for the rumble of the engine.

But, stupid me, this bike runs on *soul juice*—likely from all the influencers who have come before. There is no hum of life. No growl or puff of exhaust. Vel simply leans forward and flares his eyes bright enough to reflect off the front of the dash, and the next minute—

Our departure is supposed to be a secret one. Not even Caliko knows it's happening today. *I* barely knew it was happening today. The excessively large Reilhander mansion at our backs is hauntingly quiet as the Makayen sun slowly rises over it. Even the gardens' many birds haven't bothered to start twitterpating—or whatever the fuck they do so early in the morning.

It would be smart for Vel to ease into this. To slowly give the vehicle life. But he can't help messing with me any more than I can help—

"AHHHHHHHHH!"

I cling to him, letting out a scream that is nothing like the girly ones found in horror films.

The zipper silently moves from a dead standstill to a speed fast enough to make me fear flinging off the back. I would, too, if it weren't for the bubble of blue light Vel's conjured around us—a cushion to keep us in.

I hear him laughing over the blast of the wind and retaliate by sinking nails into his protective mythical-creature leather.

"Well, now that we've woken the entire mansion!" I shout at him over the deafening sound of rushing air.

"What do you think I am? A hack? No one heard you. No one can even see us right now."

"Then why did you make me creep around after you through the entire manor this morning?! You kept shushing me!"

"Because you look cute in your little burglar stealth mode."

This. Bitch.

I lift myself up so that my mouth is to his ear. "You will be punished, genie boy."

"Hope so." He indeed sounds way too hopeful over the prospect.

Excitement surges through me as the wheels of the zipper propel us over perfect white pavement, stark against emerald banks of grass unoccupied by any other djinn traveler. My short hair whips out from under my helmet while Vel leans forward like a motocross racer. Bet he's loving this. Bet he feels all *alpha* over it.

Good. Soak it in, Vel. And then shine for me after.

The way this feels. This rushing, exhilarating feeling. It's like getting on a plane for the first time. It's like nothing else matters but the week ahead.

Because Vel and I are a thing. Vel and I are about to traverse the *nymph* realm together. Alone and free, and no one knows it but the daddy of the manor and Evaris.

And Arrik, I guess. Arrik with his stupid tracker.

ARRIK WITH HIS STUPID TRACKER?!

The thought hits me with brick-like tenacity.

If Arrik placed that tracker on my soul, then doesn't he know I was creeping around outside his bedroom yesterday? That I heard what I heard?

And Arrik? You're disgusting.

Vel's posture tightens in front of me. "You okay?" he asks.

Fucking emotions. I don't want them. I don't want to feel sorry for Arrik.

But . . . it isn't that I feel sorry for him. That would be sympathy. What I feel is empathy. Because I know what it feels like to be torn down by another person, though I can't imagine it coming from my own mother.

Shit.

I can't feel compassion for Arrik. He's an asshole who tormented Velis and tried to steal his win, and that's the only way I need to think of him. Not as someone who helped talk me out of my head when Velis was stuck in the past, or who came to warn us at my mom's, or who complimented my art and pledged his loyalty to me.

I cannot become friends with Arrik Reilhander.

Vel says nothing more, though he can surely feel my flowing guilt. And while I know he told me not to stifle my feelings for his sake, it isn't that simple. I can't just willingly flaunt things I know would hurt him.

I won't let anything hurt him. Not even me.

It's scary to think that I could.

Love is fucking scary.

I hug him tighter and can practically feel the emotion pressing out of my chest and into his back as we continue against the wind. Empathic Vel's hand finds my thigh as if to say, 'It's okay. I love you too.' He keeps it there for the better part of an hour as the swishy blend of landscape framing the clean pavement morphs from emerald-green into the red of poppies, then back into limer shades of green. And only when the zipper begins to slow does Vel's hand squeeze my leg and slip away.

"Are you alive back there, you little masochist? It's been, like, ten minutes since your last burst of remorse."

He's offering me recovery from the vulnerability I feel.

"Don't fret your arrow, rich kid," I counter, grateful. "I'm alive."

He pulls into a turnoff at the side of the road, where sits a small tollbooth-like structure constructed of golden brick and surrounded by flowers, the sun glinting off it high enough now to soak into my neck. It feels different than the sun back home. That one pushes heat, but this one seems to hit with magical energy. It catches Vel's eyes as I release my helmet and shake out my hair.

"What?"

"Nothing."

Based on the way his mouth is kicked up at the corner, it's not nothing.

He dips low to whisper at me: "My girlfriend's hot."

I nudge at him just enough to knock him off balance, then saunter past as his grin swells. "So this is genie Customs?" I ask. "An unmanned tollbooth surrounded by a cluster of daisies on the side of a road? Isn't there, like, a portal or something?"

"Okay, I didn't understand half of what you just said. Except for 'portal.' But it isn't a portal. It's a gate. I need to go have it activated." From his backpack, he produces his Ray, swirling with that magical blue film my mortal eyes can't pierce. He nods for me to follow him to the tollbooth. "Paperwork's in order, so all I need to do is—" He stands before the empty window, twiddling his fingers over his Ray. There's a flash of light, and the next moment, the previously empty window holds a body. And a head.

It's a thirty-something djinn with long, feathered hair in a deep shade of indigo. When she sees us, she sticks up her finger prudently. "Hold, please."

There's another flash of blue, and she's gone.

"Sure," Vel responds after the fact. He looks back to reassure me, "It's a weekday. The wait should go quick."

Is it a weekday? Do they even have weekdays? With that strange four-handed clock system, I assumed their calendars were different too.

Before I can ask, a second flare of djinn blue drenches the flowers, and the indigo woman is again before us, holding a finger to the middle of her ear like she's muting an earpiece.

"Name?" she says.

"Laird Velis Reilhander."

Wow. So much conviction. It seems like he's gotten used to his title in the last week.

"Destination?"

"The nymph realm, Aphrotica."

The woman pokes at the air in front of her, though there's no screen. "It says here you've got a travel companion?"

"Dolly Jones. Human realm."

"Pet?"

I lift my chin, daring Velis to label me his pet.

"If only I could collar her," he teases over his shoulder at me, then back to the woman, "No, she's my master."

The woman stops to look past him to where I stand all snazzied up in fitted leather. "It doesn't say this is wish related." She swipes her fingers as if breezing through a dating app.

Velis shakes his head. "Not wish related. She *was* my master. Technically still is. But she's also my fiancée, the future lady of our estate. I'm not sure how she's classified in your system."

There's a long pause from the woman, and then—

"Goodness." She raises judgy brows at us while returning to pattering around on a console we can't see. "And your business in Aphrotica?"

Goodness? Okay, lady.

Velis doesn't falter. "The nymphean pilgrimage."

The woman waits for elaboration.

"Because I'm . . ." And here is where Velis does falter.

I imagine it's uncomfortable for him. Admitting to the woman he isn't full djinn and that he's bringing his human girlfriend to see his nymph relatives. He's distracted by the way she's looking at us, realizing we're going to be put into situations like this from here on out.

Only a few steps separate us. I close the distance and let my knuckles faintly brush against his.

You got this, Vel.

"I'm a quarter nymph," he finishes, stronger. "And my lady and I are undertaking a marriage ritual customary to my people. It should all be on record, though." His brows knit. "These questions are unnecessary, so why are you asking them?"

The woman eyes us overtly enough that I have a sudden desire to lunge at her. "This request is unusual," she says as her eyes flick away. "And permission to enter the nymph world is uncommon. I'm just making sure it's entered correctly."

"It's entered correctly," Vel says, unimpressed. "Open the gate."

"Er, yes, Laird Reilhander. Of course." The woman pushes a lock of escaped hair behind her ear. "Just one more question: Are you transferring anything that may be considered a weapon?"

Velis knows I don't really have a whip along, but I have an impulse to ask the woman if handcuffs count, just to see him react. Payback for that collar comment.

But to my surprise—

"Yes," he responds.

I tip my face to study him. I don't know anything about a weapon.

"Other than the one noted here?" the woman asks.

"No. And you should have an exception on file for that one."

"I do."

"Then we're good," attests Velis, his impatience stewing.

"Yes, Laird Reilhander. Please, take this." The girl extends a small artifact to Velis. A shiny obsidian ring with a red stone embedded in the center. "Your passport. Don't remove it during the duration of your stay."

Of course djinn would have arcane-looking objects for passports.

The woman waits for Velis to slide the black ring onto his middle finger before pattering at the air. "You may return to your vehicle with your pet—er, your lady. I'll load the gate."

Is it just me, or was that an *intentional* slip?

Bitch.

"Thanks for your time." Velis slips his ringed hand over mine and begins back toward the zipper, shooting eyes to me now that the woman can't see. "Annoying," he says, low.

"Let's kill her," I whisper back.

It draws a smirk from him, one that remains even after he re-snaps his helmet and straddles the bike. He leans forward in a preparatory stance as a shower of sparkling blue magic materializes over the road before us. Water-like beads catch the daylight and pellet atop the white concrete, staining it azure momentarily before being absorbed.

Vel glances back once to soak in my reaction to the beauty of it before twisting forward and juicing our vehicle to life. "Hold on, Doll."

"Holding, *doll*."

I do hold tight to him this time—fool me once and all that jazz—and prepare for the whiplash.

Only, instead of a jet of speed, Velis gently crawls us forward at a devastatingly languid pace. And it isn't just to put down my defenses so that he can reuse the same trick twice. No, he merely drives us painfully slowly into the curtain of falling light while the woman in the window watches us with obvious judgment for a good five minutes.

What a *shit*.

I won't give him the satisfaction of asking when he's going to speed up. And he's stubborn enough not to do so without me asking. So we creep forward until the snout of the zipper finally breeches the wall of blue.

When we come out on the other side, the emerald hills and

perfect white road are gone. The 'gate' that's definitely not a *portal* has teleported us somewhere new.

"Wait." I lean around Velis to get a better look at what lies ahead. "THIS is the nymph world?"

What the fuck?!

CHAPTER 5
The Black City

"Yeah, I've never been here before, but this is about what I've seen in replication—why, what were you expecting?"

I don't know. Flowers. Waterfalls. Woodland . . . stuff?

This is none of that.

The tires of the bike have dug into the peppery sand of what looks to be a desert at the outskirts of a modern city of skyscrapers backed by a gray sky. Not an overcast sky. Not a night sky. A *gray* sky. Completely devoid of all temperament, like someone painted over it with the dullest color in the box. There are no clouds, no breeze. The air is stale. And that city is all black, alien almost, and shiny, though there's no sun to catch it.

"Does color not exist in this world?" I take off my helmet to ensure the lens isn't distorting my vision. The city remains black, the sky gray, the soft sand around us colored like old ash. Velis and I and our warmly hued flesh stand out like a stain.

"It does, it's just less abundant here than in our realms. If I remember correctly, color stores energy here," he says.

I crane my neck to search the horizon for a spot of it, but all I see is gray. "Didn't you say nymphs can control the weather? I guess I thought it would be more nature-y."

"Oh yeah, they can. But according to my class on realms,

there's a stunter in place to keep the world from falling into chaos. It used to cause a lot of problems, all those people being able to control the elements at once. Nowadays, they have rec rooms in their dwellings where they can play around with it, but out in the open, it's like a blank slate. It's been that way for a few hundred years, I think." His tone is distracted as he removes his helmet and sniffs at the air. "Hey, do you feel weird here?"

"Weird how?"

He gives his head a shake. "Not sure. Just different. Maybe it's that stunter I mentioned. Maybe my nymph side's picking it up. I just feel a little . . . off."

I dismount the bike to get a better look at him. "I feel normal. Is it your magic?"

"Could be," he says. "Here, let's test it. Wish for something. But make it a good one. Really *command* it out of me."

"You'd like that, wouldn't you?"

His mouth twitches at the corner. "I live to serve."

"I wish I had a bag of Cheetos." An almost always true statement. I say it like I'm wishing for revenge on my worst enemy, just to satisfy him. Vel's eyes flare, and the next minute, he's holding an unnaturally orange bag, which he tosses at me after a small shiver of pleasure. They're not Cheetos. These say 'Chestos.' I give the bag a pop and taste one. "Definitely knockoffs," I note, crunching a chip that's not quite salty enough to satisfy.

"Well, my magic's semi-working," he says, licking the pads of his fingers that have just brushed my shiny soul as I lick at my own cheese-dusted ones. "It does feel off. But that's no surprise. I've been to a few other realms, and it's always hit or miss. I'm supercharged in the goblin realm just because that place is so *basic*. All that matters is that I have enough juice to get us out of here if needed."

I glance behind us, finding nothing but more bleak desert. "The tollbooth is gone, though. So how do we get back?"

"We don't have to bother with any of that again," he says. "Ours is a two-way ticket. I can zip us back whenever, no penalty. We just can't come back once we do."

Good. Because this place is a lot lamer than I was expecting.

"We won't be able to ride into the city, though. My bike can't handle this kind of terrain." He lowers the vehicle onto its side on the sandy ground. "Stand back a ways? I'm gonna have to shrink it."

'Have to' he says. He *loves* shrinking things.

The sand consumes my feet to the ankles as I step away to give him space. It's more like dust than anything else. Moondust. This stylish little jacket fits right in. Kind of a dystopian punk vibe. I unzip it to expose the dark T-shirt underneath. Now I kind of wish I'd picked a brighter color. I push up my sleeves to complete the look, which won't ever truly be completed without a sick pair of fingerless gloves. Maybe I'll wish for Vel to whip some up for me.

—Is what I think until I see the way his 'shrinking' magic works out for him.

There's a burst of blue light, and he's suddenly standing beside a comically large version of his zipper bike. The thing's at least quadrupled in size.

"Oh shit!" Velis leaps away from it. "That was the opposite of what I wanted to happen! What the fuck?"

Well, that doesn't offer much confidence for us getting home!

"You had better luck with the Chestos. Want me to try wishing this one too?" I ask.

"That might work . . ." He zeroes in on me, his gaze even more piercing than usual with no other color to compete against.

I almost feel like taking a step backward. "What?"

"If we do that, it'll be a bigger wish. I'll actually have to connect with your soul this time, instead of just grazing it."

And I haven't made many wishes since arriving at the manor. He looks almost hungry at the thought.

I lift a brow at him. "Do . . . you want to come over here for it?"

Wishes feel good for him. Even better now that my soul is unlocked. That shiver he released over those counterfeit Cheetos —I want to see it magnified by a hundred. His jaw flexes when he feels it in me, his expression taking on something more serious than he's shown me all day as he makes his way over through layers of dusty earth, our difference in height becoming more apparent the nearer he draws.

"Hey, Vel," I say, looking up at him through lashes I swear have been magically lengthened.

"Yes, Master?" His voice is steady in the dead space.

I motion with my head. "See that zipper over there?"

He doesn't look. "Yeah?"

"I want you to shrink it."

"Do ya?"

I give him a nod. He leans forward, the heat of his breath against the smallest hairs of my ear. His fingertips coil around the back of my neck.

"You have to say the words."

But I don't say the words. Instead—

"You're a tease, Master."

He says so because my hand has found its way firmly to his junk. Based on the response of his body, he's not disappointed by it.

Totally normal. Feeling up my genie boyfriend in a world devoid of color as some bizarre yet erotic foreplay to a wish he's about to grant.

If only he were wearing sweatpants.

I don't even have to say it. With a brilliant blue blink, the restriction of his jeans melts to pliable fabric.

Okay, but these aren't sweatpants. They're disgusting neon windbreaker pants because my wish has been mutilated by his wonky magic.

But does it stay my growing horniness?

The fabric makes a fuss as I dip my hands below. "Velis Reilhander. Shrink that bike. As your master, I wish you would."

His eyes start to glow.

"—But I wish you wouldn't do it quite yet."

"*Tease.*"

As I'd hoped, his eyes become stuck between lit and unlit. I feel him further harden as my fingers tighten around him, and his kiss finds my neck. I make him stay that way for thirty seconds.

"Master." His pant hits the crevice beneath my chin.

I don't know how it works for sure, but I suspect his fingers are just feathering the reaches of my soul's light. Coupled with the feeling of my fingers around his flesh—

"All right. I wish you'd do it now, Velis."

"Fffffuck." The sinew of his neck tightens as his eyes flash bright enough to douse both our cheeks in electric blue. He uses one of his hands to force me to his chest and the other to half-assedly throw magic in the direction of the zipper.

"Did it work?" I muffle against him in the aftermath.

"I don't know. I don't care." He brushes his lips against my hairline. "Goddamn, Dolly. Why haven't we ever tried that before?"

Well, this is new. And fun. So much *power*.

"I can feel that, you friggen' sadist," he says dryly.

"Let's hope your rellies give us lodging," I retort as I withdraw my hand from his unsatisfied warmth.

The bike is nowhere in sight—just the pack holding Vel's Ray and his vessel, where our other belongings are stored. The wish worked a little too well. I'm pretty sure the zipper is shrunken to the size of a single fleck of sand.

Velis kicks at the dust. "Guess you'll just have to *wish* for it next time we need it," he says. "But next time, *we're finishing*."

Okay, so there's darkness at the end of his statement, but it's reeeally hard to take him seriously with those gaudy windbreaker pants swishing every time he steps. He's either got enough confidence or not enough human fashion knowledge not to flinch.

This guy.

He's my favorite.

"You gonna stand around giving me goo-goo eyes all day, *Master*, or should we begin our quest?"

"Well, I was going to grab your dick again, but if you'd rather—"

"N-now, now, not so hasty."

But I've already brushed past him. "You know, you haven't actually told me anything about this pilgrimage we're supposed to take. I assumed it was going to be to some ancient ruins where we'd have to kiss on top of a magical pedestal or something, but now that we're outside black and white Chicago—"

"Ancient ruins? What the hell are you talking about? And what's Chicago?"

I snort. "Never mind."

His puzzlement probes me as he sticks a hand in his back pocket and pulls out a piece of folded paper. "We have to go here."

Whatever language is scribbled on the page, it's neither English nor Makayen.

"I can read it if I squint," he says, doing just that. "The nymph in me can. It's directions my mother left for me. Cross your fingers I've got enough skill to read the street signs."

A note from his mom? He mentioned he keeps one in the locked cabinet in his room. This looks like a piece torn off.

"Where does it lead?" I ask.

"The matriarch of my mother's family—her cousin, Joell. I don't know much about them aside from the lore my mom told me as a kid. Apparently, it's rare for females to head family lines here, but my line doesn't produce many males, so it's traditionally been females. According to Evaris, my nymph grandmother stepped down when my grandfather's vessel led him to her. My mother was raised in the djinn world, but she did come back here the once. I guess she would have been matriarch had she decided to stay, but she chose to be with my dad when he finally came around, so it went to her cousin instead."

"I can't really picture your dad on a journey like this. He seems like one of those people who was never young."

"Right? But he did. And his magic would have been messed up like mine, and he wouldn't have been able to read their language at all, so he would have had to rely on my mother when they were here. Same with my grandfather when he was here with my grandmother."

And now the quarter-nymph djinn is here with his human.

To get his family's blessing to marry me.

Admittedly, I've been thinking of this little quest as a vacation for us, but the closer we get to the gates of that blackened city, the deeper that truth is starting to sink. I'd never, ever even have considered marrying a human boy I'd met only weeks ago.

Vel's basically my soulmate, right?

So why is the thought of marriage still so . . .

Velis feels it in me and halts. "You know it's okay to say stuff like that out loud."

Empaths.

"I mean it, Dolly. You have been through an extreme amount of shit in a short amount of time. It's okay if you don't feel normal about what's happening. I know it's fast. And I know you're still recovering from everything you went through. If you start to feel like you need a break, tell me. You get a say in this. I don't want to hurt you."

To search him is to see the soft emotion behind his eyes. That sacrificial longing. Those perfect features so willing to bend for my sake.

Marriage. It's big. Too big.

But I don't want a break from him. I want to spend every moment with him because our moments together are sexy and fun and sweet.

They're my favorite.

"You're my favorite."

I don't say it intentionally. It just falls out of me, like it's the one sentence that matters most. The one that would correct any miscommunication. Get us out of any argument.

The way he's looking at me. The things he says to me. How could you not fall flat-on-your-face in love with a person like that?

For a moment, his expression is completely fixated, his stare even more devastating than usual. And then he suddenly hunches forward with his hands on his knees and unleashes a long, shaky breath. "H-holy shit. That felt next-level good, Dolly. I felt every shard of color as it collected into that release of emotion—like your soul was in my mouth and against my tongue." His expression flickers to something darker than I've ever seen it. "I wanted to take a bite."

Woah. This world is influencing him for sure. My eyes linger on his mouth, curious to see how he might react to different prompts in this state, how else we might satisfy that *thirst* clearly gleaming in his eyes.

"Vel—"

"*Move and I shall kill you where you stand!*"

We really are enamored with each other to a sickening degree. It's enough to have distracted us from a figure approaching, one who now stands within shouting distance on the edge of the sandy city, pointing what appears to be the nozzle of a hose at us.

And inside that hose is liquid the most intense color red I've ever seen.

Vel's fingers find mine, and he gently coaxes me behind his back, saying so that only I can hear, "Be ready to make a wish, Master."

CHAPTER 6
Magical Seed

THE WOMAN HOLDS the hose at the ready, the body of it snaked over her shoulders and connected to a small box on her hip. The magic inside the plastic sheathing throbs vibrantly against her neck, a sharp contrast to her own dull skin, which shows only a whisper of pink through the gray. She's as dull as the rest of this world and dressed in a dark jumpsuit that looks like it belongs in a warehouse, a shade so muted it might as well be black. Colorful Velis and I stick out like a sore finger and thumb.

He's obviously the finger, I'm obviously the thumb.

The woman jabs the hose at us, sending the brilliant liquid inside sloshing. "State your business," she demands. Despite the severity of her tone, Velis doesn't answer right away.

"*Vel?*" I urge, clutching his arms from behind.

"Hm." He digests whatever was giving him pause, then confidently faces off against the woman. "My name is Velis Reilhander of Makaya, and I have a passport to enter your land."

Nice. Very official sounding.

"You are jinnee?" the woman questions.

"I'm also part nymph, of the bloodline Evangeline, here to meet with the matriarch of my line for permission to wed my betrothed."

The hose lowers slightly. "Evangeline?"

"Yes."

"You are male."

"Yes?"

It's pretty obvious by the look of him that he is, indeed, male. The smell of him too, if you're lucky enough to get close.

"What is your mother's name?" the woman persists.

It earns another pause. "Adelle," he says. "Adelle Evangeline."

It's a name befitting of the beauty kept in those golden frames in every room of the estate. It's also a name he's never told me before now. And if he's never offered it freely before, I imagine it must be with reason. I slide a hand of comfort to his back.

I've got a name like that in my life. 'Danny Jones' has a way of feeling tart on the tongue.

The woman seems to be processing the information she's just been presented, though it's unlikely that in a city this size, one name would stand out among—

"Velis Evangeline, son of Adelle Evangeline," she repeats. "Passage is granted." She secures the hose nozzle into a holster on her thigh and beckons us with her opposite hand. "Approach."

I take it back. Apparently, one name is recognizable even in a place with dozens of tall buildings invading the horizon.

Velis acts as a partial shield for me as we make our way to the wall surrounding the city where the woman waits—a wall that starkly separates those ominous, towering skyscrapers from the lonely desert stretching beyond. The woman keeps her hand on the fastened nozzle and nods to Velis. "Your coloration will fade. It is normal." She shifts her eyes to me. "Hers will remain. She is a valkyrie, yes?"

Velis snorts. "Human. But I can see why you'd think that."

Why she'd think I was a *valkyrie*? Um, why?

"Human?" The woman studies me. "Rare."

This is the last she says before showing us her back and hoisting herself up the rungs of a metal ladder propped against the city's wall, at the top of which sits a small watchtower Velis and I completely missed amid our *goo-goo* eyes. This spot must be common for portalling—excuse me—*gating* into this realm.

Velis watches the woman with his forehead furrowed until she hits the top.

"Weird," he says.

"What is?"

"You know how I said I was more susceptible to your emotions here? They seem to be amplified in this realm. Well, with her, it's the opposite. I usually have a harder time reading non-humans, but . . . this was different. I've never been around someone that felt like that before. There wasn't even a trace of emotion. Is it because she's a nymph?"

"Could you feel your mom when she was alive?"

"Y-yeah. I couldn't read her, but I could feel her warmth."

"So it's not a nymph thing. Must have something to do with this world."

"You're right." He shakes his head to shake away his speculation. "At least we got in. Let's go figure out where this matriarch lady lives. We've only got a two-day lead until Arrik tells Jeb we're here."

And Beckham. Let's not forget Beckham.

We move through the dust ebbing up to the city's entrance, eyes locked on the woman as she peers down from her perch, talking into a small radio-like device.

Nymphs use walkie-talkies. Noted.

And since we're on the subject, 'walkie-talkie' is kind of an absurd word, isn't it? It's really no better than 'caffeine machine,' and this one's not made up.

If I had to guess, she's informing others of our arrival.

Velis grips my hand as we move through the opening in the outer wall and take our first steps into the place where his grandmother was born.

"What?" he gasps. His eyes frantically search the long thoroughfare stretching before us.

Glassy skyscrapers edge up to the sidewalk, reaching far enough into the ashen heavens to make you sick if you look up at them too long. The roads between are too narrow to fit cars, because cars likely don't exist in this world, and sharp-cornered enough to appear like the whole city was plotted out with rulers. It's all bizarrely modern and Earth-like, and at the same time, a little extraterrestrial. Here and there, glimpses of color show, so faded they're barely discernible. And despite the dust outside, the streets are pristine, I assume due to the lack of wind.

Too bad. If we had wind, we might see a tumbleweed rolling through, which would be a welcome change. The city is completely without motion. It's totally deserted.

Where the hell is everyone?

"It's so lifeless," I whisper, inching closer to Vel's warmth, scanning the streets for some sign of life or death but finding neither. All I see are wastebaskets, dead branches spouting out of pots, seating areas before storefronts, all looking like props from a black and white movie set.

"I don't like it in here," Vel says, looking distracted as he watches our reflection distort against a sheet of dark glass. "In every other realm I've been to, there's this hum of emotion in the air, sort of awake and buzzy, and even if I can't always pick up specifics from it, I can at least feel *something*. But this place is empty. Your soul is the only thing out here. Without it, it feels like I'd get—I don't know, lost."

"Do you think there's been some mistake? It's hard to believe your grandmother came from a place like this. Your mother was so beautiful, I just assumed the nymph world would be paradise." I gesture to the signage over what appear to be a strip of shops. "Maybe we're in an unused part of town. What's it say?"

"It's all generic," Vel says, squinting. "Stuff like *medicine, food, clothing*." He turns to me, a little sharper than is natural. "Dolly, I fully intended to milk this trip for all it was worth, but now, I say let's get in and out of here as quickly as possible, okay? I'll take you somewhere nice after. This is . . . not what I expected. I mean, I knew color was conserved here, but I didn't think it would *feel* like this." He brings a strained hand to his chest. "I don't like it."

I edge in closer to him, feeling watched. "Me neither. And if this is a shopping district, where are all the shoppers?"

He shakes his head and slips an arm around me territorially, retrieving the piece of paper from his back pocket with his other hand. "If I'm reading this right, we need to find Evangeline Tower in the residential area. It says there will be . . . Shit, this word is blurry. An angel? A big angel on it?"

Okay, well, there's definitely nothing angelic as far as I can see.

"Maybe we should just forget it. I mean, who says we need their permission any—"

"There." Vel's pale eyes are set on the distance. "That's it. It wasn't *angel*. It was *halo*."

A halo?

I set my gaze even to his and find it. Hard to discern in this grayscale world, but there's a thin halo of light circling the top of one of the skyscrapers.

Not just one of them.

The tallest one in the entire skyline.

Of course his family tower is the LARGEST ONE IN THE FUCKING CITY.

And now that Vel's caught sight of it, he's stalwartly marching toward it, his arm abruptly removed from my shoulder.

"V-Vel?!"

He acts like he hasn't heard me, so I hurry to catch up to him, my footsteps a forlorn echo against the sleek gray pavement.

"Velis?"

"Come on." His voice is strangely hollow.

Again, I glance behind us, and this time, I swear I catch movement in the windows of one of the storefronts.

"VEL!" I snatch his elbow. "I think we're being watched."

"Guh!" He gives a jolt like he's just been struck through the center of the chest. "Fear." He tears his eyes from the halo of light to set them on me. "You're afraid."

Accurate.

"Hell yes, I'm afraid! This place is freaky! And I'm pretty

sure we're being watched. There! Did you just see that? In that window up there? Movement. Not, like, people working movement. Like, people darting around sneakily movement! And—and what was that just now? You were getting all freaking trance-like!"

"Fuck." He grits his teeth and scratches at his hair. "I don't feel right, Dolly. But I feel like it will get better when we reach that tower." His eyes connect with the halo of light again, and his voice drifts. "It's almost like it's drawing me . . ."

I jump between him and the tower and take hold of his collar to break his concentration. "As in *magically* drawing you? Because I am not on board with that shit. I think we should leave, *now*."

"We can't." He shuts me down quickly. "I have to do this."

"Why, Velis? *Why* do we need approval from people we've never met? I didn't question it before because I thought we were taking a magical vacation together, but this? I did not sign up for whatever dystopian horror show this is."

"My dad said this was necessary if I—" He stops. "We need to do this if we're to become laird and lady of the estate."

But WHY, though? This is nymph stuff, and Vel's only a quarter nymph, and the estate is inherited through his djinn side. There's something he's not telling me.

Ignoring the movements of whoever's watching us in my peripherals, I pull him so that he's facing away from that dangerous halo of light. "Velis, *why* do we need to make the nymphean pilgrimage?"

"Because they need to bless us."

"That's fucking vague, and you know it."

He says nothing, but there's clear worry drawing over him contagious enough to sink into me.

"Velis?" I release him. "What is it? Whatever it is, just tell me."

He searches me, weighing options in his head, while my pulse escalates in my ears.

"Fine," he says, a little guilty, a little defeated. "But first, let me tell you why I didn't tell you, okay?"

Now I search him, trying to anticipate whatever he's about to confess, suffering his shared anxiety. "O-okay."

His hands take my shoulders. "The reason I didn't tell you is because you aren't an object, Dolly. I never want you to feel that you are. And I would never use you to fill some role. But . . . I know it looks that way sometimes. And I know you've felt it, by agreeing to start down this path of becoming our lady. I need you to know that when I told you you were my favorite, I meant it. You mean more to me than all the rest of it, okay?"

Okay, but . . . wasn't *I* the one who called him *my* favorite?

Now he's stealing all my best lines.

He waits for me to nod before continuing. "Becoming laird doesn't just mean taking ownership of the estate. It means committing to producing the next heirs of the estate too. If I can't commit to that, then I can't become laird. I already tried. My hand won't sign the contract."

"What do you mean? Why not?"

"It's that whole stunter magic. It isn't just on their world. It's on us too—those of us with nymph blood." His focus is steady, like the world's sexiest doctor about to reset a dislocated shoulder, making sure I'm ready for the *pop!* "Without their blessing, I'm physically unable to produce an heir."

Admittedly, we've been having reckless sex without fear of consequences because I assumed he'd been taking care of things magically on his end. But—

"Like, you're infertile?"

He gives one small nod. "This is a controlled society, and one of their ways of maintaining control is a spell on our blood. It's like a curse in your lore. And because of the magical terms in place over the estate, I need it removed before I can claim my title, and I need to present them my mate in order to get them to remove it." He takes a long, reluctant breath. "Basically, I need you to help me prove we're deserving of children."

Now I understand his hesitation. Because playing fiancée is one thing, but I am definitely, definitely, DEFINITELY not ready to play mommy.

All the commitment phobia I've ever felt swells up in my throat.

"F-fuck, Velis, who says I even want to have kids?!"

This hits Velis hard enough to make him teeter. "Umph!" He doubles forward, clutching his shirt. "*I know*," he manages through grinding teeth, fighting the sting of my emotion. "*And I knew it would freak you out even more than you already are. But it's not like I want us to start having kids right away. I'm not ready for that either. This is a formality, that's all!*"

A formality . . . that's all?

This human, should you so choose her, shall be lady of our estate—though I strongly suggest you use a surrogate for the bearing of any heirs.

Vel's dad doesn't intend for us to have children anyway. Meaning I really am just here to fulfill some role.

I wasn't feeling like a pawn before, but I sure as hell am now.

"I swear I didn't know." Vel's hand is again on my shoulder, his expression earnest. "Not until recently. And by then, it all seemed like too much. You claim to be doing okay, but I can feel those pangs of doubt in you. With everything else—moving in together, a forced engagement, being stuck in our world alone most of the day—I thought this might be enough to make you . . ."

He stops himself and digests what he was just about to say, his truth coming to light only when it's on the tip of his own tongue.

Yes, he kept the truth from me to spare me.

But he also did it because he thought the truth might be enough to make me bail.

Fear. He feels it too.

Does that mean he doesn't fully trust me? Does my own fear mean I don't fully trust him back? Well, that's not good. If I can't even trust my star-crossed fated lover, then how am I ever going to—

"Let's go back." He says it abruptly.

I look him over. "What?"

"I struggled with whether to tell you, and I chose wrong. I can't just decide what you do and don't get to know because I'm afraid of how you'll react. I fucked up, and now I can feel your distrust." He gathers my hands. "This isn't the way we're starting our life together. Let's go back and try dating like a normal couple in your world for a while. I'll just go AWOL and deal with the consequences later."

He's serious. Ready to blip me away.

I don't want to hurt you.

I don't want to hurt him either.

I'm going to make all your wishes come true.

I want to make all his come true too.

"Don't . . . be afraid of me, Vel."

I'm not sure what he expects me to say, but it isn't that. His brows squeeze, and he cracks a small grin. "Yeah? Well . . . you don't friggen' be afraid of me either."

Now I understand the grin. When he says it like that, it sounds so ridiculous. Of course I trust him. I've trusted him my whole life.

We stare at each other a long minute, letting that truth sink in.

"So, what do you say? Want to get out of here? Go hang with Steve the Cat for a few days?"

I love that he seems to think that's my cat's full name.

And of course we aren't going back. Of course I'm going to go help my mythical boyfriend lift the curse on his magical *seed*.

I take a breath and crack my knuckles, setting my sights on the halo of light around Vel's family tower. "All right, Daddy—"

"Oh, EW. Don't call me *that*. You called me something like that in the past too, and it was—" He shivers.

I adore making him skeeve.

"Ass." The next grin he flexes quickly falls to concern. "But are you sure, Master? You don't have to do this for me."

"I'm sure, Vel. Just tell me next time. I can't promise I won't freak, but I'll do my best."

"Sure. Next time we go on a pilgrimage to prove we're not total fuck-ups so that strangers can judge us and deem us worthy of bearing offspring so that I can take over my family legacy despite basically the entire world being against it, I promise to tell you."

Such a shit.

"Hey, by the way, how's your pigment doing?" I lift my arm, and he sets his own next to it, like we're comparing summer tans. "You look the same to me," I say, glad to find the normal bronze of his skin untarnished. "So I guess we've got that going for us. But I swear to god, Velis, if you start getting all weird and trancey again, I'm wishing us to the safety of the goddamned goblin realm."

"Do that," he says. "And thanks. For just being super cool, all the time, about everything. It's kinda a dream. Dating someone like you."

Oh. Flutter, flutter.

"It's a dream dating you too." First I'm soft, then I'm prickly. "But I still don't want kids."

"Ever?"

"I . . . don't know. You?"

"Well, I sure as fuck don't want them right now," he says. "And later? We can talk about later."

Good.

Excellent, actually.

He entwines his fingers with mine and shields his face from the alluring tower. "Lead the way, boss. I'll do my best not to become entranced."

Not a booth. The boss wants a table.

Our fingers flex around one another over the shared emotion that comes with the shared memory, those transparent eyes safely on me as I lead him deeper into the bowels of the cursed city.

I'm not afraid of him.

But I am afraid of something.

I'm just not sure what that something is.

CHAPTER 7
Evangeline Tower

THROUGH DESERTED STREETS harboring only flashes of concealed movement, I lead Velis past the rows of dark skyscrapers in the direction of the haloed building. This place is like a cheaply made video game, lacking the NPCs to feel real. The gray sky is unchanging, the wind missing. There's no scent in the air, and it's getting to the point where even the faintest color showing on neon-like signs is enough to rouse excitement. I can't tell if that's pink or orange, but it's something, at least.

Why did I expect a hundred Velis lookalikes splashing at each other gaily in pools of water and throwing flirty glances from behind trees?

Because Velis. And because *Fantasia*. I really need to stop relying on animated films for my lore.

"Hey, couldn't I just wish us to that building?" Something I probably should have thought of sooner than the dozen blocks we've already trodden.

"You could try, but with how supercharged that shrinking wish was, I'm worried I might teleport us into a wall or something," he says.

"And if I don't fondle you this time?"

His perfectly designed lips cock. "I don't think that was the problem."

Perv. I can't read minds, but if I had to bet, he's thinking of ways we might incorporate wishing into our *canoodling* time from here on out. Imagine springing one on him right when he was about to—

"Keep it in your pants, Master."

Maybe I'm the perv.

"It's coming up, Vel."

Evangeline Tower. The tallest tower of them all. In the exact center of the city. Surrounded by its own courtyard of gray flowers and neat ropes to keep people off the manicured lawn. Seems like overkill for a place without people, but okay.

I lead Velis up the walkway, feeling the warmth of his affection as he places it uncompromisingly on my profile. He's using this as an excuse to ogle the dip of my nose, and it's damn hard not to ogle him back.

The doors of the tower are dark glass with a sleek handle. It looks like somewhere executives would congregate in the mortal realm to do ambiguous things like 'advise' and 'hedge.' To be safe, I take the handle, unsure what it might do to trance-prone Vel.

"Be ready to wish us out of here," he tosses at me.

"On it."

I pull the door, but he's first to enter.

"UMPH!" Velis doubles over, clutching his chest, as color and sunlight saturate us.

Okay, now *this* is what I expected. There are flowers. Everywhere. Whether that door was a portal or *gate*, it's transported us into a space that cannot have physically fit within the confines of the tower. It's a conservatory. And it's huge.

Ripe, fragrant flowers settle around winding footpaths and up terraces, sparkling as if coated in ultra-fine glitter, through an expansive fairyland overrun by tendrils of cascading ivy vivid enough to confuse my gray-adjusted eyes. The air around us is translucently colorful, like the delicate sheen from a bubble. I turn my face and watch the colors shift. The ceiling is vaulted glass, to protect from a sun I know can't possibly exist. In the distance, a concentrated rain shower falls into a pond with swan-like birds that are light blue in color. In the rich moss around it, petaled trees sprout through the ground, with bark that is aged and knotted.

And golden.

The beauty of it all is almost crushing.

"S-sorry, Vel!"

"*You're good,*" he croaks under the weight of my emotion. "*Marvel away.*"

It appears to be a dwelling. Small pieces of furniture hide here and there, curled up in vines and implanted in trunks. Mosaic statues of alien-looking fish and stars comprised of colored mirror fragments dazzle from between tall, twisting hedges. Windchimes catch on easy tosses of breeze, alongside the chirp of birds hidden in the trees.

Nowadays, they have rec rooms in their houses where they can play around with it.

Yeah, I could see Velis frolicking around a place like this, shirtless and mischievous, coaxing me over from between the parted branches of a willow.

"I can get on board with that fantasy, Master." The empath has recovered from my assault of emotion and is now marveling right alongside me, though he's spending equal time looking at it all reflected in my eyes.

"So, were there magical nymph playpens stowed away inside all the towers we passed on the way here?" I ask. "It explains why the city was so deserted. Anyone would choose a place like this over the depressing stretch of urban wasteland out—"

A rustling in the foliage compels Velis to pull me behind him. He crouches at the ready, fingers sparking blue, until—

"Mayster Evangeline! You have arrived!"

An excitable voice breeches the chipper sounds of nature, swiftly followed by an excitable girl who has just come bursting through a wall of fairyland vines vigorously enough to send glitter flying everywhere.

"Ah!" she cries when she sees us. "The Mayster is here! And he is *handsome!*"

"Mayster?" Velis questions under his breath at me.

"*Handsome?*" I mutter.

A second, nearly identical girl steps through the hole ripped open by the first, much less boisterous, her interest immediately caught and held by Vel's presence. She doesn't seem to take any notice of me.

Both girls look to be a year or two younger than Vel, who is already younger than me. I'm the grandma in this situation, and I feel every week that separates us as I study their long, golden hair and fair, beauty-faced features. They're gorgeous, youthful, *vibrant*, with thick thighs exposed by romper-type clothing cut high on the hip and dirty feet that make them look like they've been outside all day, running through fields.

Like how this one is bounding toward us now, having never stopped after breaking through the vines, face flushed and sights set doggedly on Velis. I snatch his hand, prepared to make a wish, but the closer the girl gets, the looser my grip falls because . . .

Is that a *rainbow?*

Yes, a rainbow is steadily forming around the nymph girl as she vaults toward us in slower and slower motion, her silky hair trailing behind her and her eyes sparkling. And they aren't sparkling in a figurative, glossy way. Her eyes are literally SPARKLING, like the cover of an early 2000s manga, her pupils growing larger and more opioid-like the closer she gets.

Nymphs can control the weather, and a lot of them specialize in a specific element like wind or water.

So is this one, like, a *rainbow* nymph, then?

"Fiona! Contain yourself!" the other girl scolds, having hung back by the destroyed vines. She pushes her arms out from her body, and a strong plastering of wind slams into rainbow girl from behind.

Rainbow girl comes to a waffling halt just short of us, her eyes de-sparkling and the colors around her dissipating. "A-apologies!" she says at Velis. "I am working on my control. Joy is not a sensation I have experienced often." She throws her head forward in a hearty bow. "Welcome, Mayster Evangeline. Welcome to your namesake. May I greet you?"

"Namesake?" Velis questions.

"Greet?" I mutter.

Though she asks, the girl doesn't wait for permission. She takes him around the head in a playful embrace, one of her legs popping off the ground, as she presses the tip of her nose cutely to his.

A boop.

This bitch just booped my boyfriend.

Velis leans his face away and pulls me to his hip by a quick hand around the waist.

The girl flits her violet-colored eyes to me as she releases him. "She is your mate?"

She sounds less than pleased. Velis rubs his chest, likely feeling the same.

Rainbow girl shakes her head at herself like she's silly. "Of course it is your mate. Why else would you be here? I am Fiona. I am of your blood. My sister and I"—she nods in the direction of the other girl—"are of your blood."

The second girl bows her head. "I am Gabri. I am of your blood."

"Velis," Velis introduces himself. "And this is Dolly."

"You are part jinnee, yes?" asks the one called Gabri, venturing closer. "Do you retain your benediction?" And when it's clear Velis doesn't know what she means by 'benediction,' "Do you have nymphean magic?" she clarifies.

"Oh, yeah. Just a little."

I expect Velis doesn't get asked often to show off his nymph powers. Looking warily between the pair of them, he fist-bumps his own chest and coughs out a baby burst of fire.

Rainbowy Fiona's eyes begin to sparkle anew in excitement. "A firebreather!"

"Er, and I can do this." Fueled by the girl's reaction, Velis lifts his eyes to the sky, conjuring a fresh flurry of snow that catches my eyelashes on the way to my shoulders. He quickly dries it with a funnel of sunshine and a whoosh of warm wind. "And a few other things." He snaps, and a tiny zip of white lightning cracks between his fingers.

Ooh, never seen that one before.

"Multiple elements," remarks Gabri, catching eyes with her sister.

"I-I am a flutterer," says Fiona. "Gabri is a tempest. But you—"

"We should take him to Mar," says Gabri. "She will be impatient to meet him."

Little twinkly lights form in the space around Fiona's face as her hand eagerly reaches for Vel's. "May I be your escort, Mayster?" But her sparkles quickly fade when she notices the way his free hand has already taken mine. "O-or, I am sure you wish to escort your mate. Please, follow us. We shall lead you to our mother, the matriarch of the line Evangeline."

Their mother is the matriarch? The matriarch is Vel's mom's cousin. Meaning these are his cousins too. To some degree or another.

Fiona nymphs away to join her sister, and both start down a winding path in the direction of a great, Redwood-sized tree. Velis allows a little distance between us and them before following after, through a colorful forest landscape, noting the way they both keep glancing back at us amid murmured conversation.

"This is weird, isn't it?" he says so that only I can hear.

"You mean Lisa Frank over there?"

"Who?"

"Never mind. Yes, it's weird."

"Their emotions are *strong*," he adds. "It almost knocked me on my ass when that one came popping out of those vines. The other is suppressing hers, but still. Humans' emotions are supposed to be strongest, and these are at least double of any human I've met. Well, aside from you."

"I guess that whole stunter magic makes sense, then. A race of hyper-emotional people being able to control the weather? Seems like something that would lead to chaos."

"Let's just hope they give us their blessing quickly so we can get the hell out of here." He helps me over a fallen log in the middle of the garden path. "And then I'm taking you somewhere normal for vacation, like the celestial realm."

Because the *celestial realm* is somewhere *normal*.

"And I'm assuming there's no way for me to just wish the curse off your nuts?"

"My *nuts*? It's on my blood, you turd. And no, unfortunately, this counts as a doom ailment. It can only be removed by the same magic that placed it. We had Ardy take a look."

A doom ailment. Those that can't be cured by normal means. The ones he was studying before being forced into the soul-collecting contest.

Like what his mom died of.

His eyes widen at the thought, and I hurry to cover with—

"Aww, you went to go see Ardy without me?"

"Trust me," he says dryly. "I was sparing you."

But he gives me solemn gratitude because he knows what I was thinking. I squeeze his hand tighter the rest of the way to the tree, keeping eyes suspiciously on his newfound cousins' backs until we reach it.

Our destination is a goliath amid the other younger trees surrounding it, like something that would have its own gift shop in the human realm. An opening large enough to step through has been bored into the bark at the base and blocked off by an accordion-like gate, which spunky Fiona pushes aside to invite us in.

It's completely hollowed out and wide enough to be a bedroom, though there is no furniture inside. Vel nudges me to look up the rest of the trunk, which is hollow as far up as we can see and lit by tiny fairy lights embedded in the walls.

"Please, stand at the center," says Fiona, gesturing to an area where the ground changes from the softness of earth to the hardness of a wooden platform flush with the mossy ground. "And Gabri will take us up."

Up?

How far *up*?

The floor judders, and I fall into Velis, clinging to the warmth beneath his unzipped jacket as the center part of the floor begins to rise. I don't see a pully or mechanical arm, just Gabri's curled fist compelling something to push the giant steppingstone from below. It isn't a smooth ascension. Rather, it feels like the whole thing is being bolstered up by the ejaculation of a geyser.

"There is not a risk of falling, Mayster Evangeline," Fiona says after a long minute, when she notices the way I'm using him for support, her cheeks illuminated by the passing light held in the walls creeping in closer and closer the higher up we go.

Vel keeps me tucked close anyway, asking, "What does Mayster mean?"

Fiona opens her mouth to respond but stops when Gabri slips her a look.

"Mayster is what we call foreigners," Gabri says without turning to look at us.

Vel slips me a look similar to the one just exchanged by the nymph sisters.

Yeeeah, are we starting to build a picture here? That was *clearly* a lie. They seem oddly excited over and/or respectful of Vel. And 'Mayster' sounds a bit fancy, doesn't it?

I press my stare into his as if to say: *Christ, Velis, you aren't royalty here or something, are you?*

He makes a face back as if to say: *I sure the fuck hope not.*

As if she can feel our unspoken exchange, Gabri finally turns back to look at us, showing us for the first time a closeup of her eyes. The irises are green. A deep, dark, wicked shade of green that laps along the shores of black. They're narrow, acute, maybe even a little sly. They take no notice of me on their way to Vel and don't shy away when Vel meets them. Vel doesn't either. If anything, he locks on harder. I know that look. He's trying to get a read on her emotions.

But Gabri doesn't know that look. Subtly, nearly unnoticeably, her expression begins to drift into something edging on seductive. I notice it first, but dense Vel is slower on the draw. When it finally hits him, his eyes dart to mine.

I've never been fearful of him cheating on me, but it is nice to see just how guilty he is over one questionable glance. He looks like I just caught them making out. I pat his arm sympathetically.

The moment Gabri gives us her back, he turns up his palms as if to say:

What the fuck was that?! You saw that, right?

I'm not sure why someone 'of his blood' would be looking at him that way, but there is definitely something off about the way Gabri keeps taking sneaky little peeks of him while declining to look at me. Something off about Fiona's anxious nature and her eagerness to *greet* and *escort* 'Mayster' Velis while sounding a teensy bit disappointed that he's brought along a mate.

"Here, Mayster Evangeline," Fiona says as the lift slows to a stop beside a place brighter than the rest of the shaft due to another large opening in the bark, this time connected to a short walkway supported by branches and covered in a canopy of leaves.

Fiona undoes another set of accordion gates and waits for us to exit. We aren't at the top of the tree, but we are a fair way up, high enough to make me queasy if I think about it. Velis positions me directly in front of him and holds my shoulders as we walk single file into a small, wooden structure suspended in the branches, those kitschy wind pants swishing the entire way.

The tree fort looks like a study for squirrels, packed with a mix of nature and office accoutrements. Shelves burst with rolls of aged parchment while a cluttered desk holds stacks of paper intermingled with stray strips of ivy. Similar ivy drips down the walls, some of which has been pulled aside like a curtain to allow for a view of the sprawling conservatory through pane-less windows.

It's all much bigger than I imagined, and we're up much higher than I realized.

I back into Vel, who's standing stone-still and silent beside me, his gemstone eyes transfixed on something in the corner.

Uh-oh. A little *trancey* if you ask me. But as I follow his line of sight, I realize it isn't magic making him that way. There's a woman waiting in the study for us, holding a radio-like device akin to the one used by the guardswoman at the gate.

She is staggeringly beautiful, with vibrant blue eyes and soft gold hair and the world's most perfect nose.

I've seen her before.

And so has Vel.

"M-Mother?"

CHAPTER 8
A Large Fucking Bird

YES, the features are nearly identical to those massive, gold-framed portraits hanging in every room of the Reilhander manor. The difference is that Velis's mother had the darkened skin of a djinn, and this woman is all nymphean fair.

Velis's was a knee-jerk reaction, and he quickly realizes his mistake. But before he can correct himself, the fort floods with the delicate chiming of a nymph's laughter, and along with it, sunless warmth fills the space.

The woman straightens from the shadows, showing off a pair of linen overalls with a fitted tank top underneath. "My name is Joell Evangeline, cousin to Adelle Evangeline, and I am of your blood."

Wait, THIS is Fiona and Gabri's mother?

Vel swore he was only twenty-two and that there was no age-gap trickery going on. But this lady looks to be late twenties, at most. Her body is much like her daughters': sturdy, fit, with legs built for kicking and climbing. Long swathes of golden hair fall over her shoulders and curl at the ends. She pushes a helping of them aside with a graceful brush of her wrist as she approaches. "You have your passport ring, yes?"

Velis holds up his hand to show off the black ring the tollbooth lady gave him.

"Very good." Joell's smile deepens, and she sets the walkie-talkie down on the edge of the untidy desk. "The gatekeeper alerted us to your arrival, but I admit I was skeptical until beholding your features, Velis Reilhander. We knew Adelle had birthed a male, but we did not expect you for another few years. You are young to be making this pilgrimage. Is your love for your chosen mate so great that you would think to wed her in youth?"

Joell's eyes are good-natured enough to lower defenses, her demeanor confident and at the same time warm. Her clothing makes her look like someone who clips baby's breath from her own garden to decorate her cottage in the country.

Velis's chin is level, his fingers stitched tightly through mine. "Yes, her name is Dolly. I love her and desire to make her lady of my estate."

So unflinching. So certain.

Joell's mouth and gaze are kind as her bare feet sink into the cushy moss that carpets the floor of the treehouse on her way over to examine us. Gabri and sparkly Fiona have settled a short distance away—Gabri leaning with arms folded against a branch blistering with red flowers, Fiona situated on a swing suspended from the fort's ceiling. Her hands clutch the rope as her toes curl playfully into the peat.

"He is an encompasser, Mar," says Gabri. "He showed us."

The nymph mommy's expression remains genial, though her eyes show a sharp pang of shrewdness as they breeze over Vel's structured jaw. "I expect he would be, albeit not a very strong one yet."

An encompasser. Is that because he can control multiple elements? They seemed to think that was pretty cool.

Velis isn't interested in finding out. "Thank you for seeing us, Joell. Unfortunately, we don't have a lot of time. Your blessing is necessary before I can take over as laird for my family's estate. Please, tell me what we need to do to receive it."

Joell, on the other hand, seems to have all the time in the world. "We will get to that. First—come, let me welcome you, son."

Vel stiffens at the face before him and the hands opened wide and her usage of the word 'son.'

The similarity is uncanny. Enough to dredge up deep-seated memories of an embrace he never thought he'd feel again.

Oh, Vel.

He gives Joell a nod, and she closes in on him, resting her forehead against his, her hands spread over the backs of his shoulder blades. "*Harrette, mona Velis,*" she hushes against him.

Vel's hands flinch before he slowly hugs her back. "*H-harrette, mona Joell.*"

Joell's smile shines with clement delight, her knuckle sliding to the warm pocket below his chin when she backs out of the embrace. "Adelle taught you."

Velis swallows, his eyes set on her. "Some things."

"Good. You may not be full of our blood, but you are still *of* our blood. It is good you retain some of our knowledge. We wish for you to pass it to your offspring as well."

And on that note—

Vel shakes off the phantom of his mother's memory and steps away from the matriarch, reasserting, "I don't mean to be blunt, but as I said, we don't have a lot of time in this realm. I have some family politics I'm dealing with. Your blessing, will you give it?"

Joell flicks her hair again, sending a burst of warmth that smells like summer in my direction. "We shall." Her eyes slide over me only briefly before returning to Velis. "So long as you can prove your affections for your mate. She is human, yes?"

Both Gabri and Fiona lurch forward, finally allowing me the gazes they've been withholding this entire time.

Wait . . . did these guys think I was a valkyrie too?! And are humans really rarer than VALKYRIES here?

Velis doesn't waver. "How do I prove my affections for her?"

"It is the same trial undergone by your mother and father

when they made their pilgrimage. You must spend the night in Aphrotica and tell us in the morning whether your affections have stayed."

"That's . . . it?" says Velis, suspect.

"That is it," affirms Joell.

Fiona slips fluidly from the swing and steps closer as if to hear our discussion more clearly. Gabri, too, is closing in, making way for a nearer branch.

"Let me confer with my mate—er, with Dolly."

"Of course."

Velis shoots suspicious eyes at them before ushering me back out to the lift area so that we're surrounded by a cyclone of fairy lights. His skin is a little shiny from travel, our pack draped over his shoulder, making him look like a sexy vagabond. "What do you think?"

"That it's not as simple as they're making it," I say.

"Same. But what's the twist?" Velis sizes up our magical surroundings as if searching for boobytraps. "I'm obviously not going to fall out of love with you overnight," he says.

"*Obviously.*"

He flicks his eyes to me because of how cocky that was. "I mean, night's when *you're* most smitten. *Let me play with your feelers, alien bo—*"

"I did not say that."

"You did say that."

I wait for him to walk it back, but the longer he goes without doing so—

Oh my god, seriously?!

"*When?*"

"Last night."

The horror.

"Dolly, Dolly, Dolly." His eyes darken as his voice lowers to a range meant for devilry. The magnetism between us fights to make us keep going. If we were alone, this banter could continue for hours. But we aren't alone, and the rellies are starkly watching.

"One thing I should clarify," Joell's voice comes sweeping between us on the back of another burst of sunny warmth. "When you spend the night in Aphrotica, it will not be in a bed."

Vel snaps out of our flirty little vacuum to watch her as she approaches the lift.

"It shall be upon a sacred dais."

Ha! I KNEW there was a magical pedestal involved!

Velis rolls his eyes at my smugness.

Unfortunately, only one part of my prediction was correct.

"On top of this tree," Joell finishes.

My hand finds and wrenches Velis's cuff. On *top* of it? But this thing's got to be at least three hundred feet tall!

It seems we've found our twist. Maybe the test will be whether or not Velis can survive an entire night of my anxiety. Or maybe it will be whether we can sleep without rolling to our deaths.

My thumbnail makes its way for my teeth, but Vel intercepts. "There's likely more to it than just the height," he says quietly, "but my parents and grandparents survived it, and they both made it through without being tethered. You and I are at an advantage there."

My gnawed thumb falls away from my mouth because he's right. While the vessel may have led Velis's djinn grandfather to his nymph grandmother, and then his half-nymph mother to his djinn father, neither of those pairs were tethered together as master and wish granter the way Velis and I are. Neither of those pairs involved a human.

And if it really is a test of affection, our love has got to be as strong as those who came before us, right? At the very least, it's certainly lustier, and that's got to count for something.

"You're still my master, and you can still wish us out if things get hairy," says Velis.

He waits for me to climb fully on board before giving Joell his nod.

"Very well." With her golden mane glimmering in a ray of

unnatural sunlight, Joell moves closer to brush a hair over Velis's ear in a way that reads motherly with fingers that were built to dig into clay. "*Mona Velis*, I hope you will spare time for us to converse in the morning, but I am sure that tonight, you tire from your journey. If you hunger, eat any fruit that you see fit." She turns to her daughters. "Gabri, escort them to the dais."

I was right. The lift was being powered by a geyser of air commanded by Gabri's curled fist. But if I expected a gentle rise to the top of this tree, I was sorely, sorely mistaken. With Fiona dismounted in her mother's office, the lift is one person lighter and that much easier to control. We zoom up through the tree faster and faster, until I'm clutching at Velis to keep from topsying. And now I'm wondering what the hell the plan is here! If we're going to burst out the top of the tree, won't there be, like, a shit ton of leaves and sticks and birds we're going to have to smack through to get there?!

But no.

Ohhh no.

It is so, so much worse.

Gabri is a *tempest*. That was what Fiona called her. Tempest. Pretty sure that's another word for storm. A really bad storm.

Somewhere in the top reaches of the tree, the lift suddenly halts beside a hole in the wooden shaft. There's no accordion gate this time. Just an opening waiting for any loser to misplace their footing and go careening down. Holding tight to Velis, I make the mistake of chancing a glance through the opening.

That's a LONG way down. And unlike when Vel and I visited the uppers, Vel's magic is wonky here, so I can't entirely count on it to save me should I happen to fall.

Velis feels my oozing fear and cups me to his chest. "What now?" he asks his cousin.

"Step out, and I will lift you to the dais," says Gabri, voice as chill as if she'd just offered us a piece of gum.

"You want us to step through that hole into empty air?!" I lash.

Gabri ignores me, instead addressing Velis: "I will catch you, Mayster Evangeline. I am of your blood, and I would never let harm befall you." Her deep emerald eyes are set evenly on his. "Please, place your trust in me."

Velis is silent a moment, searching her for truth. And then he sets his mouth to the top of my hair. "Close your eyes, Dolly."

I clutch onto the leather of his jacket, hissing, *"Velis!"*

"Hold on to me, Dolly. And close your eyes. And if I tell you to make a wish, make one, okay?"

Fuck. This.

Velis pulls me against himself and spins his back to the opening in the tree, saying over my head, "I'm trusting you, Gabri. Don't let us fall."

Oh, dear lord, it feels like we're about to bungee jump, and that is a thrill I would never willingly seek. My eyes are clamped to the safety of darkness as Velis takes a step backward. And then, with me flush to his chest and his arms sheltering my body, he falls back-first out the opening in the mammoth tree's trunk.

Is it possible for something to smell high up? Because if so, IT FUCKING SMELLS HIGH UP!

My stomach plunges as we start to fall.

WHOOSH!

And then we're scooped up by a force from below. A cyclone of wind, if my imagination serves correctly. Though, to be fair, my imagination is picturing a cartoon tornado. The force below us hovers a moment before pushing us higher.

"We're almost there, babe," Vel says into my ear, squeezing me tighter.

The noise of the wind flogs at my ears while its physical presence whips at my hair.

And then it stops. My hair settles at my shoulders, and Velis relaxes his grip. I slowly blink open my eyes. We're standing on a mantle of leaves, tightly woven together, that stretches over the entire top of the tree. It's flat. Squishy but flat, except for the edges where the tree's leaves are loose and harbor fruits of all shapes and colors.

"That was not fun," I tell Velis.

His mouth ticks. "I mean, I kinda thought it was fun."

In the center of the tree's foliage sits a mattress-type object. A dais? Only in the most basic, basic sense. It is a large, circular pouf with pillows lining the edges and a blanket with feathers sewn into the top.

Weird.

WEIRD.

W-E-I-R-D.

Very *nesty*.

And now I'm beginning to think we're meant to be sacrifice for some large bird creature.

Velis's dad didn't seem too athletic. True, his body was fit, but he didn't seem the type to willingly exert energy that might make him become ruffled. If Daddy Djinn could survive a fight with a giant eagle, then surely Vel, with his fast footwork, strong shoulders, and that firm, *lean* chest could—

"Keep it in your pants, Master."

At least this canopy is wide enough that it will be easy to avoid the edges.

That ceiling is steadily turning from daylight to dusklight, as if the magic in this place is adjusting for us to sleep. I wasn't feeling hungry until Joell mentioned it, but now that I think about it, knockoff 'Chestos' are a far cry from the nourishment a mortal body needs to survive. But I'm not about to chow down on unknown fruits from an unknown fantasyland. As the sky continues its quick trek into night, Velis and I decompress on a safe stretch of greenery, partaking in cheeseburgers I'm pretty sure are fake vegetarian meat, though I wished for beef.

At least it isn't pegasus.

After, we stand at the edge of the nest.

"Go ahead, Doll." Velis kicks at it with his foot.

"Tch! You go ahead, *doll*. It's your seed."

"My SEED? Is that what you've been calling it?"

Guilty.

Vel's lips may purse over it, but humor shows in his eyes. He folds his arms. "Fine. How about a few precautionary wishes before either of us tucks the other one in?"

"Velis, I wish we wouldn't get attacked by any large birds tonight."

"What?" Though his mouth falls dully, he can't keep his eyes from searing icy bright. "Another super-charged one," he says as he feels it throb in him. "Pretty sure we won't be attacked by anything tonight, let alone large fucking birds, weirdo. What else?"

I'm trying to think of anything else general enough. "How about: Velis, I wish no one would be able to come up here until morning when the test is complete?"

Velis's eyes sear a second time. "That one was close, except no one will be able to even think about coming up here until five minutes after the test is complete."

Oddly specific, but okay.

"Feel safer?" he asks.

"I do. You?"

He bobs his head. "I'll get in first." But he means only barely. He grapples my waist and pulls me on top of him as he drops onto the padding. It's three times thicker than a standard mattress and marshmallow soft. Together, Velis and I sink in, his arms still tightly around me.

Not bad. From this angle, I can't even tell we're up high. Velis and I could be in his vessel for all I—

"OH MY GOD." I scramble away from him, kicking up a few loose feathers. "Why don't we just sleep inside your vessel? If there's some trick to this night, then your vessel will shield us from it, right?"

"Except, if we go into my vessel, there will be no one out here to *guard* my vessel," he says, patting his bag where it safely rests.

True.

I make one or two more vague wishes against outside attack

before settling into a lover's nest that is surprisingly comfy for the circumstances.

"I think you've covered our bases," Velis says, chewing his lip as if running through scenarios in his head. "I'll keep a lookout if you wanna get some rest."

I don't. Want to, that is. But we got up early and walked miles, Velis's chest is warm and the nest snug. I scoop myself into the crook of him, nuzzling my mouth near the beating vein of his neck.

"*Master*." Velis feels my desire to bite it.

"I know, I know." I sigh. "Not until we hit up the vampire realm."

"NO. I am definitely not taking you there. They're so fucking emo, it's not even funny."

Of course there's a vampire realm.

Velis sets his cheek against the edge of my forehead, exhaling long into the darkening sky. Whatever the circumstances, it feels good to be alone with him. "I really friggen' hope there's no twist," he says.

There's very likely a twist.

"So why aren't you more freaked out?" he says.

I shrug. "I don't know. This is all a little sus, but . . . it feels like we can get out of whatever it is. I guess the things I'm afraid of are just a different kind of beast."

"I know what you mean." He settles his head and drifts his eyes to the fake night sky. "I'm sorry I didn't tell you sooner the real reason we had to come here. Maybe I was a little embarrassed too."

Embarrassed? Crap, maybe I should have been more sensitive about all that.

"I-I hope you know that infertility curse doesn't mean shit to me. Like, desirability-wise. I mean, you know that, right? You can *feel* it, right?"

A mantle of unnatural quiet settles over us, as if the gardens below have curled up for the night, as if the creatures hiding in the greenery have fallen into hibernation. There's slight tightness to his body that makes me think he's building up to something.

I wait for it to come.

"I wish you could feel how much I love you, Dolly Jones." He says it like he's saying it to the sky instead of to me. Like it's a secret he wants me to overhear.

I peer up at him with searching eyes, my lips gently brushing his sandpapery jaw. "I do feel it, Vel. I'm not an empath, but I can still feel it." This time I'm the one to whisper a secret: "I hope you can feel mine. I know it can be guarded."

Usually. But right now, it's like it's rising in every vein of me, as if my affection is a swelling light bursting to get out.

"I can. Even when you suppress it, I feel it." He moves his mouth closer. "I *crave* it."

I sink deeper into him, absorbing his warmth and musk as he absorbs mine, listening to the cadence of his breath and the small shifts of his throat as he trails a finger up and down my arm. Our bodies are like magnets. One kiss. One stir of my hips. One nod of invitation, and I know he'd devour me.

It goes without saying we are not going to bang atop the magical feather dais because who knows what sort of ancient ritual that may incite. But I want to. I want to straddle him and show him just how little his curse means to me, with his hands supporting my arched back. I want him to see me at my most vulnerable—the moment he pushes me to juddering oblivion—and to know that he was the one that caused it.

It seems foolish now, those twinges of fear too stubborn to join the rest of us over on the love boat. His dodging around the reason we had to come here. Those hours alone in our manor suite wondering if I'd made the right choice.

In his arms, it's so obvious that there's something real and rare we're harvesting, something we need to hold on to for dear life. Maybe this is us passing the test. Maybe there's something magical about this bizarre nest on the top of a giant tree in the center of a nymphean playpen tucked away in an otherwise dead world.

I close my eyes against my genie, feeling more secure in the choices that have led me here than ever before. He must be feeling the same way. His lips graze me on the way to my ear, and as the dark settles into me, he tells me the sweetest, gentlest things.

I have a dream I'm clawed through the heart by the talons of a giant bird.

CHAPTER 9
The Rellies

MORNING HITS.

The chirp of birds and the kiss of warm sunlight hide the fact that we aren't really outside. Velis's arm is still around me, in the same tucked position as when I dozed off. "Hey." I clear my throat. "You get any sleep?"

He says nothing. Maybe he did fall asleep.

I spit aside stray feathers that have clung to my lips and crawl out of hibernation to get a better look at him, then stop as stilling panic washes over me. "V-Velis?" He isn't sleeping, but he is staring into the glassy abyss above us, body stiff. I lean over him, and he blinks at me like he doesn't know who the hell I am.

Shit, shit, shit!

And then a slow, mischievous smile begins to spread over his mouth. "Morning, Master. Want some breakfa—"

I smack him with one of the pillows lining the nest. "NOT COOL, Velis!"

He chuckles to himself as he sits up on his elbows. "Sorry, I couldn't help it."

"Fucker." And despite that wicked little grin and the clear adoration in his eyes, I can't help asking, "S-so you still—?"

"Do I still *love* you?" His expression softens when he realizes

I'm asking in earnest. "I promise you, Dolly Jones. The answer to that question will always be yes."

Thank. God.

"That was mean, though," I tell him. "And now you owe me omelets. Fat Nat's Breakfast Shack. They're the best in the world."

"Psh. You know, *I* could conjure up the best omelets in the *worlds*, and I guarantee they'd be better than whatever place you're thinking of."

"No. I want shitty burnt coffee and human-made omelets that are three times the size they should be, and I want you to not so much as blink when I eat the whole thing. No judgment, no compromise."

Vel's smile is content. "You got it, boss." He rolls off the edge of the dais to the weaving of leaves below.

"So, is that the test, then? If we weren't really soulmates, we'd have fallen out of love overnight?"

"Who the fuck knows. Pretty uneventful night from what I could tell. Since you're dying to know—no, we weren't visited by any large birds. Though you did sleepy-coo for them to 'stay the fuck away from our eggs.'" He snickers to himself. "So territorial, Master."

A second, more aggressive pillow pelts into him.

True to his magic, five minutes after he professes his love for me, the sound of rushing wind alerts us to the arrival of a nymph on the breeze. Romper shorts fluttering, brony-dream Fiona comes sailing up over the edge of the canopy on a gust of her sister's magic.

She and her half-formed rainbow skid to a halt when she sees Vel's fingers entwined with mine. That disappointment she's wearing is pretty transparent. Same with her sister, who's just come flying over the edge on a second burst of wind, looking extra judgy over the way my shoulder is pressed into the side of Vel's arm.

It's obvious this was a test they wanted us to fail.

Sunny Joell comes in more gracefully than either of her

daughters, riding one last blast of wind commanded by Gabri's curled fist. Her long hair settles gently around her face as she lands, the warmth of daylight intensifying as she approaches. "*Mona Velis*, it is good to see you well."

"Joell. We've spent the night in Aphrotica, and my feelings for Dolly have stayed. I still love her and wish to make her lady of my estate. We've passed your test, so grant us your—"

"I cannot." Joell shuts him down, sweeping over to close the remaining distance between us. Velis stands momentarily dumbstruck as she scoops up his chin with what appears to be remorse. "I am sorry, *mona Velis*. You have not passed the test."

He shakes quickly out of another memory of his mother and pulls his chin from her grip. "What do you mean? I love her. I spent the night up in this weird altar with her, and I still love her, so—"

"You have cheated. And because you have cheated, I cannot grant you the blessing of our line."

Cheated? Was it one of the wishes I cast? Were we honestly meant to fight an enormous bird?!

"How so?" challenges Velis.

"Your connection with your mate is being influenced by outside magic that has interfered with the trial. It must be removed before the test may be completed."

"Outside magic?" Vel repeats. "You mean our tethering?" He glances down at me. "They . . . think our love is being influenced by our bond as master and wish granter?"

"Well, it's not," I scoff. "Er, right?"

Velis turns his body completely toward mine. "No, Dolly. If our tethering had anything to do with our feelings for one another, I would have fallen in love with all my masters. Most of them I could hardly stand. I love you because of who you are, not what you are." He returns to Joell. "The magical bond between us has nothing to do with our feelings for one another, and I don't have a way to drop the bond without returning to my realm and—"

"We will remove it for you," says Joell.

A spasm of emotion hits Velis's face. "You want to untether us?"

"It is the only way to determine whether your feelings for your mate are true."

"And how do you expect to do that?" asks Vel.

"We are of your blood."

You don't fuckin' *say*.

"We can extract it from you, though it will not be pleasant. But if you are certain your feelings are without outside influence, then you have nothing to fear. Your predecessors faced the test without this magical bond."

She's right. Our relationship is unique among the rest. And it was always the plan for us to untether once completing this quest anyway. But knowing how temperamental Vel's magic is in this world, there's no guarantee we'll be able to safely return home without me wishing us there.

Velis is contemplating the same. "What if it's only a temporary drop?" he suggests, low. "We pass their stupid test and then re-tether right away. You can keep my vessel with you in case they try to pull something."

"I'd just have to kiss it to re-bond us?"

"Or me." One of his dimples shows. "I'd prefer it be me."

Fine. If, and when, things inevitably start to backfire, I'll kiss the vase that started it all, and he'll blink us out of this shitshow.

And then we're getting some goddamned omelets.

I'm not saying it's ever a bad thing to see Velis's shirt removed. His body is the sort of body that would take a human male a strict diet and grueling exercise regimen to maintain. Those shoulders. Good god. They always look just a teensy bit moist. Like he just lifted something heavy. So I'm not entirely disappointed when Velis is made to remove his shirt for whatever weird nymphy ritual that's about to ensue.

But what I don't like? The way his cousins' eyes are glued to his flesh as the fabric of his T-shirt glides up the warm, golden skin of his chest. Why does he always have to disrobe like he's in a PORNO? Even Mommy Nymph looks lusty over the sight of him stripping.

Based on the way Velis's lip is lifted disagreeably on one side, I'm not the only one picking up on it. Standing in front of the feathery dais, he locks eyes with me where I wait off to the side, and tosses me his shirt, which I tuck in our bag alongside his vessel to offer a quick, kissy getaway.

Joell sets a hand on Vel's muscular shoulder. "I am sorry for the hurt we will cause you, *mona Velis*. Try to bear it. It will be over soon." Her fingers smooth down his arm in a way that's no longer motherly, which I imagine feels quite skeevy coming from a woman who so strongly resembles his mom.

The daughters close in, each taking one of their mother's hands and forming a ring around delicious, half-naked Velis, while the light of day paints the gardens far, far below.

Gabri says nothing, but peppy Fiona makes it a point to stand in front of him. "I will try not to be rough, Mayster Evangeline."

Velis ignores her, looking past her to where I stand clutching our few belongings, throbbing with anxiety. "Remember what I said," he tells me. "The answer to that question will always be yes."

I know, logically, that our wishing bond has no bearing over our relationship. I know our arrows are pointed and that we're written on each other's souls. I know Velis has never had feelings for any of his other masters, and that his parents and grandparents were brought together by the vessel too.

And yet, I'm scared. I've never known him without being his master.

Velis smiles softly. "You'll always be my master, Dolly Jones." And then his face contorts. He grits his teeth and throws back his head and releases a pained, "ARRRRGH!"

"Vel!" I can't keep from crying out at the sight of his veins bulging in his neck and his kissable mouth fighting to keep himself from whimpering. A film of airy light has started to form around him, conjured by the three blond women encircling him, their eyes emblazed like mini suns and their skin delighting in nymphean power.

"ARRRRRRGH!" Vel's growl sends a swarm of fluffy creatures flying out from where they were hiding in the canopy.

I stuff my hand into our bag to grip his vessel around its neck. Ready to abort. Ready to save him if his pain becomes too—

The arcane bottle that will never become a vase tears out of my fingers and flies across the canopy, where it lands in Vel's outstretched hand the same way it did back when he was trying to prove to me he was a genie.

"V-Velis?!"

That was our escape route, and now I'm feeling significantly worse about the séance happening before me. I run to the edges of their circle but am pushed back by a pulse of golden light.

"STOP!" I shriek, unable to take the sound of his torture. "Velis Reilhander, I wish you would—"

I feel a very small pop somewhere deep inside my chest.

And I know.

I know. I know.

The circle of arms falls as the girls release their hands, and the light around Velis bursts, flooding the space in a wave of stardust that stains the leaves, the fruit, the feathers. And after, the person who was once my genie stands in front of the dais, vessel in one hand and bare chest heaving. Velis and I have become unhooked. My soul has been freed.

"Dolly."

My name on his mouth is like a siren's call. I run to him, pushing Fiona out of the way to throw my arms around his neck, feeling that specific beat in my chest that lays to rest any fear I have ever had.

I still love him. I still love him just as deeply as I always have. I may no longer be his master, but that entrenched love, lust, affection remains. Mr. Alien. My time-traveling genie boyfriend. My greatest desire.

I absorb his warm hand on my back and feel my cheeks wet

from the swell of emotion I'm pushing out at him. My voice cracks against his chest: "I still love you, genie boy." I look up at him, laughing, "I don't know why, but I was actually worried that—"

He isn't smiling back. His mouth is flat, his eyes cutting into mine like he's trying to understand a complex theory. "Dolly Jones, I . . ."

I wait for him to say it. The words are just there on the tip of his tongue. I wait for them to form and quell my racing heart.

"Don't," he finishes.

"You don't what?"

"Love you."

Not funny. Not when I'm literally crying into his chest. Not when he already pulled this on me once this morning. I wait for him to correct himself, momentarily forgetting we're no longer bound by the truth oath.

But he doesn't correct himself. He just continues to study my face like he's trying to read something in the dark. "Huh," he says after a minute, shaking his head. "That's surprising. I thought . . ."

I take a step back from him. "Velis, that's not funny."

"I'm sorry." His tone is a little off. "I can tell you want reassurance, but I can't give it." He sets a hand to my shoulder, not to comfort me but to distance our bodies, then looks away to locate Joell. "It's gone. I don't love her."

Crushing.

A crushing blow.

Joke or not, hearing those words from his lips is staggering. I take hold of his arm for support, but he carefully *extracts* it from me, like I'm an animal about to bite.

What is this game? He wouldn't make a joke this cruel unless—

I think back to the things I said when I was tricking his brothers into giving us their contest earnings. I imagine my face resembles what his looked like at the time. Disbelief. Drowning. I scan our surroundings, seeking out the puzzle piece I'm missing.

"Stop," he says. "There's no trick. That infatuation, it wasn't real. I just didn't realize it until now."

I search him for something. A hint. A trace. In those icy eyes that are colder than I've ever seen them. "I feel nothing for you, Dolly." And then at last, a spark of humor. But not the kind I want. "I mean, you're a human."

A second blow connects, and I realize:

He isn't kidding. He really thinks he doesn't love me.

How is that possible?!

I promise you, Dolly Jones. The answer to that question will always be—

His fingers. The tips of his fingers are steadily beginning to gray.

I turn my efforts elsewhere, grabbing hold of the nymph nearest me, which happens to be fluttery Fiona. *"What did you do to him?"*

Her eyes flee past me to the safety of her mother. "I-I did not do anything to him. We-we merely severed the magical bond—"

"Bullshit!" I gather the cloth of her collar tighter. "We loved each other even before we were fully tethered—before he ever latched onto my soul! We're goddamned soulmates! He loves me, you rainbow bitch. Now tell me what—"

A strong, fully grayed hand latches onto my wrist. "Let her go, Dolly Jones. She's of my blood, and I won't let you hurt her."

Oh, for fuck's sake. 'Of his blood'? What kind of brainwashed bullshit is that?

I don't buy it.

"Mayster Evangeline." It's the first time Joell has called him that. "Please leave the human to us and allow your body to cleanse. The connection we severed was strong, and I would like you to dispel all remnants before I gift you the blessing of our line."

Hold on.

So even though he failed the test and supposedly doesn't love me anymore, she's still going to unlock his magical seed?! Meaning all that intuition pecking at me since we got here was right. This was a test we were never meant to pass.

Velis obeys her, not even bothering to look at me as he releases my wrist. Not so much as flinching as I'm plowed into from the side by a burst of magical wind from Gabri's curled fist. Not so much as blinking as I land dangerously near the edge of the canopy.

Fucking *ow*.

"ARGH!" I hop to my feet and begin to charge them, only to be blasted by another, more violent gale.

"M-Mar," stutters Fiona. "Are we sure she is not a valkyrie?"

No, I'm not, but I'm about to rain down on them with all the fury of Valhalla if they don't un-brainwash my alien-genie boyfriend right this—

I stop, transfixed on the scene before me.

Velis has returned to Joell's side before the feathered dais, his own hand lifted to his face so that he can watch the color drain from his skin and clothing. It moves up his arm, spreads up his legs, until all that remains is a small spot on his chest.

And then that, too, fades.

Your soul is the only thing out there. Without it, it feels like I'd get—I don't know, lost.

Was our tethering the only thing keeping him afloat in this world?

"Y-you took away his emotion!" I accuse.

Because what else could it be? Velis could feel no emotion from that grayed gatekeeper, and he seems to now be in a similar state.

Joell ignores me, instead offering Velis a hand to guide him along the edge of the canopy overlooking the twittering, glittering landscape. "Glory be, Velis Evangeline. Adelle did well to conceive you. You are the first male born of our line in over two centuries. And an encompasser, at that. You are diluted, but you retain your benediction. You shall inherit the riches of our world and return us to the paradise we once knew." She places her lips to his forehead and sends a ripple of golden light through his face, down his chest, and deep into the reaches of those gaudy windbreaker pants. "With this, you have received our blessing. Stay, and let us tell you all that lies ahead for you, our greatest treasure."

WHAT THE FUCK?

Velis's nuts are definitely glowing, and his head is definitely nodding in agreement.

Tempest Gabri moves beside him and slides a hand to the dip of his muscled back. "Please, lie with me first, Mayster Evangeline. I wish to continue our line with you."

Oh, hell no.

Rainbowy Fiona's hair is quickly becoming all supercharged again. "No," she pleads, taking his hand. "I wish to lie with you first, Mayster Evangeline."

"Patience," says Joell. "We will all have a chance to lie with the Mayster."

Even the mommy one?!

This is some weird concubine-y shit, and Velis is clearly not himself, and once again, these bitches want to use him for his body. Maybe when I get him back, I really should wish to make him fugly and old.

He says nothing against it because we're no longer bonded, and he can no longer feel my desires.

Ouch.

That's such a sad, cold realization.

But I'm not about to let this all go down. He defended me when I was in a vulnerable state, and I'm going to do the same for him. The nymphs seem to have all but forgotten about me. The vessel is firmly in Velis's grip. If I could kiss it, I'd be able to shield him from whatever stunter magic is influencing his feelings. I just need to find a way to it. I flick my eyes to ensure the rellies are still distracted by that herculean bod and begin to edge forward.

"Fiona. The human is plotting something. Exile her from the tower."

Joell's voice hits me with another bout of happy sunlight, though her tone is anything but warm. And the next moment, I hear—

"Sorry, human. There are many humans in your world. You will find another mate. The gatekeeper will help you get home."

A half-assed apology from rainbow girl before I'm pelted in

the face with a torrent of sparkles. The next thing I know, I'm standing on the grayscale lawn in front of Evangeline Tower.

Yeah right. I'm the mother of all cockroaches, bitches, and I'm coming back for my alien. I run up the steps, my footsteps even lonelier without the swish of my favorite person by my side. I take hold of the tower's door handle, ready to heave it open, but find it's stuck solid. Shit. Last time, it opened easily.

Because last time, we were being coaxed into the web of three horny spiders.

"FUCK!"

My cry is the only thing to echo in the dead air.

Now what?

My pulse begins to swell in my ears with the thunder of panic. No, no, no, no. Panic isn't productive. I need to exchange it for anger.

"FUCK, FUCK, FUCKITY FUCK!"

Argh! We never should have come here! Children are SO not worth—

Wait. Fuckity fuck?

Fuckity fuckity fuck.

I need backup.

And there's one person in this entire multiverse who knows where I am, with the gall to have placed a tracker on my soul. One person who is under the constraints of a wish not to betray me, with zero nymph blood and full djinn power, and who likely doesn't give a shit about filing paperwork and entering this realm through the proper channels.

But how do I get his attention?

I'm not Arrik's master. That bond broke when Velis unlocked my soul and fully tethered me. So I can't just summon him the way I did last time in my apartment. But if he can see my soul's positioning, then maybe—?

Huff. Huff.

I begin to run. In a circle. Around Evangeline Tower.

If he's tracking the position of my soul, then it would seem abnormal that my soul is suddenly running around in literal circles, right?

Yeah, not so much. I'm out of breath far sooner than I should be, but I've circled that moody, obsidian skyscraper at least a dozen times, and there's no sign of everyone's favorite tatted triplet.

New approach.

With my sweaty jacket tossed aside, I run up and down the street, ignoring the obvious motion of shadowy people in the windows around me as I work to spell out the word: H-E-L-P. Over and over again, I spell it out, praying to God, Odin, *Maka*, that Arrik notices I'm doing so. And when that doesn't work, I switch to a word we both appreciate: F-U-C-K.

F-U-C-K.

F-U-C-K.

F-U-C-K.

But who am I kidding? Arrik's probably busy screwing someone's mom in their childhood home. What are the chances he's paying enough attention to my soul to notice it's acting erratic—

"What the FUCK are you doing, Dolly Jones?" A familiar rasp hits the back of my neck, and I spin to see a shirtless figure doused neck-to-waist in ink and with the embers of a lit stick falling to the ground around him from the wag of his mouth. "And why is your soul in so much turmoi—"

"Arrik!" I run at him enthusiastically enough to make his eyes pop with surprise, and land my hands on his bare shoulders out of sheer desperation. "Ohh, I am so glad to see you." I let my head fall forward, feeling the clear slide of sweat at my hairline.

"Um, hi? What the hell is up with this depressing world, and why are you sans lover boy?"

"Dude," I pant. "His nymph relatives—they're after his magical seed."

"What?" It comes out of him like dust.

"Just listen. They untethered us and turned off his emotion and plan to use him to make a bunch of nymph babies and—"

"They untethered you?" His aquamarine eyes glimmer at me curiously. "How?"

"I don't know," I huff, straightening. "Some weird nymphy ritual. They said they extracted it out of—"

"ARGH!" Arrik suddenly doubles over in apparent pain as sparks of white lightning appear all around his body, flaring his skin so that his skeleton shows through like something from a cheesy Halloween display.

What the heck?!

I stagger away from him so that I won't get hit by whatever electrical current is buzzing through him. "A-Arrik?!"

"Fuck!" he swears, bending farther forward, grunting. "It's—some—kind—of—security system. It's—trying—to—boot me from this world."

No! I cannot lose my last lifeline here!

He winces, now crouched to the ground, hand resting on the pavement. "Do—something!"

"Arrik! I wish nymph magic couldn't hurt you!"

My wish resounds. The only noise to exist in this dead world. Followed by a single, deadly syllable:

"Heh."

With the lightning abruptly snuffed out, Arrik straightens, an obvious smirk forming at the edge of his mouth. He spits out his blunt, and suddenly, he's towering over me, eyes aglow. "As you fucking wish." And then, before I can fully grasp what's happening, his hand is clutching the nape of my neck, and his lips are pressed to mine.

For a moment, I am limp as I digest what's happening, as my mouth absorbs his tobacco and happy hour taste, as I replay the last minute that led to me kissing Vel's asshole older brother.

Be careful. He knows the most about humans. And he's got the least to lose.

He'd do anything to make himself feel better about himself. Anything.

I prefer to watch things . . . implode.

It's not until I feel the wet of his tongue slide against mine that I realize both his hands have taken command of my face.

I shove him away and wipe my mouth on my shoulder. "What the hell, you *mouth rapist!*"

"Hmph." Wickedness overtly glistening in his eyes, he tips up his chin and slides his tongue fully up the pad of his middle finger. "Hey, Master, did anyone ever tell you your soul is delicious?"

Uh-oh.

CHAPTER 10
The Other Side

"I am not your master, Arrik!"

"Mm, nope. Pretty sure you are. You can try slapping me if you want. Or I could slap you, though I should mention, we technically *can* hurt one another so long as it's in the pursuit of pleasure. Anyone's guess, really, whether or not it lands." He snaps his fingers, conjuring a fresh roll of paper between them, and takes an indulgent drag from it. "Bet golden boy hasn't figured that one out yet."

The horror of my own stupidity dawns on me as I stumble away from him. "There is no nymph security system."

His eyes narrow with all the smugness in the worlds. "You know, I don't think I could have pulled it off if you weren't so *frantic*. You're sharp, Dolly Jones, but even smart girls have a weakness. I'll have to thank my little brother once he's done impregnating those nymphs."

Arrrrrrrrghhhhhh!

Wait.

"You're lying. You can't tether me because you're under an oath not to betray me."

"Yeah? I don't remember you ever asking me *not* to make you my master. Therefore, I haven't betrayed anything. Not to mention, you invited me here for help, and I'll be much more *helpful* as your wish granter than as some stray djinn. This weather's not good for casting solo. This cigarette tastes like shit."

And the stain of his own smoky taste is still on my tongue.

Disgusting.

You're disgusting. Clean up your skin and wash the stink of human off you, and maybe your father will stop favoring that halfbreed.

His eyes zip to mine because now he's got a direct tap into that vein of empathy I've been trying to stifle.

Ughhhhh. This is not ideal for multiple reasons.

I back away farther and then turn from him, trying to clear my head and come to terms with the fact that I really just contracted Arrik Reilhander as my genie. Velis is going to kill me.

Correction, Velis is going to kill *him*.

Because Velis isn't an asshole.

Like a lost puppy, the bastard comes trotting up beside me and glances sidelong. "Are you mad at me?"

Why does he still sound like he needs my approval?!

Of course I'm mad at him! And 'lost puppy' is too cuddly for him. He's like a lost snake, slithering up someone's pantleg.

"As soon as we get Vel back"—I fight for composure—"we're *figuring out how to switch the tether back to him.*"

"Sure," says Arrik, but he adds under his breath, "assuming you've got any soul left."

A gasp fights its way out of my throat. That's right—Arrik now has access to my soul, and every wish he grants will chip away at it until it's gone. I can't let that happen. I need his magic, but my soul is mine, and there's only one djinn I would ever let have it.

"Arrik, don't take any more of my soul."

He exhales smoke into the monochrome sky. "Sorry, love, that's not—"

"Well, I just asked you not to, so I'll consider it betrayal if you do. And if I recall, you already granted a wish not to betray me."

The cigarette drops low in his mouth. "Shit."

Well, I wasn't totally sure that would work, but that fallen jaw is a good sign. He appears to be calculating the algebra behind a word problem I've just presented him, and by the ashen look sinking into his features, the conclusion is that he, indeed, can no longer take from my soul as payment for any wishes granted.

Now it's my turn to feel smug. "Guess you'll be working this case for free."

A string of creative curses follows me as I turn my back to him and gape up at the ominous tower in front of us. We need to get back in there asap. Those bitches looked thirsty.

"Arrik, I wish—"

"Hey!" A hand with tattooed knuckles lands on my shoulder. "Don't wish for anything too extravagant, okay, you little con artist? I'm not an unending tap, and I don't like borrowing from the estate. So unless you're going to revoke your other wish and let me have your soul, I need you to be conservative."

Yeah, no. I'm going to do whatever it takes to get Velis back.

"Arrik, I wish we were inside Evangeline Tower."

"Fucking hell." But he can't stop his eyes from washing his cheekbones in blue. I wait for warmth and color to hit us. For the feeling of lazy summer air and the chaotic sound of shithead birds. But when the transportation is through, the world around us is even grayer than before.

We stand in an empty office building with cement walls and drab floors and not a single noteworthy detail.

"Wow, good wish, Maste—"

"Take us to the nymph conservatory where Velis is!" I correct. "Arrik, I wish you would!"

"Hold on, would yo—" Arrik is cut off by his own flash of magic. His eyes seem to absorb the wish but quickly dull, and after, we're standing in the exact same place as we were before. "Sorry, that was an impossible wish. There is no such place."

"There is, though! I was there!" Panic rising, I take Arrik's shoulder to steady myself. "Arrik, I wish Velis was here with us!"

"Damn it, slow down, would—" His eyes flash again, and again, they fade without delivering. "The wish thinks he's already here."

No!

How do I word this wish? Is he in some parallel space that doesn't actually exist?! That is some sci-fi bullshit!

I don't love you.

I can't breathe.

That infatuation, it wasn't real.

I can't stand.

I feel nothing for you, Dolly.

I can't hold it in.

"Geezus, what the fuck is this noise?"

That's Arrik's voice, but I can barely make it out over the sound of heaves. MY heaves. Forcing out of me like a clogged bellows.

I think I might be hyperventilating. I might be in shock. This might be a panic attack. My peripherals are vignetted, and they're closing in. All I can see is some painted piece of Arrik's flesh.

It looks like a peach.

"This is so not as fun as I thought it would be," says Arrik's dry, muffled voice, before—"Ung!" He releases a grunt of pain, and I feel his body bending alongside mine. "*Your emotions!*" he strains. "Why are your emotions this strong?!"

Because it feels like the part of Vel written on my soul is being carved out of me. My skin crawls with prickling sweat. I might vomit. This self-suffocation has only happened to me one other time, and when it did, it felt like it was never going to stop.

"Master!" A growl hits my ear as a defined hand secures my back. "You need to hold it together, or you're going to put both of us down! I'm going to help you, but you can't be mad at me after, deal?"

I can't respond. It feels like my lungs are collapsing.

My chin is seized, and a cloud of thick, fruity smoke hits my face. I open my eyes to see Arrik's posh lips a hair's breadth away from mine, funneling purple smoke into my mouth. I flick my attention upward to find him gazing at me through lowered lashes. I'm already in the middle of gasping. The push of his tainted air easily makes its way down my windpipe.

Instantly, the constricted muscles of my throat loosen, and I'm left panting, my cheeks left damp. His hand is left at the middle of my back. The panic, urgency—it's all still there but buried beneath layers and layers of what feels like feathery down.

My lungs suction air to recover. "Th-thanks."

"Don't thank me yet."

"Why? What did—?" It hits. I cling to his arm for support because it suddenly feels like my legs are much, much too puny to support the mass of my body. Like I'm a watermelon being held up by toothpicks.

"Angel's breath." Arrik's eyebrow arches as he coasts his eyes over me. "Seems to have worked. Stay there." My legs give out the moment he releases me against the cold cement wall and steps away to assess my current state.

My current state is . . .

The sail of a boat above his left nipple looks like it's thrashing in a storm. "Arrik, are your tattoos really moving right now?"

There's a small flicker in his stony expression as he looks down to process what I've just asked. "Heh. No." When he looks back up, he does so with the refined amusement of a sphinx. "All right," he says. "Let's hear it. Now that we've got your emotions under control, tell me what's going on with our new *laird*."

I do. I tell him everything. Probably too much, actually. About the rellies and their lust for Vel's seed. About how he's their first male born in two hundred years, and how this all seemed to be some trick to get him to stay with them in the hidden nymph pocket that exists somewhere beyond this plane. After, I wait for Arrik's reaction, watching waves of ink slither over his smooth body. The sailboat has now sailed to his other pec, and his nipple seems to be the bait for a fishing line.

But rather than responding, he stares at me like I just failed hard at the school talent show. "What the fuck was that? What language was that?"

"Huh?"

"Listen, most realms have magic on them so that we can understand each other's speech, but that . . . that was nothing.

That was gibberish. Are you messing with me? Or is the magic failing?"

"I can understand you just fine," I say.

He shakes his head. "You're, like, clucking and stuff."

I'm *clucking*?

Now that he mentions it, my legs do feel disproportionately small, and my hands have sort of tucked themselves into their own armpits.

"Hmph, based on your expression, it's not anything you're doing intentionally. Maybe it's the angel's breath. Never given it to a human before. This should be interesting."

Never given it to a HUMAN before?!

"Okay, you get a pass because you just saved me, but no more *feeding me random fantasyland drugs*, got it?!"

"Cluck, cluck to you too, Master." Arrik snickers to himself like a bully delighting in the misfortune of the kid he just pantsed. "It's pretty funny. You're like an angry chicken."

No, it's not funny! Vel's going to get sexually mauled by his cousins, and Arrik suddenly can't understand me?!

He returns to the wall where I'm propped, crouching down beside me like a spider moving down its web. "You know what I think, Master?" The warmth of a toned arm slips around the back of my neck. "I think you should give up on him. You two were never going to last anyway. Not with the vipers in our family. Trust me, it's not worth it. We were born into it. But you? You have a chance to be something other." His thumb frisks along my shoulder. "Why not forget about him, and I'll show you a good time?" His mouth lowers so that he can tease my ear with the heat of his breath and the riling quiet of his voice. "I know you're attracted to me, Dolly Jones. I can feel it now for sure."

Attraction is involuntary.

Action is voluntary.

I elbow him and shove away, horrified to see a flustered trail of feathers in my wake.

And something worse.

Is that . . .

DID I JUST LAY AN EGG?!

There is, indeed, a speckled egg residing in the space I just sat.

Arrik releases an actual laugh this time. "Whatever you're seeing, it's not real. Damn, though. I'll have to remember this stuff makes you guys hallucinate."

Creep.

His eyes flare with dark comprehension. "I am not creepy."

"It's creepy to just abandon your own brother in some twisted world—"

"Oh, come off it, *dramatic*. He's not exactly being tortured. From what you said, it sounds like he's screwing a bunch of nymphs. Likely in an incestuous orgy. What's the problem?"

There are many problems, but more importantly—"You can understand me again?"

"No, no, no. I'm *reading* you, chicken girl. You're incredibly transparent, especially now that we're tethered. By the way, that soul of yours, why does it taste so . . ."

"You may not be here!" A stern voice echoes off the concrete of the room.

We didn't hear them enter. I don't even know which hallway they came from. But there are three gray women, each wearing one of those jumpsuits, each holding a nozzle connected to a hose, each hose filled with intensely vibrant colored liquid.

The one with the blue hose is pretty. The one with the yellow hose has bangs. And the one with the green hose is the shortest.

"Great descriptions, Master," Arrik mutters.

"Cluck?"

"Nothing."

"Leave whence you have come, jinnee!" A splatter of what looks like green paint sprays the floor in front of us, jarring enough against the gray world to blind.

Arrik slowly rises from his crouch and strolls over like he's greeting his groupies backstage. "Hey, you ladies know anything about a half-breed and some nymph conservatory?"

Arrik has no idea what's really going on.

"We do not welcome you into our land, jinnee! Leave now, and remove this valkyrie with you!"

"Valkyrie?" Arrik shifts his focus to me. "Ha. I see it." Then he rolls his neck. "Yeah, no. I'm not going to do that, and you're not going to tell me what to do. Now, until my *valkyrie* companion can speak for herself, I'm going to need you to tell me where my little brother is."

A splatter of yellow shoots from the banged woman's nozzle directly at Arrik's chest, but with a swipe of his hand, a spew of ink-like magic clashes into it, turning the yellow gray.

Okay, that was pretty slick.

Arrik steps forward so that the bottom of his combat boot is disrespectfully in the center of the puddle that is their pooled magic. "Do three nymphs really think they can take down a full-blooded djinn and his valkyrie mast—" Arrik stops and looks down to the gray puddle, which is undergoing a change around his boot, slowly returning to yellow. He attempts to jerk his foot away only to find it stuck. "Well, shit." He looks over his shoulder at me, shaking his head. "It's this weather."

Is he seriously trying to save face right now?! Is he not concerned about the three dystopian battle-women closing in on him?!

"Want to take care of this for me, Master?" He gestures to his stuck foot.

"Cluck, cluck, cluck, cluckums," is what I imagine he hears.

"Yeeeah, that's not going to help me out." He turns to the three women. "Listen, I'm not really the whole 'magical showdown' kind of guy, so if you could just tell me what the risk is here before we get going, I might save you the trouble. What does that do—besides being *sticky*?"

"Yellow will turn you to stone," says the pretty woman holding the blue hose.

Again, Arrik looks over his shoulder at me. "Yeah, that's not good."

"Focus!"

"Heeey," he mocks in an 'aww' kind of way. "I understood you that time." He returns to the women, his voice returning to its bored resting state. "And the others?"

"Green you cannot cross, and blue will melt your skin."

"Seems a little imbalanced, but okay." He beckons at me with two overly confident fingers. "All right, Master. Get over here and wish us out."

Absolutely NOT.

"Ugh." Whether he can feel my push of resistance or simply read it on my face, Arrik shakes his head at the nymph women, who are taking this situation way more seriously than he is. "Can you give us a minute? This one." He points his thumb at me like he and the nymphs are all on the same page, and I'm the only outlier.

Frustration rising, I storm up next to where his boot's stuck.

"We are not leaving Velis here! His relatives practically kidnapped him, sucked him into their little flamboyant world, and plan to use him for mating!"

This time, Arrik gathers enough of it.

"Meh. My stance remains. Nymph boy's got himself a nice little nymph harem. And now he won't have to worry about our other brothers coming for him. The estate will go to Beckham, where it was always going to end up. And you and I can have a little fun together without any guilt. Win-win."

I slap his hand away and give him my steeliest expression. Ice cold steel to let him know I'll never 'go have fun' with him, and that his delusions of me giving up on Velis are just that. I'm nothing if not determined, and I would never, never, ever abandon Velis. All my instincts are swirling like a halo at my back. Vel must be protected at all costs.

"Arrik, I wish you would—"

My lips are pinched shut. "Have you learned nothing? You don't get to just bark out wishes. That's not how it works with me, sweetheart."

Sweetheart.

A totally different connotation than when Vel says it.

And fine. Then I'll go for them myself. Without any kind of

plan, I charge at the nymph women, hoping they're scared of whatever abilities valkyries have, when—

Wham! I feel the hard recoil of slamming into a brick wall.

I rub at my throbbing forehead, looking down to where my toes are edged up to that line of green.

"Ouch," Arrik calls, arms crossed over his head like he's waiting for his girlfriend to finish shopping. "I mean, they did say you couldn't cross it—"

"Shut up, Arrik!"

Argh! He is so not about to help me! I am so on my own!

"*No.*" His voice suddenly sounds like it's directly against my ear, though he's still standing in that same bored position. "*I wouldn't have come here if I wasn't going to help you. But listen to me, Master. There's no use fighting when you aren't on an even playing field. My magic is not its best here, and theirs is, and you obviously aren't any help. So you really shouldn't be the one staring them down right now.*" His voice zips away from me, and the next time he speaks, it sounds normal. "Don't shoot her. She isn't a valkyrie. She's a human, and she's clearly distraught."

I don't need him sticking up for me. I need him to start using some of his dark genie magic on them!

"A human?" The short woman with the green hose lowers her nozzle slightly. "You are not bred for battle, and we do not wish to waste our color on you. As thanks for delivering one of our Maysters, we will let you leave peaceably, but the offer remains only one minute more."

My fists shake on the opposite side of the painted line. Shaking at three women who hold no shred of emotion. Shaking over the things Velis said to me. The coldness I felt from him. The emptiness I still feel.

"I . . ." It's no use. "I wish you were unstuck, Arrik."

"Good girl." His eyes flash blue, and in a similar flash, he's at my side with his hand on my shoulder. "Do it."

With my eyes firmly on the three women across the green line, and with despair sinking in my stomach, I close my eyes. "Arrik, I wish you'd take us away from here."

Our surroundings rip away and are replaced with—

The room looks nearly identical, though the nymph ghostbusters are nowhere in sight.

"We're still in the tower?"

"Three floors up. Apparently, I need a more specific wish than that to get us out of here. Their atmosphere is weird." He drags his fingers through the air, and the space around them ripples. "It's too stabilized. There's no chaos to pull from."

Whatever that means.

Unlucky for him, I won't be wishing us out of this realm until we find a way to Velis. Plenty of wars have been won without magic. We just need to see what other resources we can find in this world. I begin scanning the room for anything that could be of use, but it's the same as the first floor. Exceptionally blah. Fine. Then we'll wait for those women to leave, and we'll exit this tower and scour the city for something useful.

We're not leaving without him.

"Huh." Arrik is scrutinizing me. "That's strong enough that it almost makes me want to rise up and fight. *Almost*. Whenever you think about him, it feels so . . ." He chews his lip, eyes fiercely concentrated on something that isn't there. "Let me see your soul."

Like. Hell.

"I'm going to find a way to make you open your mouth, so why not just save us both the trouble and do it willingly?" His dark confidence closes in on me. "Be a good girl, Master, and you might get rewarded."

"Don't call me that."

"That's all I'm ever supposed to—"

"Don't."

It feels wrong coming from anyone else's mouth.

He rolls his eyes, abandoning the fuckboy approach, and throws his arms out at his sides. "What do you want from me, Dolly Jones? You're the one that called me here. I stupidly tethered myself to you, and now I have to obey you, and I'm not even getting payment for it. Worse, I'm paying *for* it. So not exactly a great deal for me. I'm basically your magical hostage. And this is a

Class H realm. People aren't just supposed to show up here. I'm breaking the law for you, and there will be consequences if I'm caught."

He's got a point.

"Not to mention, you've been dishing out wasteful wishes left and right knowing it's eating into my savings. I told you back in your apartment—it's our job to help you figure out what you desire and to form that desire into a wish, but you haven't even given me the chance. And then challenging three guards from a species you know nothing about and just—what—hoping for the best? You need direction. Unlike your boyfriend, I actually know what I'm doing, and I'm good at my job. So you're damn lucky I showed up in this broke-ass world for you."

True.

He did care enough about my peril to come see what the matter was. And he tethered me knowing all my wishes would be spent trying to get Vel back. And I tricked him into using his own savings to do so.

Guilt claws at me until I succumb. "You're right."

He stiffens like he didn't expect concession, like he expected to go on and on until I fired back at him. "What?" he says.

"I said, *you're right*. Thank you. For coming here. I didn't know what else to do. And I'm sorry. I fully intend to use you and not give you anything in return."

His eyes fall over me with zero readability. "Yeah, so be nicer to me."

"I'll ask Vel to reimburse whatever soul juice I use up to get him back. I think he would."

"You mean out of the earnings *you* stole? I'm good. Just let me have a peek at that soul I'm smelling. It might clue us in to how they were able to break an unbreakable bond. I don't know a lot about nymph magic."

At least he's not asking to take a look at it from below.

His eyes glow a soft blue in preparation as I reluctantly part my mouth. The scent of expensive cologne mixed with last night's party floods me as he closes in, using his thumb to pry my jaw open, his eyes intently fixated down my open throat.

And then those shrewd eyes abruptly widen, and I see the shimmer of gold reflected in them. "Why is your soul like that?"

"Ike what?" My tongue inadvertently brushes his knuckle.

"It's . . ." His protruding Adam's apple swallows against the inked flower petals sheathing it. "Nice."

Nice?

He shakes his head, dark brows bent in concentration. "It's expensive. Maybe the most expensive I've ever seen, and I've pacted a LOT of church girls. How is your soul so clean if you're so . . . ?"

Spicy? Sassy? Scrappy?

"Bitchy," he finishes.

I nearly bite him but stop, curious about the face of disgust he's now making. "Wait—your heart's greatest desire is—? Oh, *puke.*" He releases my chin. "I expected better of you, Dolly Jones. I guess it explains your little obsession with him, but still! We're definitely going to need to work on changing that." Arrogant cackles ricochet off the surrounding cement. "It's Velis? That's so lame."

I see fire. "It's not LAME! It's sweet . . . I'm his greatest desire too."

Arrik makes a gagging noise.

"And you can't change my heart's greatest desire. That's impossible."

"Psh. Says who?"

Says—

Oh.

Did anyone ever say that?

"Do you really think a five-year-old's greatest desire is the same as a thirty-year-old's?" he scoffs. "No. Hearts change. I should know. I've seen more human desire than any other Reilhander." There's a moment where he seems slightly distracted. "I saw a really strong heart change once . . ."

"Whose?"

"None of your business. And don't try to wish it out of me. I've found creative ways to make my masters compliant, but I'll save my tricks if you agree to play fair." He waits for submission that will never come. Is he sucking in his cheeks right now, or is that really the structure of his face? He sets a hand atop my head like I'm his pet. "Come on."

I promptly buck him off. "Where?"

"You're hungry."

I—!

Am.

But I'll starve before I leave Vel.

Arrik shakes his head. "No, we need to think through this. Like I said, I don't know a lot about nymph magic. Throwing out empty wishes won't get us anywhere. There's data on the races stored in our Rays, but I need time to dig into it. It's clear he's in a self-contained dimension of some kind, but I don't know enough about the magic that created it to help you craft your wish. We'll warm up your soul away from this lifeless cacotopia, get you something to eat while I look into it. I already know what you're in the mood for, and I know the place for it, so all I need is for you to wish us out of this realm." He stops. "What? Why are you looking at me like that?"

"You're . . . a good genie."

I don't think I meant to say it out loud.

"Tch. Of course I'm a good fucking genie. Who do you think you're dealing with?"

To be honest, I just thought he was kind of a slut.

"How come when I asked you if you thought you deserved to win the contest, the truth oath made you say no?" I ask.

"Because that oath is a fucking joke. Technically, I didn't think any of us deserved to win because we were three-on-one-ing the kid. But take that out of the equation, this is kind of my thing. I've put in the most work. Those other guys are just posers. And you have no idea how frustrating it is to see some inexperienced kid best us just because he got a special vessel and a smart girl to help him. This thing was rigged from the start."

Wow. Is that really the way the other side sees it?

But knowing the things he's done over the years? Not only to me but to my friends? My girlfriends? It's just hard to stomach the thought of you caring about him.

No, there's still a lot more to this story than I know. Too much to just jump aboard the Arrik train.

I feel my eyes narrow. "Are you implying that it's abnormal for women to be smart? Like it's just a small sect of us?"

That was one hundred percent a diversion technique.

One Arrik immediately sees through.

"Oh, calm your feminist shit, Susan B.," he snarks like he has no time for childish behavior. "Look me in the eye and tell me most men are smart. Hell, tell me most women are. Come on, you already said I was right once. It shouldn't be that hard to do it again." That hand is back atop my head. "Now, give me your wish, and let's go. I'm taking you out for brunch."

CHAPTER 11
The Experienced Brother

I blink.

Blink. Blink.

The heated kiss of a familiar sun settles over my cheeks. The world is alive with the chaotic sound of impatient humans. Humans, because this is not the same sun that lights Vel's gardens. I can feel the difference. This is the sun that cultivated me.

I blink.

Blink. Blink.

Because I'm trying to blink back my own weakness.

The dingy sign before us reads *Fat Nat's Breakfast Shack*. It's a sign Nat's never had to replace because the food is good enough to stand on its own. At least, those oversized omelets are. The shitty coffee's just a bonus.

Arrik smirks at me. "See, Master? A real djinn doesn't even have to thi—H-hey! What the shit? This is the place you wanted, isn't it?!" His cool exterior shows a rare crack over my reception.

Yes, I wanted it. Earlier today I wanted it. But I don't want it now. And I didn't want it with him.

It's like the universe stretches the farther I am away from you.

Oh no. Standing here, with my shoes on the warmed pavement, it feels like all the strength I've built up over the last year has completely dissolved. I knew I was becoming dependent on him. I opened myself too quickly, and the proof is the crumbling feeling deep in my soul over that sun-faded sign and the smell of sizzled bacon.

I didn't want to turn into this. A person that breaks at the sight of a breakfast place just because I intended to go to that breakfast place with some guy. I've experienced this all before in a different flavor, and shame on me for letting it happen again.

I've hardened myself once. It shouldn't be that hard to do it again.

"Come on, Arrik," I say, fists tight. "I'm hungry." I take a step off a curb that shelters blow-away receipts and old cigarette butts—

"*Wait.*" Those tattooed fingers are clutching my shoulder. Arrik yanks me to face him and snatches my chin so that my cheeks are contorted by his fingers. And he peers. *Delves*, his brow laced with concentration, his face close enough to feel the heat rolling off it. Until it sharply stops, and he releases me. "I know how to console you in two ways, and because you aren't yet open to the first, let's try this." Again, his hand is atop my head, this time in a gentler manner. "Strength and weakness can exist inside the same person. It is normal to feel sad when your heart's greatest desire has been stolen from you. Feeling sad is a good thing. People who never feel sad are not good people. Emotion does not always dictate the body's response, and however you try to suppress it, it's still got to release in the end. These truths are universal across realms." He removes his hand and bends again to inspect me, voice dulling. "Feel better?"

There was no fluff to it.

But I definitely don't want fluff right now.

"Was that you, Arrik? Or was that you reading what I needed to hear?" I ask slowly.

"That was me reading you and then telling you what I know from experience." His lip lifts playfully to reveal one side of his teeth. "But I'm glad I got it right."

The whirr of a car comes and passes. Across the parking lot, a child is being an ass.

Arrik's eyes are so crafty, his chin so haughty, his stare so invested.

"Why . . . are you being nice to me?" I probe. "I tricked you."

He shrugs. "I tricked you first."

Well, if we're going all the way back, I was the very first, but . . .

"It doesn't matter. You're my master now, and that means you're now the most important person in my life." His demeanor turns suspiciously nonchalant. "So, really, you could undo that silly betrayal wish you made back at Marcy's house—"

"You're not allowed to call my mom 'Marcy.'"

"—back at *Marcy's* house because I would never betray you, Master. Never . . . Now that you're mine."

Well, I'm beginning to see how he's managed to pull so many masters into his bed.

"Nice try, Arrik. Whatever happens during this short, short stint of you being my wish granter, you are *never* going to devour my soul."

He's caught off guard by a speck of amusement. "*Devour?* Is that how you picture it?"

I wasn't picturing it. But I am now. He'd likely summon you with one finger and then make you kneel at his feet with your mouth open, leering down like he's the 'master' in the relationship.

"Heh."

The world turns dark, and the next moment, we're standing in a chic-looking café alive with the sound of clinking silverware and subdued conversation. Sheer curtains billow with life, mingling the scents of outside air with the thick smell of chewy, baked bread. The tables are small and round, the glasses and silverware finely polished. The people here are at least three class levels above me. The kind of people that only wear their clothing once.

"Where are we?" I ask.

"This place has decent breakfast," says Arrik. "It was my last master's favorite."

"Okay, but why do I feel like I should be wearing a really big hat?"

There's a snap, and suddenly, my line of sight is cut by the overhang of a floppy white sun hat. I swiftly remove it and push it against Arrik's bare chest, which sticks out like litter among this classy crowd. I could see him working the kitchen. But definitely not front of house.

And certainly not as a diner.

Those pierced nipples have drawn the attention of a woman in a collared blouse tucked into navy pants. She's making a beeline for us, the tray in her hand dangerously balancing orange drinks in fine goblets. "Monsieur! Excusez-moi! Vous devez porter une chemise!"

"Wait—is she speaking *French?*"

Looking bored, Arrik waves his hand over the waitress's face and at the same time materializes a black T-shirt over his bare skin. When the woman un-stupefies, her face has gone from harsh to pleasant. "Que voulez-vous pour le petit-déjeuner?" she says.

"Avez-vous un menu en anglais?" Arrik responds. "Merci."

The waitress brisks away, tray rattling.

"You speak FRENCH?"

Arrik eyes me up. "You know, I thought it would be much harder to impress you. Did I not mention the translation magic? I can speak any language. Except whatever the fuck you were clucking about back there."

I really hate him because of how cool he thinks he is.

Even more so because there seems to be a shred of validity to it.

He pushes me into an open seat.

"Arrik, are we in France right now?"

"Don't worry about it."

Cluck, cluck, cluckity cluck.

"We don't have time to be in France. We should go tell your dad what happened to Vel and see if he can help—"

"Sorry, our father's on a business trip with Evaris in Dhiant.

Won't be back for a week, and I don't have the clearance to go there."

"Dhiant?"

"The reaper realm."

Reaper? As in *grim* reapers?!

Ohhh. How is this life?

The waitress returns, stringing together more stylish prose I can't understand, and hands me a menu in English. This feels wrong. Casually eating brunch in a place like this while those nymphs suck Velis deeper into their web?

But . . . Vel isn't going to get any more stuck in the nymph world than he already is, and Arrik can't lie to me, so I know their dad really is in another realm and that Arrik really does need time to research nymph magic. Not to mention, it smells amazing in here. I eye the embossed paper before beginning to order the fanciest scrambled eggs I've ever seen, until Arrik abruptly snatches the menu from me. "Come on, Master. That's not what you want. Why did you second guess yourself?" He lifts his face to the waitress and reorders for me in French—a pastry, from the little I can pick up.

I watch her go, and when I look back to scold Arrik, he's summoned his Ray from wherever it was hiding. It had to have been shrunken. There's not much hiding space on him.

"*I'm fine ordering for myself.*"

"You'll thank me." He plucks a spoon off the table and tucks it into his cheek before leaning back with the Ray resting against his knee, casting magical blue onto his face. "Huh." His eyes read something lost to the waves of light. Then he swipes his fingers to move to a new passage.

Ughhhh. Time feels like it's crawling by, every ticking minute an hour as I think about Vel's weird, emotionless state and the things he said to me and the fact that all his cousins want to bang him. I mean, if he has no emotion, does that mean he has no conscience? Does that mean he can't be blamed for whatever's happening over there with Rainbow Brite? Actually, I'm more concerned about the other one. Gabri and her jade stare licking up and down his body.

Lest we forget Mommy Nymph.

Fucking gross.

"Hmph. Nice it's not directed at me for once." Arrik doesn't look up. "What an idiot. He's getting so much shit for this after we get him back."

He says it like it's a subconscious thought. But it strikes me with all the intention in the world.

After we get him back.

Arrik is serious about helping me. He's serious about helping me form a wish to get to Velis. If it weren't for him, I'd be raw from throwing myself against the locked door of Evangeline Tower.

I look up to find him looking at me, but he quickly shifts those shifty eyes away before I can catch them. "Interesting," he murmurs, like he's been looking at the Ray the whole time.

"W-what?" I lean to get a look at it, knowing it won't show me anything.

"Well, I know why we can't get in. We don't have the blood for it." He pulls a sucker from the pocket of his mouth—Wait, wasn't that just a spoon?!—and pokes it in my face. Cherry, by the smell of it. "Only nymph blood can access their cubiculums."

"Cubiculum?"

"That's what their little sparkle jungles are called."

"But I was able to access it," I argue.

"Yeah, but it was Velis's blood that opened the door. And now that it's shut, you can't get back in without the proper blood to activate it."

"Fine. There was another nymph guard lady that welcomed us when we first got there. Can't we just . . . I don't know, *wish* her into helping?"

"*Wish* her into helping?" Arrik looks amused in the way an adult looks amused at a child. "I'd like specifics as to what you had in mind, Master."

I have no specifics, and he knows it.

He leans back in his chair, that sucker clunking against his teeth. "And no, not unless she's part of their clan. It has to be family blood."

"Okay, so I just need to wish for some of Velis's blood, then."

"Close. You need some of Velis's blood, but you can't wish for it."

"Why not?"

"The math doesn't work out."

I wait for him to elaborate.

"The math?" he persists. "Did Velis not go over this with you? Of course he didn't. Our entire magic structure is based on us hunting and farming *human* souls by manipulating the *human* world. One of the reasons our kind chose yours is because your magic plays nicely with ours. Step out of either of our worlds, and you never know what you're going to get. The whole wish thing isn't really designed to counteract another race's magic. I've tried it, and it never works out the way you'd want. Which is why none of your frantic wishes back there took the way you thought, despite draining my account."

Okay, but he doesn't know that for sure, right?

"Go on and try it, then, but if it doesn't work, you have to promise to say it again."

"Say what?"

He cocks his cocky brow. "That I was *right*."

Yeah, I'm not agreeing to that. "Arrik, I wish we had a vial of Vel's blood."

Arrik lazily points his finger at the table between the salt and pepper shakers, and after a flash of blue, an empty vial appears. "I cannot get his blood right now because it doesn't exist in a plane I can access. It's the same as if you'd asked for a dead person's blood. Not recently deceased—I mean rigid in the ground."

ARGHHHHH. WHY is everything so COMPLICATED?!

"FUCK!"

The universally understood word comes out of my throat just as the urbane waitress approaches with our food, but she doesn't seem to care. Turns out Arrik ordered us both the same thing.

Some kind of puff pastry filled with lemon curd. I tear into it like it was the thing that imprisoned Velis.

This time, I swear because it hits the spot.

"*Relax*," Arrik nags. "Just because the blood thing's a bust doesn't mean there isn't another way. Be a good girl and eat your breakfast while your genie looks into it."

Fucking demeaning prick.

He was right, though. About the blood. And about the pastry.

But he wasn't right about one thing. I'm still hung—

His plate slides across the table at me, his eyes not bothering to look up from the Ray as his fingers push it purposefully enough to cause friction. "I got this one for you too."

Mother-clucker.

He's good. *Experienced*. Able to pick up on my desires with little to no effort.

"How old are you, Arrik?"

He doesn't look up. "Why do you care?"

I'm silent, swallowing the last bite of the second pastry in all its lemony, curdy glory.

"Maybe I'll answer if you ask the thing you really want to know," he says.

Sigh. Whatever. "How long have you been a wish granter?"

At that, he flicks his eyes at me, arrogance coiling. "Yeah, I told you I know what I'm doing." He tosses the Ray onto the table with a dull clatter. "I'm twenty-eight. And I've been doing this since I was the kid's age."

Vel's twenty-two. That means six years. Arrik must have a small fortune by now.

"Hey, Master."

I'm not paying attention. I'm thinking about all those poor, poor 'church' girls and their Arrik-devoured souls. When I turn to look at him, his neck is keenly stretched in my direction, his mouth closer than it should be to my ear.

"Are you starting to like me yet?"

I push him away with one pointer finger against his shoulder.

"'Like' is a strong word, but I'm grateful you're helping me get Vel back."

"Yeah, but you don't still think I'm creepy, do you?"

All those poor, naïve church girls.

"Why does it matter what I think of you?"

His expression lapses into a slight frown because I dodged the question. He makes a drama out of retrieving his Ray. "I can't compute a way to make them come out to us, either. It's the same situation. I can't interact with a place that technically doesn't exist."

"Arrik," I say again. "Why do you care so much what I think about you?"

Silence.

Humans always want to fuck me. You don't?

Why am I here if not to pleasure you?

I'm not creepy, Dolly Jones. And I'm not gross.

His vessels usually pick out his masters. A certain type of master built for a djinn like him. I am not one of those masters.

Sorry. I'm not used to being turned down. And I can't figure out what that little shit has that the rest of us don't. It's frustrating.

I turned him down in that genie club, and at my apartment, and again at my childhood home. But until now, human women have been a source of validation for him.

And Arrik? You're disgusting. Clean up your skin and wash the stink of human off you, and maybe your father will stop favoring that half-breed.

Because . . . his mother's a total cunt?

If I had to bet soul juice, I'd bet Arrik's interest in me boils down to mommy issues. I mean, the guy practically screams mommy issues, right?

"Stop, stop, stop." He waves his hand at me. "Enough psychoanalyzing me. You're wrong, but nice try."

He can tell even that?!

It's mommy issues. It's got to be.

Or . . . just jealousy toward Vel and trying to take something Vel loves.

Loved.
Used to love.
Oh no.
I don't love you.
Stop.
I mean, you're a human.
STOP.

A hand with strong knuckles covers mine, pressing my heel firmly into the table. Arrik isn't looking at me. He's still busy with his Ray.

"We can't draw them out, we can't break in . . ." he mutters, lost in thought. He clicks his tongue. "Not going to mess with time in another realm . . . Hmmm." He carries on musing, his fingers firmly holding mine, like he wouldn't let me pull away, even if I tried. And then—"You good?"

He doesn't look at me. Doesn't make any movement.

I slip my hand from his relaxed grip and slide it into my lap. "Yeah."

He's silent a moment, and then, "Help me."

"What?"

"Help me. You aren't in a good headspace, and your emotion is damaged. Don't let your thoughts just wander. Direct them at solutioning with me."

"But I don't know anything about magic, and I can't see whatever genie encyclopedia you're looking at."

"So? You're a smart girl. I'll present you the problem, and you try to come up with a solution. A *rational* one." He watches me like a professor quizzing his worst student. "Ready?"

"Er, sure?"

"Velis is in a place we can't access, and we can't draw him out. We need blood from his family to get into his family's cubiculum. Go."

"Another person from his family line?" I guess. "We could see if anyone else is in a realm we can access?"

"Yes, good. Form it into a wish."

Is he . . . coaching me?

He's supposed to guide you in making the wishes. You don't just let your masters blurt them out. Part of our job is figuring out what you really want and helping you form it.

This is what he meant when Velis was lost in time.

"Arrik, I wish we had a list of the names of all living members of Velis's nymph family."

The magical glow of wishery lights his face. Eyes locked on mine, he flicks his wrist like a magician performing a sleight of hand, and the next minute, there's a piece of cardstock between his fingers, which he discards at me.

Joell Evangeline
Gabri Evangeline
Fiona Evangeline
Velis Evangeline

"That's it?" I flip the paper over, desperate for more. "But they're all inside the cubicle!"

"Cubiculum. And yeah, dead end. Let's try again. We need blood from Velis's family line to get to him. But we can't access any blood in existence. So?"

His eyes search mine, and I get the feeling he himself doesn't know the answer, and he's waiting for one of us to spark.

I spark first.

"We need to create some."

If he's the professor, it's as if I've just found an error on his test. He weighs it, conjuring a teal-colored roll of paper in the process that begins to smoke even without fire. He pops it into the side of his mouth to replace the sucker that's mysteriously disappeared, and it waggles, clunking up his speech. "How are we going to create blood? Your first wish with the vial would have worked if we could have fabricated it ourselves."

"I don't know," I admit. "But . . . would a blood expert know?" The idea seems to form first on my lips and secondly in my brain. "Yeah! Would Ardy know?! Of some way to replicate blood or create blood or pull blood out of thin air?"

A low growl of reluctance begins to form at the back of Arrik's throat.

"What?"

"That guy and I don't get along."

I try to picture them interacting. They're both a bit *extra*. I imagine Ardy pestering Arrik, and Arrik getting more and more pissed off until he punches a wall.

"Something funny, Master?"

I waft at the aromatic cloud he's just used to distract me from the image. "How much do you smoke in a day?"

"A lot." He extends a hand to me with the teal roll plugged between his fingers. "Want some?"

I'm not sure if it's okay to smoke indoors in France. I'm not sure if we're even in France.

"No," I say. "What is it?"

"Nothing you've ever heard of."

He leaves the offer standing and gives me a look.

No means no, Arrik.

His divinely crafted chin raises, and he coolly brings it back to his mouth and exhales a stream over my head. "Let me know when you're ready for a taste, Dolly Jones."

Is he legitimately trying to score me, or is his normal behavior with his masters just a habit that hard to break? He's got to know by now, after everything we've been through, by taking a look at the face written on my very *soul*, that there's no way in hell I'll play off obvious innuendos like that, right? And is the mouth fixation related to his mommy issues? Is that wetted paper tip a substitute for a nipple?

His eyebrow is at its peak again. "And now she's thinking about boobies." He drives the lit end of his mouth's latest victim into the fine navy tablecloth. "The question is whose."

I swear to god that was no 'emotion' reading.

And a snarky response would be 'your mom,' but it hits a little too close to home.

He stands and swipes his hand over the table, removing all trace of the mess we just made. Huh. Thought he was more of a 'pop in and destroy' type. Would have been nice if he'd shown the same courtesy to MY VIOLATED APARTMENT.

"That wasn't me, you know," he says as he shrinks his Ray with an exaggerated curl of his fist. "I mean, I did enough not to stand out, but that was all Jeb."

Suspiciously, I ask, "My TV?"

He shakes his head.

More suspiciously, I ask, "My *bed*?"

No response to that one, but that smirk is a telling indicator.

Bastard.

I give him my glariest glare, opening my mouth to tell him off, when—

"You *caught* her?" A chilly voice cuts through the open window of the café in perfect view of Arrik's and my silhouettes. "Arrik—you actually *caught* Vel's pet human?"

Arrik and I recognize it at the same time, a voice practically built to shake with rage, followed by the cackle of someone who's come unhinged by dark glee.

I squeeze closer to the tattooed djinn than I ever voluntarily have before. We aren't friends. But he is most definitely the lesser of two evils if the other evil is—

"Jebidirah," mutters Arrik without turning to look out the window. "*Fuck*."

CHAPTER 12
The Cruel Brother

Breezy curtains separate us from a pair of eyes that would look most natural on the other side of a set of bars—though it's difficult to say from which side.

"Arrik?!" I hiss.

I've been so caught up in this rescue mission, I haven't stopped to consider that if Arrik's helping me get Vel back, he's officially transitioned to our side, however magically forced to do so, and that it's likely not going to sit well with the other two peas from his birthing pod.

By the look in Jeb's squinted eyes, the youngest triplet is quickly trying to sift through the situation before him. Arrik in the window of a French bistro with the human who played a key role in he and his brothers' usurping.

"We can't run," Arrik rumbles low, his hand at the center of my back. "I'm not worried about him, but I am worried about the people he'll tattle to. If we run, they'll know I'm helping you. And if they find out we're tethered, even worse."

This time, he isn't intentionally presenting me the problem, but I'm already at work solutioning.

"So, pretend I'm your prisoner," I say. "Pretend you really did capture me. I'll play along."

His eyes press into mine. "That'll work."

"*You don't have to look so excited about it.*"

Too late. There's a dark, dusky delight to his curling mouth as he calls through the window, "Yeah, *I* caught her. All on my own. Meaning she's *mine*, and I don't plan on sharing." He seizes my wrist and forces me against him violently enough to draw the attention of the surrounding guests, who seem to have completely missed his little cleanup sorcery and magical tablet of light.

"Outside," orders Jeb through the window. "*Now.*"

Arrik waits for his brother to disappear before unshackling my wrist and tending to the disgruntled diners around us who are speaking in hushed French about my safety. He wiggles his fingers, like he's waving goodbye to a butterfly in front of their faces, making them instantly go back to their meals like we aren't even there.

His use of magic is so . . . fluid.

Practiced.

But his moment of distraction is over, and that eager, wicked shroud is fully over him—all of it directed at me. It's like he's been waiting for this moment his whole life.

"Follow my lead and don't fuck it up." His hand takes uncompromising hold of the squishiest part of my arm.

I rip it from him. "Follow *your* lead? You mean on the plan *I* just thought of?"

"Oh, *come on*, Master." He rolls his eyes like a teenager from a movie made for old people. "Let me have this one. Once we're out of this, you can get back to asserting your feminine dominance, and I can get back to ignoring it. But if we want Jeb to buy that I've been hoarding you to myself in a non-Master capacity, you're going to have to relinquish some of that control you love soooo much and let me lead. Let's practice with a verbal agreement. Call me your Handler."

Like. Hell.

"Yeah," he sighs. "I didn't think I could get that one out of you. Although . . ." An idea seems to settle over him, though not a very savory one based on the way he's looking at me. "This will sell it." And again his grip is around the soft of my neck, no fear of the fake metal plates inside my knees. "You'll feel a tingle."

It does tingle. Even after he removes his hand.

I rub at my throat, suspect. "What was that?"

"Just a little bruising."

"If I were your prisoner, you would STRANGLE ME?!"

"Only in the way you'd want, love. Only in the way you'd want."

Okay, but does that kind usually leave marks?! I don't actually know. I've never tried anything too exotic. But Arrik likes to have control, and I could very much picture him choking someone while he climaxes. I don't think he'd even remove his joint for it.

Perv.

Although, I am the one who just imagined the whole scenario, so what does that say about me?

And you know what I've also been wondering? How the fuck does he know who 'Susan B.' is if he didn't even know Santa's name? Is this, like, a selective human knowledge situation, or is he just finding loophole ways to be annoying?

The culprit is stopped at the door, the sun through the window turning his eyes almost white as he pierces me with them.

"What?"

No answer.

"Arrik, *what*?"

"It's the other way around," he says, eyebrow at peak.

I have no idea what he's talking about.

"The choking. It wouldn't be during *my* climax."

Implying it would be during mine.

Oh, dear god, his intuition is a LOT sharper than I realized.

There's an unwelcome push of tension from my heart into my neck over how serious he sounds, and a residual throb over the way he continues to look at me like I'm an ornate box he'd like to open.

Obviously, I'm not interested in pursuing this conversation further.

"You aren't allowed to use words like 'climax' for the remainder of this rescue mission," I bark.

"Is that a wish?"

"It's a *request*."

"Hmph." His eyes drip over me. "Take it from someone who's been doing this a long time. Don't use words like 'like' in your 'requests.' Ambiguity leaves room for interpretation." He leans forward, lowering his voice: "Better keep that desire of yours close to the chest, Dolly Jones, lest I begin to feel it."

NO.

There is no desire.

It may be damn near impossible to ignore a hot, tattooed snake when it coils itself around your neck, but my only true desire is to get Vel back as soon as possible.

You're adorable, Master, and ever since the first moment I touched you, it's all I've wanted to do.

Vel.

I can practically feel the funnel of affection from those eager, lovesick eyes, always probing for my needs, so grateful for my reciprocation. Vel's love is a warm, safe love. But it's also a tense, rushing one. He's got so many sides, and they all seem to resonate with different parts of me.

It's how I know I'll never get bored of him.

The thought of Arrik's fingers around my neck—it makes me feel dirty, like I could be easily tossed away. But imagining what it would be like if that same grip were Vel's? He has no desire to own me for real. He wants to have me, but he doesn't want to own me. So, temporarily giving up my power to him would feel . . .

There's safety in being alone behind a locked door with a person who's exposed so much of his weakness yet consistently tries to act as a shield for my own. If his were the fingers tightening around my neck, obsessively watching for the moment I lost it to the pleasure he was meticulously curating in me—

An obnoxious gag shatters my fantasy.

Arrik is pushing the back of his tongue against the roof of his mouth like he's just tasted something nasty. "You want to talk creepy and mother-fucking gross? That was the most *disgusting* thing I have ever experienced out of any of my masters." It's not an exaggeration. The truth oath doesn't make him correct it. "And so Maka-damned *vivid*. Haven't you and my brother been going at it like goblins in your little honeymoon suite? Why are you so *horny*?"

Though I don't feel all that great about making genie Bathsheba experience it, it is comforting to know that my lust for Velis works as a buffer to keep Arrik out.

"I can't believe I actually have to say this, but for the love of god, control your sexual desires, *Master*." Arrik pulls the café's door. "And for the record, I didn't give you *strangulation* marks—geezus—I gave you love marks. Two of them." He slides his thumb against the skin of his neck and then again beneath his opposite jaw to show the location of said hickeys.

I really am the pervert.

So as not to let him home in on my embarrassment, I shove past him onto a crowded thoroughfare susurrant with foreign tongue.

Turns out this café is on a corner. The streets beyond are narrow with a backdrop of light-colored buildings. I don't know anything about architecture, but I think that's sandstone, and the overall feel of it is worn and historic, with cute little signs jutting into the street to mark the names of shops, and greenage spilling out of flower boxes.

Still no idea where we are. France or somewhere else where people speak French, or maybe this is all an illusion Arrik created based on what my soul needed after its stint in dystopian nymph horror land.

But it is pretty.

Pretty enough to make me suck in a breath and graze my eyes over the whole of it, fixating on the small details found therein. Foreign words on fancy shopping bags clutched in manicured nails. The rounded edges on aged cobble that's long outlasted the people who laid it. The bursts of passion cutting above the hum of conversation. And in the center of it all, iceberg eyes pegged on me with unyielding focus.

I know I'm supposed to be acting like Arrik's plaything, but I can't help grasping the back of his shirt.

I forgot how scary Jeb is.

Jeb's stare is like cold, hard, in-the-ground death. Such a contrast from that coral sweater and those trendy above-the-knee shorts. He looks like the prep school rebel, like his dark nails and piercings are a quiet yet open invitation for conflict. Like he's got the grave he's planned for you already dug.

Arrik nods to his brother and then to a covered alleyway farther down the road—one overtaken by full bursts of ivy and less occupied than the main stretch of shops.

It will take us half as much time to get there than it will Jeb. If I had to guess, Arrik's buying us time.

His hand is on my shoulder, driving me forward. He mutters, like he's trying to keep those around us from hearing a secret they'd have zero context for anyway, "Hey, why are you so scared right now?"

"Because your brother is freaking scary!"

"Jeb? He's the one you're scared of?" Arrik *tchs* it off. "I told you—you're the most important person in my life right now, so I find your fear a little insulting. Like you don't think I can protect you."

Arrik is in a position where he wants to protect me?

Unlike Velis, I enjoy the company of humans, and I always take care of my masters.

Even now, it isn't so much that he's forcing me toward the tunnel—it's like he's *escorting* me, like a tatted genie bodyguard.

With a purebred on your arm, you wouldn't even have to wear that tacky disguise. Such a shame to cover such pretty eyes.

"Better," says Arrik, his hand strict on my shoulder. "Now keep it that way. Your emotions are extremely sharp, and I find them distracting. Focus on staying close to me in case I lose control of the situation."

To be fair, if HE loses control of the situation, I'll be waiting in the shadows to scoop up the reins.

I chance a glance over my shoulder at the scary brother, who's swiftly tailing us through the crowd, pushing people out of the way without remorse. "Hey, I think there's someone with him," I observe.

Not only with him. Talking to him, keeping his steps in line.

It's a college-age guy with buzzed hair that has two of those diagonal strips shaved into the lower back side. I always thought those looked cool. But even when my hair was shaved, I knew I couldn't pull it off. I feel like there's some secret to getting the positioning just right. His skin is dark, his hairline crisp, and though there's no branding on his clothing, it just *looks* expensive. Like he probably pays quadruple the price for a pair of sweats than the rest of us.

Arrik sneaks a look. "Probably Jeb's current master."

"But . . . he's a guy."

Arrik tosses his shoulders. "All Jeb's masters are male."

Huh. So far I've only heard about female masters.

"The question is *why* he would have a master right now," continues Arrik. "Unlike me and Beckham, this isn't Jeb's chosen field, so there's no reason for him to seek new masters now that the contest is over. He could have just used a one-off wish to find me, but instead, he pacted someone. At least it will restrict how he can use magic." We come to the mouth of the alleyway, and the tunnel beyond is spotted with whatever light can find its way through the ivy latticing the overhead beams. In the shade, Arrik's eyes are a much more discernible shade of blue. He ushers me in deeper, then directs my shoulders against the matured, moss-covered stone on one of the walls. "Ready to play?"

Never.

Not when Arrik's the goalie, ref, and opposing team.

He snaps his fingers anyway, and a lacy collar manifests around my neck, complete with a miniature bell, which he prods with his finger. "There."

IS THAT REALLY NECESSARY?!

I glare up at him while he gloats down at me. "Enjoy this, Arrik. Because it's the one and only time you'll—"

I taste his most recent cigarette as the pad of a finger stamped in Makayen letters squishes against my lips. "Shh."

I smack his hand away, but my tongue feels suspiciously numb in the aftermath.

Um, what was that for? When I open my mouth to ask, nothing happens. Because it feels like my tongue has just ballooned to the size of a tomato inside my mouth.

"Like I said, follow my lead and don't fuck it up." Arrik ruffles the top of my hair like I'm his kid cousin before turning to face the alley's opening.

MOTHER-FUCKING FUCKER! He just totally hijacked my plan! Does he honestly think I would be stupid enough to give us away?! The alleyway floods with the angry chiming of my voiceless body attempting to tell him off, but his response is to set his elbow to my shoulder.

Like I'm his armrest.

"Your annoyance is pretty cute, Master. Feels like a nip from an angry gerbil."

The bell quivers.

I throw all my weight into shrugging him off as Jeb's silhouette appears before us, backed by the French light of day and framed by unruly growth around the tunnel's mouth.

Jeb must have told his master to stay back. Alone, he comes storming through the passageway like a blizzard in spring, his chilling gaze pinning us the whole way, his tight lips spitting, "*Arrik!* What do you think you're *doing?!*"

"What does it look like I'm doing? I'm playing with Vel's human. Or should I say, MY human." Arrik gives my bell a flick.

This time, I don't even care about the bell. Because Arrik's presence is a calm, confident contrast to the beast charging us, and my body is hunkering against him without any conscious effort.

Jeb stops short of us, seeing my willingness to cozy up to Arrik. "What did you do to her?"

"I took care of that mouth, for one."

"What *else*?"

"Does it matter?"

Jeb shakes his head in salty disbelief before finishing his assault. My neck jerks as his fingers curl under my collar and yank me forward. Jeb's glare pierces me more bitingly than any other time before. "You have caused me more trouble than you know, *little human meddler.*" His rage shakes the choker, his knuckles hard against the soft flesh of my neck.

Is Arrik just going to stand there and let him hit me?!

Well, I'm sure as hell not going to stand idle and let anyone hit me! Least of all this preppy psycho. I breathe deep and prepare for a slap I assume is coming, readying my chewed-to-shit nails and my non-plated knee—

And then I feel it. Warm fingertips. Smoothing down my wrist, out of sight of Jeb, and curling into the palm of my hand.

What is that? Some sort of *secret caress?*

Whatever it is, I can't help wrapping my fingers around him and squeezing in anticipation. Jeb is before me, his face reddening, tightly compressed and giving only the smallest judders of release—

And then it stops.

Jeb forcibly releases me and speaks over my head. "Where's the brat?"

Wait. What?

"Detained," says Arrik, slipping his fingers from my wrist. "And he will be long enough for me to get to know every *crevice* of the infamous Dolly Jones." He catches my shoulder and uses it to pull me to him, then slides his arm across my chest like I'm a child about to cross a busy street.

It's a little bit warm. A little bit secure. A little bit *foreign*.

His fingers burrow into my ribs as his nose buries itself in my unwashed hair as if to prove that I'm his.

I hope it smells stale and sweaty.

He, on the other hand, smells like chaos. Musk and smoke and male energy all covered up by rich cologne meant to stain the sheets of his next sleepover. I shoulder him in the jaw, hard. Exactly what I'd do if he'd captured me for real.

"Lecher," says Jeb, disgust apparent.

"Yep, that's me." Sounding a little tired, Arrik straightens but doesn't release me. "What are you doing in the human realm, Jeb? I thought Amoira forbade you from coming back here after the contest."

Amoira?

Jeb and those other cads' mum.

Arrik calls his mother by her first name?

Yeah, that tracks.

"What do you think, *moron?*" scathes Jeb. "I'm here looking for you. You missed Beckham's meetup, and he's not happy. He assumed you were here screwing around. You're lucky you actually captured her, or you'd be dead. Come on, let's go." Jeb makes a try for my wrist, but Arrik smoothly teleports us deeper into the tunnel.

"Jeb. *Jeeeb.* You can't really expect me to give up an opportunity like this, can you? Think about it. Velis *loves* her. He took everything from us, and he *loves* her, and now she's mine. Keep quiet, and I'll let you have her after I'm done."

"Right. What am *I* going to do with her?"

Wait, why is Jeb questioning it? Wouldn't he want to, like, cut me up?

Jeb's a fucking sociopath.

Jeb will literally tie you up and starve you until you give in to him.

And Jeb, well, he'd like to dissect her, I'd imagine.

Jeb's got a definite reputation for being the crazy one.

Arrik shrugs. "I don't know. Get revenge? Live up to your name."

"Oh, shut up. I am so sick of that joke."

"Yeah," says Arrik, quiet. "But don't you ever just want to prove people right?"

There's something to it, obscured by ink and smoke, but I don't know Arrik well enough to know what it is.

Jeb is silent, breathing through his nostrils, his eyes dead set on mine. "*No*. Now quit messing around and come on."

"Where?" Arrik pokes as he teleports us away from another of Jeb's failed swipes, his arm still around me like a crossbody strap. "Not home. Not unless you're planning on bringing that human with you." He nods to the mouth of the alleyway, where said human has just appeared. By the disapproval on Jeb's downturned mouth, it isn't an expected appearance. "Why a master, Jeb? Why not just strike another one-off deal to locate me? You miss having a human companion that much? I told you you'd get your cock sucked here."

"No, you rake!" lashes Jeb. "It's because I'm broke! All of us are! Dad cut us off from the estate funds the moment those two left for the nymph realm, which, if you remember, *you were supposed to warn us about!* I had to bum off Mother to even get to this realm! Do you think I want to be here in this—this—!"

"Do it, Jeb. Say '*shithole*.' I won't tell on you."

Jeb again looks like a blister about to burst. "ARGH!"

"Relax. I'm just messing with you. Of course I know about the estate funds being locked." It's a lie loosed easily over Arrik's tongue. "Why'd they send you, though? Why isn't the good son out searching for me himself?"

Jeb releases a shaky breath. "Dad confiscated Beck's vessel right before leaving on his business trip. You're lucky you weren't in your room. I bolted before he got to mine."

"Huh." Arrik shifts his arm so that it's hanging around my shoulder, like we're buddies. "Bet Beck's pissed. Is that why he didn't let you borrow from his personal account before sending you here? What a dick."

"No . . ." Jeb's eyes turn scrutinous. "Dad sealed that too. Dad didn't seal yours?"

He must not have. If Arrik's not soaking off my soul, and he's not using magic from the estate, he's got to be pulling from the savings he amassed before starting the contest.

Meaning either Vel's dad spared Arrik for some reason, or . . .

"You think our father knows everywhere I keep my money?"

Hm.

"Arrik, you know you can't keep her. You *need* to hand her over so that we can be done with this. I *want my life back*."

"Yeah, yeah." Arrik wafts at his brother. "How long's it going to take pretty boy over there to blow through his wishes?"

Jeb hesitates. "I don't know. He still thinks I'm a demon. Probably a few days."

"See? I'll have her back at the manor before you're even done. One girl can only entertain me so long." Arrik's tone darkens. "Let me have this, Jeb. You forget you weren't the only one ripped from your life for the sake of someone else." That last part feels like the most honest thing he's said since entering this alleyway.

Jeb's jaw tightens. "You are aware this is a bad idea, right? You're forbidden from going after humans who aren't found through your vessel for a reason. We all know what happened the last time you decided to go rogue."

Wait. What? I tornado my neck to get a look at Arrik, wondering what did happen the last time he decided to 'go rogue' with a human.

"Jeb, Jeb, Jeb. It's not like I plan on tethering her. She's still attached to Velis."

Okay, but we're already tethered.

"Make sure it stays that way. They're not going to give you a third chance. *She's not worth it*."

"Go have fun with your new pet, Jeb. Don't do anything I wouldn't do."

Jeb throws his cold eyes in a circle. "There would have to be a limit for me to surpass it, *freak*." He releases thin air through his teeth. Then he turns on his heel, adding curtly over his shoulder, "You have two days. Don't damage her," before marching away to join his master, who's been a spectator for the whole second half of this brotherly love tragedy.

His master locks eyes with me for a long moment before Jeb gets to him and blinks him away. Poor guy. Who'd want *Jeb* as a wish granter? Who'd want any of them?

I definitely lucked out with Vel.

After, Arrik releases me like a boa unconstricting. "Well, that was a bust."

I can't yet speak, so I give him the inquiry in my gaze.

"He knows something's up, or he would have fought me harder. My guess is he'll call Beckham the first chance he gets away from his master." Arrik sighs. "But at least now they'll think we're sticking to the human world. They won't expect us at the manor." His eyes sidle toward me. "It IS the stupidest, most dangerous place for me to take you right now."

Yeah, well, we're going. Because Ardy's our one and only lead, and every moment spent in the middle of triplet politics is another minute away from my captive soulmate.

Not that I can say any of that. I can only *chime* it. And I'm not about to go begging for my voice back, either. I'll wait for Arrik to offer it on his own, banking on the fact that this will get awkward eventually.

Quiet settles over us. His eyes remain slyly on me. "That wasn't so bad, was it?"

I'm not sure which part he's asking about. Does he mean Jeb? I shake my head 'no' because the violent triplet wasn't as violent as I expected.

"Did you . . . kind of like it, though?" he asks.

He's joking.

He's not joking?

He's genuinely waiting for a response.

Yeah, no. I am not whatever type of human he usually pacts, and I am not the kind of girl that's into being dominated by some smug, arrogant—

"What I mean is, when something's out of your control, isn't it kind of nice to let someone else take charge?"

He's not talking about this interaction with Jeb. He's talking about the fact that my duress over Velis being stuck in Aphrotica has become buried under waves of annoyance over his actions.

He snaps and materializes a new cigarette. "Smoke?"

I shake my head, eyeing him and his motives up with new

curiosity as he leans against the tunnel's aged wall, staring off in the direction Jeb and Jeb's master disappeared.

"You want to know why I do so well with my humans, Dolly Jones?" He flicks his ash. "*That* is why I do so well with my humans. Contrary to what you may think, I don't just draw easy girls or vulnerable girls. I draw girls who feel aimless and want to be *aimed*."

And then he fucks them.

He smiles. "And then I fuck them."

All of them?

"Most of them." He tips his head against the brick and shoots his smoke into the ivy dangling above. "Most of the ones my vessel picks."

You're forbidden from going after humans who aren't found through your vessel for a reason.

Jeb's words remind me of something Beckham said.

Unfortunately for you, our vessels aren't allowed to go after people we could become attached to.

"If I return your voice, you're going to ask me about that, aren't you?"

Before giving a nod of admission, I search Arrik's eyes. They're hard to read. A mesh of curiosity and tedium. He motions for me with two fingers. "Come here."

Why?

"I'm going to make you forget everything you just heard."

Why?!

"Because you're a smart girl who can figure things out using context."

I fervently shake my head and take a few quick steps back from him, having just gleaned far, far too much insider information to let that happen.

We aren't monsters, Master. We have our own backstories too.

I'm only just now starting to believe what Arrik told me when I was bonded to him the first time.

Maybe he can feel it.

"Fine," he says, "you don't have to forget it yet, but the

moment you put it together is the moment I'm taking it from you. Enjoy your *sleuthing*, Master." He exhales over my head, adding with toying amusement, "Your voice is back, by the way. Not sure why you're carrying on like that."

"It is?" I question and then gasp, "IT IS!"

Fucker! When did it come back?

"Arrik! I wish you wouldn't ever silence me ag—"

He zips at me faster than any track star, and it's startling enough to cut short my wish. "What did I say about throwing out wishes on your own? Let me just verbally agree that I won't, okay, Miss Wishy-Pants? No point in wasting magic on it. Conservation. Who knows how much more we're going to need to get your boyfriend back."

I wish I knew how much magic he actually had.

"And that, kitten, is what we call a paradox."

Kitten?

His gaze has fallen to my neck, the smallest hint of wickedness playing at his mouth.

The collar.

It's still on.

Though the bell has gone silent.

I claw at it furiously. "ARRIK, TAKE THIS THING OFF ME RIGHT—"

The world blips to darkness.

CHAPTER 13
Prisms

"Ugh. This is not where I meant to land."

A flood of light washes over me like I've just been abducted by aliens. The place we've landed brings conflicting feelings. It isn't my home, but it's been more of a home to me than anywhere else lately, and just being within these pristine Reilhander halls reminds me of—

Arrik clutches his chest and bends forward to take my shoulder. "Ung! Can you try to do that without the whole sorrow thing attached? It feels so much better when you aren't all weepy over it."

"I'm sorry that thinking about my lost boyfriend isn't *pleasurable* for you, Arrik."

"Boyfriend?" Arrik straightens. "I thought he was your fiancé."

"He . . . is."

The word just tends to stick in the back of my throat, like gum.

"It's his fault we landed way over here. You must have influenced my teleportation with your *pining*." He shows his displeasure with a lift of his nose. "I'm not wasting another teleportation spell. We're walking to find that dipshit Ardy. Chop, chop."

I recognize this wing. It's one of the ones I passed through that day with Caliko, close to the area sealed off for Vel and me. If I'm not mistaken, there's a statue of a dolphin-like creature coming up. Yup, there it is. I avoid glancing up at the walls as we walk, afraid to see Vel's familiar eyes peering out from one of those obnoxiously large portraits of his perfect mother. Never did I think I'd be returning here without him.

"Hey."

"Hm?"

"How are you doing? With him being gone. You okay?"

Well, this is new.

I search Arrik for motive, but it looks like he's just asking me, like a regular human person. Maybe he feels bad about manhandling me for the last twenty minutes.

Or maybe he's reading my needs and reacting to them.

Because he's a good genie.

"Not really," I answer with caution, "but I've been thinking about it, and—" I prepare for the fallout of what I'm about to say. "You were right when you said he wasn't in immediate danger." I wait for him to gloat over his favorite phrase, but it doesn't come. His expression is as disinterested as ever, but his stare is intently on me, waiting for me to say more as he escorts me down the hall. "Joell isn't going to hurt him. He's important to them. My fears are of a different kind. Arrik, do you know how big of a role emotion plays in decision making? I assume it's big, but . . ."

He digs for my real question. "You mean big enough to change a person's moral compass? It depends on the person. There are a lot of factors that contribute to the choices a person makes. One of them is emotion."

Vel's is heartily founded in emotion, for sure. Yet, even without his emotion—"Vel told me he wasn't ready to have kids, and I don't think that would change just because he lost his emotion."

Arrik looks like I just told him we were into something super niche and nasty. "You guys have been talking *kids*? You've been dating, like, two weeks, right?"

"Trust me, it wasn't a conversation I planned. It came up when..."

I left out the part about Vel's infertility curse when I told Arrik the rest.

"When we realized why his rellies wanted to use him," I finish.

"Oh, you mean for his super special *splooge*."

Yes, technically, for his super special splooge.

I redirect. "Anyway, I've decided to just focus on what I can do instead of dwelling on what might be going down in the nymph world—sort of like ignoring the shark in front of you so that you can focus on swimming to safety."

"*So wise*, Master. Am I the shark in this metaphor?"

I can't tell if he's kidding. "No, I mean—"

"I know what you mean. Staring at a problem straight on means you can't always see the solutions around you. Don't mansplain to me, Dolly Jones." This time, he does gloat, and it's over his own deception. But he continues to inspect me. "You're good at burying it. When your emotions come out, they're strong, but I can barely feel them right now. You must have practiced suppression."

Um, yeah. Understatement.

"This way." He motions down one of the hallways at a crossroads lit by a sparkly chandelier. I ignore yet another sparkly picture of Vel's mother. The walls in this area have flecks of opal-like rock in them that catch and toss the light. "I can't tell you exactly where Ardy is. The man migrates. But there are a few places he frequents. We'll start with the closest."

"Do you really think he'll know of some way to fabricate blood we can use to get into the nymph cube?"

"Do you want the truth or reassurance?"

"The truth."

"Nope. He's not going to know shit. And to be honest, I don't think we're going to figure anything out until our father is back from his business trip. But what else are we going to do?"

I should have gone with reassurance. There's no way I'm

hanging around here for a week while Velis rots in the nymph world.

"Don't worry, Master, my bed's open if you need a place to camp out. If you're lucky, I might even let you see inside my vessel."

I glance at him. His chin is raised with clear hints of seduction. I give him a moment to reconsider what he's just said because *I* was under the impression that we were in the middle of a real-people conversation.

"Sorry." He licks at the corner of his mouth. "Habit." He digs a foot into the ground with no regard for its polish, just to leave a scuff, not bothering to show his home the same respect he did that café. "Can I ask you something?"

"Is it another roundabout way to get me to sleep with you?"

"Heh. No. Maybe, but I don't think so."

"*Suuure.*"

"Don't you think you're too mature for our brother?"

"What do you mean?"

"I mean, he's only twenty-two."

"I'm only twenty-four. And he is mature. He's emotionally mature."

"He's *soft*," counters Arrik.

"No, he's *compassionate*, which is good for me because it helps me soften. But that's only one side of him. He's still stubborn enough to challenge me. And snarky enough to keep me interested." I feel the capsule of my heart fill and throb. "He's actually really incredible. Multidimensional. And tenacious. It's a shame you don't know him."

"I know him," says Arrik. "I just don't like him."

Fine. Whatever. I tried.

After, it's quiet.

"Over here." Arrik rounds another corner.

All the hallways in this place look the same. Ever since that day with Cal, I've wondered if Velis was always kept in separate quarters or if there were events leading up to him getting relocated. Did little Vel ever wander down to the wing where his brothers lived? His three big brothers, who hated him. Knowing their age gap puts it into perspective. Six years would have made them thirteen when he was seven. A gap ripe for bullying.

Poor Vel. I bet he was adorable as a child. With those wide blue eyes, so ready to absorb love. He was able to comfort me as a child. I wish I could go back in time and do the same for him.

"Puke. Why can't you just be normal and desire money? Or me?"

Arrik ushers me through a set of doors that lead to another wing, and the moment they close is the moment I root myself in place.

This hallway isn't like all the others we've passed through on the way here. This one's occupied by someone standing in a beam of fuzzy sunlight coming through windows high up on the wall.

"It's fine," says Arrik. "You're invisible. Just keep your mouth shut."

It would be nice to know these things.

And it's pretty annoying that his use of magic is so subtle, less like he's casting magic and more like it just exists around him and responds to what he wants.

The someone in the hallway is a girl—one of the manor's maids. From what I've seen of them, they all wear these cute little uniforms, skirts with suspenders. Some of them wear striped shirts underneath. And some of them are topless.

This one is topless.

With the amount of titties I've seen since entering this realm, it's a wonder Velis has any interest in mine.

It looks like the girl was in the middle of adjusting the various flower arrangements kept in the hall. At her side sits an ornate pushcart overflowing with bunches of rainbow verbena and other fantasyland garnishments. She jiggles with excitement when she sees Arrik—"Young Laird Arrik!"—and hurries to ditch her gardener's gloves.

It's the first time I've ever heard someone call him 'Laird.' Of all the Reilhander men, he probably enjoys having a title the most and would at the same time be least suited for the job.

Besting Vel aside, there's no way he'd actually want to give up his freedom to file paperwork and do . . . whatever Vel's dad does.

I should really figure that out. 'Governing lands' sounds ambiguous and made up.

I digress. What I'm really wondering is—isn't it a little weird that Daddy Djinn chose to hold his contest in a field where Arrik was the clear expert? Even knowing Arrik was the least suitable choice? Was he just that confident in Vel's abilities, or did he assume Arrik would help his other brothers out?

Maybe this really was rigged from the beginning. Maybe it was always meant to be a showdown between Velis and *Beck*.

The approaching girl is pretty, her collarbone pronounced, her silky hair clipped up with a jeweled hairpiece. She looks to be full djinn.

Because I am a person that recognizes these things now.

"Gem," is Arrik's only greeting. Who knows if he's happy to see her. Who knows if he hates her. It's impossible to tell because he looks like he's a blank slate that could flip from mocking asshole to dark lover at any moment.

"Pleasantly surprised to see you, my young laird," the girl purrs. "We thought you'd be back in the mortal world by now."

"Me too," he lies. "Unfortunately, my mode-of was confiscated. Apparently, we were a little too naughty this time."

Gem sticks out her bottom lip, her cute eyes set squarely over her nose at him. "I heard about that. Shame. It was a good try. It's hard to believe our new laird's going to be some halfer. Woof. What is your father thinking?"

Apparently, Velis isn't friends with *all* the help.

"I never know what my father's thinking," says Arrik.

"Well, I can't say I'm disappointed you're grounded." She comes right up to him so that her perky nipples are nearly to his chest, one of her hands trailing against the shaved part of his head. "Since you'll be stuck here, do you want your room cleaned?"

Hoes. Everywhere.

Seriously.

Why have I not met any normal women since coming to these realms?!

Arrik's eyes are artful. "You clean Beck's room this week?"

"I like cleaning your room best," she says, conveniently skirting around the real answer to his question. She stands on her tiptoes and brings her mouth to his ear, her chest fully pressing against his tattoos now. "Your room's always the *dirtiest*."

Okay, I'm just going to come out and say it. It's a little hot, and I'm surprised she didn't ask if she could help him put away his toys. And if Arrik is in master-seducing mode, this might not be a bad way to put some space between us.

But Vel's been locked in the nymph world for a few hours now, and we're not letting this turn into an all-day endeavor.

I step around them so that I can cast invisible judgment on Arrik, but he's already in the process of rejecting her. "I'm good. I cleaned it myself earlier."

"Just once? That means there will be plenty more for me to take care of." She goes in for his neck like a vampire.

Arrik puts his hands on her shoulders, where only thin elastic straps reside. "No. Not today, Gem. I've got shit to do."

She leans sharply away from him. "What's going on with you lately? Elastia said you wouldn't with her either."

Elastia. Pretty name.

"The last time you were like this was when you were with—"

"Goodbye, Gem." Arrik doesn't even care how it looks. He snatches my invisible wrist and lugs me after him like an angry mime.

After, it's quiet but for his annoyed footsteps.

"You're not going to ask?" he says a few moments later.

"Are you going to tell me if I do?"

"No."

Then I'll save my energy.

"You can't hold my hand, Arrik."

He rolls his eyes as he releases it. That, like his magic, was fluid, slipping covertly from my wrist to my fingers.

He stops in front of a set of double doors at the end of the next hallway. "If Ardy's around, he's likely to be here—in the Glass Hall." The hefty doors open, and I nearly buckle from the beauty of what lies beyond. "H-hey! Easy!" Arrik clutches his chest from the push of my emotion.

I can't help it. The setting before me is one of those things that could never accurately be captured on film. Through a long, open hall, enormous prisms of glass shoot up from the ground, ricocheting sparkling light all over the white walls and floor, like crystal windchimes dangling in a window to capture daylight. But there are dozens, and they're huge, all refracting rainbow light from a source I can't see.

It looks like magic incarnate.

"Oh my god." I cling to Arrik, absorbing a billion slices of glittering light that paint the hall. "It's so beautiful. What is this place, Arrik?"

Arrik furrows his brow while studying my reaction before shifting his gaze to the beauty before us and fixing his posture as if experiencing the room for the first time. "Huh." His hand remains on his chest. "It's an energy nexus. It's to help creatures from other worlds acclimatize to ours. You don't need it because our worlds are similar enough, but for people like Ardy, who comes from a world of eternal light, he's got to soak in it every so often. He usually does on the weekends."

"A world of eternal light?" I question.

"Dhiant. The place our father's visiting. It's an underworld where Daems and Reapers hail from. I know what you're going to ask next, and the answer is, I don't know why human lore always depicts underworlds as places of darkness. It's the opposite. Places touched by the soul tend to be stained in light. A-anyway, let's get this over with. There's a waiting area in the middle where Ardy typically reads."

Arrik shows me the way, weaving through the giant crystals while I gawk, trying to absorb a place so hard to conceive. The floor is a patchwork of geometric colored lights bleeding together from the various refractions. It's a lot for my mortal brain to take. I'm definitely lagging.

Until I realize Arrik is lagging even more, his determined pace now overtaken by something else. Something foreign on him.

"Look at this one, Master," he urges. "It's the prettiest one."

Awe? That's . . . odd for him. The way he's rubbing at his chest, I assume it's because he's experiencing this place under the influence of my emotion. I assume he's showing me for his own sake more than for mine.

And he's right. This crystal is the prettiest one. The way it's cut makes the light look like glitter. I stop to let it sparkle in my eyes, taking short breaths and feeling the shivers invoked by such beauty running through the hair of my arms.

I want to come back here with Velis and let him feel this through me instead. This is the sort of beauty one could never get used to, but I'm sure that first moment packed a particular punch. It's a shame Vel couldn't have been there to experience it with me.

"Don't," Arrik hums from beside me, his voice a murmur. "Don't ruin it with sadness." He closes his eyes a brief moment. "It feels so good."

He's acting weird. "Arrik?"

His eyes are still closed. "It's such a fucking waste—an emotive like you being with someone who can't even fully feel what you feel. I bet there's a layer of numb separating him from what you're really experiencing at times like these." He sucks in his bottom lip and tips back his head, skin colored with patches of light. "This nexus is amplifying you, pulsating your emotions through me. I've never been so connected to this feeling before, like I'm the one feeling it. Fuck. You're going to make me high."

"A-ARRIK?!"

No. We can't have my one and only djinn ally getting high while we're sneaking around in enemy territory!

"Arrik, I wish—"

His eyes snap open darkly. "Better not. Unless you're willing to swap it out for something equally pleasurable."

He'd do anything to make himself feel better about himself. Anything.

"Argh! Come on. We'll get you out of here to cool down as soon as we find Ardy."

But after weaving through a few more crystal towers, it becomes painfully apparent that this is going to be a *problem*.

I feel the sneaky slide of his arm around my shoulder. "Master, you are so *awesome*. Your hair is soft, and your neck smells good."

"*Arrik?*"

"Isn't this fun, Master? We're on a quest together, like I'm a good guy. *Dawww*. Bet you didn't see that one coming."

Uh-oh. He sounds straight-up DRUNK.

I steal a frantic glance behind us, feeling more and more like I'm supporting his weight the deeper in we go. "*Pull it together, right now, you idiot!* If anyone sees us, you'll clearly look like something's off, leaning on someone they can't see!"

"Oh, you're visible." He floo-floos his hand at me. "I turned you visible. I was going to trick you into thinking you were still invisible, but I can't comprehend that shit right now." He straightens off me, tip-toeing his fingers along my shoulder as he skitters his hand away. "Speaking of scheming—you didn't even flinch when I mentioned my vessel earlier. You aren't even a little curious to see what it's like? I've been trying to figure out a way to get you in there. I was like, do I present some fabricated danger? Or do I make it sound really desirable so that she asks? Or do I just teleport her in her sleep? Help me out. Which one will work best on you?"

Oh, this fool.

"Better shut up or you'll lose all your cool factor, Arrik."

"Don't tell me to shut up unless you're going to do it with your *body*."

What does that even mean?! He's a cocky motherfucker to be delivering pure nonsense with so much confidence. I keep a lookout at our rear as he ambles onward, as I work to suppress the emotion fueling him, worried we'll be caught, worried he's in no state to blip us to safety or fight whatever other corrupt maids might be patrolling this part of the manor.

"You know, this is not a bad high." He nods and looks around like he's appraising the lawn on a golf course, my anxiety having no effect on his enjoyment of the situation. And then, totally casual, like he's calling out at a party—"Hey bro, look! I caught the human!"

I come to a screeching halt behind him.

We've reached the center of the hall, where a sitting area is arranged within four columns of crystal. There is no Ardy. But there is—

"You owe me five souls, Beck," Arrik brays. "I told you I could get Dolly Jones here willingly."

The oldest triplet sits looking very much like he's been waiting for us.

CHAPTER 14
The Golden Brother

TIME FREEZES. Not all the way, but for a stretch, each second feels like ten. Maybe it's because we're in a *nexus*. The scene before me: a fancy little sitting area; a floral-patterned chair lined in gold; a table with a game on it that looks like a distant cousin of chess but with half the pieces and a board that's teal; a crisscross of rainbow light smattering the floors. And in the center of it all, a familiar, disarming smirk.

He's leaned forward, mouth cocked like he's the hot TA in your first college math class. His shirt is unbuttoned, his sleeves pushed up casually, and his elbows rest on his knees to present a posture that's fraudulently open and warm. "Hm." Beckham slaps his knees and stands. "I have got to say, Arrik. I'm impressed."

I look at Arrik to see him straightened, all traces of the inebriation I saw on him just seconds ago gone.

He was ... faking it?

Disillusionment hits me. Reality seems to shatter. Because the moment I lock eyes with Arrik, my body knows, seconds before my mind, and takes a step away from him. His grin grows, his jaw lifting to show me he's better than me, smarter than me.

My eyes feel wide. "You can't betray me."

"Oh, really?" His demeanor is crisper than I've ever seen it.

"Look!" His eyes flash blue. "I just granted you a wish. Look!" His eyes flare once more. "I just granted another one." His eyes narrow, wickeder than ever before. "This whole thing was so, so easy because your boyfriend doesn't know anything about being a wish granter. The moment you thought I couldn't lie to you? That was when I knew I had you."

Does that mean . . . we never even tethered? Is Arrik not really my genie?!

Three against one's getting a little old, don't you think? And now you've got something shiny. I don't want to see it fall into the wrong hands.

There. Now I can't betray you even if I wanted to. I'll give you a two-day head start when the time comes, fair?

I wouldn't have come here if I wasn't going to help you. But listen to me, Master. There's no use fighting when you aren't on an even playing field.

You're my master now, and that means you're the most important person in my life.

That was all a lie?

No.

Even if he pretends to help, it's just the long game with him. Trust me, I've dealt with him my whole life.

Be careful. He knows the most about humans. And he's got the least to lose.

But knowing the things he's done over the years? Not only to me but to my friends? My girlfriends? It's just hard to stomach the thought of you caring about him.

NO.

"Pretty fun faking the truth oath when you bought it every time. And do you know why you bought it every time? It's called *grooming*, stupid girl. I made you feel desirable and smart. No full-blooded djinn would want someone who's already been fucked by a nymph."

Oh my god.

Is this . . . the real Arrik?

Sit here. Pretend I'm that fat red guy. He's much creepier and much grosser than me.

Do you want me to wait with you until he gets back? I can sense you don't want to be alone.

It is normal to feel sad when your heart's greatest desire has been stolen from you. Feeling sad is a good thing. People who never feel sad are not good people.

I want to try Master's mother's cooking.

I'm an artist too.

"Where *is* our friend?" says Beckham. "All you said in your message was that he was 'detained.'"

Message? When did Arrik ever have time to send Beckham a message? Unless—was that what he was doing in the café? While pretending to research ways to rescue Velis?!

Seedy, skeevy—!

"He's stuck in the nymph world, emotionless and masterless, and with the structure of the weather there?" Arrik shakes his head. "He's not getting out without a wish. *I* barely made it out without a wish."

"Excellent." Beckham's smile stretches as he stands, his overall demeanor remaining unsettlingly calm as he begins to approach like a dragon stalking its prey.

I take another step backward for each encroaching pat of his feet, my heartbeat escalating with each push of air from my lungs. Don't panic. Don't panic. Don't panic, DJ. Flight is the only option here. There's no way I can fight.

The look in his eye—he's enjoying every wave of fear radiating off me. He's perfected the act of looking good-natured. The stranger you'd feel comfortable falling asleep next to on the bus. But his darkness is too strong to completely suppress. It shows deep, deep in his eyes and in the subtle facial movements he tries to hide.

He's excited at the thought of capturing me.

I'm going to run. In three, two—

"Ah, ah, ah," Beckham scolds, curling his hand into a fist in front of his chest. "Have a *seat*, Dolly Jones." The slide of a heavy piece of furniture scraping against the smooth ground plays preview to a decorative armchair pummeling into me from behind hard enough to knock me on my ass.

Beckham is still approaching, but he's no longer the one I'm looking at. "Are you fucking serious, Arrik? All that stuff you said? About three-on-one-ing him? About how I was allowed to be sad for him? You have the capacity to voice things like that yet don't believe them? That's worse than being too stupid to see another point of view! You see it and willfully choose wrong! I was right about you from the beginning—you are creepy, and you are most certainly gross. You *disgust* me."

"Do you think I give one shit about what you think of me? That I care what any human girl thinks about me? Are you fucking kidding me? Do you see the kinds of women who throw themselves at me here? Why would I choose to waste my effort on a feminist asshole I'll never even get to sleep with? The only thing you're worth, DOLLY JONES, is the payoff." Arrik pushes himself back against one of the nearby crystals and folds his arms, all *snooty*.

Mother-fucking, fucking, fucking, FUCKER!

Beckham has been patiently waiting just before me. "You done?" he asks his brother without even a trace of charm before trapping me once more with his kind, clever stare. "Dolly Jones, you did a bad, *bad* thing." His hands press my wrists to the arms of the chair as he leans forward. "And now you've come to meet your new warden. Are you excited? I have so many fun things planned for us. When I'm done with you, no man will want you, least of all my little, half-breed brother." His face is close, his stare dominating. The kind of confidence he breeds, it's different from Arrik's. Arrik sides with cockiness because his confidence isn't sound enough to stand on its own. Beckham's confidence is a whole other level, so certain that it barely needs to manifest.

A melting pot of fear and hatred and regret boils in me.

Beckham leaves his eyes on mine, and that calm smile stays as he slowly rises. "You can go, Arrik. I don't need you anymore."

"Sure," says Arrik. "As soon as you pay me."

"Five souls, was it?"

"Of my choosing," says Arrik.

"Mm. I don't remember that part of the deal."

The brothers enter a stare down.

Good, quarrel amongst yourselves, you dicks. I'll use the time to seek out all exits. I acknowledge there's no way to get away from them, but I at least need to try. At the thought, a cold, dark substance sieges up the arm of the chair and chills as it passes over my arm. It isn't material. It exists *under* my skin.

Arrik's tattoo magic winds around my wrists, binding me to the stiff arms of the chair.

I thrash against it. "ARRRRGH!"

The brothers ignore me.

"Beckham. Five souls of my choosing," says Arrik. "I got her here *willingly*, on my own. Those were the terms, and I met them. Despite you sending Jeb to fuck it up."

"Oh, I didn't send him to mess with you." Beckham's tone is light and patronizing. "I sent him because I was *annoyed* with him. It's not my fault he found you. I thought you were in the nymph realm."

Arrik wrinkles his lip. "Yeah, well, he tried to drag her back by force."

"I know," says Beckham, unnervingly chill. "I just got off the Ray with him. But, you already knew that." This time, his hands are on his knees, but the lean is the same as he comes at me.

He wants me to challenge him so that he can gloat over my inferior positioning. He wants me to narrow my eyes and hide my fear so that he can soak it in and feed his ego. I pretend he isn't even there, sending my rage elsewhere.

"Arrik, I am extremely disappointed in you."

That's the sum of what I'm feeling. Because, you know what? I was getting the impression that we were starting to become friends. He was showing me glimpses behind that whole playboy persona, and he wasn't a bad person to spend time with. It's pretty horrifying to know that after all this time, after all I've been through, I'm still a terrible judge of character. Why do I always trust in the wrong people? Is Velis truly the only man out there who won't betray me?

But then . . .

I don't love you.

This is a lot for one day. Velis looking at me without breaking eye contact and flat-out telling me our love was a lie? Arrik weaseling his way into my life, only to lure me into real danger?

Arrik ignores my admonishment. "What's the deal with Jeb?" he says. "Is he still being a wuss?"

"Yeah, he still doesn't want us to kill her." Beckham doesn't remove his gaze from mine. "I promised him I wouldn't, but he'll get over it. Jeb was always such a soft boy. Good thing he has that face to compensate for it."

Kill.

Kill?

Wait, actual *killing* is on the table?!

I thought this was more of an avoid-their-naughty-antics-while-waiting-for-them-to-cool-down-so-that-we-can-all-coexist situation and less of a try-not-to-get-murdered situation!

A rapid beat has been upsetting my chest, but it begins to elevate into my neck until it's as intrusive as the bass from a shitty car. I'm in real danger here. Daddy Djinn and Evaris are gone. Velis is locked in a pocket of space inside another realm. The only djinn ally I thought I had just brutally sabotaged me. And apparently scary, sociopathic JEB, who is stuck pacted to a master in the human world, is the voice of reason in this situation?!

My world has completely turned upside down.

"She isn't even that pretty. Solid seven." Beckham takes my chin hostage. His nails begin to sink into my flesh. "Your pussy must be magical."

Ow, ow, ow—!

Snap! A whip of ink adeptly strikes Beckham's hand sharply enough to make the ringleader brother release me and straighten. Arrik! A pearl of hope surfaces that maybe this is all an act. That Arrik is about to effectuate the ultimate redemption arc.

Is there some chance I wasn't completely naïve?!

I seek out his eyes and clench every part of me in anticipation.

Arrik looks like he hasn't even moved. He's leaned against that same pillar with his arms folded and gaze bored. "Until I get my payment, Vel's pet is mine. If you can't pay up now, I am more than happy to take her for the night." His tone darkens. "Hand them over, Beck. I placed strong hex magic on that deal we made. To break it would cost you more than five measly human souls."

Beckham shows his first flash of annoyance as he rubs his sore wrist, now stained black. "Give me the names."

Arrik has them ready to go. He kicks away from the crystal, producing a folded piece of paper from his back pocket that he slaps into his brother's hand.

Beckham scans it and laughs. "Oh, come on. Really? I should have known that was what this was about. That was so long ago! You're really still stuck on—"

"Those are the names I want, Beck."

Beckham shakes his head in a 'whatever dude' way before returning to the note. "Who are these other people?"

"Nobodies. But they're clean."

Beckham folds the note and tucks it into his back pocket. "Are you sure you want *that* one? What are you planning to do with it? It's not like you can give it back to her, and I know you're not about to desecrate it."

Her.

"None of your business. Just like whatever you're going to do to Dolly Jones is none of mine." Arrik won't even bother to look at me. Not because he's ashamed. Because I'm not worth the energy of flicking his eyes. "Look, I have spent the last three hours building trust, and I'm exhausted, so quit stalling. Transfer the souls, and I'll leave you to your new toy. Just be sure you don't leave a trace. Father can't know I had any involvement."

The hope I allowed to grow melts. Arrik is beyond redemption. This is real, and whatever that soul is he wants from Beck, it's worth the cost of my life.

Beckham twitches his wrist to materialize his Ray. "Calm down, bro. I'm transferring them now." Beckham's face washes in blue as he peers into the disc-like object and tappers his fingers in the air above it. Arrik waits for a ding to sound before pulling out his Ray and verifying.

There is a moment of relief from him that is quickly flushed away with dark smugness. He swivels his wrist, and the Ray disappears. "Pleasure doing business with you. Enjoy." He waves over his shoulder as he turns away.

That's . . . it? After helping me in my apartment, showing up at my mom's, taking me out for breakfast in France? I can't take it anymore.

"You're a coward, Arrik."

His boots stop mid-step. "Excuse me?"

"You are so much worse than these other two. I don't know how I'm going to get out of this, but I promise you I will, and then I'm coming for you. And if I don't, I'm coming for you from the fucking underworld, and I will haunt your ass, I swear to GOD—"

In a zip, Arrik is in front of me, his fingers curled around my throat.

"Hey!" Beckham shouts, Ray still in his hand. "Don't even *think* about teleporting out of here with her. You aren't strong enough to make it through my barrier. And if I see you even start to try to tether her—"

"Yeah, yeah. Like I'd be stupid enough to try." Arrik turns to me, his fingers tightening around my throat. And then—

It's weird. His mouth is moving in a way that makes it look like he's insulting me to my face, but the voice I hear doesn't seem to be coming from his mouth. It's pressed up against my ear, just like how he threw it when we faced those nymph guards.

"*You did great, love. Thank you.*" Arrik's free hand slides to my face, his thumb flattened against my temple. "*I'm giving you back your memories now. Get ready to make that wish.*"

Wait.

What?

CHAPTER 15
What Happened in the Hall

"Ugh. This is not where I meant to land."

I blink at our new surroundings. We're no longer in France, but I recognize it. The Reilhander manor. It's a hallway near the wing Velis and I have been occupying—one of the halls I passed through with Caliko the other day. If I'm not mistaken, there's a statue of a dolphin-like creature down yonder.

Arrik lets out a long, grainy sigh. "Ughhh, fuck. Now what am I going to do?"

I search the deserted hallway flooded with beams of golden daylight. "Can't we just walk?"

"No." He fans at me like I'm an annoyance. "That's not what I mean. I mean Jeb. Now that he's seen us together, I'm going to have to alter my plans."

Blink. Blink. "*Plans?*"

He says nothing, just sets his back a little harder than is necessary against a wall.

"Arrik, *what plans?*"

He studies me a moment, eyes gliding down my features. "Come here. I need to talk to you. And then I need a favor."

First 'plans' and now a 'favor'? Velis is rotting in the nymph world. I don't have time to be dishing out favors for some *plan* I'm not privy to! I will my mouth to conjure something sassy, but it won't budge. Maybe it realizes that Arrik is in the middle of doing us a pretty solid favor this very moment.

"You can consider it payback for me coming to get you," he says. "If it's easier for you to justify the time it will take, I can pose it that way." He waits for my cooperation and feels it the moment I thaw. "Come sit by me." He slides himself down the wall. "No tricks."

Mmkay, this is . . . odd for him. His demeanor is significantly less complacent than literally minutes ago. I allow my back to wilt down the wall opposite him. The hall is quiet. The daylight warm.

It feels like the manor is asleep, and we've both snuck out during naptime, which makes my stomach feel off.

"You mean it feels naughty?" he says.

"What?"

"Nothing."

Okay, Arrik can definitely read thoughts, and it's FREAKY. I wait for him to speak, and the longer he goes without doing so, the more obviously my heart begins to thud. Because everywhere else around us is so vast and empty. The quiet stretches.

"Ask me if I'll ever harm you," he says.

Something about the interaction we just had with Jeb has completely transformed his mood. "Arrik, you're kind of freaking me out right now."

"Ask it," he insists.

"Will . . . you ever hurt me, Arrik?"

"No," he says. "Not intentionally. But you need to know that leaves room for unintentionally, okay? I have a confession."

Depending on when his last confession was, we might be here a long time.

"Funny. But shh. The sooner we do this, the better the chances it will work. When I came for you, it wasn't for altruistic reas—" His mouth twists, the oath compelling him to correct, "It wasn't for *entirely* altruistic reasons. Not in the nymph world. Not when lover boy got lost in time. Not even when I let you go at Sudoré."

"Sudoré?"

"The nightclub," Arrik clarifies, followed by a shooed hand. "Quit sidetracking me. One of the reasons I didn't snatch you there or anywhere else is because I'm a master planner, and I'm patient. And ever since I saw how badly Beckham wanted you, I have been laying the groundwork to get something I want equally badly." He lifts his chin. "Did you mean what you said about helping repay the souls you've cost me?"

"Er, yeah," I say. "Of course."

"Then listen." His eyes connect with mine, so striking against his bronze skin. "I'm not taking you to see Ardy. He's not even here right now. He's at a different Reilhander manor. I'm taking you to my brother, Beckham. I wasn't planning on doing it this soon, but now that Jeb's seen us, we have to expedite the plan."

Of all the things he could have said, that was the most damning.

"Arrik, I wish I had a knife!"

One materializes in my hand, heavy and sharp.

"What the fuck?" he says as his eyes simmer down from the wish. His mouth pops with a small tell of amusement. "You planning on stabbing me?"

"If I have to. I don't like guns. You were joking, right?"

"Have I been forced to correct myself?"

No.

"Hear me out before you go stabbing me, all right, you little psycho? My brothers think I'm trying to lure you to them willingly. It's a game I proposed to them after I met you at Marcy's house."

"At *my mother's* house," I cement. "And what do you mean *game?*"

"Beckham has something I want. It was always meant to be mine, but he swooped in and stole it, and I want it back. I've been waiting for something to come up that I could use as leverage, but there's been nothing—until you. I'm not planning on giving you to him, but I need him to think I am. Do this for me, and I'll do everything in my power to get Velis back to you."

"*You mean you haven't been?*"

"... I'll try harder."

To either side of him, light from the windows hits the floor. But he's backed by the shadows between.

The knife makes a small clink as I release it onto the chilled ground beside me. "Why even tell me. You've earned my trust. I would have gone with you anyway."

"Besides the fact that I'm not a fucking monster?" His eyes pass over my face. "When this plan was first built, I never thought we'd be tethered. Now that you're mine, it changes things. Everything I do is supposed to be for you. This isn't for you. This is for me. As my master, I'd like you to agree to it."

Honest. And aimed.

Honesty is my weakness.

"Tell me the details, Arrik."

"Beck will already suspect we're working together, and he'll choose a place for us to meet where his power is most amplified. I doubt Velis has told you about core power or how magic actually works, but high-level—there's realm-specific magic, and then there's absolute power. We have a room here lit with absolute power. Whatever your realm's magic system, it heightens your abilities. It's called a nexus. He'll insist we meet there so that he'll be able to read your emotion more accurately, even without being tethered to you. He'll also set up a barrier so that I can't take what I want and run. Beckham's stronger than I am, but he isn't smarter. I will be able to teleport away with you, but only if you wish it. The problem is that I need you to believe I'm taking you to him. I need your shock and fear to be real for this to work."

"You want to take my memory of this conversation," I conclude.

He nods. "I have to. You need to think you've been betrayed. Any trace of you believing otherwise, and this whole thing goes to hell. Beckham cannot know we're tethered, and he won't be able to tell without looking at your soul, so I'll need to get us out of there before that happens. One thing I'm worried about is how being in that room while tethered to a human will impact me. It might make me lose my head, so we need to work that out ahead of time." He stops to swallow. "What do you say?"

This is a lot.

Arrik is asking me to put myself in an extremely dangerous situation without full knowledge of why I'm doing so.

"After this, Velis becomes our one and only priority?"

He nods.

Fine, then.

"So . . . you'll do it?"

"Of course I will, Arrik. I owe you."

His head falls back against the wall, and he breathes. "Okay. I need you to wish for a few things now, and then save one for later. I need you to wish that as soon as we enter the nexus, the truth oath will be temporarily revoked. It's a stretch, and it won't work completely, but I'm hoping to get a few carefully worded lies in. He'll be able to tell if I pose everything as questions. I also need you to wish that the moment we see Beckham, my powers will be temporarily dulled. There's a good chance being in there with you will fuck me up, and I need to keep a clear head."

"Okay, what else?"

"I'll find a way to get close to you and return your memories of this conversation. I think I know you well enough to provoke you into provoking me, so we'll go that route. The moment your memories return, you need to wish us out of there. You don't need to specify where. Just out. I'll take care of the rest."

"What happens if he catches on?"

"He won't."

"What happens if he does?"

Arrik is quiet. "Sometimes, you need to ignore the shark in front of you if you want to swim to safety."

"Are you the shark in this scenario?" I joke.

"No, what I mean is—"

"I know what you mean. You don't have to mansplain it to me. And okay. Anything else I should know?"

"Yes," his truth oath compels.

But whatever else there is, he doesn't offer it. He merely pulls his Ray from behind his back, unsheathing it from whatever invisible magical pocket it's been hiding in. "Make your wishes." His eyes are a sea of reflective blue. "I'm going to contact Beckham and tell him I'm ready to meet. He'll have likely already been contacted by Jeb. This is better for me than him hunting us down."

He waits for me to make the wishes as instructed, his eyes flashing twice. Then, he boop-beeps around on top of the lit pad for a few moments before making it disappear behind his back.

"It's done. Are you ready?" He stands, offering a hand to help me do the same.

A flicker of hesitation flutters at the base of my neck.

"I mean what I said, Master. Right now, you're the most important person in my life. I won't let anything bad happen to you."

I look at him, searching him for honesty, questioning whether or not I'm really ready to place all my trust in Arrik Reilhander for the sake of getting Vel back.

"You better not let me down, Arrik," I say as my fingers fall into his palm.

He pulls me to standing. "I won't. I'm not done playing with you yet. Now, hold still. I'm going to erase your memory like those green fucks do."

"You mean *aliens*?"

He takes my face in his smoke-stained hand, thumb brushing my cheek on the way to my temple. The last thing I see is the intensity of his genie-lit eyes as, indeed, a flood of light does wash over me like I've just been abducted by aliens.

When the memory drains away, Arrik is in my face, leaning over the decorative armchair I'm still strapped down in, his eyes different than they were just a moment ago. The truth of it floods me with overwhelming relief that this is the real Arrik, and that he's still on my side, and that everything until now has just been an act.

"We really are tethered," I whisper up at him.

"Of course we are," he responds. "I don't have that kind of self-control, are you kidding?"

"*Arrik?*" A menacing growl cuts through the rainbow room. Beckham likely felt that burst of relief, and Arrik's next line is a rushed one:

"Do it now, Master." His tattooed hand is still on my cheek. Over his shoulder, I see Beckham charging us, eyes lit not that standard wish-granting blue but a wicked, fiery red.

He's an ACTUAL DEMON.

"A-Arrik, I wish you would take us to safety!"

It isn't a normal pop of absence the way teleporting normally is. Instead, the sparkle around us distorts and stretches. Arrik's palm grapples the back of my head, and he smooshes my face against the fabric of his T-shirt. "*Hold on, Master,*" he says through is teeth. "*I have to get through his magic.*"

"Have you lost your Maka-damned mind, Arrik?!" Beckham's voice is near and shaking, his face distorted along with the rest of the stretched world. "What is it about this little human bitch?! This was your last chance, and you just blew it! Release her to me right now, or I'm telling Mother!"

Wow. Big boy BECK is going to tattle to mommy?

"*Wish it again, Master,*" Arrik huffs against me, his forehead dropped to mine. The world around us feels like we're in one of those fake freaking skydiving tubes. Wind pulls at my skin, trying to tear me from the world. I clutch onto the front of Arrik's shirt.

"Arrik, I wish you would take me away from here! Arrik, get us away from Beckham, I wish you would!"

My desperation runs through, charging up Arrik's eyes blindingly bright. I squeeze mine shut against him and wait for it to end—

"ARRRRRGH!"

Beck's frustration is the last thing to evaporate from the world, and after, Arrik is left panting against me. "Don't open your eyes yet," he says, forehead still touched to mine, his hand still gathering my head to his chest. "We're in between spaces. I just need a breather before getting us the rest of the way."

That would explain why I can't feel my legs.

"Why is Beckham so strong?" I whisper, recovering from the intensity of what just happened.

"He's the firstborn. He absorbed the most magic in the womb. I took what I could, and Jeb got shafted with the rest."

"You . . . remember it?"

"Yeah."

Weird.

"Keep your eyes closed. There's nothing to see out here."

He must have felt my urge to open them.

"Humans aren't supposed to linger between spaces. It isn't good for you. But I want to make sure I get us to the right location, so just give me another minute here. I'm replenishing myself."

"Er, sure. So, what's Jeb's deal?"

"What do you mean?"

"He's . . . He was arguing not to kill me? But he tried to bash me in the face with his vessel when I tricked you three during the contest."

"I would argue that hitting someone in the face is a far cry from killing them, but that's just me."

"But Vel was genuinely afraid of him getting me. He said he'd tie me up and starve me if he caught me. And Ardy said something about him dissecting me, and—"

"It's that bitch face of his," says Arrik.

"What?"

Arrik's chest falls with a weary sigh against me. "Think about it. You've got Beckham, who was blessed with charm despite being a fucking demon underneath. And then you've got Jeb, the weakest one, the youngest one, and also the one who looks the meanest, so . . ."

"You're saying he's the fall guy?"

"Usually. I mean, I took the fall for my own shit growing up, but Jeb? He took the fall for Beck's. I'm sure you've heard about Velis's fox?"

I have not, in fact, heard about Velis's fox.

"His mom gave it to him. His last birthday gift from her. He probably still thinks Jeb was the one that killed it."

A sharp, sudden sickness hits me.

"Shit," says Arrik. "Sorry, I thought he would have told you by now."

It's embarrassing to admit Vel hasn't opened up to me about a lot of that stuff yet.

There's an awkward ripple of silence.

"I'm almost done. This . . . doesn't usually happen to me. Extenuating circumstances."

He sounds like he's trying to explain away a limp dick.

"Heh. You're funny," he says.

Another ripple of silence.

"Hey, Dolly."

Dolly. I don't think he's ever just called me Dolly before.

"Thanks . . . for doing that."

"Sure. I mean, I owed you, so—"

"It hurt you. What you thought I did hurt you. Even with my powers dulled, I could feel it the whole time."

"Er, yeah. It hurt." I pause. "Are you going to tell me about the soul you reclaimed from Beck? The reason we had to—"

"No."

To the point. Noted.

"Fine. But at least tell me this: You haven't, like, erased my memory any other time that I don't know about, have you?"

Silence.

Silence.

Silence.

"All right," he says, completely glossing over my question. "That should do it. Hold tight."

"A-Arrik?!"

"Shhhh."

My lids snap open to the nothingness surrounding us.

There's a burst of light, and when it all refocuses, I have a hard time making out where we've touched down through my smeared vision. It reminds me, almost, of a laser tag arena, all black-lit with pops of neon. But the longer I stare into it, the clearer it becomes.

Fish. Coral. Strands of slow-dancing seaweed. All glowing neon, bright enough to cast the room in alien-looking light that's fuzzy against the dark. Tanks in various sizes line a waist-high ledge along all four spacious walls, one of which backs the head of an enormous bed, half-assedly made up with a dark comforter and a spray of pillows. Unlike the other beds I've seen here, this one doesn't hang from the ceiling. That's because the entire ceiling is made of an inky black substance that churns with swirls of metallic dust. It's mesmerizing, like you could fall back into that bed and get lost in the hypnosis of it for hours. Various pieces of furniture litter the room, the overall vibe messy but clean—drawers closed but with disobedient sleeves trying to sneak out, tabletops holding clutter but no trash. The air is silent and still but for the trickling of water filtration systems running through those magical tanks.

I forget what we were just talking about.

"Arrik, what is this place?"

"Oh? You don't *recognize* it?" he says, releasing me. "Last time, you were right through there." He gestures to the corner. "Sneaking around and letting your guilt spew all over, where just anyone could step in it, and expecting others to cover for you."

"Wait, this is your—?!"

"Ye-p." The 'P' really pops. "Feel lucky. Only a select few humans have ever entered this place."

Arrik's room. I never thought I would be inside it, and lucky's not the word that comes to mind.

"HOW IS THIS A SAFE PLACE FOR US?! Isn't this literally the first place Beckham will look?! I thought you were taking us *away* from the manor!"

There's a cushioned trunk at the foot of the bed. Arrik takes a seat on it and rubs a palm down his face like he's tired. "Relax.

When are you going to get it through your humanoid skull that I am *always* one step ahead?"

I fold my arms. "Except for when I stole your contest earnings."

"... Yeah, except for then."

"And when I wished you out of taking my soul."

His jaw adjusts as a parched expression crosses his face. He says nothing to that one. Instead, "We can't enter each other's chambers without being invited in. Our father enchanted all our rooms several years ago, after . . . the incident with the fox. It's similar to the charm over your and Vel's little fuck chamber."

The incident.

I'm scared for when Vel finally decides to share it.

I steal another look at him and find him genuinely looking tired on the trunk. I have no idea what time it is here. Maybe he was sleeping when I summoned him.

Never took him for a fish guy. The colored glow from the tanks illuminates my cheeks as I approach to get a better view.

Okay, but those aren't fish.

Because some of them have breasts.

And arms.

And human-like faces.

"OH MY GOD, ARRIK—ARE THESE BABY MERMAIDS?!"

He looks up at me with an expression like dehydrated fruit. "... What?"

"You—Did you kidnap baby mermaids?" Now I'm talking to myself. "Mermaids are real? But they're so tiny. And that one doesn't look human at all. That one looks like an eel with a face."

The trunk creaks under Arrik's shifting weight as he stands to come up next to me. The room is warm, but his skin is warmer. His arm grazes mine as he crouches to inspect the tank.

"Yup. I steal them, and then I cultivate them, and then guess what I do?"

He doesn't—?! *Gasp.* But how? They have fish tails!

Arrik unbends. "Let me get this straight. You genuinely

believe I'm the kind of guy who would kidnap baby mermaids, wait until they grow to full size, and then fuck them?" One incredulous burst of air laughs over his tongue. "What I said before was a lie. Mermaids turn to foam when they leave their realm. These are water sprites. They help me sleep. Can't you feel their essence?"

"Feel?"

The bubble of aquatic plumbing fills the silence.

"Hm. Maybe you can't. Here—" He scoops up my hand and sets it to the heated glass, spreading his inked fingers over mine, the glow catching the crafted hollows of his cheeks. "How about now?"

I shake my head.

Determined, Arrik slides the cover off the tank and dips a painted finger inside. The surrounding water sprites flock to him, the light of their little faces lighting up his knuckles. Those with arms cling to his finger like they're hugging him. He watches them with humor, neon pinks and greens reflecting in his eyes. Then he swirls his finger to release the ones clinging to him, and the creatures go dizzying around. They're quick to try and reclaim him. But he slips his hand from the water and captures mine once more —this time so that he can wipe his wet finger down the vein of my wrist.

Oh.

He catches my head in his palm as it falls backward, as intense relaxation washes through me. It feels like being a teenager half-asleep at ten a.m. on a Saturday morning. It feels like getting your hair shampooed. It feels like stretching.

"Interesting," Arrik notes, like a scientist of the dark arts. "You may not be able to feel it in the air, but when it's direct, it seems to hit pretty hard. Feel good?"

I nod limply, gazing into the swirling ceiling above us.

"They only give off this kind of aura if you take care of them," he says. "It's a reflection of their mood. One time, Jeb was in here, and the whole atmosphere went to shit. It took me a week to get them back to normal." He eyes me over. "They don't seem to mind you."

"How long will it last?"

He shrugs and releases one of his 'I dunno' sounds. "Never seen the effect of their essence on a human before."

Meaning whatever other humans have been in this room, it was before he adopted-slash-abducted these creatures.

Have I not already told him not to use me as a human experiment?

"Oooh yeah. I can feel it spreading through you. It's kind of nice for me. Your worry over my little brother has been like a dull prick in the back of my neck all afternoon, but it's finally blurred over. It'll do you some good to chill out with them for a bit. They'll come up to the glass and listen if you feel like talking to them. They like stories. I'm going to jet off to our cousins' place to find Ardy."

"Wait—" I shake my head, which now feels loose enough to spill off my neck. "I want to go with you."

"Ah, no." He touches my shoulder, and the next minute, I'm standing at the side of his bed. One weak push from him makes me fall into the mattress.

Into. Not *onto*.

Because it feels like I'm falling down a rabbit hole of cushion and fabric, lush and soft and welcoming. "Take a nap," he barks. "There's no way I'm taking you with me."

And yet he makes no move for the door. I find him through the haze, and his eyes are passing over my fallen form, his inked body a silhouette against the glow of the tanks. I know he can't hurt me. And I know he can't betray me. Maybe that's why this situation isn't pulling me back into a moment as it so easily could.

So why does the room suddenly feel very, very still, like the invisible particles in the air have all abruptly stopped their clashing?

"Arrik?"

"Can I . . . show you something, Master?"

"It depends on the something."

He slips off his shirt by clenching one hand between his shoulders and discards it beside me.

Oh geez.

"Not impressed. I already know you guys do nothing to get your abs like—"

He moves to the edge of the bed, zipper practically at eye level. "Give me your hand."

I'm not totally capable of scrambling in my current state, but I do my best to get away from him, pulse flushing because: "I-I love Velis, Arrik. I love him, and I would never—"

A classic eyeroll. "As you've made *abundantly* clear. This isn't about that. Look closely. You missed it before, and I don't know when I'll get another chance to show you."

It?

I follow his line of sight downward through the inky lines of his body set in that distinct, confident-yet-chaotic style, washed in the pale neon of the room. A Makayen bird with eerily long legs, the plumes of a jagged-leafed fern, a curvy silhouette funneled up in smoke, the thicc tail of a dragon . . .

The THICC tail of a dragon?

Most of it disappears below the border of his jeans.

"Hold on, is that—"

"If you want to see the rest of it, you can either give me your hand, or I can get nakey. Your choice."

I do want to see the rest of that *unnervingly* familiar tattoo, and I'd like to maintain some shred of integrity in the process. I spare him one finger, which he pokes into his own firm stomach.

Poke is a stretch. There's not much give. It must be rough being *enchanted* to look hot.

"You don't know my life," he says.

Yeah, but I do know Vel's never so much as done five minutes of cardio to get what he's got, and that Arrik had, like, five servings of pie at my mom's.

"You're kind of mean." He says it like neither an insult nor a compliment as he closes his eyes and lets his head fall backward.

"Keep your hand there, and give me a sec. This might look sketchy."

Not sure I want to know what Arrik's version of sketchy is, but at least he warned me. Especially because his abs are within licking distance.

Ah, there's the sketchiness. He's just released a *moan*, his eyelids fluttering in apparent ecstasy, with his hand around my finger, firmly holding it against his own muscle. The room bubbles. The sprites nearest Arrik flock to the glass. The dragon's tail begins to thrash, like it's wiggling itself free of his skin.

The next moment, the head of a tattooed dragon slithers up from below Arrik's jeans, past his belt loops and over his ribbed flesh until reaching my finger.

"Flatten your hand," he orders, head still rolled.

"Arrik—"

"It's okay. It doesn't have to mean anything."

It doesn't *have* to *mean* anything? That makes it kind of sound like it would otherwise mean something. Our situation doesn't call for that kind of phrasing.

To prove it, I flatten my hand to his stomach and feel like I'll need seven or more Hail Marys for doing so. Though, to be fair, I have no idea how potent each Hail Mary is supposed to be, or if seven is anywhere near enough. I watch as the tattoo transfers from his skin onto mine, crawling over my knuckles before filling in the whole of my hand and skittering up my arm, feeling sloppy and wet on my skin.

"I liked your drawing," says Arrik, no longer in his magic-mojo state, just observing the tattoo settling around the bend of my shoulder. Clifford, my chubby childhood dragon sketch, glowed-up in Arrik's own unique style. He's presenting it to me like the artwork he made at school. "Do you like it, Master?"

Yes.

BUT—

"The tattoo is neat, and I'm glad you got your lost soul back and that we didn't get murdered by Beckham and that Jeb is secretly a semi-decent person, but—

"Yeah, yeah. Your nymph is still stuck, and I swore to you I'd do whatever it took to get him back. I'm going to be honest with you. Taking you to Ardy would be nothing more than pandering to make you feel better right now. I don't believe he'll be able to help us. We can still go if it's what you want. But we might have better luck here. We've got the biggest collection of books of all the nobles."

Wait, nobles?

They're *nobles*?

Vel's never, ever mentioned them being NOBLES.

I mean, I guess the whole laird and lady thing—

"Focus, Master." Arrik flutters his fingers in the air over my face to remove the influence the sprites were casting on me, compelling me to scamper—for real this time—out of his bed. "Our family has texts that aren't registered in our Rays. Things that are forbidden. To me, conjuring blood sounds like it could be considered core negative magic."

"Core negative?"

"Like dark magic," he says.

I saw what one of their libraries looks like. Unless we get extremely lucky, digging through old books for a secret way to get into a nymph cubby is going to take forever. We don't have forever. And how are we supposed to just casually flip through books when his Hollister-model-turned-serial-killer brother is out prowling the manor?

Every once in a while, I stop to consider that this is an actual family inside an actual house.

And murder is on the table.

Okay.

"Quit worrying," Arrik orders. "You'll just have a wish waiting on the tip of your tongue to send us back here. Teleporting into our rooms is cheaper than anywhere else. It's like our default location."

"Do you think Beck's vessel really got confiscated, or was that part of his excuse to send Jeb away?"

Apparently, Arrik knows for sure. "It was confiscated." He

beckons me to follow him to the door but stops at the handle to give me a bro-nod over his shoulder, saying, "So, you going to keep that tattoo?"

I pull up the sleeve of my shirt to get a better look at it. It does look sick, its sharp mouth open to my neck and its scaled tail coiling around my shoulder blade. But I'm not sure how I feel about having Arrik's lasting legacy imprinted onto my body.

"You can have it back."

A trace of amusement wafts over him. "Keep it for now. I'll get it back later. And how about the collar? You keeping that too?" He turns and gives a flick to the silent bell I completely forgot was still adorning my neck.

"Oh. My. God. This thing is still on?! Fucking creepy, Arrik! I am not your pet! You are not allowed to think of me as your—"

Arrik opens the door, a self-satisfied grin plastered over his face.

And is subsequently pummeled into from the side.

"UNGH!"

CHAPTER 16
Ambush

"Master!"

The scene before me is very abruptly chaotic. Arrik, sliding along the ground slow-motion style, Spiderman-slinging a slew of black inky magic from his wrist and straight at my throat. The string of gooey magic connects to the collar STILL ON MY NECK and solidifies into a leash.

Oh.

No.

NO.

I'm magically recoiled into his arms.

"Arrik, take this leash off, OR I SWEAR TO MAKA—"

"Haven't you ever heard of the eleven commandments? No taking our lord's name in vain."

I'm pretty sure 'Maka' isn't an individual. But not sure enough to say anything against it.

"*Have you noticed,*" I spit at him, "that you constantly find excuses to gather me to your naked body?!"

"Sure have."

I push him off so that I can figure out who just slammed into him and where they've gone to.

"This way, milady!" My palm is captured by a bony hand, and

I'm pretty sure those are garden shears that just snippity snipped the leash connecting me to Arrik.

"Take her, Cal!" cries a female's voice. "I'll distract the young laird!"

"Don't go announcing it, Bellamy!" shouts the person holding my wrist, who, upon further inspection, is indeed Vel's greenish-haired half-leprechaun bestie. Obviously I don't know if they're besties for sure, but he's the only friend I've officially met, so that's what we're going with.

And wait!

Could it be?

A friendly female character is being introduced?! I swivel my neck to get a look at this magical unicorn of a person.

Vibrant purple hair twisted up into a big, messy knot. A sleek black ensemble I can get behind. A heavily freckled face. "*Heyyy*," she croons. "It's the new *lady*! Can't wait to meet you someday, milady!"

That's the last I see of her before Cal tears me around a corner. His cheeks are flushed, his eyes showing the sparkle of a narrow escape. "Your cheek, milady?" I forget why he's asking until he sets his lips to my cheek to cloak me in a . . . a *cloak* of his luck.

I look behind us, where purple smoke is now spilling out from the triplets' wing.

"Don't worry about Bellamy," huffs Cal, jogging beside me. "She's a moondropper, and it's high moon this week."

She's a what and it's what now?

And it's not her I'm worried about. I'm pretty sure that sequence of inspired cursing means Arrik isn't faring all that well.

"Hold on, Cal." I root myself. "This isn't necessary. Arrik is actually helping me right now."

"Nope! Arrik wouldn't be helpin' you, but he'd be good at making you think he was."

"No, no." I fight to keep him from running off. "He's really helping me! I know because—" It feels like a dirty thing to admit. "I'm his master."

It hits Cal like a splat of tar to the neck. He slides to a stop beneath an ostentatiously large chandelier. "You said you're Arrik's master?"

"Er, I am now, yeah. Hold on, why were you two waiting outside his room? Do you know what's going on with Velis?"

Based on his expression, he clearly doesn't. "What did that dastard do with him this time? Bellamy and I was just coming back from dinner. Was my luck that brought us down that way. Happened to cross through just as the young laird was opening his door. Heard your voice, figured we'd best act fast."

Okay, this could actually be really good for us. This could mean more allies for getting Vel home!

Excitement burns in my cheeks as I begin to pull unsuspecting Cal into our drama.

"This has been one shitshow of a day, Cal. Vel's . . . I don't know if I can really say he's in danger, but he is stuck somewhere, and our bond was severed, and his emotions were kind of lost, and Arrik tricked me into pacting him? And now he's helping me figure out how to get Velis back. It's a whole thing. I'm really, really glad we ran into you. Or that you ran into Arrik."

"Really?" Cal rubs at his neck bashfully. "Didn't know how you felt about me after our excursion yesterday, being you wore that face the whole time."

I need to start making a conscious effort to be more approachable. "I . . . had fun," I tell him. "With you, I mean."

A smile crosses Cal's face, though he can't bring himself to meet my eyes. "I had fun with you too." He ventures a glance behind us, where that purple smoke still drenches the hall and from where the clear sounds of magical battle are trailing. "Bellamy's another of my and Vel's friends. We'll help you get him unstuck, just tell us what you need. His pop's not here, and Evvy's not here. Not much way to reach 'em where they're at, either. But we can enlist anyone else. Though I should warn you, the oldest one's home, and he's been brutal."

"Yeah, we encountered him once already. I'm surprised Arrik's even letting me out of his room."

"Well, that'd be on account of the spell, I'd wager."

"Er, the spell?"

"You can't feel it? He's using real strong magic on you right now. I doubt Beckham'd be able to get within twenty meters. You must have a costly soul for him to waste power like that."

Oh.

How far is twenty meters, again?

And how long has he been casting that over me?

"I suppose you'd have a little control over him, being his master, but I've got to warn you—you can't trust a thing he says. He's only in it for himself. Always. And he's good at getting girls to trust him, so be careful. You sure he wasn't behind Vel getting stuck wherever he's stuck?"

People really don't trust Arrik.

"I'm sure," I say. "He can't lie to me."

"Can't say I like it, but it's your call, milady. You're cloaked in my luck now, in addition to his protection, and you should be for at least a twelfth day's mark."

Not that I have any idea what a 'twelfth day's mark' is.

I really need to learn their clock system.

Caliko lets out a shy, "Woo," followed by, "guess we'll just see what happens, then!" Energized by the thought of the danger this situation might elicit, he begins jogging back the other way, green hair bouncing. "Bellamy! Cease fire! The lady says she's tamed the wolf."

I'm not sure 'tame' is the right word.

A thick layer of purple cloud has settled at the mouth of the triplets' hallway, perfumed and parting with each push of our feet. "What is this stuff?" I ask.

"Smoke of the hidden moon. It won't hurt ya. It's just a byproduct of Bellamy's magic."

"What is the hidden moon?"

"Er, the one you can't see? Wait, does Earthen only have the one moon? I can never remember." Cal holds out an arm to stop me from moving forward while he assesses the quiet-turned hallway, the length of his slender arm causing his sleeve to ride up. "You said Vel's lost his emotion?"

"Yeah, the nymph world has some kind of magic capable of removing emotion. Their color too. Like, from their skin, clothes, everything. It was freaky. The lady at the gate looked like an old photo. And so did Velis, after we were untethered."

"Photo?"

"Portrait?" No, those wouldn't be black and white. "Never mind. Not important. The thing is, though, that they have these little magic pockets where they're normal. Very earthy and incesty, but normal *looking*. Then, they had us sleep on this sacred altar on the top of a big tree—like a nest—and it's clear they thought Velis was going to wake up a zombie or something, but his connection to my soul seems to have been keeping him intact. So when that was severed . . ."

I'm not about to tell Cal that Velis said he no longer loved me. That's not a thing I'll ever repeat.

"His lusty relatives—they were all normal, but Vel turned gray. And it's clear they all thought it should have happened sooner. The lady at the gate even warned us it would."

"Interesting," the leprechaun ruminates. "I didn't know the zombie realm crossed into the nymph realm."

"No, that's not—"

"Wonder why his skin didn't react the way of his kin even after you came unhooked. It's not like *they* had masters to keep them bright. And *your* skin stayed bright. By logic, that means the less nymph ya are, the less affected ya are. If that's the case, he should have grayed less, not more."

Cal's right. That does seem strange.

"Could it be because he's male?" I speculate.

"Mm. Maybe. I don't know much about the realms themselves, but I can apply logic to things."

Maybe I'll ask Arrik his thoughts. Now that I know he's smart-ish.

Cal lingers at the head of the hallway, waiting for the purple smoke to thin. Likely, he's waiting to see if Arrik's behaving himself. He mentioned he wasn't scared of Jeb, but we didn't talk as much about Arrik and what kind of relationship they all have.

The smoke clears to reveal a figure standing like the survivor of an old timey duel: Arrik, his shoulders squared, his chest heaving, and his arms stained black up to the elbow like he's just dipped them in ink.

"Where the *fuck* is she?" he snarls.

At first, I think he might be talking about me, but his eyes find mine once before slipping to the side, like he's listening for someone sneaking up on him. And then he spins and grapples at the air. There's a pop of colorful smoke, and after, he's holding the purple-haired girl by the neck.

"Gotcha."

The girl's eyes flash violet, and a push of smoky energy blasts Arrik away from her. He hits the glossy wall with a *thud!*

I run to him.

I *run* to him?

"Arrik, are you okay?"

He swats my hand away like he's *me*.

"Oy! Bellamy!" Cal hustles over to where Bellamy stands over Arrik, lavender smoke whipping around her fists. "Hold on!" he urges. "The lady's the young laird's mistress!"

It sounds like a tongue twister.

The purple-haired girl's hands fall. "Huh? I thought she was Vel's mistress." It was clearly not something she meant to say, and her back zings like she's just made a terrible mistake. "Or the *laird-in-waiting's* mistress." Her eyes widen, and she says in a voice that's deep and a little goofy, "I mean the laird-in-waiting's MASTER."

Cal's gaze meets mine. "You don't mind, right?"

"No. Call him Vel. And it's true, I'm technically Arrik's master right now."

"Tch. *Technically?*" Arrik slides himself up the wall, leaving inky streaks from the magic stained on his hands on the otherwise immaculate marble. "There's nothing *technical* about it." He draws his fingers down my arm, leaving a sooty trail along my pale skin. "Come on, sweetheart. How can you say that when you were just in my bed?"

Bellamy and Caliko stand blinking at me, and the marks Arrik previously left on my neck, and the door they caught us coming out of.

"NO. Oh my god, no. There's nothing going on between us. No, no, no. Not like that, no."

Cal leans over to Bellamy. "Why is she protesting so hard?"

"This is like you-know-who all over again," says Bellamy back.

"Mm," agrees Cal. "Looks like he's out for another of Vel's betrotheds."

Oh no. There's clear judgment being cast! This CANNOT be the impression I leave on Vel's friends!

Dick move, Arrik!

With the not-so-gentle encouragement of my emotions, Arrik rolls his eyes with more effort than the entire little showdown I just watched. "It was a joke, you fucking nerds. This one's annoyingly devoted to my little brother." He flicks his eyes to Bellamy. "And our lady is nothing like Elastia."

Elastia?

Was that 'another of Vel's betrotheds'? The one that ditched him at Mayree's? The same Elastia that maid said Arrik won't bang anymore?

Knowing the things he's done over the years . . .

Seriously?! SLEEZE.

"Easy," Arrik mutters at me. "It's not what you think."

Sure.

He and Cal and Bellamy are still involved in a faceoff centered around my assumed infidelity.

"She's wearing one of your kitty collars, mate."

MOTHERFUCKER! WHY DO I KEEP FORGETTING THAT'S ON?! Is it—Did he enchant it so that I'd forget about it? That seems like something he'd do.

"ONE of your kitty collars, Arrik?" Somehow it feels worse knowing that I'm not the first girl to have worn one of these for him. "Take it off me right now! *I wish you would.*"

"Aw." His lip curls up in disappointment. One flash of blue later, and the collar is lying at my feet.

I turn back to the others, showing them disbelief in the shake of my head. But Arrik is back there swiveling his fingers, and the thing fucking flies back onto my neck.

"*Arrik.*" I take out my scariest voice. "*Take it off and keep it off.*"

"No."

"I wish you—"

His blackened hand is over my mouth. "Don't. You need to keep it on."

I search his eyes for a reason worthy of my patience.

"Ah," says Cal, tapping his neck. "That thing I mentioned, milady."

Arrik's . . . protection spell? It's inside the collar? Oh. I bring my fingertips to its noiseless bell. Well, that's kind of sweet. So why not just tell me? It would have earned major brownie points if he had told me.

He kidnaps my arm. "Come on." Then he turns to Cal and Bellamy. "You guys work here, right? Clean up this mess. And while you're at it—since when is it okay to attack one of your *lairds* outside his own chambers?"

"Since one of the *lesser* lairds captured the estate's new lady," challenges Bellamy.

"Does she look captured?"

A stupid question for him to ask with the KITTEN COLLAR still around my neck and his hand still around my arm like he's just apprehended a burglar.

He realizes it and releases me, while I hurry to explain, "Vel's stuck in the nymph world, Arrik came and got me, and now he's helping me figure out how to break in and get Vel back." A bout of bashfulness sweeps over me. "I'm Dolly, by the way. Hi." I give Bellamy the lamest, shruggiest little wave and feel immediately stupid.

Why am I getting *flustered*?!

Because if this is one of Vel's gal pals, then she's likely got some pull. She's one to impress. Also, I mean, look at her outfit. And she totally beat Arrik.

"*Hey.*" He sounds grouchy.

"Hi, Dolly." She winks at me. "Bellamy. Tell me the truth, girl. This isn't, like, a hostage situation, is it?" She seems to be kidding —until her freckled face flattens harshly. "Blink twice if you need us to save you."

She's cool. And she seems like she's used to dealing with genie boys. The kind of girl that can throw her hair up into the perfect bun that just looks so easy and at the same time glammy.

"Oh," says Arrik. "You like chicks too?"

Tch. *No.* I don't think so.

I ignore him.

"I know how it looks," I tell the others, "but he really is helping me. And we could use your help too, if you guys are willing."

Arrik's mouth slouches. "What?"

"Arrik and I are off to look in the library for secret ways to get into a nymph cubby," I say.

"*Cubiculum.*"

"From what I've seen, there are several libraries in this place. Why not divide and conquer? I want to get to Vel as soon as possible, and we can cover double the ground if you guys are looking into it at the same time. What we know so far is that it requires blood from Velis's family line to enter his family's cubby."

"Cu—" Arrik starts to correct me. "You know what? Forget it." He conjures what looks like a stick of cinnamon and tucks it into the corner of his mouth, then strolls away.

"Right, then. Sounds good to us," says Cal. "We'll spread the word, pull in others."

"Yeah, but keep it quiet," snaps Arrik. "Only people like you."

"Excuse *you*," scoffs Bellamy. "Like us?"

"Velis sympathizers."

"Oh."

Arrik continues, "Our lady and I will take my father's

personal library. Spread your little minions across the others and have any new intel sent to my Ray."

"How are *you* going to get into the laird's library?" asks Bellamy. "No one has access to that wing."

"Don't worry about it."

Cal's eyes pass from Arrik to me with soft analysis, then back to Arrik with soft understanding. "You're really helping her, then. Helping our lady rescue Velis?"

Arrik says nothing—just palms the top of my head like it's a basketball. I recognize that he's about to blip us away, but before I can let that happen—

"W-wait! Thank you, guys. Come visit our quarters anytime. Open invitation . . . I'm not screwing Arrik. I'm not. Please come."

Oh no.

Why do I sound so fucking *desperate*?

Evil snickering floods the darkness as we transport from the scene.

When we land, I don't recognize our surroundings. Probably because I'm staring at the floor out of embarrassment for how that all just went down. A wet cinnamon stick bops me on the nose.

"What was that back there?" Arrik says wryly. "You acted like you've never had friends."

I focus on the hall of doors we've found ourselves in, seeking out any that look like they might be hiding Daddy Djinn's private library. "Well, to be fair, I don't have any friends," I say as I try the door directly beside us.

Arrik halts. "What do you mean you don't have friends?"

I shake my head as I move on to the next door—the first was locked. "I lost them all last year. Vel's my first friend since. My only friend. Until you, I guess. And hopefully those two back there, if I can manage to get my shit together and remember how to interact with people again."

Arrik's hand is now spread over the first door, his palm glowing in a magical kind of way. "You . . . consider us friends?"

"Yeah," I say. "Kind of. You don't?"

He shakes his head.

Oh.

Well, now I feel stupid. I hang back and watch as his glowing hand imprints into the wood of the door like it's a hot iron melting ice.

But should I feel stupid, though?

"Are you sure you don't consider me a friend, Arrik? I mean, you've saved my ass multiple times now. When I was freaking about Vel being lost in time, and then when I was freaking out about him being lost in the nymph realm, and even when you came to warn us at my mom's. You've been helping me chill out and take my mind off things all day—we had breakfast, you showed me your room."

"Those events were all circumstantial," he says.

I stand by it. "We've spent a fair amount of time together. I'm starting to learn things about you. If I do the good news test, you'd pass. Would I?"

"The what?"

"The good news test. Like, tomorrow, if I had good news to share, I'd tell Velis, I'd maybe call my mom, and then . . . I'd probably tell you. You know, if I saw you in one of the courtyards or something."

I stop to consider A. how absurd that sounds when there are people here who legitimately want to kill me and B. that it's very likely not the same for him. I can't imagine him telling me anything personal that happened to him. I honestly don't know what kind of news he'd even have to share.

His ink-stained hand has removed itself from the searing imprint and fallen to the unlocked handle. He doesn't open it.

"I painted a mural on the roof last week, and no one knows about it." He says it like he's testing out the way it feels and then awaits my reaction.

"Cool. Can I see it after we rescue Vel?"

He stares at me a long minute, then—"We need to talk."

"Arrik?"

"*Now.*" He pushes the door open but immediately slams it shut. "*Shit.*" He clamps onto my shoulder like he means to teleport us away, but though his eyes brighten, nothing happens. He blinks down at the palm that just failed him. "Shit!"

And now we're running, his arm circled around my waist.

I paw at his skin to get adequate grip as he sprints away at djinn speed with me tucked in the crook of his arm. "W-what the hell, Arrik?!"

He gets to a cross-section and practically throws me down the righthand hall, around a corner, and then drags me up a flight of stairs with a pretty, curling handrail. "*Amoira*," he growls. "How the hell did she get in there?"

The triplets' wicked mother was in Vel's dad's library? And we almost just ran into her?! So much for Cal's condom of luck!

Arrik tears me further down the connecting hall and around another turn, up more steps, then flings me in front of a set of closed double doors. "Open them," he orders.

Heart palpitating and ears straining for sounds of pursuit, I grip the handle and pull it open for him.

He shakes his head. "I can't go in. But it looks like you've got permissions. Get in there and stay inside until I come for you." With a hearty shove between my shoulder blades, he sends me stumbling into the room, then slams the door behind me.

What the heck? Why couldn't he teleport us? Is his magic glitching out or something? And why was Vel's dad's ex-wife in his dad's locked library while his dad is away on a business trip? This whole family dynamic is effed.

I turn to figure out where I've just landed, wiping Arrik's smudges from my arms.

A room with a bed.

Also known as a bedroom. Thank you, Dolly.

Their rooms are all so big here. This one has a modest bed in the corner with dark bedding and those same ropes to hold it off the ground. Equally dark curtains stretch floor to high ceiling, closed so that only a crack of dusty light shows around the edges. The way they're pulled reminds me of being somewhere after hours. A little isolated. A little forbidden. An intricate shelving unit fills the entirety of one of the walls, with drawers and cabinets and space to display collected objects. A jar of marble-like spheres that swirl with milky liquid, a stack of antique books with Makayen script on the spine, a globe showing the continents of another world.

And there, in a small frame, a portrait of a staggeringly beautiful woman, an adorable little boy, and a fox.

The fox is indigo but for a burst of white on the tail.

"It's your bedroom, Vel."

A prick of loneliness hits me at the realization that I'm standing in his space, drawing in his air, but that he's not with me.

Vel's room. The only other time I was in here, I didn't see much of it because I was inside a locked cabinet inside a locked closet.

It's funny. I can totally see the 'young laird' version of him in this room. The one that donned that dorky collared shirt when Evaris summoned us to his father's office last week. A heavy contrast to the inside of his messy vessel, where his genie version likes to strut around all cocky in those gray sweatpants.

I miss those sweatpants.

I skim my fingertips over the silken varnish of a fancy looking dresser. Yes, Arrik is out in the halls somewhere dealing with family drama. But I kind of don't care.

I feel Vel here. I miss him here.

I promise you, Dolly Jones. The answer to that question will always be yes.

I pick up the portrait from the mantle and hold it to the crack in the curtains to examine all the secrets hiding behind the brush strokes. Vel looks like he's in primary school here. I don't know exactly how old he was when his mom got sick, but I suspect this might be around that time. The fox is pretty. Vel looks happy.

He's so cute. Those icy blue eyes and that dark blue hair.

He would make cute children.

Ugh. Gross.

So why am I picturing it? Our shared offspring. Vel as an actual daddy.

Vel as a really, really good daddy.

I return the frame to where I found it.

Sad to think of him abandoned to all this once his mom passed away. When my dad died, I had Grandpa, my mom, Steve the Cat. When Vel's mom died, he had a distant, wounded father and three mean older brothers—one of which literally wanted him dead. Has it always been like this? Or has Beckham just gotten worse and worse? Was Vel's dad blind to it? Or was he pulling strings in the shadows like he did with the contest?

I'm disappointed in Arrik for not stepping up and being a brother to him. Even now, he's doing all this for me without even a shred of care for Vel. Why? Arrik doesn't even want to be laird. Not really. He doesn't seem to care about gaining approval from his brothers. He just blatantly double-crossed Beckham. He has no fear. So why wasn't he ever a friend to Vel?

A pang hits me like I already know the answer, but I can't seem to put it into words.

I didn't think any of us deserved to win because we were three-on-one-ing the kid.

Now, until my valkyrie companion can speak for herself, I'm going to need you to tell me where my little brother is.

"*Dolly.*" Arrik's voice is in my ear, though he's nowhere to be seen.

"That is so creepy, Arrik."

"*Shh. Change of plans. This wing is on lockdown. It triggered when I opened my father's library. I have clearance, but Amoira doesn't, and when I opened the door, it tripped the security. I have no idea how she got in there or what she was doing, but it means we have to sneak our way out. I have a teleportation route secured. I'm coming to get you.*" He pauses. "*That your first time in his room?*"

A weird thing for him to care about.

"Yeah?"

There's another long pause. "*Check out what he's got in his closet.*"

How does Arrik even know what Velis has in his closet if they can't enter each other's rooms?

"*Be there soon.*"

For some reason, I expect to hear a click. But there's just silence. I warily make my way to one of two other doors in the room. The first is a huge bathroom with a clawfoot tub I could totally picture Velis sponging me in. The second opens to an enormous walk-in closet housing rows and rows and rows of *clothes*. None of which I could ever picture him wearing.

And then, there. At the far back—I assume this is what Arrik was talking about.

It's a tree. An actual, living tree inside a glass case. Its trunk is white, its branches decorated with clusters of tiny flowers glowing with a mellow, blue light.

I believe I've seen a tree like this before. Earlier today, in the nymph realm. Is this another of his mom's mementos?

I come up to the glass, seeing the reflection of blue haze on my own cheeks.

"*I can feel that from way over here,*" says Arrik's voice in my ear.

"You're still here?!"

He ignores me. "*You react strongly to beauty. It feels pleasant. If we had more time, I'd show you some shit. But we don't. Be there in two minutes. Get ready.*"

I spend another thirty seconds of those two minutes gawking at the tree illuminating a closet that could be its own room, until my eyes shift to a white cabinet sitting inconspicuously on the floor beside it.

Come to think of it—

We're inside a locked cabinet inside a locked closet inside a locked room inside a locked manor.

I crouch and inspect the etchings around the face of the cabinet. Worn and scuffed, it looks like something that's been passed down from generation to generation. And it's no higher than my knee. Is that really where Velis and I made out right before we made love the first time? Feeling the warmth of my own smile on my mouth, I pull the latch and immediately stiffen.

What am I doing?

This is totally snooping.

But as it turns out, the genie version of a 'lock' isn't actually a physical lock but an enchantment to keep undesirables out. So if I am able to open this cabinet, does that mean it's okay to open it?

I let it creak.

Because I can't help myself.

It's almost like I'm being *compelled* to open it.

It's where I used to keep my vessel. And also, there's a necklace in here my mother used to wear. The one from the painting you saw. And . . . there's a letter she wrote me before she died. Just some personal crap.

A slip of folded paper. A small ring box. And a necklace. A delicate silver strand with one red stone at the base. I begin to reach for it, unsure why I'm reaching for it, feeling like there's no choice but for me to reach for it—

"Dolly Jones." A hand lands on my shoulder. "What are you doing?"

I jump as my brain digests the rasp of that voice. I turn to look at him. "Arrik? How are you in here?"

He steals an anxious glance over his shoulder. "I've been calling for you. Come on."

I definitely didn't hear him calling for me.

"Arrik, how are you in here? I thought you couldn't enter each other's rooms?"

He certainly acted like he couldn't enter this room not more than ten minutes ago. He flat-out told me he couldn't.

Meaning he lied to me.

Meaning . . .

How did he get around the truth oath?

He lets out a long sigh and again flicks his eyes behind him as if checking for pursuers. He seems to weigh a decision, and once that decision's been well weighed, he walks over and closes the closet door, blocking off what little light there was from the outside world and leaving us alone in the quiet dark with only the glow of the tree to light us.

"Do you want to see it?" he asks, voice strangely tempered.

"See what?"

He hesitates. "The other memory I took from you."

". . . What?"

"I did take one other from you. A bigger one. We . . . had a conversation once. I took it from you because it didn't fit within my plans. I think you need it back."

The blue glow from the tree shines on his skin, making him look arcane and a little wicked, as he first slowly kisses then extends his thumb to me, eyes sharply on mine the entire way. The pad of his thumb is still moist when it makes contact with my temple. He lifts his chin and watches the memories sink into me.

And after, I recoil to distance myself from him, eyes widened and heart racing.

It was the basement.

That night at my mom's.

"Are you sure you don't want to fuck me, Master? Even now?"

CHAPTER 17
Cartoon Sheets

The memory of it douses me. Nighttime in my mom's cold, musty basement.

"Hey." Arrik catches my wrist from the edge of the couch as I start to back away. "Are you still afraid of me?"

"No, I'm not afraid of you."

"Does that mean you like me?"

I look past him to where Velis is coming down the stairs, having placed a barrier that will ensure no more uninvited guests break into my childhood home. "Yet to be determined. Helping Velis is a good start."

He frees my wrist, and Velis and I leave him sitting on the edge of the couch, shirtless and musing as we hole up in my bedroom.

Velis shuts the door behind us with a hearty dose of force. "Fucking asshole." Because only stringed lights illuminate this legendary place, Velis's magic-charged eyes are a bright contrast as he makes a magic-charged sweep of his hand across the door to seal it from entry. "You can still leave, like if you have to go to the bathroom. But let me know if you do. I can go with you." He turns to me, framed by the poster on the back of my door featuring a band I'm proud to say I still stand by all these years later—and I probably will until the day I die. "I can't believe he had the nerve to come here," says Vel.

"To be honest, I think it's kind of funny," I say. "Like, he's stuck out there crashing on my couch right now with a pink and yellow blanket my aunt made. What the hell?"

"I don't think it's funny. I think it's dangerous. He's got to be planning something. He would usually never be caught dead sleeping with cartoon characters on his pillowcase."

Oh no. I just remembered something.

HOW COULD I HAVE FORGOTTEN ABOUT THAT?!

Velis follows my line of sight to the bed waiting for us. "Wait—"

My eyes jet to the cord fueling the stringed lights next to the bookshelf. Maybe I can make it before he sees what's hiding under that comforter.

I fail at being covert. Mischief tugs at the corner of his mouth. "What are they?"

Not anything he should know.

But intuition has already stricken him. "It's aliens, isn't it? *Please*, tell me it's aliens."

I prepare myself for a race I know I'll lose as he takes a sneaky step closer to the bed. I know I can't beat him. He's too fast. He's genie fast. I shoot my shot anyway and am swiftly captured around the waist and tossed onto the bed.

Velis's eyes gleam evilly over me, his hands dipped into the worn mattress on either side of my head. "Never run from me, Master. I'll catch you every time." He reaches over my head to where the defensive line of pillows rests, tearing one from under the blankets to reveal its damning pillowcase. "YES." He cackles wickedly to himself. "Are these sunglasses they're wearing? *Awesome*."

"I bought them back when I thought you were a cool alien, not a derpy, lovesick alien," I grumble.

He leans his face closer, dark-djinn mode commenced. "Oh, I'm still cool, Doll. I bet I can still make you just as nervous as I always have."

There's little I can say against it with his face that close, with him looking from eye to eye like he wants to *play*.

"Prove it," I bait. Technically, I think he already has, but I taunt him anyway with a lift of my brow. I feel like a teenager on the verge of making out, and it is one-hundred percent hot.

The pillow is chucked to the foot of the bed, and my toes curl over the feel of his mouth on my neck. He takes liberties to kiss and suck at my nape, his knee sneakily pushing my thigh aside for easier access while my hands are preoccupied with gripping at his hair and back.

This bed is so much different than the swinging beds at the manor. The center is a slow, laborious dip, and the build is like a lasagna of unmatching blankets collected over time. Vel doesn't seem to notice as he moves from my neck to my jaw and then to my lips, his hand unwavering around a wrist he's just taken captive.

I love the taste of his approaching breath. I love the moments of anticipative kissing before it escalates. Each time, I half expect him to pull out a second tongue to mess with me, but it hasn't happened yet. As things begin to heat, I give him an opening, and he takes it, sliding his tongue to meet mine. I don't know how or why, but I think djinn are designed to have the perfect amount of saliva in their mouths at any given time.

He is such a good kisser.

The hand around my wrist relaxes and spreads, fingers threading through mine. The softness. The love. All amid such wolfish desire. His other hand has found its way to my thigh wrapped around him.

That earlier tomfoolery under the table has me pent up. I want him. So. Badly.

He must feel it. His mouth smiles mid-kiss.

"Take off your shirt," I whisper in the sliver of time before our mouths reconnect.

Pulling away slightly, he teases, "Geez, make up your mind, Master. Weren't you only recently demanding that I put one on?"

Humor apparent, he reaches into the air over us and snaps his fingers.

The magic of the snap hits, but after, it isn't his shirt that's been removed.

I lie below him in a bra and jeans. Yes, I even broke out the jeans for this homecoming. It's a lot easier to wear them when they've been magically adjusted to fit the day's bloat. Vel conjured me an enormous plate of nachos last night, so this was necessary. Velis, meanwhile, remains in his V-neck, probably enchanted to always smell like fresh laundry, and his classic Vel sweatpants.

"You must not have heard me. I said *your* shirt, Velis."

"Oh, I heard you." His mouth moves to the smooth area above the demi-cup of my bra, while his hand pops beneath the wire and gathers my breast. "This is how they do it in *Brazil*."

How does he even know about that?!

His intuition is getting scary good.

"You don't even know where Brazil is," I protest.

"You're right." He tugs the strap down my shoulder for easier access. "But your mom's been asking me questions about it all night."

Oh. Better.

My head falls back as the warmth of his mouth takes me in. His other hand, meanwhile, is messing with the button of my jeans—which is pointless because we both know he's just going to magic them off in the end. I think he just likes it because it's different from the elastic waistband he usually has to play with. My back tenses as he nibbles, suckles, as his fingers skate along me like he's reading the braille of my body. He leaves my bra disheveled and his thumb on my nipple when he pulls away to position his face directly before mine.

"Hey, Master." He glimmers with dark intent.

"Yeah?" I breathe.

His pale eyes secure mine. "I'm gonna make you come. And then I'm going to turn you around and make you come again. And I'm going to start right now."

Vel's a lot more vocal than I'm used to, and every time he

throws something like that out, I have no idea how to respond in a way that isn't completely goobery. I've had plenty of sex. But not like this. Not so open and expressive, like the secrets we share here will never leave this room.

It makes it all feel so new.

I'm still fumbling for something sexy to say in return when he offers me a wink and slips lower on my body, palm to the curve of my waist, mouth above my bellybutton. He uses his breath to play with me. And this time when he snaps, he leaves me in my bra and panties.

Called it.

His shirt's gone too. Gone to whatever magical pocket he used to stow my pajamas, allowing full display of his statuesque build that looks no less perfect under this shitty lighting.

That is one hot, hot alien.

He kisses my stomach and looks up at me, eyes impossibly rapt. His shoulders are tight from the way he's holding himself. The glimpse of his abs showing from this angle is cruel, really.

"Tell me what you want me to do to you, Master."

Oh, we're going to play *this* game. He knows I'm not good at *this* game.

He also knows it makes my adrenaline rush.

I've never told any of my other boyfriends what I wanted from them. They always just did whatever they felt like. I feel stupid demanding sexual favors from him now.

Though, I do know what I want.

"It's okay. It's just me, babe. Tell me what you want."

I swallow the feeling of vulnerability in my jugular. "I want you to fuck me."

"How?"

All the ways.

One of his dimples puckers. "Which one first?"

He already knows. He's already halfway there.

"Say it, Dolly." His voice drops, sexy, as his heated kiss meets my navel. "*Demand* it."

My chest draws air deeply as he waits with shoulders flexed.

Anticipation pools on my skin. My heartbeat quickens. Velis's eyes pulse a miniature wave of blue as he absorbs the desire radiating off me.

"With your mouth," I finish and feel a burst of release in my chest that I've admitted it to him.

His other dimple joins the first. "As you wish."

He won't snap my panties away. Those, he likes to remove himself. He peels them off slowly, kissing as he goes, leaving me scorching in his wake. His hands slide like satin up my arching back. His perfectly mocking lips start to work. I always feel bad asking for this, but he's soooo . . . oh . . . ho good at it. That mouth. I thought it was built to kiss, but . . .

He isn't shy with it. Every drag of his fingertips along my waist, every dig of his thumbs into my hips. Every intentional push of his tongue. It's all for me. It's never about him. It's always for me. I take his hair in all its Goldilocks glory and force him to me because I don't want him to pull away too soon. Because this is the best feeling ever, and I don't want to miss out on a moment of it.

I tell him it's about to happen.

And then I shiver his name when it does.

And one of the best parts about Vel is that he doesn't overstay his welcome. He has no ego to feed. He doesn't think he's going to conquer the limits of my body and force a second out of me right away. He feels what I desire, removes himself, and gives me a moment alone to release a breath with one arm strewn across my own forehead.

He doesn't ask me if it was good. He knows it was good. He just slides up beside me, takes command of my jawbone through my hair, and kisses me. "That was fucking hot. You're wet as hell."

Is hell wet, though?

He gives me a grin and a shrug. "I haven't been there yet."

His turn.

I crawl over him, straddle him, take his face as he claims the curve of my back. I kiss him. "You did so good today, Vel. My mom loves you."

His smile pops. "Thanks, babe."

I kiss him again. "I was proud to show you off." And again. "That's a first for me." I kiss him hotter, deeper. The momentum between us accelerates. I move my passion from his mouth to his body. Tasting, warming. Velis releases the unintentional moan of a man lost to lust as my bra becomes unclasped, as he evaporates the cottony fabric, as he gathers my flesh and sets his mouth around me again.

Before, he said he was going to turn me over, but it doesn't seem to be going that way.

"No," he huffs, hair starting to moisten from sweat. "Just like this. Ready?"

I nod.

He doesn't snap this time. But our bodies find each other as the last of his clothing is removed.

His chin rises as we meet. "F—*uck*." And then he pulls my hips closer, removing any distance between us. "Fuck, that feels good."

Okay, I do love how vocal he is. I wish I could drop my pride and do the same. I'm getting there. I usually default to his name because it feels safest. And because it excites him.

"Vel."

I roll my body, thinking of the way this must feel for him, the way it feels for me, as he props himself up by one arm and moves in sync, worshiping me with his mouth, his voice, his free hand encouraging my thighs closer. Even after an addictive number of times, I find it sort of remarkable that he makes love to me like this —like I'm some goddess. I've seen the other girls who are after him. I know I'm not perfect or desirable the way any of these fantasyland bitches are, but when he looks at me, he never lets it show.

I wonder if it's our arrows that make him feel this way about me.

"No." He stops our momentum but leaves his arm behind my back to let me know he means to continue. "You are so perfect, it's not even funny. Dolly, you're desirable enough to make me nervous."

How is that possible? I know I must have lost weight during that year of atonement, but I still feel so . . .

"Trust me, I'm not the only one who sees it." He uses the opportunity to lift me and roll us so that I'm the one on my back.

Simple. Classic. But this way might be my favorite. I like to feel like he's caught me. *He* likes to feel like he's caught me.

"I want to fucking consume you," he whispers, eyeing me over with a harsher hunger, the lust in his veins rising above the empathy of his heart.

With his eyes locked on mine, he slides himself out of me, taunting me at the outskirts, eyes pulsating to match every throb of my body, hair tousled from my fingers. And then he drives into me, determined enough to make me grip the comforter hiding alien sheets. He lowers his chest over mine, taking all that he can, with his mouth on my neck and his hand sliding up the meat of my ribs. Over and over, on and on, in our own untouchable vortex until we feel like one beast, one body. His forehead finds my forehead, and when he releases, he does so with his mouth open against mine. I mirror him, crying out for him like he isn't right there.

He was right. He made me come twice.

And we did indeed bang in my childhood bed.

The part that comes after is something to look forward to on its own. There's after-sex cuddling. And then there's after-sex cuddling with Vel. He doesn't just grab me and conk.

He cherishes the feel of my exhausted self curled up against him as he takes my shoulder like he's been waiting for it and pulls me into a secure cocoon. He sets his nose to my hairline and exhales the steam he's built up. "I mean it, Dolly. Every beautiful thing we've seen together. They're nothing next to you. I could look at you all day."

He makes me feel girly.

I love him.

So much.

"I can feel that." His tone lightens as he nuzzles at me. "I love you too." His voice dips to a heart-melting whisper, "You're my favorite."

Thank god for empathic boys.

And I like that. Simple and effective. He's my favorite too.

It used to be that I was a sleeping snob, unable to get comfortable unless I had the proper amount of cool air and weight. But lately? I've been falling asleep all drooled up on him, messy and sweaty.

I blame the onesie incident. It changed me.

The basement air chills, but we've collected our own heat within these walls. His voice rumbles through his sticky chest as he tells me how work is going, how he enjoyed my mom's potatoes, how he doesn't think our cat likes him. And why do humans have separate computers and television cubes, Master?

Somewhere in there, I doze off, safe with him, happier than ever. I've been a little bit of a mess lately. I feel like I keep flipping between being bonkers in love with him and feeling so, so afraid to commit, to protect myself from being shattered if this all goes south. I know it's annoying. I'm annoyed with myself. But how else can I possibly behave when the thing in front of me is Velis? I want him so badly that I'd rather never have him than lose him.

When I open my eyes again, it's dark. It's so hard to tell what time it is in this room. There's a window I can likely no longer fit through high up on the wall. I could get there if I could figure out how to hoist myself on top of the dresser, but, what? Am I seriously going to do that if there's a freaking fire in the room? Anyway, that window doesn't face any streetlights, and the bay is buried deep.

I doubt Vel actually got up to unplug the lights. More likely, he gave one of his little snappy snaps to turn us dark. By the sound of his breathing, he's asleep. He waited until I was out to let himself go. I kiss his throat and feel him swallow. What a loveable, loveable creature.

I have to pee, and I know what he said, but I'm not waking him. I'm not afraid of Arrik. He's had plenty of opportunities to grab me and run, and he hasn't, and now he's under a wish not to betray me, so the chances are even less. I'll be quick, and I don't need a light. This was my piddle path for years.

In the belly of the basement, I make my way to the bathroom, feet crossing the cheap, shallow carpet, going extra wide to avoid the area where a second djinn is sleeping with our spare set of creepy circus-themed sheets. The walls are this weird, spackled texture down here. I trail my fingers over it as a guide until reaching the open frame, where I step onto the linoleum and carefully close the door behind me.

Patter. Patter—

"Wait, wait, wait." A croaky voice hits the darkness. "I'm not into watching girls piss."

Oh. Em. GENIE.

Is Arrik taking a shit in here?!

There's a snap, and the darkness of the closet-like space is broken by a small, flickering flame. A ball of fire rests in Arrik's palm, smoldering in his eyes and casting light on his tired face. He's not on the toilet. He's sitting on the floor in the corner.

"What?!" I say.

"What?" he says.

"W-what are you doing on the floor?!"

He swells the fire in his hand and sets it on the ground beside him, where, by all logic, it should melt the linoleum. But logic doesn't totally come into play when genies are involved.

"I came in here so that I wouldn't accidentally read you in your sleep," he says. "Learned my lesson when you two started fucking earlier. I'm not about getting a secondhand hard-on from the things my little brother's doing to you in there. No thanks."

I didn't realize we had such a problematic spectator.

And now I'm replaying everything I felt while Vel was pleasuring me. Yikes.

And okay, but—"We aren't doing that anymore. So why are you hanging out in here still?"

"I was reading a book on my Ray," he says, dull, "but I got bored."

So he just stayed in here alone in the darkness? That's weird. I fold my arms to cover my chest, which sits unbridled against my tank top. "What were you reading?"

He fires back, "Why do you care?"

Because based on how long Vel and I were at it, plus sleep time, he's been in here at least a few hours, sitting alone on the floor of someone else's creepy basement bathroom where all kinds of nasties like to hang.

"Just . . . wondering what kind of books djinn like," I lie.

"What kind of books do you think I like?"

"You don't want me to answer that."

The room is silent, and then, "Heh." He swipes to reclaim the flame, setting it on his shoulder like a pet squirrel. "I'll leave you to it." He pushes himself from the floor.

"Hold on." I tag his elbow on his way to the door. "I'm serious. What were you reading?"

His cheek is hued with the light of the fire from his shoulder. "It was a book on chemistry for humans."

The only thing more surprising would have been if he'd said the Holy Bible.

"You're messing with me."

"I assure you, Dolly Jones, I can think of much, much better ways to mess with you than to lie to you about what book I'm reading. Your world's magic is interesting. Usually. But this was dry, even for me. Have you read it? *Organic Chemistry*, second edition, edited by a whole shitlist of people you don't want me to ramble off."

Hold on, hold on. Arrik Reilhander spends his free time reading *college chemistry textbooks?*

"No, I haven't READ it. I bought something like it once because I had to, but I skimmed it, at best—Arrik, why are you even awake right now?"

He loiters at the doorhandle. "Sleep and I don't always get along." The door thuds as he closes it behind him on his way out.

Okay, that was not normal, right? People don't just sit in bathroom corners in the dark, alone, for hours on end. Is there something wrong with him?

Questioning reality, I relieve myself and wash my hands in the pedestal sink that has the hot and cold water mixed up. Grandpa never bothered to fix it before he passed away, and Mom doesn't know how. I flick my hands dry because that's what you do when your mythical boyfriend accidentally uses the hand towel to wash some part of his mythical body.

No sign of Arrik outside the bathroom door.

Interesting. That seemed like a prime Dolly-ambush location. I retrace my steps, searching through the dark for a sign of the flame he was shouldering. It's gone out, but a much smaller one has taken its place, hovering above a worn armchair in the corner.

I recognize the smell.

While it isn't the first time weed has been smoked in that chair, it is the first time it's been smoked by a creature from another realm.

I stop at the door to my room. "Do you want a different pillow, Arrik?"

"I'm fine."

"Blankets?"

"No. I like these. They smell like human."

Predator.

Indeed, he looks like a demon, eyes dark and glinting, his symbol-marked body all wrapped up in haze. He flicks cinders that disappear before hitting the ground. "Go ahead," he says. "You don't need to work up to it. Just ask."

"Ask what?"

He shakes his head and unleashes a thin, controlled stream of smoke. "No need to beat around the bush with me, love. We may never be tethered, but we have been bonded, and that's a link that will never go away. You've got a question wriggling in you. I can feel it."

Super.

"Fine," I say, venturing deeper into the family room. "Why are you here, Arrik? You came to warn us. Fine. You want to stop the whole three-on-one. Sure. But why are you here *now*? Why did you insist on spending the night? And what are you doing awake?"

"I'll tell you if you join me." He extends a hand to me, and the smoke coming from his fingers pulls in the opposite direction, wafting toward his nose like it's been enchanted to seek him out.

Yeah, no. Velis didn't even want me out here alone. He definitely wouldn't be cool with me toking in the dark with his crafty older brother.

But Velis and I aren't in the kind of relationship I've been in in the past. He's never looking for a reason to make me apologize. He doesn't seek out conflict. And to be honest, I'm worried about Arrik. Whatever he's doing—coming here, hanging around in the dark—it doesn't seem healthy.

Plus, it would be helpful to know his real motives.

I take the paper from between his thumb and pointer, and his eyebrow reacts like I've just asked him to go make out behind the bleachers.

I inspect it. "Is this normal weed?"

"It's really fucking good weed, but yeah."

I set it to my lips, muffling the question, "Are you high right now?"

"I don't get high off stuff like that anymore. I metabolize too quickly."

Of course he does. Because his body is m-a-g-i-c-a-l.

The paper tries to cling to my lip as I pull it away. "Well, I'm not about to be the only one getting high out here." Because, somehow, that seems worse.

"Easy fix." His eyes roam over my face. "Wish I'd get as high as you get."

"And then what?"

"And then we'll have a chat. Maybe I'll even tell you some secrets."

A chat. Secrets. He knows the right buzzwords.

I bring the blunt within tempting distance of my lips. "Arrik, I wish you'd get as high as I get. AND that you'd answer all my questions truthfully while we smoke."

Those eyes wrapped in darkness show a flash of amusement. "Smart. I'll allow it."

The room bursts in blue, and I'm temporarily blinded with the imprint of his glowing eyes stained into my vision.

"Granted," he says as it fades.

My lungs burn with the pull of foreign substance, and after, I cough into my shoulder, the residual smoke clouding up the area around me.

Arrik makes a bored sweep with his hand, and my lungs clear. As the impact of what I just smoked hits me, I lean against the textured wall beside the well-loved chair. Arrik's head falls backward in sync. "Oh yeah, I can feel it. Your tolerance is low."

That would be because I gave up smoking over a year ago. I can't afford to take more than one or two hits, but I've faked it before. No smoke rings. The world's tiniest pulls.

"Why are you really here, Arrik? Tell me."

"No need," he says. "You already know."

I don't, though.

He spreads back in the chair. "Come on, Dolly Jones, you're a smart girl. Why would I be *here* in *your* basement, keeping lookout for *you* and someone I hate, knowing full well I won't be able to sleep for shit?"

It hits my tongue without effort: "You're here to protect me."

He affirms it like I've just answered a trivia question correctly. "I am here to protect you."

"Why?"

He gives me a bro nod. "Smoke up."

I return the lit roll to the corner of my mouth, but I don't inhale.

Why does he want me to get high so badly?

Arrik leans forward in the chair, his hands folded under his chin. "Say what you want, but there is an element of fear in you, Dolly Jones. I can *feel* it. A little offensive, a little exciting, but ultimately in the way. Why not just get it over with and ask if I'll ever harm you?"

I think through any possible loopholes, finding none before asking:

"Will you ever harm me, Arrik?"

His eyes sear. "Not intentionally. Now smoke up."

He releases his neck backward as the smoke from my next hit sinks into me, his arms spread around the head of the chair like royalty. "Yeah. That should help. Thanks."

Oh. Is this less about him getting *me* high and more about him using me to get *himself* high?

So that he can sleep?

"Arrik, why are you here guarding me?" I try again.

His eyes flare. "Because of a promise I made."

Purposefully vague.

"So, you being here has absolutely nothing to do with you trying to take me from Velis because you want to hurt him?"

He takes the blunt from me, making sure to show a peek of his tongue as he pulls the end of the paper into his mouth. "If I take you from Velis, it will be because you want me to take you. The hurting him would just be an added bonus."

There's no humor. He means every word.

That's so . . . mean.

I think about how happy Vel was to meet my mom. Him eagerly hugging her. Arrik swooping in to try and ruin it.

"Seriously, Arrik?! Aren't you, like, thirty? And if you're reading fucking science textbooks, then you aren't stupid. You can't possibly still blame Velis for your family getting broken up when you were young." I feel myself being incited over the ludicrousness of it all and the fact that Vel literally did nothing to earn the hate his brothers have for him.

"I'm twenty-eight," he corrects. "And you don't know what you're talking about."

"You're right. I don't. And the more I see of you and him, I understand it even less. Don't you feel at all brotherly toward him? You share a father. You grew up in the same effed-up family.

You're both empaths, so why is there no empathy between you? The other two seem beyond help, but you? You seem like you have some shred of decency, so—"

Like blue lightning, Arrik is no longer in his chair. His palm is suddenly pressed to the textured wall above my head, and I'm taken back to that night at the disco when he caught me and played with me and then let me go. I sink under the intensity of his presence looming over me, a far cry from the lazy stoner he was just seconds ago. "You know what's maybe more frustrating about all of this than anything else?" His eyes narrow to hold me in place. "I have had hundreds of masters. *Hundreds*. And the kid has had, what? A couple dozen? And of *course* he finds a white fucking knight. I've never seen any master stand up for their wish granter the way you've stood up for him. The way you're still standing up for him, face to face with a dangerous djinn."

Dangerous. In this moment, he does feel dangerous.

I swallow. "You're jealous of him."

"*No*. I'm not jealous of him, so you can stop pushing that fucking narrative. I'm *annoyed* by him. Your boyfriend is too clean for his own good. He's incapable of seeing the darkness in people. His mother coddled him from it, but ours? She *bred* it in us. Look at fucking Beckham. It is so stupidly obvious. And yet, he's had the kid under his thumb since we were teenagers. And despite having everything he's ever loved ripped from him—his grandfather, his mother, his *familiar*—he continues to pull victims into our web without regard for what it could do to them. He continues to think he deserves a happy ending. He's never getting a happy ending. None of us are. And the sooner he realizes that, the sooner we can all move on."

I stare up at him, searching through the miasma around us for the true source of his frustration.

"Fucking empathy?" he questions. "Even now?" His hand falls down the wall and lands on my shoulder, aura quickly reverting to one of composure. "Sorry. I didn't mean to take that out on you. It's been a long few months." He pushes himself from the wall and then moves to the edge of the couch where lies the upset nest I made for him.

That barrage he just hit me with. It's a lot to unpack, and at the same time, only snippets of a larger story.

"The Beckham thing confuses me too." I search for common ground. "It's obvious he's a snake. I don't get why Vel doesn't see it."

"Part of that's magic," says Arrik, rubbing his face. "But there is an element of willful ignorance, or he wouldn't be susceptible to the magic in the first place. Velis wants it to be true, so the spell works."

Okay, well, there's takeaway number one. Get that fucking spell off Velis.

He takes another drag before handing off the blunt to me. This time, I take a bigger hit. Arrik's eyes close momentarily.

"Arrik, what do you mean none of you get a happy ending? Why not?"

He shakes his head. "Because when you're part of a legacy like ours, everything and everyone around you is at risk—a tool that can be used to cause pain or coerce. He's not going to get his 'lady,' just like I'm not going to get a 'lady,' just like Jeb's not going to get a fucking 'lord.' And to think we could is naïve. Only one person in our family will ever be allowed to mate, and it sure as shit isn't the guy with tainted blood." He swipes the blunt from me. "And now you have gotten yourself all sticky in our web. And good fucking luck getting out. I was hoping I could make it self-destruct before then, but you complicated things the moment you betrayed us for him. That's when the others realized you were something more. And now, it's no longer just your soul they're after. You don't have any idea how much danger you're really in here."

Implying—

"You honestly believe Beckham and Jeb would, what, *kill* me for being with Velis?"

"Pfft. *Jeb*. Jeb just wants this all wrapped up so that he can go back to his life in the city. But yes, there are others who would end your life over this. The last human who got caught up in our affairs wasn't even a real threat." He shakes his head in dark remembrance. "She wasn't even his."

She?

"Arrik, was there someone that you—"

"Off limits."

I'm sure he can feel the ripples of curiosity and empathy streaming off of me. But more importantly, he can't lie to me, meaning he truly thinks my life is in danger. *Murder*, though?

What kind of *Days of Our Lives* bullshit is that?!

"Hold on. Why are you telling me this, Arrik? Are you really switching to our side?"

He looks at me like I just told an unexpected joke. "You still think I'm on a side? The only 'side' I'm on is my own. And right now, that side happens to involve keeping my little brother from destroying *you*."

"Because of a promise you made?"

He gives one unreadable nod.

"To whom?" I ask.

"Whom. Ha. Fancy."

"To *whom*, Arrik?"

"Off limits," he says again, then through his teeth, *"but you've already asked it, and now I'm fucking compelled to answer it, so . . .* a human female."

A human female? The last one that 'got caught up in their affairs'?

"When?" I ask.

Another burst of blue. "Six years ago. After they killed the fox."

"Fox?" I don't know anything about a fox.

"That fucking fox. I should have just left it alone. But have you ever heard the noise an animal makes when it . . ." He stops himself. "Locking the kid in closets, outing him at school, that was nothing. But that fox. That was something else. That felt different. And fuck me for trying to stop it, because they took someone from me in exchange and still killed the damned thing." His stare is vacant, as if he's lost in the memory of it. "At least I got special permissions out of the deal. Suppose tattling has its advantages. Must be why Jeb likes doing it so much."

I'm not sure what he means by 'special permissions.' And in general, I'm having a hard time piecing together what he's saying. Lack of context. Four pulls deep.

In the dim quiet, Arrik takes a long scan of my face. "We're no longer smoking, so I should let you know I'm no longer compelled to tell you the truth. Might want to quit while you're ahead."

He's right. The blunt has disappeared, and I'm not even sure which one of us was last holding it.

"Arrik—"

"I get that the underdog thing is cute, but you'd do well to think long and hard about why you're with him, Dolly Jones. Is that really what's going to make you wet for the rest of your life? You're so goddamned hard for my little brother—Can you honestly tell me that, if it had been my vessel waiting for you in that thrift store, you wouldn't have let me take you home and fuck the living Christ out of you?"

The last part is striking, Arrik's tone flat and at the same time devastatingly direct. Posed as a rhetorical. But not rhetorical.

I search him, his dark presence, his complex motives, his unknown history. "Arrik . . . did you come to protect me or to steal me from him?"

In another burst of speed, he's before me, eyes agleam with dark energy, this time holding my chin. "Both."

His mouth is close, his aura coating me, his rising chest nearly pressed to mine as if to prove I'm still the mouse he once let go. I pull in a sharp breath as he continues.

"Let me take you from him. It wouldn't even be a job for me anymore. I like smart girls, and I like girls who fight back. I have all the confidence that I could break through your defenses eventually. I could trick you into it, or I could take my time and cultivate it. But it would be much more pleasurable for me if you'd just do it on your own." His eyes close partway and his lips graze my ear. "Come on, Dolly. You're all fucked up. Imagine the kind of orgasms I could land."

Dolly.

I don't think he's ever just called me Dolly before.

My response may be delayed from the smoke lingering in the air and in my lungs, but it's still just as sound as ever. "I love Velis, and I would never, ever, ever cheat on him, Arrik. Ever."

"We'll see."

His thumb presses to the side of my forehead, and the memory of the night is stolen from me.

CHAPTER 18
The Truth about Arrik

I RECOIL to distance myself from Arrik, eyes widened and heart racing from the memory he's just returned to me.

"Are you sure you don't want to fuck me, Master? Even now?"

It makes sense now.

Why their father chose a field he was an expert in to hold this contest.

The reason Arrik has special access to his father's library.

The reason his dad didn't seal his account when he sealed his brothers'.

How Arrik knew Beckham's vessel had been confiscated. How he was able to enter Velis's room.

And also . . .

Why he has the 'least to lose.'

Why he's been seeking my approval since the moment he met me.

Why he can't sleep.

"Who was she, Arrik?" I ask as the pieces flood together in Velis's blue-drenched closet. "Beckham said your vessels can't go after people you could become attached to, so she couldn't have been one of your masters. Unless you found her on your own. That was the soul we took back from Beckham, right? Was she someone you cared for? The one they . . . because you told your dad about the fox?"

He keeps his mouth shut. Then—"That wasn't the moral of the story I just showed you. Forget about her and worry about yourself. Is my little brother's cock really worth your life?" He stops himself. "What? Why are you blinking at me like that?"

"Arrik. You're—" I reach out for him, making his lip curl in disgust. "A good person."

"Tch. Of course I'm a good person! Who do you think I am?"

"You have a conscience."

"Again—"

"Arrik, you're a good guy. For real. Not just because I'm forcing you to be. I'm so proud of you."

"You're fucking *proud* of me? Gross. I don't need you to be proud of me. I need you to want to fuck me. I told you I can feel your attraction to me for sure now that we're tethered, and it's grown. I know you want me. So let's just do it already. Perfect opportunity. There's a bed right back there."

He's serious enough in his proposition that I feel a familiar push of tension from my chest into my neck. This time, it stays and throbs. Okay, so he might be a good guy, but he's still very much—

"You truly believe I would have sex with you in VELIS'S CHILDHOOD BED?!"

He shrugs. "You thought I would fuck baby mermaids, sooo . . ."

I tip my head, just straight-up ignoring all that because I have *questions*. "How are you so good at avoiding the truth oath? You told me straight to my face you couldn't enter this room, and then you did."

"I meant it as in, 'I can't enter or I'll blow my cover.' Like I said, that oath is super basic and really more to make you guys feel at ease than it is to keep us honest." He begins a long pace of the closet like a caged tiger.

Wait a second.

So he's telling the truth when he says he thinks attraction exists in me and has grown?

Well, of course it exists. Look at him. He is unignorably hot. Unquestionably charismatic. The way he moves his body, it's like it's intentionally designed to make you picture him having sex—his confidence, his experience, his *control*.

He slips those artful eyes of his over his shoulder. "For the record, I want you too."

"I don't *want* you, Arrik."

"Sure, you don't."

I'm not humoring this conversation any further. "Why did you decide to show me all this now?"

"Because you, like, want to be friends and shit."

And the memory he just showed me will make me want that even more. Meaning—

"You . . . like me. As a person."

"Like is a strong word," he says dryly, copycatting my earlier statement. "But I do think you're interesting. When you played us during the contest, I didn't see it coming. And then you had the balls to do it again when you kept me from taking your soul. You're so . . . cunning. And you fight dirty. It keeps me from getting bored."

He appreciates totally different characteristics in me than Velis does.

And it worries me. The way his eyes seem to be working out thoughts behind the scenes.

"So, the contest," I divert. "Were you even really playing?"

"I was. At first. Our father told me he wanted me to participate and that it was going to be a fair fight, which was . . . odd. But refreshing. Until I found out Velis already had an edge with that special vessel from his nymph-loving grampy."

I wonder how much Arrik knows about Vel's vessel. He seems to think Daddy Reilhander gave it to Velis as a handicap for the contest, but that isn't right. Vel's vessel was always meant to lead him to me.

His *arrow-pointed lover*.

Can we not think of something cooler to call it than that?

The truth about my magical bond with Velis, what happened with Vel's mom and their shared father—it isn't my place to tell Arrik. It would be like saying that he and the other two triplets were never meant to be born. It would be like feeding his demons.

"Things have escalated," he continues. "Beck's one thing. He's powerful, but he isn't all that smart. But Amoira? She's a whole other animal. And if she was in my father's private library, the only place in the manor where there might be recondite information about the nymph realm, it means Beck escalated to her much sooner than I expected. I need you to tell me—is there anything you left out about this morning before I came and got you? Small details matter."

Within the still, ethereally lit closet, I think through the day. Waking up to Vel's big stupid grin. Then his warm mouth against my ear. The curtains were blowing. The sky had all the promise in the world.

Every time I wake up to you, I'm afraid it's a dream. A little sweet. *Let me taste you to see if you're real.* A little spicy.

And then the bike. When I crumbled under the weight of another beautiful morning and the sheer terror of how it would feel to lose it.

The way I've been feeling since Velis said those words.

I don't—

"Focus," says Arrik, in my face, dark brows pushed together. "Ignore the shark."

Right.

"There was one thing," I say. "I thought it was weird. The tollbooth chick. She asked Vel if he had a weapon along, and he said yes. What kind of weapon could he have possibly had? It was right before she gave him the passport ring."

Arrik's eyes narrow. "What did you just say?"

"Yeah, supposedly he had some kind of weapon along? But he never mentioned—"

"No, not that. The weapon would have been his vessel. I

assume he took it with since you guys were still tethered. I'm talking about that ring."

"At the gate," I repeat. "The toll lady checked us in, and then before she'd open up the gate, she gave Velis his passport ring and told him to keep it—"

"We don't *have* passport rings. And he should know that."

"Maybe it's unique for entry into the nymph world?"

"Do you see me wearing a magical ring? No. There's no physical requirement to cross realms. See, this is what I was talking about. He just keeps trucking on, arrogant enough to assume fortune's on his side. It's *annoying*."

My gullet drops.

Oh shit. Oh shit. Oh shit.

"And if he's not arrogant?" Arrik continues. "It means he's just a moron, which, in my opinion, is worse—"

"Enough!" I lash, stomach twisting over the fact that Velis accepted that relic without knowing better—and taking it out on the *shark* in front of me. "I don't need you to be nasty right now, Arrik, I need you to be helpful, and if you continue that train of thought, I'll wish your fucking tongue away!"

I won't.

And this isn't Arrik's fault. But there are things I need to say.

I sigh. "You've got six years of life experience on him, Arrik. Of course he doesn't know as much as you. That doesn't make him a moron. And for the record, I don't like him because he's an underdog; I *love* him because he's courageous and clever, and he puts his whole heart into everything he does. He didn't win that contest because of me or that vase. If anything, we were a hindrance to him. The *only* reason I did what I did and sabotaged you guys is because he was winning before I slowed him down. And you know why? He's a good wish granter too. I mean, he basically cracked me on day one, and I was a tough customer. The contest wasn't handed to him, Arrik. He may not have your experience, but Velis is an incredibly driven person, and I'm not just going to stand here while you cut him down."

Arrik's skin gleams with the dreamy glow from the tree. "See?

The Dolly Jones defense force. All because the cutest, saddest brother gave you his puppy eyes." It's his turn to sigh. "This world is going to eat you alive. Come on, let's hear more about that passport ring my little brother was super *clever* and super *courageous* to have blindly accepted from a stranger before going into a realm he's never entered before."

Yeah. One pep talk isn't going to do much with this one. But at least he knows where I stand.

"It was a ring with a glassy black band, and it had a red gem."

"You mean like a ruby?"

"No. It was cloudy. Actually—" I return to the white cabinet and crouch to retrieve the silver necklace stored within—the same one that's plastered all over the manor in those giant portraits. "The stone looked kind of like this."

Arrik scoops the bead with his finger. "Did it look 'kind of' like this or exactly like this?"

"I didn't get a close enough look. There was a lot going on. But if you're thinking there's a connection between the necklace and the ring, there's a ring box in here too." I relinquish the chain to him and then return to the cabinet, fishing out the small golden box that looks like something royal.

Inside, there's a cushion. And a ring. But it isn't another antique passport ring.

Oh.

OH.

And speaking of wifey, I know this is a lot. I know you don't really believe in the scroll and arrows, and I know that before a week ago, I was just some mysterious alien visitor to you, but is that in the realm of something you'd be interested in?

"Yikes," Arrik says from over my shoulder.

"When did he have time to go out and get a ring?" I mutter, transfixed on the way the diamond-like stone catches the light. It's beautiful. Simple. Very sparkly.

Vel is so serious about this.

Why does that scare the shit out of me?

If anything, being away from him has resolidified my feelings for him. I like having him around. Marriage would ensure he's always around. Marriage would cement the security I feel in him. I don't have a problem with marriage as a concept. My parents had a good one.

So why can't I shake this fear?

"You guys are different," interrupts Arrik.

I wasn't looking at him, but he's been looking at me, and now that I know it, he moves in for the kill, taking my face and peering into my soul like a hot hypnotist.

"Hold still."

He looks from one eye to the other, his perfect mouth slightly ajar as I hold my breath to keep it from hitting him directly in the face.

"I don't know your story, but I've picked up enough of it to know you've been through shit. He has too. But you process differently. One example—his last 'fiancée' was a spoiled cunt, and he knows that. But in his mind, the reason it didn't work out is because he didn't get her committed quickly enough. But what I'm reading in you is that you believe the pain you've felt is *because* you committed. Exposing your wounds made them easier to salt. You guys want the same thing, but your methods for getting there aren't aligned." He unhitches himself from his hold on my emotions. "Or something like that."

Oh my gosh, I can totally see that.

"A-Arrik, have you ever thought of being a therapist?"

"That's basically what I am, babe."

Babe.

Yours is the fantasy world, babe.

Vel.

I don't love you.

No.

The strength of Arrik's hand is on my shoulder. "Chill out. Put the box back where you found it and worry about it later." He lifts that same surly brow, but instead of conveying haughtiness, this time, it seems to be for reassurance. His hand wobbles my shoulder. "Okay?"

He's right. I slide the ring box back where I found it beside a folded piece of paper missing its corner. I consider that the note might hold useful information, but we're not snoop-reading Vel's letter from his mom unless it's as an ultimate last resort.

Arrik snaps his fingers to conjure a black T-shirt over his body. "My thoughts about you being with my brother aside, I'm still compelled by you to go find him. I was cool letting him rot there for a week while our father is away, but now that I suspect Amoira may be involved in all this, we need to go get him tonight. So, let's focus. Basic knowledge wishes are technically possible. The math is hard, but you can get there through fancy footwork. I didn't propose it before because they're more expensive than they're worth. There are much easier ways to find information. I don't think we have time for that. What I need you to do is wish to know what kind of stone this is." He hands the necklace back to me.

"Do . . . you have enough soul juice to do it?" I ask, feeling guiltier about our arrangement now that I know the truth about him.

"Ha!" After an arrogant chuckle, he bends forward with his hands flattened in his jean pockets. "If I'm going to *feast* on your soul, it isn't going to be for a lame-ass knowledge wish." He tosses another of his bro nods. "This one's on me."

"So you DO devour them. I knew it." I say it offhand because I'm a smart-ass.

It hits more intentionally than that.

"No," says Arrik. "We don't devour them, but . . ."

His distracted eyes list across my face, and I'm suddenly very aware of the fact that I'm alone inside a locked closet inside a locked room inside a locked manor with Arrik Reilhander.

I love Velis, and I would never, ever, ever cheat on him, Arrik. Ever.

We'll see.

I feel that push of tension in my neck, a bit choking. He feels it too. His eyes hold mine darkly.

This closet is too small.

His eyes slip away. "Make your wish, Master."

His magic washes out the already blue glow from the capsuled tree as I wish to know what kind of stone this is. And after, when the light falls, his mouth twitches over the relief I'm emoting.

"We just got lucky," he says.

"Very," I confirm.

The stone is a nymphean bloodstone, and it's made from the pressurized, heated remains of a nymphean progenitor.

CHAPTER 19
Very Lucky

"I mean, it makes sense, right? That Vel's mom would wear around the key to getting home? She was a half nymph, so she'd be able to come and go easily, and so would baby Vel, but not Daddy Djinn."

The sucker stick poking from the pocket of his mouth wobbles. "I still can't believe you call our father that."

You're just jealous.

—Is a thing I'd say if Arrik were my boyfriend. But I'm starting to recognize that I might need to monitor my interactions with him. Showing me that memory. Telling me the truth about his relationship with his brother. Letting me in enough to see a bit of authenticity and motive. It's what I wanted, but I didn't expect to find someone so . . .

Arrik is complex.

And if we're talking least favorite tropes, obviously miscommunication gets the gold, insta-love is right up there, but love triangles? A nice bronze.

Strangely, I'm okay with reverse harems. So, what, adding one extra person suddenly makes it okay? I know, Dolly, it makes no sense.

"That," says Arrik. "That right there."

I pull my eyes from where they're zoning to see what's 'right there' and find that, apparently, *I'm* what's right there.

"Such a random mess of emotion, I can't even guess what you're thinking. It's a nice change. Stimulating."

Stimulating.

I cross my arms protectively. "I thought you'd met a lot of humans. 'Random mess of emotion' is kind of our thing."

Then again, Arrik's vessel picks out a specific type of person that needs a specific type of wish from him. And if it's true that he's not allowed to contract people outside his vessel, then there's a good chance I'm an outlier to him.

Because I'm messy.

"I'll help you out," I deflect. "One of the things I'm feeling is anxiety. How do we think Vel's passport ring comes into play with all this? And how does your mom?"

"Don't call her that." His answer is biting enough that I feel the need to apologize, but he moves on before I can. "I don't know about Amoira. But the ring, I have a theory." He twirls his finger, and there's suddenly a whiteboard in the closet with us, pushed up against a hanging row of snooty clothes.

The board fills with the squeak of chunky, heavy-handed doodles as he speaks. "My theory is that there's an inhibitor enchantment over their entire world, except for their cubiculums. The ring likely interrupted the protective magic of the cubiculum, allowing the outside inhibitor magic to reach him even while inside. Velis was clearly meant to lose his emotion the longer he was in that realm, regardless of being inside his family's protective zone. But whoever set this up didn't account for your bond keeping his emotion intact."

What I assume to be a Makayen formula has just finished phantom scribbling across the board behind him along with a figure that resembles DNA. Arrik, meanwhile, looks like the kid in detention who got up and started playing professor. All he's missing is a pair of boxy glasses.

"Er, sure." He snaps, and a pair of dark-rimmed spectacles appear beneath his brows.

No, that's definitely not what I—

He pushes them up his nose. "We're assuming blood in the form of stone will allow us entry into their cubiculum, but what we still need to determine is why the ring made Velis lose his emotion—whether that was an intended purpose, if the stone in this necklace would do the same, and what Amoira's involvement is." He steps back to review his mess of notes.

"I can't just wish for that information? It seems like a lot of what I've gone through the last two weeks could have been *easily* solved with a wish like the one I just made."

He shakes his head. "The one you just made was tangible. You had a physical object, and I was able to give you knowledge about its composition. And it still cost much more than it should have. Without something to connect it to, a lot of the information you'd wish for would turn up dry, just like when we tried to conjure blood from nothing. We wish granters have our limits. And a lot goes into producing the things we conjure. Sometimes, we even have to freeze time while we work out the calculations before producing what you've wished for. Like this—"

He swirls his fingers, and they're suddenly holding a fresh, inflated bag of non-knockoff Cheetos that he tosses at my face. "You're hungry, but you don't want to stop for a meal. Eat up."

"You just froze time?" I ask.

I could freeze time. It's hard, but I could freeze it.

"Mm. And I also swiped that necklace from you and put it on, and you didn't even notice. Do better, Master."

He's right; the necklace is chicly around his tatted neck.

"How long did you freeze it for?"

"Couple minutes. The chips were easy. But those took a little finagling."

"Those?"

His eyes flick to the space above me, but a glance upward offers no answers.

Unsettling.

He offers no further explanation before clapping his hands once to compact the whiteboard into nothing. "Let's go. We'll figure out the rest on the way." He teleports to my side, but his glasses remain where they were, falling to the closet floor in the absence of his body. "Want some?" The last of his sucker is in my face, blackberry this time.

I ignore it. "Arrik?"

He looks from the sucker back to me. "What?"

"Will you tell me about her?"

"No time." He pops the sucker back into his mouth and sets one of his talons on my shoulder.

"Hold on! We need to tell Cal and Bellamy not to waste their—"

The dark takes us, and as one world falls away, another is constructed in its place. Shoots of black sprout from the ground, devilishly shiny, until towers line the streets like sentinels guarding the way to the gray courtyard, where stands the tallest tower of them all, Tower Evangeline.

The lack of wind is instantly apparent. Bizarre to be outside without even a whisper of a breeze. It all feels like the walls are going to fall away and reveal the real world beyond. It's stagnant, lonely.

But not deserted.

Three familiar baddies stand in all their ghostbuster glory before the manicured lawn that surrounds Vel's prison. The one with the yellow hose has bangs. The one with the green is the shortest. And the one with blue is pretty.

Yellow will turn you to stone, green you cannot cross, and blue will melt your skin.

A green splattering of paint has already been drawn to keep outsiders from approaching the tower.

"Finish your chips quickly, Master."

Forget the goddamned chips! The one with the blue *flesh-melting* hose is already moving into position at the front of the formation!

"Jinnee!" she calls. "You have used your last chance, and now you shall be punished!"

Arrik turns to me like he's telling an inside joke. "Story of my life."

It's that same flippant attitude he had during our first encounter with them.

Seriously?!

I gather his shirt to pull him to my level. "Arrik! This was stupid! We just charged in without any sort of plan! What happened to not fighting on an even playing field?!"

His eyes taper cleverly as his hand snatches my wrist. "Did I not spend twenty minutes researching their magic system in that café? Never underestimate me, Dolly Jones. I am *always* one step ahead. On that note, I need you to wish for something called an effusorium. Quick, now."

Oh.

When something's out of your control, isn't it kind of nice to let someone else take charge?

I think Arrik charged in like this to make light of what could have been waiting for us. And he's acting so blasé so that I don't freak out about it.

With all three women poised to shoot at us if we so much as flinch, I follow his instruction, eyes evenly on his. "Arrik, I wish you had an ... effusorium?"

"Good. But with conviction. I need you to mean it."

It isn't a stretch to mean it. The one with the blue hose just pulled back on her lever.

"A-Arrik, I wish you had an effusorium!"

"Bingo." A flare of hued magic lights him up, and the next minute, he's standing with a hose weapon of his own. With that sucker still protruding from the pocket of his mouth, he holds the nozzle steady while the hose winds around his back and plugs into a box on his hip.

But unlike the other three, Arrik's hose is filled with inky black.

"That greenie gave you his luck, didn't he?" he says, spitting out his sucker stem as the women storm us.

"Y-yes?!"

"Good. Don't get hit." He tears away at genie speed, and the first thing to go is that protective strip of green the women placed around the tower. Arrik washes over it with a splattering of his own inky black. The short one sprints after him, trying to corner him with a restrictive strip of green while the pretty one prepares to fry his skin with blue the moment he's caught. Meanwhile, the yellow one is coming after me, the much less harrowing threat, hoping to land a shot that will turn me to stone.

Oh hell. I am so not athletic enough for something like this!

"ARRIK!" I shout as I begin to run at a much slower pace than the woman pursuing me. I sprint—or whatever you'd call my version of a sprint—around a vendor stall as a splatter of yellow magic ricochets off its front.

NOT GOOD.

I dart—again, dart is a stretch—from my hiding place, ignoring the splashes of green and blue in my peripherals as the woman chases after me.

Crap, crap, crap! There's nothing close enough to hide behind. The spray of her next shot will get me for sure!

And then she just completely biffs it. Walks right into the curb and spills forward.

Cal's luck is doing some heavy lifting. I use the lapse to create distance between us, then jump out of the way as a second blast of yellow fails her. It's like her machine malfunctioned, sputtering out only half its normal potency. "OH MY GOD!" I won't be able to keep this up for long. I haven't done cardio in . . . ever. And luck can only take me so far. She'll be able to hit me if I stop moving for sure.

What's Arrik even doing right now?

No, I can't worry about him. Not with this lady coming at me like an exterminator after a roach. But he seriously just abandoned me like this?!

Evil cackling hits my ear via his freaky ventriloquist voodoo.

"Arrik?!" I howl.

"Do you really think I'd leave you to fend for yourself? I've got a cloak on you, remember? You can stop that show because she

can't get within two meters of you, and neither can her magic. But keep her distracted for me, would you? Just don't kill yourself doing it."

Bastard!

I slow enough to see what he's up to.

The middle triplet is clinging to the side of Evangeline Tower by one arm, his feet squatted, a strip of inky paint trailing up the wall to show the path he ran up. Just your friendly neighborhood Arrik fucking DANGLING from the side of a building TWENTY FEET IN THE AIR.

Down below, the green nymph is favoring a black-stained arm while the blue one makes continued spurted attempts at hitting him, each of which he cuts off with a douse of black.

And Arrik seems to be trying to *woo* her, of all things. "Hey, nymphy. Looks like you may have a bit of a dick shortage around here. You ever been with a djinn?"

I suspect not, but with the way those rellies blatantly thirsted over Velis, it's only a matter of time before this whole effed world gets a taste of him.

"*Geez, you never feel jealous like that over me,*" Arrik scoffs in my ear.

He's trying to take my mind off the fact that the blue-hosed woman definitely has no intention of taking him up on his offer and now seems to be changing her tactics.

"*Arrik,*" I hiss through my teeth so that my yellow pursuer won't be alerted. "Did you see that?"

Arrik's phantom voice is in my ear. "*I see it. My friend over here just slipped something off her finger and put it into her pocket.*"

Immediately after, the color comes rushing into her, her skin turning nymphean fair, her hair like silken gold. And it turns out those jumpsuits are actually deep purple. Plum, for the fancy folk.

That means Arrik's theory was incorrect. Vel's ring didn't break through the magic that protected his kin from the stunter magic. His ring WAS the stunter magic. They must all have one on out here!

"Yeah. I... wasn't right," says Arrik.

"There's a word for that."

"Shut up. If that's true, then this abnormal weather could just be the result of natural trauma on the atmosphere from conflicting elemental magics."

Talk nerdy to me.

—Is what I could imagine someone saying if they wanted to flirt with him.

"Th-that's great!" I avert as the unfortunate nymph tasked with my pursuit trips for the tenth time—this time over a wastebasket. It's a good thing her emotions are being suppressed, because I imagine this would be a frustrating experience otherwise. "If the rings are what make them lose their emotion, then all we need to do is get Vel to remove his ring, and he'll—"

I clamp my mouth shut. I almost just said 'love me again.'

"Ick. No one wants to feel that. Shove it down and focus."

Right. Ignore the shark.

Arrik's got a shark of his own to deal with. Now that the pretty woman's ring is removed, her entire demeanor has changed. "I would never soil myself with the seed of a jinnee, *jinnee*," she sneers, tossing her hose weapon aside.

Seed?

Hey, that's what *I* call it!

After that bit of sass, the pretty nymph extends her arms above her head, muscles shaking with enough force to make it look like she's lifting an invisible boulder. Once at full extension, she throws her neck backward, and something begins to crystalize in the air above her.

It's hard to decipher because the landscape is so drab, but by the shimmer of it, it's either glass or ice. This being a realm where people control the elements, logic dictates it's ice.

"*Talk nerdy to me,*" says a voice in my ear.

My stomach drops.

Apparently, it's not enough to not say flirty things. I have to be careful about not thinking them too. But those one-liners usually just come whizzing at me! How do I block Arrik from reading them?

"*Don't bother. I've become intimate with your soul now, DJ, and it'll only get deeper. Action may be voluntary, but chemistry is a force all its fucking own.*"

We have no chemistry. And what's with the 'DJ'? Only WE can call us that. And isn't he a little cavalier for someone about to be *slaughtered* by magical ice?!

"*Yeah, yeah.*" He fires his weapon and douses the forming ice chips with black, but the ink merely turns to dust upon contact. Meaning that ice is *extremely* cold. Meaning Arrik needs to worry about more than just that spell puncturing him.

Arrik doesn't have a leprechaun's luck. He doesn't have a kitty collar of protection. It's just him, with fast reflexes and wonky magic.

I don't even bother distracting the yellow-armed soldier anymore. I stop where I am and watch her ram into the air like there's an invisible wall between us before shifting my focus up to Arrik, awaiting instruction for the next part of his plan. The cluster above his pursuer's head has doubled in size.

"*Dolly.*" His voice is level. "*Wish to take the necklace from me, and the moment you have it, make a run for the door. I'll be behind you.*"

Wait, what?

I assess what I've just heard.

'I'll be behind you.'

Not, 'I'll be *right* behind you.'

"You have a plan?" I ask.

"*A plan, yes.*"

"One that involves you following me to safety?"

He's quiet.

I scan the scene before me. Arrik propped high up on the glassy wall of the tower, his magic doing little to combat the maelstrom of ice forming before him. The other nymphs confident enough in its power that they've both stopped all other efforts.

Hold up.

Hold up, hold UP.

"You expect me to believe you're going to *sacrifice* yourself out here, Arrik? Yeah right! That's not your move. And especially not now, not for something like this."

"*Tch. I'm not planning to sacrifice myself, idealist woman. But I need the power back that I'm investing into your protection spell, and I can't pull it. Not while you're out here.*" Our eyes connect from where he's perched, his voice sounding like he's got his hand cupped around my ear to tell me a secret, though his mouth isn't even moving. "*You're my master. Meaning you are my number one priority. Always. I can't risk your safety out here.*"

Always?

I wasn't his number one priority when he used me to rescue that soul from Beckham.

"*That was the one and only exception. Always from here on out. Now, obey me and let me do my job, Master.*"

I glance at the cubiculum's entrance, countering, "But there's no guarantee I'll be safe in there. They could ambush me the moment I go through that door."

"*You're right. In there, they could. But out here, they will. And you've got luck. Not enough that I'm going to leave you out here to fend for yourself, but enough that I think you'll be able to get in there unnoticed.*"

"Okay, but why can't I just wish for something to help you?"

He says nothing. That ice cluster is now the size of a small car. "Arrik?"

"*I already ran the math. You can't. For some reason, I have to get out of this on my own. Apparently, aiding me with a wish would manipulate my destiny.*"

As in . . . he's destined to be defeated out here?

"*NO. I'm not sure why, but I felt a shift in the plausibility spectrum the moment she took off that ring. It severely limited our wishing potential. I can feel your worry, but I assure you, I'm not going to get offed by fucking nymphs for the sake of rescuing one of my brothers.*"

'One' of my brothers. Offhandedly putting Velis on the same level as the other two.

"Gross. Stop. *I don't need that kind of emotion right now. I need to focus. Come on. Wish for the necklace. Run your little ass to the door. And then I'm taking away the gift of protection I so generously gave you. If you're a good girl, I might give it back.*" Semi-distracted, he tries shooting a bit of his own magic—directly from the fingertips this time—at the collection of ice. It doesn't even get within two feet before turning to dust and flittering away. "Go on," he says, swallowing any hint of worry, "*and trust that I'm always one step ahead.*"

He seems to have a lot of confidence, as always.

"Arrik, I wish—"

I scan from him to the front door of Evangeline Tower and all the gray city in between. A city so dull that lights just look like white breaks in the canvas.

Something about this situation is nagging at me.

Because Arrik *isn't* always one step ahead. He wasn't one step ahead when I took his contest winnings, and he wasn't one step ahead when I tricked him out of taking my soul.

Sometimes, the person one step ahead . . . is me.

"—that you would make me super, duper fast," I finish.

His response is delayed, tart, and dry. "*What?*"

"I wish you would make me crazy fast!" I double down. "Like, hummingbird fast!"

"*Jesus Christ.*" There's a flash of light from the side of the building, and after, I feel it, the stored-up energy itching at my feet.

Exactly like a hummingbird, I unleash the power prickling in me, charging past the yellow-hosed woman, around the green-hosed woman, and straight at the ice-wielding woman, shoving into her with all one hundred and seventy of my blessed pounds and catapulting her onto her ass.

She even slides from the momentum.

I CAUSED MOMENTUM.

My mother would be so proud.

The moment I slam into her, the ice collecting above her releases and comes shattering down onto the gray pavement. I'd never be able to dodge that under normal circumstances. But I've got luck on my side and freaky-fast feet.

I leap.

And I ROLL.

Arrik uses the moment of distraction to kick off from the wall. I still don't know how he got up there, but the way he gets down is to repel himself backward like a rock climber. As if there are invisible bungees holding him up, he pushes away once, twice—before landing in a crouch on his third. He rises out of it like Hades ascending from hell, scoops up my arm, then blitzes away with me across the spongy gray grass and to the door of the tower.

With the necklace within sniffing distance, the door opens as Arrik captures the handle, and he hurls me into a world of massive butterflies and enchanting waters.

CHAPTER 20
Smoky Little Swish

It's as beautiful as before, shimmery, sparkly, flowery—did I say shimmery?

Okay, but we're in an entirely different area than we were last time. There's an enormous blue toadstool over us, the underbelly of the cap disgusting from this angle, with filter-like flappies filled with what I assume are SPORES. This place is huge. And thanks to Arrik's rash arrival, we have no plan. At least not one I've been let in on.

"You are SO lucky that necklace worked as theorized! Can you imagine reaching the door and having it—" My words catch.

Because the expression Arrik's wearing is an odd one.

"That was . . ." he starts.

These genie boys and their genie stares. Capable of causing madness. This one feels like it's boring directly into my soul.

"Fun," he ends.

Now mine is the response that is both tart and dry. "*Fun?*"

"Maybe I am a magical showdown kind of guy." He pushes past me, peering around our surroundings and swatting away a full-winged butterfly like it's a gnat. "Sparkly," he sniffs. "You said their center of operations was a big tree, right? That one right there?"

We're on a splattered stone path that weaves through waist-high emerald growth. Around us, the iridescent air looks like the milky sheen of a pearl. The horny chirping of birds chitters in the foliage. That accursed tree and its accursed nest taunt us from the distance.

"Yes!" I feel a rush of relief at the sight. Velis is close, and we know what needs to be done to return his emotion.

I could feel how badly you wanted one of these. It's on the house.

Oh, you're gonna like my flavor, Dolly Jones. I guarantee it.

What can I say? You're a spunky, unapologetic little dork who isn't afraid to stand up for herself and call others out on their bullshit.

Vel.

I don't love—

An intrusive finger squishes into my cheek. "You mind if I revoke that hummingbird spell? It's a lot cheaper if it's temporary. You didn't specify duration in the wish."

"Er, y-yeah." I feel the tingles lift from the pads of my feet as he drags his finger along my face.

After, I study him. "I don't get it, Arrik. Why couldn't I use a wish to help you save yourself, but I could use a wish to help me save you? Was I . . . *destined* to save you for some reason?"

Arrik pokes at a fluffy burst of plumage interrupting the path. "Come on," he says without answering the question.

"Arrik?"

"Later. We've got a blond damsel to rescue. Quit scratching your ear and let's go."

I didn't even notice I was scratching my—

Or, no, my ears are down here. So then what's up—

The chips were easy. But those took a little finagling.

"ARRIK! WHAT KIND OF ANIMAL EARS ARE THESE?!"

He allows a minute to absorb his own smugness. "I think you already know, kitten."

"*Remove them right now.*"

"Tsk. No fun." His eyes flash blue, and after, he looks crusty. But not crusty enough.

"You're so transparent, you dick. I know you can flare your eyes to fake a wish. I WISH you would remove them right now."

There it is. The crustiness.

I feel my head after to ensure the KITTEN EARS have been removed.

Oh lordy, this has been a day.

I step in line with him as we push our way through similar meddlesome boughs, their feelers tickling at our arms. This whole section is very *Wonderland*-y. I'll bet eating any of those toadstools would result in some interesting visuals. The flirting of critters fills the silence. Pops of color show in through the green—scarlet flowers shaped like bells, marigold lizards scampering away from the path, a squat willow-like tree that has crystals dangling where leaves should be. Arrik is quiet—contemplative, almost. And the next time his disinterested eyes slide to get a skim of my face, it feels a little different. It seems like he's working up to say something.

"What is it?" I prod, before deepening my voice, "You know, there's no use beating around the bush with me, *love*. You invasively stuck your hook into my soul, and now I can tell you've got a question wiggling around in you."

"Cute," he says like he's about to stick out his tongue. And then, "When we get him back, they'll have me temporarily unregister so that we'll be untethered. You'll be released from my care and put in Velis's charge again."

He's making it sound like I'm an orphan and he's my ward.

"Yes," I say.

"You . . . sure you want to do that?"

"Arrik, I think you know it would be problematic for you to remain my genie while I'm engaged to Velis."

Huh. It slipped out easier that time. The whole 'engaged' thing.

"The reason I'm asking is that there's danger waiting for you back at the manor. This doesn't end when we get Velis back.

Untethering from me means you'll no longer be the most—" He stops. "Means I'll no longer owe you my protection. It'll be up to him. I'm stronger, smarter, older. I can keep you safer."

"Except, if I'm not with Velis, there's no point in me even being at the manor, so . . ." It's not like I'm just going to hang around there if we happen to break up. I'm not *Amoira* or *Elastia* or whomever.

"Okay." He smacks away a tuft of vegetation like it affronted him. "I just wanted you to know you won't be my problem anymore if we unhook."

I'm fine with that.

I stick to the edges of the growth as the path opens into a clearing with another of those scenic ponds. They probably already know we're here, based on those bested guards and their whole little walkie-talkie system, but I'd rather we maintain some sense of ambush-ability.

Arrik, meanwhile, struts blatantly out into the open, lip snide. "What is it you're doing?"

"Sneaking?" I say.

"Yeah, no. You're good. My magic's working better in here. Not perfect, but better. You can have this back now too." He flicks a wrist at me, and I feel the tickle of something delicate hitting my neck as Vel's mother's necklace falls into place beneath Arrik's protective collar. "I wanted to make sure it wouldn't do anything averse to us here before letting you have it. Seems to be just a key. Those rings must be something different."

I bring my fingertips to the fine chain that belonged to Vel's mother and then to the soundless bell above it.

"Arrik, we have time now. Can you tell me more about what happened to your, er, friend—the one that . . . They really killed her? Who did it? And how did it . . . happen?"

A barrier of cattail-like reeds flitters with the movement of something large swimming beneath the water. Similar movement bends the stalks of grass edging the clearing. This whole place is rife with hidden life.

"I *can* tell you what happened to her," answers Arrik.

Crickets.

"*Will* you?" I ask.

He shrugs. "I don't know the future."

Dink.

"*Would you please* tell me about her now? If there really is danger waiting for me back at the manor, if you're really concerned about me falling out of your protection, then can you at least tell me what I'm in for? I figured this would all end after the contest, but it seems to have amplified to a whole new level. I just want to be prepared."

"It's not relevant. Your fate will be different than hers. You pose a different kind of threat. Their path to you will be more direct—my brother, my mother, my grandfather, and my uncle."

Wait, wait, wait, *what?*

His shoulders toss. "You wanted to know. Velis becoming laird really put a kink in their carefully hewn plans to take over the Reilhander fortune through Beckham." It rolls off his tongue like it's common knowledge, and he allows no time for me to absorb. "We might be triplets, but Beck is the oldest. That title was always meant for him. Jeb or me winning the contest? That would have been one thing. But Velis? Oh, no. That's not gonna fly. And after your display in front of Beckham when you overturned the results . . ." He crouches to inspect a place in the ground that's foaming rainbow foam. "I knew this was going to be an issue when I saw the way he was with you at those salt flats. Could practically smell it at Sudoré. I was hoping that drugging you up and getting you to confess would make him drop you. And when that didn't work, I figured fucking you would be a mutually pleasurable way to get you out of a situation you don't belong in. No one would care if you were mine. But because you're his? There's going to be a constant target on your back. My father knows it, too. So he's either got some grand plan he's withholding, or—what's more likely—he's putting far too much stock in our little brother. Forced rearing or some shit." He stands and shakes the foam from his fingertips. "Velis's biggest weakness is that he's naïve. Maybe he'll grow out of it. Maybe you'll help him get there. But why would you want to put your life at stake for some guy you met two weeks ago?"

Because . . .

Remember what I said about boys who pick you second. Not worth your time.

We didn't meet two weeks ago.

You're adorable, Master, and ever since the first moment I touched you, it's all I've wanted to do.

And I love him with all my cold, black heart.

"Fuck, that feels good." Arrik grips his elongated neck as my adoration for Velis hits him. "Your heart is the fucking opposite of cold and black. Love like that, I bet it feels fucking incredible paired with sex." That last piece he says to himself, his eyes closed to imagine it.

Is—Is he implying that he's never felt love during sex? Because that's so . . .

"Oh, *relax*," he's quick to correct. "I meant feeling it from someone who's tethered to you. It's rare for wish granters because of how our vessels are set up. Unless you're special like *Velly* boy, apparently."

Meaning he and this mystery girl were likely never tethered. She was never one of his masters.

"No." His voice is light, his face turned to the shimmering pond beside us, where a flock of pink swans lists. "She was one of Beck's."

Oh.

I wasn't expecting that.

Beckham and Arrik both worked as wish granters before all this, so they've got their own savings not tied to the estate.

Beckham has something I want. It was always meant to be mine, but he swooped in and stole it.

"If you want to know more, I'll tell you, but you won't be allowed to keep it," he says, then licks his thumb like he's about to separate plastic bags at the grocery store. "Your choice."

I suspect he just wants another excuse to steal my memory, which, quite frankly, I'm over.

"Can I at least know her na—"

'Danny Jones' has a way of feeling tart on the tongue.

I stifle my curiosity. I never would have badgered Velis for the name of his mom. It shouldn't be okay just because it's Arrik.

But Arrik doesn't take the exit offered. His attention lassos on me, his all-pervading gaze searing through me into the fantasy jungle beyond. "Your emotions . . . they're so sporadic and *alive*." He seems to lose himself a moment, but his mood quickly darkens with conniving. "Come here and let me tell you all about my sad, sad childhood."

Um no. I'm not about to get him HIGH off my empathy—or OFF on my empathy—while Velis is up there being fondled by his cousins!

"Quit messing around, Arrik." I blow past him, but the iron grip of fingers around my wrist stops me. "You can know her name," he says, demeanor collected. "On one condition. You can't ask me about her after that. Deal?" He doesn't give me a chance to decline before bringing his fingertip to the place where his cheekbone meets his eye, where rests a tattoo in the shape of a smoky little swish. It almost resembles an—

S

A

R

A

H

The rest of the letters fall down his face, wispy and licking at his skin.

"Sarah," I utter.

He nods. And then he sweeps his fingers to rescind the letters until only the S remains. "Now you know it. And because I've asked you *not* to, I'll consider it betrayal if you ask about her again."

I'm under no such wish constraints, but I'll respect it anyway. It seems like he can't even bring himself to say her name.

Oh, come on. Really? That was so long ago! You're really still stuck on—

"I'm sorry for whatever happened to her," I tell him and nod further down the path, wishing I could know the full story, though it's a wish I would never force him to grant.

We come to a part in the jungle where the trees are a bit taller, a bit thicker than the garden variety we've seen so far, enough to create a canopy. The trunks in this section look as if they're made of vines that have twisted together and solidified, their middles stuffed with misty light that bursts from various openings in the framework. Shallow water pools between the exposed roots, housing traces of neon darting here and there. Fish? More sprites? Whatever they are, Arrik makes them scatter as he trudges right through in his boots that always come out clean afterward, because human souls are worth looking fresh, apparently.

I stick to the banks, finding drier passage and stealing glimpses of that tree in the distance through whatever openings I can find. No clue what happens when we reach it. I've learned not to ask Arrik what the plan is, though I assume he's got one.

Not assume. Trust. I trust that he's got one.

"Good girl."

Ugh.

Unseen creatures splash away from my footsteps as I follow him through the marsh, daydreaming about the scent of Vel's T-shirt. The texture of his skin.

I'm so sickly addicted to him. The minute that ring comes off, I'm going to maul him. I'm going to bombard him with all the affection of my arrow. I'm going to—

"*Master.*" Though he's still a ways ahead of me, I hear Arrik's secret voice all up in my ear. I expect him to rebuke me for mind-banging Velis, and I prepare to tell him to bug out of my thoughts, but instead—"*We've drawn one of them out. Get ready for round two.*"

Drawn? But I thought we were invisible!

There's a pause. "*What gave you that idea?*"

Because he said his magic was working and that we didn't have to sneak?!

He clicks his tongue several times in my ear. "*You know what they say about assuming. You make an ass of you and—just you, really. I did nothing wrong. Why do you think I didn't just teleport us to the tree?"*

So that he could conserve magic?!

"Because an invisibility spell would conserve magic. No, I prefer to pick them off one by one. I don't think you'll make it to me in time, but try anyway. Create a diversion. Do it now."

"H-hey, Arrik!" I call to him like it's unprovoked, eyes flitting around the trees for signs of movement. "Are you forgetting that I can't magically dry my shoes? Slow down!"

He spins around, hands lazily tossed behind his head. "It would be really nice if you humans could figure out how to harness your own magic. You've got alchemy down, but you're shit when it comes to physical channeling."

He's right. I don't make it to him. The moment his back is turned, that's the moment she strikes. From somewhere in the treetops, a hip-heavy girl comes leaping, golden hair trailing behind her like a cape and those shiny bishoujo eyes asparkle.

And this time, she's got wings.

CHAPTER 21
That Rainbow Bitch

NOT THE FEATHERY KIND. They're made of translucent rainbow and shaped like butterfly wings because of course they are. This seems to be Fiona's magical girl form because naturally she'd have a powered-up anime mode.

Arrik staggers backward to close the distance between us. "What the fuck?"

I edge up next to him, pulse escalating. "She's something called a flutterer. Ever heard of it?"

"Briefly." He slides eyes to me. "This morning."

The path ahead is lined with feathery curls of grass that go up well past our heads and are stained deep teals and seductive purples. Fiona lands at the mouth of them, her wings spread open like a gate. "Y-you cannot be here!" she stammers. "Mayster Evangeline does not wish to see you! He has chosen to stay with us!"

'Mayster Evangeline' may not want to.

But that's not who we came to rescue.

I step forward with righteous indignation. "There's no way Velis would ever willingly stay here with you in this messed-up neverland if he had his wits! Not after just getting everything he's ever wanted! Not after getting his title and his father's approval and his heart's—"

That infatuation, it wasn't real.

A tatted claw takes my shoulder as my confidence trips. "I should warn you," Arrik tells her darkly, "I'm a full-blooded djinn with a master."

"I know what you are, jinnee, and I am not afraid of you!"

"Your emotions say otherwise." Arrik's eyes rove over her fist clutched to her chest and the fact that she looks almost ready to burst into tears. "You know, you could just let us pass and tell them we defeated you. I'd let it slide."

"No! You do not understand! I MUST defend our family line! We cannot let you have Mayster Evangeline! He is our *savior*!"

"Tch. *Savior*? Of course he is. I assure you, we're not leaving here without my little brother. You fight us, you lose. Your choice whether you want to go through the trouble of getting dirty."

Arrik's so confident. So certain.

Like we're unstoppable.

Fiona diverts her efforts to me. "Why have you returned? I have told you, there are many humans! You may pick a mate from those. Or if it must be a jinnee, why can you not mate *this* jinnee? There are many humans, there are many jinnees, but there is only ONE Mayster surviving of our line!" Yes, those are tears welling in her eyes, but so much more glistening, so much more tangibly collected than normal tears, like shiny, animated gelatin. "He is our one and only!"

"No!" I cry back, lurching forward. "He is MY one and only! YOU'RE the one who doesn't understand! Velis is—He's—"

I don't love—

I fight through it. Fight through my dread of rejection to fortify my tongue.

"He pulled me from the dark. He sees the absolute best in me. He loves me so deeply that it reminds me to love myself. He's patient and understanding and handles my heart so carefully because he knows repaired hearts are the ones most easily broken. I'm something precious to him, something he wants to nurture. The way he looks at me, I just know—he'll never, ever hurt me. Never, ever abandon me. He's—"

You don't need a boy to solve your problems.

"He's my favorite."

That talon on my shoulder grips hard from the drive of my emotion. And after, that same hand softens and slides into the crook of my neck.

I push my own tears away with the heel of my hand, offering Fiona ferocity through my teeth. "And I know you've got some weird, last-of-his-line prophecy bullshit or something going on here, but I can't let you steal him from me. Come at me, bitch, for real."

She looks almost sorry over it as she lifts from the ground, arms opened like an angel and one toe pointed like a dancer about to pirouette, and hovers. "Very well." And then, with a mighty push of her rainbow wings, she comes blowing over the top of the glassy water at us, leaving ripples in her wake.

"Arrik, I wish you would immobilize her without injuring her!" I command with a djinn master's conviction.

A flash of blue hits him hard enough to make him teeter. It may have been the most authoritative wish I've ever given him.

Albeit an inconvenient one.

"Well, how the fuck am I supposed to do that?" he grouches, caressing his hand away from my neck and down my back in a way that's . . . hm. He stays where he is until Fiona is nearly upon us. And then he uses that hand on my back to teleport us to the opposite side of the marsh. *"Now we're invisible,"* says his secret headset voice in my ear. His mouth doesn't move, but there's motion in his sly eyes as he asks, *"The things you just said about him, that's what you meant by compassionate?"*

I nod.

"And emotionally mature?"

Again, I nod.

"Hmph."

"Arrik?"

"Stay here. I'll go capture the butterfly." He clutches at his own chest once before blipping away.

When he reappears, his tattoos coat him like armor, no trace of the T-shirt he was just wearing. He stands on a dry patch of grass with his feet apart, his shoulders tense and his fists tight, like he's about to perform martial arts. Based on the way Fiona's making a beeline for him, he's made himself visible.

This. THIS is a magical showdown if I've ever seen one.

As Fiona approaches, her wings swell until they're no longer butterfly wings but massive dragon wings, the surface of them transformed into something *psychedelic*—still rainbow but all swirled together like a nebula—her eyes now inhumanly large and twinkly.

It's like a ten-year-old's birthday party got possessed.

Arrik stands at the ready, waiting for her to get close. His chin is high, his eyes taunting. And then, when she's halfway to him, he throws his arms backward and releases all the tattoos from his body. They go flinging from his skin to land on the spot of ground behind him, spread out like a shadowy mural.

Okay, that's cool. This is going to be a sick-ass spell.

But Arrik himself? Now looks a bit *nakey* without any tats or a shirt.

"*Nakey, Master? That's my word.*"

THAT IS STRAIGHT-UP THOUGHT READING.

Over on Fiona's side of the world, Queen Butterfly flaps to an abrupt stop inches from Arrik's face, and when she does, all the magic stored in her wings comes flying forward like a pop of rainbow confetti. It hits Arrik in the face. He sneezes, and a flurry of blueberry-sized bubbles shoot from his nose.

Ur, is that normal for djinn? I'm trying to remember whether or not I've ever seen Velis sneeze.

Arrik abruptly stiffens, straightens, and hoists his shoulders forward like he's repositioning a backpack—a motion that sends all the tattoos spread over the ground recoiling back onto his body—and after, he stares straight ahead at hovering Fiona.

"Jinnee!" she cries at him with new confidence. "I am your master now!"

His eyes surge blue like a robot resetting. When he speaks, his voice comes out from the back of his throat, affirming, "You are my master now."

What?

"Jinnee!" Fiona roars. "Expose the human to me!"

Arrik flicks a hand at me without looking in my direction.

By that pointed violet gaze, I know I've just been un-invisiblified. WHAT?!

"Arrik! I wish you would—"

Another little genie flick, and what feels like a strip of duct tape slaps itself across my mouth. I hurry to peel it off and find it's hardened like cement.

ARRIK! I snarl in my mind, clawing at the silencer. *Snap out of it right this second!*

He's proven he can basically read my thoughts, so I assume if my desires are strong enough, he should be able to read them through whatever that rainbow allergen was.

ARRIK, I wish you would get this thing off my mouth or so HELP me!

I squint at him for a sign he's back to normal. There's nothing. No smirk, no twinkle, no blink.

"Next, Master?" he croaks at Fiona.

Seriously?! If only he could have been so obedient with me! And for real?! He was freaking *bewitched*?! I thought he was an all-powerful djinn!

Could it actually be that Vel's the one with the stronger magic in his blood?

"Jinnee!" Fiona cries. "Capture the human!"

In a flash, Arrik is behind me, hand securely around my throat. A flutter hits the bottom of my chest cavity from the suddenness of it. His skin is warm as ever. I feel his chest piercings wedged up against my back.

One blip later, and we're before Fiona, whose bare feet are now firmly in the mud, rainbow powers suppressed. "Carry her to Mar," she instructs of Arrik. "Mar will put her to ground." She curtly turns and starts away.

To ground? As in *bury* me?! Yeah right. Arrik can't carry me all the way—

Oh, wow. He's strong. He easily maidened me. I cling my arms around his neck—*because my core isn't strong enough not to*—and wait for a sign. I'm so sure this is all a trick. I take his face and shake him, expecting him to roll his mouth into my palm before showing me his wicked delight that I fell for it.

But no, he simply marches through the wetlands after his new master.

Uh-oh.

Walls of plume-like grass tickle at my feet and ankles as Arrik carries me down the trail Fiona previously barred from us, each apathetic stomp into the drying dirt a warning that we're getting closer and that soon it will be me against three nymphs, a djinn, and a Mayster.

All right. Desperate times. There's one thing I've seen Arrik lose his mind over, and that's ultra-strong emotion, especially when it's affection based.

I cup his cheek, where only the finest, finest stubble resides, and will that he'd feel everything I feel when I close my eyes and recall the night before Vel and I left for my mom's.

Four nights ago.

It feels like so much longer.

Velis stands in the bathroom connected to our suite with a fluffy towel around his hips and his shoulders backed by a halo of lights around the mirror. I checked those things out my first day here. There's no bulb. Just miniature bundles of light that simply exist rather than being cast.

Probably cost a human soul or two, no big deal.

Ugh. Genies.

. . . Genies and their fine, scrumptious, lickable bodies.

"I can feel that, you know," Vel says with my gaze on the lowest muscle of his back.

"How is he so fucking swole?"

It seems I've accidentally asked it aloud.

His mouth twitches in that classic Vel way. "I don't know what 'swole' means, but whatever it is, I'm glad I'm it. Your reaction to it feels nice. Come and talk to me while I shave. I'm lonely."

"I am honestly shocked you shave," *I say as I accept his invitation. The bathroom is the sort where you feel compelled to leave your clothes lying all over just to messy it up. It's fancier than fancy. And that shower over there has multiple heads. I feel like a mermaid in a lagoon whenever I get in.*

Velis taps a pinky to the granite-like countertop, his hand already full of lather. "Up here."

I hoist myself up and slide backward on the cold surface, tucking my knees into my stomach so that my heels are rudely on the edge of the counter. Bet this is the first ass to have ever graced the slippery stone. Definitely the first human ass.

Vel grins up at me. "You look cute like that, Master. And your soul feels warm. Was today okay?"

It wasn't. Not at first. Not up until about an hour ago, when he came in here and ravaged me before taking an indulgent shower break. He begins to smear his lather all around his jaw.

"Velis? Do you know who Santa is?"

I've been wondering about this ever since last week with his brother.

"Who?"

"Santa Claus?" *I clarify.* "St. Nick? Kris Krispy? Krispy? Is it Krispy? That doesn't sound right."

"Is that a politician?" *he asks.*

He's serious enough that I can't help snorting.

"What?" *he defends. His smile starts small and begins to blossom out.* "Dolly, what?" *He laughs because I'm laughing.* "Ugh. So mean to me. How am I to know who one random human is? There are a million of you."

"Billions, Vel," *I tell him.* "There are billions of us."

His impishness sparks. "Billions, then. And you know what's crazy? Out of all of them— not just them, all of everyone, in all the realms, you're the one I'm destined for."

Even with that mask of foam, I can see his grin persisting under eyes that are glimmering with adoration.

Oh, Vel. He's so cute. Just everything about him. That prince-charming smile. Those eyes that shift from innocent to sharp and pull my desires along with them. Do I want him to pin me down and have his way with me, or do I want to squeeze him to death?

Both, obviously. But in which order?

The best thing about Velis Reilhander is that he can do it all.

"Stop saying heartsy-poo things like that while your mouth is all slathered up," I order. "It feels like a trick to get me to kiss that mess."

He smooches coolly through the froth. "Maybe it is."

His razor is . . . strange looking. It's shaped like a handle-less, round-edged comb the width of a few fingers, but where the teeth would normally be, it's one long blade. He grips it like he's combing a mustache.

You know what? He's one who might actually look good with a mustache.

Here, let me picture it.

"What'd you do today, Master?" he asks as he pulls the razor deliciously through puffy foam.

"What did you do today, magical genie prince?"

"It's actually magical genie ALIEN prince." *He prods me with a move of his chin.* "And I asked first."

I sigh. "The life of a lady. Slept until noon. Ate one egg. Masturbated. Ate another egg."

"Wow. Guess you'll be needing more eggs, then."

If I say yes, I'll wake up to a basket of them. "I'd ask the neighbors if I had any, but unfortunately, you've made me your prisoner, so . . ."

"Yeah, but it's kind of hot, right?" he says. "You're like my hot human secret, hidden away like this."

"Depends. Which is the hot one? The human or the secret?"

"Both. Duh."

Good answer.

I reach out to capture his exposed waist and coax him to my side of the counter.

Now, as he shaves, he does so between my knees, bending around me while I lean out of the way so that he can still see himself in the mirror. His eyes slip from the mirror to me as my fingertips play with the rim of his towel. I'm a distraction. When it comes to him, it's something I pride myself on being.

"I'm excited to go to your mom's tomorrow," he says, the razor making an adept scrape against his neck. "I'm excited to meet Steve the Cat. Do you think he'll like me?"

"He likes no one. Except my grandpa. He liked my grandpa."

"I hope he likes me."

Vel says it like Steve is a person.

My wish granter keeps shaving, making flirty eyes with me through one of the side mirrors as the razor makes another pass over his neck, the cleaned strip within biting distance.

"Master, how many times do I have to—" He starts over. "Do I need to fear for my neck for real? You're never going to tear into me or anything, are you?"

Tear into him, yes.

The thought turns that flirty gaze a little darker, a little more 'come hither.'

So versatile.

And then he winks and returns to his grooming.

Genies. They're like vampire-incubus-empath perfection.

"Hey Vel, do you ever imagine what it would be like if I were your genie?"

Amusement moves through is features like it's an outlandish hypothetical. "What?"

"Yeah, like, if you had picked up a 'consumables' bottle, and the moment you put your mouth to it, I popped out in a cute little genie costume and started trying to MILK your darkest desires out of you? You know—basically THROWING myself at you like you did for me?"

There's zero hesitation. "I'd love it. I'd make you clean my room."

"Clean your room? That is so not sexy."

He laughs at me like I did at him when he asked if Santa was a politician.

The fact that we have so much to learn about one another, it makes this all feel continually fresh. Like I could spend a thousand days with him in this room and never stop bantering, probing, opening.

The thought of losing it is a little scary.

A little more than a little.

I don't ever want to lose him.

Vel's eyes are on me, no longer flirty, no longer tempting. They're compassionate.

"Honey."

But I don't want to talk about it.

He feels it, and he struggles not to pry before redirecting the conversation for my sake. "As to your question, I need a visual before I can answer."

He snaps, and the next moment, I'm in a full I Dream of Jeannie-esque genie costume. And not a cheap one like Beckham had, either. Sheer pink fabric loosely covers my legs and gathers at the ankle. My toes are tucked into cute little booties. My stomach is bare—but I'm leaning back, so that helps the situation—and my chest is packed into a matching bra with intricate stitching and that same sheer fabric on the shoulders. A long, dark ponytail drapes over my shoulder, propped up by a thick hair piece.

Eyes suddenly fixated enough to freeze, Velis waves his hand to remove all traces of the shaving cream and stubble that was left on his face. "This," he says. "This is what we're doing tonight."

There's clear hunger. But it's apprehensive hunger, like he's trying to plan out his meal, deciding where to start.

He takes my lower back and slides my hips over the polished counter to meet his waist. He's still got that towel. I use the exposed muscle of his back to pull him closer against me, enjoying his hands doing the same.

"Make a wish, Master," I say, giving him cute eyes.

"Holy shit."

He likes it. A lot.

"But I'm not cleaning your room," I add.

He leans forward. "That's not what I want. Dolly Jones, I wish you would—"

I cut him off with an abrupt kiss. "You don't ever have to wish for a thing like that, Master. Those are always free."

His grin is so subconscious, so reactive, so stuck on me. He looks me over like he's grateful to have captured me, grateful to have locked me away in a secret room at the far edge of the manor.

He claims my mouth, taking the kiss a bit further, tasting me, igniting desire behind my ribcage. I slide a hand up his chest and take his neck and face.

We intensify, our hips pressed, genie fabric to genie towel. My feet latch around his back. This shared desire, it's an incredible, soul-bonding thing. When one of us starts it, it's impossible to make it stop. We're rolling down a hill, catching one another up in our speed as we fall.

"Fuck, Dolly. Being with you, it's the most euphoric thing I've ever felt. You feel so good, inside and outside. I want it all." *His voice lowers to my neck.* "I want it all."

I want all of him too. I don't want to be separated from him during the day anymore. I don't want him to become laird and be busy all the time. I just want him to myself.

But I know I can't take that. Because he's made for so much more than just me.

He feels it, whispering, "So are you. But at the end of the day, we come back together always, yeah?"

He waits for me to agree to it. To promise myself to him. To seal us together at the end of each and every trying day.

I nod against him as his towel falls.

The rest of it isn't something Arrik should feel. But that was a definite cluster of love, something that would normally make the susceptible djinn falter and grip his chest and peer at me afterwards, longing for more.

Now, though, he doesn't so much as blink.

Oh my GOD. What if I can't break him out of it?! What happens when we get to Vel and I can't even speak to him?! How am I supposed to fight through three nymphs, a zombified Arrik, and an emotionless Vel? Arrik was my only lifeline. I have no others to call!

I begin wiggling in his arms, but his grip just grows tighter. And then I resort to downright flailing. I could claw at him, but I don't want to hurt him. I could elbow him in the face or butt at him with my head, but—

His mouth finds my forehead, and the next moment, my body is limp, like I'm a sacrificial virgin being carried away by King Kong.

And then the darkness hits. The back of my eyes slowly fill with black ink.

CHAPTER 22
That Green-Eyed Bitch

Rushing water.

Close enough to spray.

The scent of ripe fruit.

Cushy ground beneath my back.

My eyelids flutter open as the black coating my vision slips away. The face leaned over mine, peering down at me with eyes I've stared into a hundred times, causes a swift, reviving kick to the chest.

"Vel."

The barrier over my mouth has been removed, and I breathe his name like I've just remembered it. This is a dream. This is a memory. It's—

Not a dream. His color is still gone. He's completely gray, save for the tiniest whiff of blue in his eyes. I start to extend my hand toward him, but he straightens out of reach.

"Dolly's awake."

I push myself up from a bed of peach flowers thriving beside a gleaming pond that's got water fountaining out of it at various places. We're even farther from the tree than we were before, the area carpeted in thick, verdant moss. Vel's no longer rustling around in those gaudy windbreaker pants. He wears something that looks like what a cult leader might wear. LOTS of linen. His pants are straight and cropped at the ankle, his top a tunic with a deep swoop in the front. And are those *beads* he's wearing around his neck?

It's the least sexy he's ever been.

And behind him, against a backdrop of shiny magical growth, stand all three nymphs—jade-eyed Gabri, rainbow starshine Fiona, and the one definitely responsible for all that linen, Mommy Nymph herself, Joell.

Oh, and off to the side, staring into the abyss? Vacant, fucking half-naked Arrik.

WHO LETS THEMSELVES GET HYPNOTIZED THAT EASILY?!

You know, part of me's thinking, he's always 'one step ahead,' right? This is the perfect opportunity for him to announce to everyone that he was faking it as he curls a fist and rips hidden tattoos up from beneath the grass. He would just LOVE to be the hero of this whole thing if only to play it off like it was no big deal.

But no, Arrik fucked up this time. He got too cocky when he faced off against magic he knew little about. And as I find my technically-EX genie boyfriend, I know for sure I'm alone. I can feel the warmth radiating off my skin in his direction because there's been an electrical current running between us since the moment we first touched. But while my Dolly-watts are reaching, they aren't landing. There's nothing for them to connect with.

Velis's aura is cold and empty.

Somewhere deep inside, at the core of the soul I can't see, I feel sharp pain over the state of my heart's greatest desire and the way he's looking at me without any spark of light.

Rejection. Like he would show disgust if I touched him. Like the thought of me being here *annoys* him.

It's the thing I've been protecting myself from since the moment I first locked on to those glacial blues.

He sounds tired. "Why did you come back, Dolly Jones?"

It's so hard to restrain myself. He might not feel it, but I still do, the pull of our arrows. That magnetism, dynamism, addictivism. I want him. I want to run into his arms and see his face brighten from the feel of me. "Because we come back together at the end of the day, Vel," I tell him. "Always."

"*Dolly.*" He looks at me like I'm silly. "We only dated a couple of weeks. Let it go. You should be free of it now that we're untethered."

He legitimately thinks it was our bond as master and wish granter that was keeping us in love? Does he not realize his emotion was completely removed from him?! That he's the only gray thing in this fucked-up fairyland garden?!

My eyes sink down to his hand, where the passport ring remains. That glassy band is black as ever, the wickedly red bloodstone like an evil eye staring up at me.

"Velis, take off that ring," I order.

Joell makes a start from behind him but halts when Vel's opposite hand territorially moves to cover the stone. "No. I'll be expelled from this world."

I was wondering what sort of lie they'd fed him. I glance back at his fidgeting relatives before lowering my voice. "No. Velis, listen to me. They've tricked you. That ring isn't for passage into their world—it's an artifact for dulling their emotions. They wear them outside, we think to help keep their atmosphere stable. It's what made that gatewoman gray, the same way you are now. Arrik and I saw it."

But to all that, he only says, "Pfft. *Arrik and I.*"

He may not be able to feel emotion, but that certainly felt a little . . . hm.

"They knew you'd never stay in their land," I continue, ignoring his tone. "Your whole life is in Makaya, and the only way you'd stay here with them was if all emotional ties to your old life were removed. Look at your skin, Velis. Just like that gatewoman's. Remember what she felt like?"

His mouth doesn't so much as flinch. "So?"

I search him, my next question delayed, "What do you mean 'so'?"

"SO what if they tricked me? For the first time in my life, I feel great." He forces his shoulders into a backward flex, his stare chilly and cruel. "At least I did. Until *you* showed up."

My throat catches. Men have spoken to me that way before. But never Velis. Never with that voice, those transparent eyes, that unsmiling mouth.

My arms fold to protect me from him. "You feel great being an emotionless asshole?"

"An *asshole?*" His eyes narrow with all his normal sass but none of his normal charm. "A human like you could never understand what it's like to absorb the rest of the world's emotion all the time. It's tiring in its own right, but to be shackled to someone like you? Just a noncommittal human drag? It's exhausting."

Is . . . that how he really feels? That being tethered to me was exhausting?

You're kind of hard for an empath to be around, you know. It'll be nice when I can move on from you.

Yeah, I guess even when he was whole, he felt that way. And he was shouldering it because he loved me. Have I truly been a burden on him all this time?

But that won't be an issue because we're no longer tethered! The plan was always for us to remove that bond. Once we go back—

"Velis, how long do you intend to stay here? Your father's expecting you back so that you can sign off on that paperwork, and —You're not planning on staying here permanently, are you? Why would you want to?"

"That's not really any of your business, is it? I dumped you. You no longer need to know anything about me. And you coming back here? Kinda desperate, to be honest." His tone is smug, mocking, *slap*-able. "And why the fuck wouldn't I want to stay here? Back in Makaya, I'm more djinn than nymph, and I have had to prove myself every Maka-damned day to make up for that missing fourth. But here? I'm not even *half* of what they are, and they're ready to make me a king. So yeah, I am staying. At least parttime. And, let's be real, I barely had time for you in my life before getting a second legacy, soooo . . ."

Oh. Wow. He really feels that way, deep down. Deep down, he knew he didn't have enough time for me. Yet he was so desperate to keep me that he locked me away, and—

When I told you you were my favorite, I meant it, Dolly. You mean more to me than all the rest of it.

Being laird is my dream, but . . . I've only got one ear on it, you know? I'm always thinking about rushing back here afterwards to be with you.

I changed my mind, Father. I choose Dolly!

No.

No, no, no. This isn't Vel. And what he's saying isn't true.

A cake isn't a cake if it's missing its sugar.

You don't want to start messing with that stuff. You need your empathy.

If only I could hit him hard enough with mine to jolt his into motion. I look past him to where his harem is leaned forward, captivated by his every word. It's clear they already think of him as their leader.

He follows my line of sight. "The only reason they're hanging back and letting me *educate* you before sending you on your way is because it will cause problems for our family if my ex-master goes missing. Once you agree to give up on whatever it is you think you're doing here, my brother can escort you back to your sad dwelling. It looks like you two have gotten close anyway." His eyes fall to my neck, where Arrik's collar still resides, his voice becoming quieter and derisive. "You let him collar you, Dolly? One day away and you jumped hard on that bandwagon."

Okay, I'm sure this time. That was anger. Or jealousy. But there is definite emotion fueling his annoyance that I showed up here with Arrik. This feels exactly like running into an ex, awkward and knowing all the past intimacy but feeling it very obviously snuffed out. Is that his djinn side breaking through?

"I'm giving you an easy way out. And if you don't go quietly, Fiona will compel Arrik to take your soul. Now that my brother knows he can be easily bested by her magic, he won't come for me again. Not that it matters. Once you're gone, you won't be able to get back in anyway." He wiggles his fingers in my face, and the silver chain manifests between them. "I'm taking back my mother's necklace."

"How does it work?" I call past him to the nymph trio observing. "The ring, the necklace, the bloodstones? His mother wore that necklace in the djinn world and retained her emotion, meaning whatever spell he's under must be kept inside the band of the ring, right?"

Joell's voice comes bursting at us over the vibrant moss like summer sun through a window. "That is not knowledge you require for exiting our realm," she says.

A perfect opening.

I pivot my focus. "Yeah, but aren't *you* curious, Velis? You've admitted you don't care if they tricked you, but don't you want to know why? Based on the way they've treated Arrik, they clearly aren't fond of djinn, so—"

I hesitate. I have a plan, but it's an icky one.

The thing about letting someone in the way Velis has with me is that it becomes that much easier to manipulate them. But to do so feels so . . . It's like I'm using this beautiful thing we've created to hurt him. I never wanted to be the one to hurt him. I never wanted anyone to hurt him.

I see a flex of disgust in the lines of his face and know I have no choice.

"So why would they even want your magical seed?" I commit. "Why do they get to retain their color when you don't? Is it because of what you are? It kind of seems like the only way they're okay with your soiled blood is if it's totally repressed. How is that any better than what the djinn have done to you?"

For the first time since meeting her, I see a flash of anger cross Joelle's sunlit demeanor, one she's quick to hide when Velis turns to squint at her.

"You're right," he mutters.

The minute he's distracted, I feel something wet and slippery race over my arm, like someone just slid a piece of seaweed across my skin. But when I move to swat it away, there's nothing there. I hurry to inspect the pond behind me, which shows nothing suspicious, before eyeing up those daughters, thinking one of them might be messing with me.

But no. Both are transfixed on Joell, who has just come sweeping up beside Velis, her hand falling into place on his shoulder like an autumn leaf. "*Mona Velis*," she gushes, earthy, motherly, *warm*, "all we have done is freed you from the nature of your jinnee blood. The means are not import—"

"Tell me how it works." Velis holds up his pale hand, where the dark ring resides. "What's wrong with my djinn blood?"

"Surely these are things we can discuss once your ex-human companion—"

"See?" I scramble to stand beside him. "They don't want you as you are. They want a diluted version of you. It's the only way they can stomach the thought of—"

"*Silence!*" A sharp hiss of wind hits me from the direction of tempest Gabri, who has just stormed forward to meet her mother, the impact hurling me into the mushy banks of the tentacle-ridden pond.

Velis watches me without wincing as I hit the ground hard enough to cause splatter, then returns to Joell. "Would you accept me as one of you if I weren't wearing this?"

"Gabri." Joell waves at her wind-powered daughter but sets her sights firmly on me. "Watch the human. If she tries to move or speak, take the air from her lungs."

My butt remains moist in the gunk of those shimmering banks, my elbow sore from taking the brunt of my fall. Gabri jogs over and presses her heel onto the untied shoelace of my muddied boot as a means of leashing me. "It is better for you if you obey, human. I do not wish to take your air."

She doesn't bother to look at me, her jade gaze drilling into what's slowly becoming a heated conversation between Velis and their matriarch.

No, I think it's . . . it's that she *can't* look at me.

Discomfort in a situation like this has got to be a sign of empathy, right?

"Gabri?" I prod.

"*Human!*" she hisses, grinding my shoelace into the mud. "Did you not hear Mar? You are not to speak!" There is a moment of hesitation where her scowl softens. "And it was foolish of you to come back. Now that you know we have manipulated his senses, it is unlikely Mar will let you leave. You had the opportunity to find a new mate, and you have wasted it. It is a shame."

She sounds sincere. But, find a new mate? She says it like just anyone could replace Velis Reilhander. Has she SEEN Velis Reilhander? Has she ever seen anyone LIKE him? Equally sweet and smart-ass. With the world's most charming smile and a body licked by the flames of hell? Who has mastered the tightrope between wholesome and naughty, and absorbs love like it's oxygen?

"He's so much more to me than just a mate, Gabri."

"The attachment you feel to him would wane over time and—"

"NO. It wouldn't. Velis isn't just some guy that can be replaced. I've loved him my whole life, and there's no way I'm letting him be imprisoned here without his true consent. He isn't an object to fill some role. I never want him to feel like one."

I got you, Vel.

"It is too late," says Gabri. "Whatever he is to you, the Mayster has filled a role from the moment he was born. From the moment his mother was born, and her mother before. All were born so that he could come and revive us. As important as he is to you, he is even more so to us. Here, he is not just one person's destiny but the savior of our entire line. I am sorry, for it is the same I saw with his mother and his grandmother, but he was never yours to claim. He has always been ours."

That she saw with his *mother* and his *grandmother*?

She's younger than me for sure. But just in case—

"How . . . old are you?" I ask slowly.

"I am two hundred and forty-five years."

Oh my god, it's all my age-gap nightmares come to life!

"Is—Is Velis going to age slowly because of the nymph in his blood?!"

The horror.

"He will age the same as us," she says, "so long as he remains with us. Which he shall. If not willingly, then by force. It is better for him to do so willingly. He will be happier if it is willingly." I follow her emerald focus to where Velis and Joell are now wrapped in a funnel of sunlight, squabbling. Even from a distance, Vel's countenance is troubling. Feisty and *mean*.

"Why is he so important to you?" I ask. Maybe if I can understand the full picture, I can figure out an escape route.

Talk nerdy to me.

Ugh. Still no help from that one. He could be a tattooed mannequin for all anyone knows.

The splash of the fountains glitters in my peripherals. My shirt clings to my back from the moisture it's absorbed.

"He is more than important," says Gabri. "The Mayster is vital. You have seen our world. You have seen it is not in a natural state. The truth is, there are no mating-aged males left among us. The last died out around the time the last of the color drained."

"Only women live in this city?"

Looks like you may have a bit of a dick shortage around here.

"The few of us who remain are female-born," confirms Gabri.

Explains their thirst. Vel makes your mouth water on his own, but to have been without males for however many years? I'd want to tie him up too.

I already do want to tie him up.

"Ours used to be a world of vibrancy and chaos," says Gabri somberly, as she watches her mother fail to quell Velis's suspicions. "But our people were passionate, and we warred often, and the last . . . It was long, and it was terrible. The men were first to fight, and the men were first to fall, and after, when we cleaned the rubble from our world, we began to realize that youthful males on all sides were few. And when those males beget only female offspring . . ." Her gilded hair shimmies as she shakes her head. "I believe it is penance for what we did to our world. Now, our only option is to send out our own to procure mates, but it takes much sacrifice from our pooled magic to send one of us across realms. Our magic grows thinner. This city used to be a sanctuary, but we have had to retreat. We are only a few dozen family lines scattered throughout it now, hoping for our Maysters to return."

"Return?"

"If they are ever born at all. Our family has waited long, but others have waited longer. When our last Mayster, my dar, died a hundred years ago, the fairest of my sisters was chosen to leave our world in search of a mate. Her name was Chastel. She paired with a djinn but failed to produce a male. Her daughter is Adelle, Mayster Evangeline's mar."

Wait.

Wait. WAIT.

I was really close with my grandfather too! The djinn one on my mom's side. He's the one that went and screwed a nymph and fucked up my bloodline, but he was a good guy otherwise.

Gabri and Fiona's sister was . . . Vel's nymph grandmother?

"If your sister was Vel's grandmother, that means your mom, Joell, is—"

"Mar is Mayster Evangeline's great-grandmar."

Um, *ish.*

BECAUSE LOOK AT HOW SHE'S LOOKING AT HIM AND FONDLING HIS SHOULDER!

No wonder there's such a strong resemblance between Joell and Vel's mom! They aren't cousins! They're direct fucking descendants! This whole 'nymphean pilgrimage' was nothing more than a farce to get each generation to return home until a baby-making male could be secured.

"My sister, Chastel, returned here with her jinnee mate, as did my niece, Adelle. But neither fulfilled their duty. Both wished to return to the jinnee world with their mates instead of remaining here to produce offspring. They came and stole our blessing and abandoned us, so we had to take other measures to prepare for the return of Mayster Velis. When we learned he was male . . ." A grain of hope shows in her serpentine eyes. "A male nymph of our line, ripe for seeding? He is too precious to leave to chance. We had to ensure he did not do the same as his mar and grandmar, and so we prepared the ring to be waiting for him."

Seeding. Is that super necessary?

"But the ring was in the djinn world," I clarify. "The tollbooth lady had it. How did you get it to her if you can't leave your realm?"

"A jinnee came," Gabri says with fondness. "A very beautiful jinnee. She came last week and told us of the Mayster's coming. She took the ring and prepared for him to have it upon entering our world."

Mother. Fucker.

Assuming there are no other 'very beautiful jinnee' out to get Velis—which, let's be real, is still a possibility—Arrik was right. Amoira did have something to do with this. She may even have orchestrated it. And it was a plan separate from Jeb and Beckham's simple one to ambush us in the nymph realm.

The bitter ex-wife is working on a whole other level.

"Those rings suppress your emotion," I say. "And you expected Vel's to be suppressed, but you didn't count on him having a master tethered to him. None of the others had that sort of relationship."

"No, they did not. And you are correct. It is the band that suppresses emotion. We must all wear them when exiting our nests, our world being as unstable as it is. Your fight earlier with our guardswomen caused several rifts in the sky that must now be repaired."

"And the red stone?" I ask.

"Decorative. The blood of our last Mayster—a reminder of why we must wear them. And, as it turns out, blood enough to grant access to our nests to even those not of our blood. We did not know this prior to you coming. It seems my sister, Chastel, or her daughter, Adelle, removed the stone from her ring and placed it into the necklace you brought here. It is sacrilege to do so. Mar was hurt when she saw it."

A second time, my hand darts to wipe something goopy I've

just felt slipping past my neck. But my fingers come up clean. There's nothing there.

Maybe it's this shiny air. Maybe it has texture. Maybe this entire pocket is one large, listing bubble.

"Then I assume the reason you cursed your own blood to be infertile is so that those who are sent out into the world are forced to return if they want to produce offspring?"

Gabri is quiet. "Mar cursed it. And yes. That is why she did so. She cursed the blood of my sister Chastel before sending her out into the realms to find a mate." She pauses. "Now that you know our plight, you have no choice but to commit to it, human. I do not desire to take your air. I have heard of other lines killing the mates their Maysters return with, and it is not good for the soul of our world. I may be able to convince Mar to let you leave, but you must promise to forget the Mayster. One broken heart does not outweigh the fate of an entire world. The more of us there are, the more magic there is, and we need magic to fix what we have broken. We need him. He is our hero."

I understand where she's coming from, at least.

But she's wrong. Velis isn't a hero. Just like I'm not a heroine. We're just two flawed, recovering people in desperate love with one another. And the Velis I know deserves a say in what they're doing to him.

I could never promise to abandon him here.

"Djinn can teleport others easily across realms," I say, solemn. "Velis would teleport you, your mom, and Fiona out of here to find your own mates. I know he would. I know his blood is stronger than whoever you would find out there, but . . . I can't give him up. Not like this. I know people change and relationships fail, but if he's ever going to reject me, it needs to be the real him. He's all I've ever wanted, and if I leave this place, I'm returning with an army of djinn by my side to come back and get him."

An 'army of djinn' is a bit of a stretch. But I'm sure I could wrangle a few. And at least one leprechaun. And whatever moon-powered creature Bellamy is.

I probably shouldn't have admitted that out loud, though.

Finally, Gabri deigns to look at me. Her eyes truly are a beautiful shade of darkest green unlike I've ever seen in the human world. The spray of water frames her golden hair like an angel's shroud. "I knew this would be your answer, but I thought to try."

She holds my gaze as her hand curls and the air begins to suction from my lungs.

Zombie Arrik excluded, I gasp loudly enough to draw the attention of the others. Velis glides those perfect, absorbing, dreamy blue eyes to mine and does nothing as I'm slowly suffocated. In fact, the only one showing any reaction is Fiona. She nervously shifts her weight from behind Joell. The daughters are not as committed as the mother, but that's going to do jack for me now that I've decided to overtly defend Vel's honor rather than playing a sneakier game.

FUCK.

I shouldn't have announced my intent like that.

I just couldn't keep it in.

I'm not a quitter. I'm nothing if not determined.

But no one ever said I deserved a happy ending.

The world around me pops with sparkles of light somehow more beautiful than all the fantasyland in the blurred distance as I slump over and submit to unsympathetic darkness.

So much for Cal's luck.

CHAPTER 23
Always and For—

Wet, cold, slippery. Something slithers along my back like a frigid tongue.

There's a scream. Two screams. Three.

All the air in the universe comes rushing back into me, and I gasp. Cough, cough, cough. *Hack.* And then I fight the light on the other side of my eyelids. My palms press into the mushy ground skirting the pond as off-spray from the fountain shimmers and mists my wet, chilled skin.

No sign of Gabri. I search through delay and confusion. There's Fiona, backing up, violet eyes wide.

Oh, there's Gabri. Clinging to Joell.

And Vel is exactly where he was, fingertips beginning to spark with white-hot lightning in preparation to fight something.

And the thing they're all cowering from, fear-devoid Vel exempt, is . . .

I stand, realizing I'm cast in a shadow, and begin to turn, neck slowly craning to figure out what they're all—

Holy.

Mother.

Of.

"Clifford," my mouth mutters as my eyes fixate and my back

arches to take in the black, inky creature standing over me. "Clifford the Big Black Dragon."

It's the tattoo. It's the tattoo Arrik transferred to me in his room during that problematically intimate scene. It has firm-ish edges yet seems to be made of ink, like liquid in a dragon-shaped balloon. And it's standing upright, more Godzilla-like than the ones fought by knights. And it's *chonky*.

"A-Arrik?!"

No response.

"ARRIK?!"

I twist to find him still unmoving, like a hot robot.

I return to the dragon. Is it looking at me? It seems to be looking at me. Waiting for . . . something.

"Get them?" I say without much certainty.

Clifford's beady little eyes flare blue, and the next minute, he's stomping off, splashing this beautiful, magical canvas full of ink. Crisp white trunks with tiny twinkling flowers? *Splash!* A mosaic sculpture of a koala-like creature? *Splash!*

He is straight-up destroying things as he trudges after Joell and Gabri.

THAT THING WAS HIDING INSIDE MY SKIN THIS WHOLE TIME?!

"Er, F-Fiona!" I shout, reclaiming my voice. "Release Velis's brother! He created that thing; he's the only one who's going to be able to stop it!"

"No!" lashes Velis. "Don't. I got this." He shoots me cockiness over his shoulder. "How much you want to bet I can beat my brother's magic?"

Okay, well now this is a conundrum because on the one hand, I'd really love Velis to show up Arrik. But I really don't want *this* Velis to be the one to do it. Because in this situation, Velis is the enemy. And that makes Arrik . . .

Ugh, I feel like if I finish that thought, he'll know it somehow.

"Clifford!" I cry. "Change of plans! Go relentlessly after Fiona until she releases her bewitchment on Arrik!"

"Well, that was stupid," Velis says as ink Godzilla sloshes past him on the way to Fiona, who has just begun to sprout sparkle wings—which, yes, are different from the rainbow wings we previously saw. Velis starts for me, offering a look I've never seen on him before. Something dark and controlled and a little menacing as electricity strings across the tips of his fingers.

He's so fucking hot. And now he's, like, *villain* hot.

"S-so what, alien boy?" I take a step back. "You lose your emotion, and you suddenly lose your entire moral compass? You went from egg conjurer to fiancée killer in one day? Are we really sure that's how it works?"

That isn't how it works. People don't just become homicidal maniacs if they lose their emotions, right?

No, humans don't. But maybe djinn do. Or maybe nymphs do.

SHIT.

The moment I turn and start to flee, Velis is before me. I don't even know if he used hyper-speed or if he teleported. His hand catches my back before I can stumble from the surprise of his appearance. That darkness closes in on me, his voice light and deadly. "Did you fuck my brother today, Dolly?"

"A-are you seriously asking me if I would do something like that?"

"But you did run to him. Again." He looks at me like he's a mother who already knows which kid colored on the wall and is just waiting for them to fess up. "This is the third time, *Dollykins*."

ASS. And it's the second. The dance club doesn't count.

I'm not indulging him. The real Velis would never pull me into an argument like this, one that isn't for the sake of solving something but for the sake of hurting *someone*.

That accursed black ring is on his grayscale hand. I just need it off. HOW?

Before I can figure that part out, Velis spins me around and forces my back flush to his chest, his ample lips close to my ear. "Tell that creature to leave my kin alone, or I will hurt you."

So maybe lack of emotion leads to fierce loyalty in nymphs?!

"Take the ring off," I counter, "and I'll tell it to stop."

One of Vel's hands grips my shoulder in place while his other takes hold of my chin. He rotates my face until my ear is directly to his mouth. "I'm still attracted to your body, you know. Do it now, and we could get one more in before you go. There are a couple of things I've been wanting to try."

My stomach flutters.

Until he adds, "It would be nice to have mindless sex not tied to your every erratic need for once."

He really does know how to be hurtful. That one stung enough to water the eyes.

I wrench myself to find his faded face. To see what sort of expression he's wearing. To see how a person with no emotions could look so . . . happy. He's glad at the distress he's causing me. And that's gutting.

"Hey, *Dolly-kins*. How many weeks of atonement do you think it's going to take for you to get over m—"

"*You don't want to say that, little brother*," a smoker's voice cuts him off. "That's going to be a harder one to come back from."

"ARRIK!" I cry over my shoulder. The tatted antihero's got Velis in a chokehold, which is doing nothing to deter Velis's clutch on me.

"If I'm not mistaken, that was relief, DJ."

Arrik's not mistaken. It looks like Fiona finally gave up on him. That monster is no longer after her. In the corner of the clearing, Joell is busy loosing sunny fire at it while Gabri plants her feet and air-bends to hold it in place.

"What the hell is with that tattoo monstrosity?!"

"That? That was my failsafe," Arrik says like it's unimpressive. "Should I get incapacitated and my protection spell on you fall, that was plan C. There is a plan D, but you don't want to know what it is. But what the fuck happened? That only activates if you're in serious danger, like near death."

Velis releases me to devote all his brute strength into wrestling Arrik off.

"What happened—" I say, panting as I scamper away, "is that you totally got zombied by butterfly girl within the first minute!

You were all set up for this epic battle-off, and then you just failed! It was totally lame! Be glad you didn't see it."

Arrik isn't the kind to show his full smile. Neither am I. But there's no stopping this grin of camaraderie happening between us as I connect with his aquamarine stare amid sloshed ink and iridescent air—maybe the first we've ever shared.

Velis bucks Arrik off, and Arrik zips away at vampire-speed. Velis quickly darts after him to initiate the sexiest game of tag ever. Fiona has joined the fight against Clifford and is now flinging bursts of confetti-sized glitter magic into his slippery form. It hits him like feathers stuck on a wet craft project, gooping down his molasses-like side.

Velis stops for some good old-fashioned taunting. "Dolly said you didn't fuck her today, Arrik. What's wrong? She doesn't want your filth in her?" With a burst of speed, he closes the gap between them.

MEAN. He needs to stop. I know these are extenuating circumstances, but he needs to shut his mouth until it can remember how to be kind.

"*I think it's his nymph side,*" says Arrik's headset voice in my ear as he springs away, so much springier than he looks capable of. "*He doesn't feel right to me.*"

"We need to get that ring off him," I say. "Do you have a plan?"

"*Do I ever not have a plan?*"

"Psh."

"*Dolly.*"

"What?"

"*You really aren't impressed with me yet?*"

I'm quiet, watching him dart around, spewing magic at Velis and provoking with one-liners.

In my ear, his voice is always so much more . . . intimate. Low and secretive and rumbly. "*Come on, love. It's okay. We don't even have to call it a crush. We can just call it . . . attraction meets admiration.*"

"Shut up and get out of my head, and don't hurt Velis . . . please."

"*You make that into a formal wish, and it's going to lower our chances of getting out of this. Just saying.*"

I consider it. "I'll stick with the please. But nothing we can't easily repair with a wish, okay?"

"*Good girl.*"

Ink meets flashes of djinn-blue mixed with bursts of dragon fire—no, not from the dragon among us but from my fire-breathing ex-boyfriend, *obviously*—as the brothers begin to battle it out in another epic magical showdown. Arrik runs toward a tree, squatting deep so that he can thrust himself to its canopy, then begins rapid-firing pellets of condensed ink magic at Velis while Velis runs along the tree line below in hot pursuit.

Arrik bounds across the shedding treetops, something likely protruding from the corner of his mouth, and casts magical webs backward over his shoulder as Velis works to incinerate the leaves of whichever tree is coming next. They could go at it all day, but Joell has given up on helping Gabri and Fiona attack Clifford the nightmare dragon and is now steadily zooming toward me on what looks like a strip of sunlight.

Are we sure we aren't tripping right now? We didn't just hang out in Arrik's bedroom, popping genie drugs all afternoon, did we?

There's a soft chuckle in my ear. So much softer than Arrik's normal cackles. Like he appreciates the joke.

A second later, he's in front of me, Velis in the distance ensnared in a web of sticky ink—the same ink Arrik now spews at the mother nymph barreling toward us, her body amassing a wall of growing flame behind her as she comes.

"Arrik!"

He lands a good hit, and then another, until Joell's sun-fire dies, and she's forced to wrestle the black, taffy-like substance binding her arms to her sides.

I run to Arrik.

I run to Arrik?

"I'm still under your wish not to hurt the butterfly one." His painted chest heaves from his efforts. "Do you want to change that?"

"Do what you have to do, but only if you have to do it. I'm not about to control you right now." I'm not paying attention. I'm watching our four enemies preoccupied with ink in its various forms.

So I don't anticipate it when Arrik's hand gathers the nape of my neck, and he bends low to give me one of his piercing assessments. "Are you okay?"

It's a bit striking. The depth of his concern.

"No," my mouth admits. "Velis is horrible right now, and I'm pretty much useless in a fight like this."

His eyes stay on me, like we have all the time in the world, like he's not the least bit concerned with the chaos around us, like our victory is certain.

"I won't let anything bad happen to you, Master. To either of you. I'll get him back for you."

And then?

And then.

Uh-oh.

The plush of his lips is warm on my cheek, his fingers all up in the back of my hair, pulling upward against my skull to create delicious tension at the roots. Arrik's already taken more unconsented kisses than is acceptable in the new millennium, but this one feels different. This one fuels the top of my chest with adrenaline.

And then he zips off to work on securing Mommy Nymph.

I touch the area where the feel of his mouth lingers and know—

I can't hang out with Arrik anymore after this.

"*That . . . sucks.*" His heat is in my ear, though he isn't looking at me. "*Let's just get through this before we start making rash decisions. You aren't useless. I made that creature for you. You control it. Up the ante and take care of those two younger ones. I'll focus on these psychos.*"

He means he'll focus on Joell and Velis, and the former is

already basically taken care of. She's strapped to the ground with lines of ink, and Arrik is in the process of turning his attention to ink-stained Velis, heckling, "Bro, you need some sun."

As Arrik comes at his brother, splashing up waves of ink from the stained ground that Velis easily dodges with fancy footwork and swift teleportation, Velis appears to be in the process of conjuring something. Teeth bared, he spreads his fingers into curled claws and scoops them through the air at his sides, like he's an evil sorcerer pulling demons up from hell. The earth around Arrik rumbles, shaking Arrik's footing, and an army of pebbles lift from the ground to frame elemental *encompasser* Velis. Arrik teleports to another tree, where he stays crouched like a cat about to pounce, waiting for his brother's next move.

Velis is going to send all those rocks at Arrik, and Arrik is going to dodge around, slinging more ink.

I force my concentration away from them to where Gabri and Fiona are still fending off Clifford with glitter and wind. The wind is doing its job of holding him in place, but the glitter seems to be doing squat.

"Clifford!" I shout. "Fight back harder! Create a cage around them and then come help Arrik capture Velis!"

At my renewed command, the towering dragon's eyes flash blue, and the creature begins making movements identical to Arrik's, tossing ink at the two girls fighting him. Gabri leaps to the side to avoid a clump of it, and her steady onslaught of wind breaks—an opening for Clifford to attack.

But something is wrong. Half the dragon's body seems to be stuck, and as the ink covering him drips off, I realize the glitter magic wasn't doing nothing—it's adhered to half of his body. That half of his body abruptly turns on the other half.

A glittery dragon claw begins clubbing at an inky one, both connected to the same dragon.

He's been sparklefied.

"Arrik, can you hear me?"

"*Mmhm*," says his voice in my ear.

"When you said, 'We may never be tethered, but we have

been bonded, and that's a link that will never go away,' was that a literal statement?"

"*You've got a good memory.*"

"Focus. Did you really mean that, or was that just you asserting dominance?"

"*Tch. There's no need to assert my dominance. It flows freely. And yes, I meant it literally. I could feel glimmers of you even after you fully tethered Velis. All three of us could. Why?*"

"Velis told me when we first met that he isn't able to do some of the stuff that you three can, like make one-off wishes or contract people outside his vessel, because he isn't full-blooded. So if I were to make a wish now, he wouldn't be able to grant it because we aren't even bonded, let alone my soul tethered to him, except—"

"*Except you've already been bonded, and that's a link that will never go away,*" confirms Arrik. "Yeah, hypothetically, he could grant you a wish if he wanted, but why would he? He'll get no payment for it, seeing as you're already tethered to me."

But he doesn't know that. He likely assumes it, but he doesn't know it for sure.

"Follow my lead," I say quietly into my invisible Arrik earpiece. And then louder: "Velis! This needs to stop! You two will destroy this nymph cubby—"

"*Cubiculum, Master.*"

"You'll destroy the nymph cubby, and then you'll have wrecked the last refuge of your family line. Let's stop this," I propose. "We've been bonded before, so it's possible for you to access my soul outside of your vessel. Grant me a wish. One wish, and Arrik and I will surrender."

"Ha! So you can wish me to turn on my kin?" Velis hisses at me before sending a boulder hurling at Arrik. Meanwhile, Fiona continues to send her sparkles into the half of Clifford that remains ink while Gabri rushes to her mother's side to help unbind her from the ink strapping her to the ground.

"You can have my soul!" My voice rings of last-ditch effort.

Velis halts from surprise but immediately settles into haughtiness, setting an inky hand to his hip. "Nice try. I'm pretty sure my brother's already got his hooks in you—Why else would he be here helping you?"

Because Arrik is . . .

Kind of amazing.

"*Daw*," says a lazy voice in my ear.

Eyes pleading, I tell Velis the truth: "I love you, Vel. I would never let another djinn take my soul." And then a lie: "Arrik and I aren't tethered."

"*Do you have a follow-up plan to that, Master? Because that's a pretty bold lie he's going to see through.*"

I connect eyes with Arrik where he's perched on top of the nearby koala statue. Gabri has succeeded in blowing the ink from her mother, and both are running over while Fiona the dragon tamer continues her efforts on Clifford.

"My soul is free for the taking, Velis," I reassert. "And I can prove it."

Velis holds out a hand to stop the heat and wind charging me. Arrik quickly blips over from his vantage, trying to anticipate what I'm doing.

"Clifford!" I cry in a show of good faith. "Stop. Leave Fiona alone."

"*Master,*" Arrik's secret voice persists. Luckily, he's yet to say the title out loud in front of any of them.

Velis's hand is still out, the thought of my soul too tempting to resist. Overhead, a tree releases black droplets like collected rain.

I turn to address Arrik. "Make me a one-off."

He glances at Velis. "Er, sure?"

"I wish that you'd answer my next question truthfully."

Arrik's eyes flash blue, his voice in my ear, urging me to, "*Be careful, Master.*"

"Arrik," I say, eyes on grayed Vel and the line of angry nymph women beside him, my big black, half-sparkled dragon wilting into a heap of ink and glitter in the background. "Are we in a master/wish granter relationship where you're able to freely siphon my soul in exchange for wishes?"

"No," Arrik responds, eyes bright. "We aren't in a relationship like that. I can't freely siphon your soul in exchange for wishes."

Because of the betrayal wish.

"*Ah*," says his telepathy. "*Clever girl.*"

Velis still looks suspicious, though that hand keeping his great-grammy and aunties at bay is a good sign.

"My wish will be minor," I tell him. "And once you hear it, you'll be able to choose whether or not you want to grant it. And if you decide to grant it, you'll be able to finally sink your teeth into my untethered soul. If not, Arrik and I will leave. Agreed, Arrik?"

"Whatever."

Vel's mouth is propped up like he's amused by my stupidity. "Go on, then," he says. "What's the wish?"

"Remove that ring you're wearing. Velis Reilhander, I wish you would."

Behind him, Joell lurches forward, linen overalls stained black and her golden hair matted with drying ink. Her two daughters are in a similar state, as are all the gardens around them. Wonderland has become a mess, coated in ink and glitter and scorches of fire and lightning, the earth cracked where Velis's nymph power upset it.

"Velis!" Joell uses Vel's name with less respect than I've ever heard her use. "You cannot remove the ring! It will remove your power!"

Velis turns to her. "I've used my elemental magic in both the human world and Makaya, so I know that's not true. Your story seems to be changing, *mona Joell*." He flicks his evil stare back to me. "Quite the deal for me, Dolly Jones."

His eyes sear—polished gemstones against an otherwise muted slate—and I allow my shoulders to melt in relief because I know.

We've won.

Joell knows it too. "NO!" she shrieks.

Both her daughters react. Gabri hits Velis with a cyclone of wind to blast him away before he can remove the ring; at the same time, Fiona's rainbow wings begin to manifest again. She uses them to swoop at Arrik like a hornet.

This time, Arrik's ready for her. A wall of ink rises before us with a flick of both his hands, then his arm is around my waist, and we're both teleported to the opposite side of the fountain-clad pond. Whatever swans would normally hang around have all flown away for safety, the water no longer shimmering but invaded by oily black.

All the nymphs have now turned their sights on Velis, but the wish is already enacted. Vel's eyes are stuck blue, and that ring will come off him. It's only a matter of time.

Arrik and I stand together, watching and waiting.

"Good job, Master."

"Thanks."

I'm proud of what I've done. Proud I came through as the white knight I'm thought to be.

"You seem to respond well to praise," says Arrik. "I'll have to remember that."

I'm . . . not totally sure what he means. "Was this fight as fun for you as the first?" I divert.

"More."

We aren't looking at each other. I feel the intentional placement of his structured fingers along the curve of my side, where they remain strongly wrapped around me in preparation to teleport should we need to, and realize—this is different from the potato-sack way he usually holds me.

"Arrik—"

"Did you mean it?" he says, staring ahead. "We can't hang out anymore after all this?"

His hand on my waist. It's now the only thing I can feel.

"Why . . . did I have to save you out there? Why was I *destined* to? Did something change for you in that moment?"

He's quiet. And then—"Later. Looks like it's about to happen."

Cult-master Velis has just elbowed the last of his ravenous kin away, using a mixture of nymph elemental power and genie whatever power, and his hands are together.

And he's slipping it off.

And it's off.

His body absorbs color like a sponge darkening from water as the cursed ring finally falls to the ground.

"VELIS!" My legs act on their own, and I feel the last cling of Arrik's fingertips slip off my waist as I run toward my alien-genie boyfriend.

I know. Those eyes. Those eyes, so warm, so emotive, so compassionate, are his. True, they're replaying the last day's worth of events with absolute horror, but he'll get over it. And I'll get over it.

"Dol . . . ly." My name quivers on his lips as his brain processes the hurtful things he did and said.

"It's okay," I call as I run my way around the pond. "We're okay."

But Gabri is on her feet, desperation carrying her, and she's charging with a tornado at her back.

Arrik zips to his brother's side, prepared to fight alongside him. "Get your vessel and let's get out of here, you little shit."

I can help with that. He doesn't seem to have a mind to do it himself. "Velis, I wish you had your vessel!" I cry as I jog around the inky waters.

Still stuck between reanalyzing the last day and observing the chaos we've found ourselves in, Vel's eyes flash blue as he chooses to obey the wish. His hand outstretches, waiting for the summoned vessel to find him as Arrik flares up another even greater wall of ink. But this time, he does so with shoulders bent forward, the fatigue of it all starting to hit him.

Just a little more, Arrik.

Give us just a little more of yourself.

"*Aye-aye, Master*," says his voice in my ear.

I run to meet them where they stand, Vel clutching his face and Arrik struggling to maintain his spell against wind that's again been joined by sunny fire and pops of rainbow light. Through the curtain of falling black, an object comes zooming, landing heavily in Velis's palm.

I fall into his re-bronzed arms—which are rather nice arms, if I'm allowed to comment—and bury my face in the starchy fabric covering his chest—which, if I'm allowed to comment, is a rather nice chest.

"Dolly?" His free hand lands somewhat absently on my back. He may be in shock. "I'm—Shit. Babe, I'm so—"

"*Later!*" Arrik says through his teeth. "Master! We need you to wish us both out of here, and we need you to do it now!"

"Master?" Velis questions.

We don't have time for an explanation.

"Arrik Reilhander, Velis Reilhander, I wish you would get us home!"

Two sets of blue eyes wash over me as Arrik finally drops his protective veil of ink and places his tatted fingers to my shoulder for what should be the last time.

CHAPTER 24
Lace and Ink

Night wind blows at the curtains, hinting at the magical kingdom beyond. Vel and I are clean—the stain of ink and mud and sweat removed—and Arrik has returned to his quarters to decompress.

Beckham is in the manor somewhere, gunning for us all, but within our individual quarters, we're protected from his wrath. When Vel's dad is back, there will need to be some SERIOUS conversations around the dynamic of this family. Just how dangerous his oldest son is, Amoira's involvement, how we're all supposed to move forward from here. And . . .

I don't know. There's something off about his dad's handling of all this. He's got to know the extent of it, right? Why didn't he do better to warn us about the despondent state of Vel's rellies? And that whole pretending not to love your kid for some grand reveal?

There's more to all this. There's got to be.

But djinn and family politics will have to wait.

Tonight is mine and Vel's and that big magical moon's.

The lights in our suite have been snapped away so that our space is bathed in the romantic glow of the moon through those sheer, billowing curtains. There are fairy lights too, placed around the balcony rail. I've always loved fairy lights. I'll have to ask Velis if fairies are real. The gardens below carry the sweet and sultry scent of lilac through the window. My favorite. I've never told Vel that, but I suspect he's enchanted the air to carry it for me.

Just like those lights.

I'm noticing them more and more, the little things he does. I'm appreciating them more and more, knowing he's doing them for me and not so that I'll praise him.

That's Vel.

A good hour of our night has been taken up by me rehashing the events of the day and him groveling for my forgiveness, which I've already granted him a dozen times.

Yet there he is, in one of the fluffy robes we've both finally succumbed to. And fuck it all, they are damn comfy.

"Argh! I am such an asshole!" he says yet again, his face buried in his hands. He's spread-kneed in the armchair directly facing me. We've pushed two of them together, like we're sitting in a rowboat. *Forced* forced proximity, maybe.

Arrik's kitty collar finally removed, my damp hair bleeds into the shoulders of the robe. My chin rests on my knees and I clutch my own toes. "I mean, we've always known that," I tease gently. "You showed your hand the first day I met you."

"Yeah, well, I didn't ever want to be *that* much of an asshole. Babe, the shit I said to you—"

"It wasn't okay. I know that. And I also know that wasn't you."

But I also know there was some truth to the things he said. Of all the things his altered state told me, there's only one I really need to clear up. One that's been weighing on my heart. I think he's finally stable enough for me to ask about it.

"Vel, is my emotion still hard to be around, even now that we're no longer tethered?"

His gaze pops up out of his hands. "What? No! It wasn't bad before either! I mean, yeah, it can be a lot to absorb the emotions around me, but yours—" He reaches to gather my hands. "I feel honored to absorb your feelings, Dolly. I *want* to know them. The things I said back there, it was taking the absolute fuckin' worst situational parts of it and twisting them into something that would hurt you. My goal was to get you to leave. I knew what it was doing to you, I just didn't have the capacity to care." He yanks his hand away to press his eyeballs into the heels of his palms. "I am *such* an *asshole.*"

"Velis—"

"I swear to you, Dolly Jones. I swear it. I will never speak to you that way again. I don't know why you don't feel more hurt over—" He stops, realization hitting him. "Maybe you do feel more hurt, and I just can't read it anymore." His eyes widen, followed by a two-handed hair mussing. "Fuck! I can't believe you're fucking tethered to *Arrik.*"

"Not for long. He said he'd temporarily unregister so that I can become a free agent again. And he didn't take any of my soul, except a small taste right at the beginning when he tethered me."

"Yeah . . ." Velis contemplates. "That part still seems weird. That betrayal wish. I'm pretty sure even I could have gotten around that one. It's almost like he was sparing your soul, which, why would he? I can't see him being able to resist a soul like yours."

We haven't even begun to dissect the truth about Arrik's motives and all I found out about him today, but a lot of it doesn't seem like something that should come from me. I'd rather focus on the fact that Vel is home, his empathy restored, his SEED restored, and that he's still looking at me the same way he always has, even without our connection as genie and master.

"Does it feel different for you?" I ask. "Him being bonded to me instead of you?"

The night air circulates around us, the outside world peaceful, our suite empty but for our two beating hearts.

"I could lie to you and say it doesn't," he says quietly. "Now that I can lie. But . . . it's a lot different, Dolly. I can hardly tell what you're thinking. I'm looking for it in your eyes, but your eyes have seen a lot, so I'm not getting much."

I don't mind him searching. I don't mind being the specimen under that lens.

"Is it . . . ?" He squints. "You have a question you want to ask?"

I do.

He continues trying to read me. "It's not a question I'm going to like?"

Probably not.

I brace. "You didn't . . . bang your grandma today, did you?"

He blinks at me.

Blink, blink, blink.

Then, he jerks backward in disgust. "Maka, no! I didn't bang any of them! They . . . weren't in heat."

Okay, well they sure *seemed* in heat.

He shudders. "She looked like my *mom*, Dolly."

"Yeah! Well, it seemed like *Mayster Evangeline* would do anything to spread his magical s—"

Dark Vel mode commences, a shine from some nonexistent light source catching his eyes. "Call it my 'seed' again, and we're coming up with something equally cringy to call yours, *Master*."

"To call my *what*?"

He shrugs. "Your Dolly juices."

Oh. My. God.

He cracks a smirk. "Oops, looks like we just did."

He's such a shit. Such a lovable, squeezable shit. And I missed him today. So badly. The feel of his secure arms, his absorbing stare, his considerate hands, his devotion, his love.

I never want to be separated from him again.

I've been afraid of getting hurt. Today, I did hurt. But I survived it, and I didn't regress. And I'm willing to accept the risk that it could happen again. Because he's worth it. And the way he makes me feel is worth it. And I like the Dolly that stands up and fights for people, who outwits the villains and who repairs herself after being broken.

Vel is helping me to become this person. Nurturing me into it.

"I wish we were tethered so I could feel that better," he utters with soft determination. "It almost feels like . . ." He concentrates. "Pride? Are you proud?"

I claim his cheek and love the way he automatically moves to kiss my thumb with his eyes still fully captivated by mine.

"You know how yesterday you said something about how you've been feeling these pangs of doubt in me?"

He's hanging on to my every word with such heartwarming intensity. "Yeah?"

"Those weren't doubt. I've never doubted you or me or us. Those have always been fear. I'm afraid of losing you and this. I'm so, so afraid, Vel. Because this? The strength you offer me? The security? I have lived without it, and I don't want to go back. I realize I need to be my own person. I realize I can't rely on you to fix or protect me, but I like having another person as invested in me as I am. And same for you. Today, I nearly lost that, and all the fears I've been harboring, they came true, and it was kind of devastating. But I'm alive. I did have a moderate panic attack, but there were others out there who supported me—your friends, your *brother*. I'm not afraid of what we have. I'm afraid of losing it, but I'm not afraid of us. You won't feel that in me anymore."

Of course he won't.

Because we're untethered.

And the plan was always for us to remain untethered.

Vel's face twitches, and he swallows. He's trying to speak, but he's having a hard time releasing it because the pressure of his own emotion is strong. He looks away from me, out at that strip of delicate lights distorted by the sheeny, lapping curtains. "Dolly..."

"It's okay," I whisper, knowing the struggle of being this vulnerable. "What I'm saying is, I want to be the person on your side and at your side, Vel. Always."

Not as his fakely tamed human bride. Not as a mate to fulfill his obligations. For real. And if this all shatters, then I'll rebuild myself. Velis isn't the only other person in existence, and I can survive without him.

I just really, really, *really* like having him around.

His eyes find me again. "You're perfect. You're a perfect

person. Except—" He shows a dash of dryness. "Can't I protect you, even a little?"

I'm grinning. "A little."

Because those damn dimples.

He's so cute. His goony, cute, in-love face. Like the puppy so happy to have been taken home. And the longer I stare at it, the more mischievous it grows. His grin is reacting to mine, his features starting to look a bit naughty.

He wants to schmexx.

But first—

"Can you . . . humor me with something?" I ask.

"Not sure I like that ominous tone, but I think I owe you whatever it is, so yes."

I tell him what I want to see.

"Ha! Really?"

"I'm curious."

"Okay." Smirking, he taps a finger to the corner of his mouth.

I quickly change my mind.

"Nope. Nope, nope, nope. Abort," I say, shielding the monstrosity from view with my hand.

The result of this experiment is that Velis does not, in fact, look good with a mustache. Turns out there is a way to soil perfection.

"Too late, Doll." That smirk only grows under a canopy of hair that really needs to go. "Let's see how it feels on your *mouth*."

"Oh, ewww. All you need now are those windbreaker pants—"

"Done."

There's a pop of smoke, added sheerly for effect, and the next moment, mustached, shirtless, neon-windbreaker-pantsed Velis is looking like a fine yet semi-creepy basketball coach from the eighties.

"Oh no, Velis, that is SO wrong."

And yet, kind of right?

He winks, and suddenly, we're in bed together, his pants making a noisy protest against the plush bedding. He puckers up obnoxiously under that gross strip of hair as he comes for me, and my eyes swell in the horror of it approaching—

But at the last minute, he stops, retracting slightly, airs settling. "Dolly?"

"Er, yeah?"

"I can't feel it anymore, so I'm not sure if this is okay. After the stuff I said and did to you today, I understand if you need some time—"

I stroke his mustache in a way that I'm not sure how to feel about—kinda sexy, kinda skeevy—then give him the nod he's seeking. "I want this. I want you, all of you, all night, and all morning. Please. I missed you so much."

"Oh, thank Maka."

Rabidly, his mustache finds me—

Yeah, nope. Can't do it.

Not sure if he can feel it in me or not, but the mustache disappears seconds later. He gives me all the heat in his mouth—on my neck, on my shoulder, my cheek, my lips—as his hands work to pull the tie of the robe and find my body, as he wets his fingers in me and swells against me, as his teeth chew at me like a wolf suppressing its hunger. My body flushes as he takes command of it, still as adept at appraising my desires and delivering on them as ever. He may not be able to read my fluid emotions, but he can read my moans, my gasps, my lip pulling between my teeth, my curled toes, my gripping hands, the vocal direction I feel safe enough only to offer to him.

My genie spends hours pleasuring me, magically reverting my body back to the beginning every time I break, desperately trying to show me his love to make up for the wounds his actions caused. He tastes me. All of me. He tastes me everywhere, shifting his passion from physical to emotional and back.

"You feel so fucking good."

"I love ya so much, babe."

"You're a goddess, Master."

"Tomorrow, I'll make you the best omelet in all the worlds."

This boy loves me, and it's apparent in every slide of his

fingers, every push of his hips, every suck of his lips. Our sweat mixes, our *juices* drip, until the sheets are stained with us and our love, and my hairline is dewed with effort.

He's over me, panting, his arms shaking as they hold him up.

I set a hand to his moisture-laden chest. "I'm exhausted, Vel."

"Oh, thank Maka."

He collapses and pulls me to him, cuddling me into his cocoon. We're messy, coated in pheromones, our bodies throbbing. The bedding around us seems far too regal, far too extravagant, to have witnessed what we just did to one another. Even in the world's softest, deepest, most decadent bed, Vel is my greatest comfort.

"Honey?" His voice rumbles against my cheek.

"Mm." I inspect our fingers, woven through one another in the dark.

"I want to ask you something, but I don't want you to take it the wrong way."

I reposition to search his expression and find him gazing at the ceiling.

"Go ahead."

His swallow is deep. "I feel the same about you. I still love you and want you just as much as I always have. What we have right now is okay. But—" He stretches his neck to offer a kiss to my hair that never fully dried from our earlier shower. "I want more. It's true, it can be a lot sometimes, but I don't care. I want a connection with you that no one else has. I want to give you everything you deserve, and I think the best way—" Again he swallows, nervous over whatever he's about to ask me. "When you and Arrik untether—" He starts anew: "Dolly Jones, will you tether me. Like, forever?"

It strikes me squarely in the pulse.

"Is that . . . normal? Is that allowed?"

"I don't care if it is. It's what I want. Is it what you want?"

Our relationship isn't conventional. Because who falls in love with their GENIE? So maybe for us, a marriage proposal isn't conventional either. Maybe this is what means so, so much more.

He's fighting to retain control of his breath. It shivers against his lips, his body tense as he awaits my response.

"Yes, Velis Reilhander-Evangeline, I will tether you. Like, forever."

The glimmer of emotion shows in his eyes. He lets it stay a tender moment before burying it with snark. "Ugh. Can we drop that last part?"

I snicker because this memory is one that will stick with us.

But really, I do feel bad about the state we left Gabri and Fiona in when we left their nymph cubby. Joell too, *significantly* less because she's a boyfriend-stealing bitch. But still. Maybe one of Vel's ambiguous roles as laird can be as an ambassador to their world or something. Maybe we can do something to help.

There will be time for that later. For now—

"As you wish, Laird Velis Reilhander."

"Good." Vel squeezes me to him. "Better."

One more kiss to his delicious neck, which dances one last time in response, before we both evaporate into the night.

"You're my favorite."

One of us coos it. Or maybe both of us do.

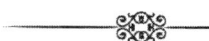

"*Master.*"

That voice isn't Vel's.

"*Dolly Jones.*"

It's up close and personal with my ear, all throaty and raspy and like it's been up all night shouting at trains. I even feel his breath.

I jerk awake, prepared to push the tattooed intruder off me, but there's no one leaning over the bed. The night looks no different. Vel is out, his inhales on the verge of snores.

"Arrik?" I hiss. "*Are you in our room?!*"

"No," says his voice in my ear, at a slightly less creepy distance. "But I *will* be in about two minutes. Get dressed. We need to have a conversation."

"You have access to our room?" Of course he does.

"I'll meet you on the balcony. I'm coming one way or another. Your choice whether or not you want to get dressed for it."

Click.

That click was definitely added for impact this time.

I wiggle out of Vel's clutch, earning me a moan of protest, but he's too exhausted to stir. I hurry to the ostentatious bathroom to clean myself up and slip into a T-shirt and sweatpants. I'm in the middle of splashing cold water on my face when I feel his phantom warmth on my ear.

"*I'm here.*"

I'm actually a little nervous. I'm not sure why.

Oh, *I* know why. Because Vel's hot older brother, whom I have a forced intimate connection with, is coming to steal me away in the middle of the night while my fiancé sleeps ten feet away.

But after what he's done for us, I feel I owe Arrik this much. Not to mention, I suspect he has as few friends as I do.

A conversation. The last one was illuminating. I'll fill Vel in in the morning.

My bare feet smudge the polished floor on the way to the balcony, where a shady silhouette shows through the listing curtains. The fairy lights have gone out, and the moon is lower on the horizon now. We're getting closer to morning.

Arrik magically swipes the curtains apart with a flashy little flick of his wrist, then reaches out to me like a devil come to spirit me away. He's barefoot, his painted chest bared, his jeans dipped low on his waist. His eyes shine like an animal of the night.

The moment my fingertips graze him, we're blipped away.

The shy wind escalates to something flirtier as we find ourselves at one of my least favorite places. What is it with djinn and heights?! I back into Arrik's muscle because we're near the edge of what I assume is a roof, looking out over the expanse of night-clad Makayen fields. The sinking moon shines over them, painting them in frosty silver.

"Sorry," Arrik says, feeling my fear. "Didn't mean to put us so close to the edge. I'm still recouping from today." His hands clamp my arms, and he slowly backs me away from a view as stunning as it is stomach-turning.

I twist to meet him. "This is the top of the manor, right?"

He gives one nod.

He looks . . . tired. He did just engage in several magical battles after living what looked to have been a mostly low-energy life. It's weird to see him this way. It's the same as that night in my mom's basement bathroom. Like he doesn't have the energy to hold up a front.

"Can you conjure me up a smoke?" I ask.

His mouth reacts like I've just asked him to go make out in the bar bathroom. "Really?"

At my nod, he produces one that's already lit and extends it out to me coolly.

"It's for you," I say. "Figured you might need one after all that."

"All what?"

"All day?"

He tucks it into his lips. "You're not wrong. Come on." He shoves his hands in his pockets and nods deeper onto the roof, lit stick dangling. I take my first step after him, and he stops. "Your feet are cold."

"Oh, they're—"

Without turning to look, he snaps over his shoulder, and my feet, though still bare, feel like they're being clasped between two warm palms.

"Thanks."

I wonder what sort of area we're walking over. Most of the manor's roof isn't flat like this. The majority is slanted, with those cupolas coated in reflective mosaics. So ridiculously extravagant, it seems like it would take a solid month to map the place out. And Velis is going to lord over all of it. I picture him behind a huge desk, dicking around, re-shuffling paperwork and low-key freaking out. I'm guessing he'll need to grow into it like shoes that are too big.

"How is he?" Arrik says without turning back.

"He's good. Lots of groveling, but he's good now."

"Yeah," Arrik says with a bit of a scoff. "I'll bet he is."

The way he says it, I'm instantly, horrifyingly reminded of the fact that he can damn near read my thoughts and was emotionally connected to me during my past few hours of nasty with Vel.

OH NO.

I wonder how much he picked up. He couldn't actually *hear* the things I asked Velis to do to me, right?

"Eh." He shrugs. "It was just like really vivid porn."

THAT'S SO MUCH WORSE.

"Heh."

"H-how are you doing with it all?" I ask his back.

"Clearly not as good as him."

Errrrr.

"I mean, how are you doing with everything that went down. Today was intense."

"Fuckin' understatement." He doesn't turn to look at me. And he doesn't answer me fully. He's locked into a truth oath, so maybe not answering is intentional. Or maybe he's just too tired.

"Thank you, Arrik. For everything you did today. Not just today. At my mom's. At my apartment. Even all the way back at that dance club when you chose not to take me. You've done a lot. For me and for him."

He glances back at me like I just said something highly offensive. "That's not necessary."

It is, though.

His bored eyes shift over me twice before turning away. "Almost there. Keep up."

Okay, grumpy.

Cinders pepper the ground as he gives his cigarette a flick. "It was good thinking. Getting him to take off the ring. Smart."

"Yeah, well, my other option was to wish for you to make yourself into a souped-up superhero version of yourself—Ink-Man, naturally—which I'm honestly kind of sad we never got to see. *Although*, I *could* always just wish for it randomly . . ."

This time, his glance back is humored, like he can't hold it in. "Up here." We've come to a place where the roof hits a wall up to another level. Arrik offers me a hand like he's going to escort me up a set of stairs, but there are no stairs. Chary, I accept, and he springs into the air with me as if propelled by an invisible coil.

I'm NOT okay with going even higher, and definitely not in this fashion!

"AHHH!" I cling to him.

His arm pulls me closer with no uncertainty. "You're okay."

I wonder how he makes his voice that way. Always so dull and unexcitable and at the same time harboring a million secrets. My warmed feet touch down gently. Arrik slowly releases me from his chest and then waits for my reaction.

Oh.

Oh.

Oh.

This is a small vantage that overlooks the rest of the roof. And the entirety of that lower level is being illuminated by the dancing light of candles lined around the perimeter.

I painted a mural on the roof last week, and no one knows about it.

Cool. Can I see it after we rescue Vel?

We've rescued Vel, and Arrik's showing me that mural. The reason for that rectangle of candles fighting the dark.

I grip his arm. I'm tired, my body weak, and the sheer beauty of it threatens to make my knees give.

"Oh, Arrik."

It's a woman's profile. A girl in her early twenties with long lashes and a perfect chin. Long, dark hair curls around her face like it's being coaxed forward by the wind. And she's blowing into her open palm to scatter flower petals across the rest of the open roof. The unfilled space is a lace-like pattern, almost like henna, intricate and detailed.

Arrik grips his chest and hunches from the warmth of my reaction to it.

"Is this her?" I ask with as much care as possible. "Is this Sarah?"

He straightens to observe his own work. "Mm."

"By magic or by hand?"

"By hand."

"It's beautiful. She was beautiful." I stand in awe of his talent, watching the light of those tiny flames prevail against a world of darkness to light this beautiful, whimsical girl, and imagine Arrik bent to the ground, meticulously crafting each lattice and loop.

"You like it?" he says.

I nod, finally wrenching my eyes away to see what kind of expression he's wearing. His face is serious in a way that's different from his normal boredom.

Oh.

This now feels wrong. This feels like a situation I shouldn't be in. This feels different.

"Arrik, why was I destined to save you outside Evangeline Tower?"

He's quiet.

"Arrik?"

He gives me a look like, 'come on, sweetheart.'

I knew it. The moment I saved him—that was the moment Arrik—

"You can't have feelings for me, Arrik. It doesn't work for you to have feelings for me. For so many reasons."

"I'm aware." He releases a bout of smoke into the night. "But the problem with that, sweetheart, is that you like me too. Maybe you haven't realized it yet, but I know you do. I feel it every time you touch me. Even more when I touch you."

He refrains from doing so now.

I take a step back from him, tightness in my chest. "I don't *like* you, Arrik. I love Velis. A lot. And I'm not a cheater. Whatever you're feeling in me, it's not—"

"*Relax.* I'm not some adolescent. Hormones don't dictate my actions, Dolly Jones. You're cute, but you aren't that—" His mouth catches on itself. He ends on 'that,' picturing any number of *that's* to get around the truth. You aren't that tall. You aren't that good at karate.

This is not good. I know I can't possibly have a crush on him. A physical response does not mean an emotional one.

But he definitely has one on me. And I know him now. And that complicates things. Arrows or not, the bond between a djinn and their master is a lot more intimate than I realized.

"Like I said, *relax*. I'm not telling you as some broke-ass effort to win you over. I'm telling you so that you can protect yourself." The mural draws his gaze. "If I don't, you're going to wind up hating me for real. And I didn't like the way that felt when we played pretend."

He'd do anything to make himself feel better about himself. Anything.

"You want me to make a wish?" I guess.

"I want you to make a wish," he affirms. He holds his roll between his fingers at his side and gazes into the Makayen night sky. "I want you to wish that the only way we can ever become physical is if you initiate it."

The wind drops to give us silence. "Arrik, what?"

"There's a reason our vessels can't go after humans we could become attached to. When I feel your attraction for me, it amplifies my own for you. That resonance could get hard to resist, especially now that I've tasted your soul and know what's under there."

I study his profile and notice his arm is now tattooed with one of those swan creatures we saw today, his neck boasting a shape that resembles the prettiest crystal in the nexus.

"Okay," I say. "Thank you."

"Sure."

He doesn't make eye contact—merely gazes off into the night sky. Wind that reminds me of early autumn in the human world pulls at the sleeves of my oversized T-shirt. The flames below react.

"Arrik, I wish that you and I would never become physical."

"H-hey!" His complex gaze strikes me. "That's not the way

you were supposed to—" His demeanor reverts. "Hmph. Won't work anyway. Too much destiny manipulation."

Implying our destiny is for us to become physical?! No way. There's got to be some loophole being exploited. Arrik thrives on my questioning of reality.

Now, he's giving me 'you tried a bad thing' eyes, and there's a bit of seductive bulliness to him when he tells me to, "Do it the right way, Master."

Dear lord, his hotness is the sort that should be exorcised by a priest.

"Arrik—" I prepare to offer one last wish to the genie who will someday become my brother. "If we ever become physical, I wish that I would be the one to initiate it."

The flash of his eyes is crisp and haunting in the night.

"Granted."

After, we stand side by side awkwardly, the night chill most definitely nipping him out. I wonder if he feels any different after granting that wish.

The girl painted below us seems to be caught in a moment of longing for something over the horizon. The style of Arrik's art is so heavy-handed. It looks like he presses down hard with every stroke, and yet he's able to pull it together into something like this. Something delicate as a whole.

I saw a really strong heart change once...

I wish I could ask him what Beckham did to her.

There's quiet, and then—

"*He gave her everything she ever wanted.*"

It's barely words. Phantom enough to have been the wind.

"*He gave her things that weren't good for her. Things I wouldn't give her.*"

Things that were bad enough to end her life? I wonder how Arrik even met her.

But even the wind won't answer that one.

"Come on." Arrik gestures with his head. "I'll take you back to your 'big-lipped lover.' Your bedroom thoughts are weird, by the way. And dorky."

OH MY GOD NO.

Smirk bordering on evil, he blinks us away and back onto the balcony, where swishing curtains beckon. His hand falls from my elbow, and he meanders to the Cinderella-esque railing to finish a cigarette that must have been magically prolonged. He blows a string of smoke rings, which, upon closer inspection, are actually smoke *spheres*, against the moon. "Nighty night, Master."

This is it. This is the end of our . . . whatever that was.

"Thanks for today, Arrik. Really. But no more nighttime telepathy, okay?"

"Is that a formal request that will count as betrayal if I disobey? What if there's an emergency?"

I'm thinking. "Fine. In cases of emergency—"

"You never learn. Who's to say what is and what isn't an emergency? Careful, love. There are wicked djinn everywhere, out to get a taste of that soul."

Hearty eye roll. "Night, Arrik. Get some sleep."

But he pulls my attention as I'm about to start for the suite. "Wait."

I do. I wait a long moment. But he just stands an abnormally long time while those curtains swish and the night air whispers. "All right," he says. "Nighty night."

Weird.

I start for the room but notice something before I do.

That cigarette is gone. It was just between his fingers, and now it's gone. And the moon. It's definitely lower than it was just seconds ago.

"A-Arrik?! Did you just ERASE my memory again?!"

There's the slow, anarchic stretch of a grin on his mouth. "See ya around, Dolly Jones." With a two-fingered wave, he leaves me standing on the balcony drenched in moony glow, the curtains licking at my back.

Mother. Clucker.

A Bomb-Ass Genie
Epilogue

CHAPTER 25
Up All Night
ARRIK

Fucking sucks.

Of course fucking Laird Velis would have a soulmate like that. Just like he had a mother like that. And a grandfather like that.

She's cool.

The ceiling lists with core neutral energy. I give it my eyes and wait for the calm to come. The sprites are vibing. It feels good in here. I suffocate myself with a long pull and funnel cherry red smoke out my nose.

I never got to show her the inside of my vessel.

Probably for the best. The only other person who ever got that far—

I wish you wouldn't ever speak my name again!

Sigh. Even in death.

They're different. She and Master. There are similarities. But they're different. I bet *Dolly Jones* would have treated that whole situation differently. She isn't impressed by mediocrity. She sniffed Beck out within minutes.

Sharp girl.

I pull the joint in with my tongue and feel the burn on my cheek before evaporating it away. I stare at the ceiling.

Sleep.
Sleep.
Fucking SLEEP.
Ping!
A ripple hits the eye of my mind.
No. It's fourteen after night. I'm not picking that up.
Ping! Ping!
Take a hint.
Ping! Ping! Ping!
Fucking hell.

"Ugh." I snap to summon my Ray from the abyss and roll onto my side, blinded by the light of the veil. Jesus Christ, how many times did Beckham call me today? Even a few from the ex-lady herself. But this one is, "Jeb?"

Some nerve after he tattled on me.

I dip a finger into the veil to open it for him. "What do you want, loser?"

The tantrum comes before he's even materialized within the frame. "HAVE YOU LOST YOUR MIND, ARRIK?! What are you THINKING, crossing them like that?! Mother is—! And Beckham is—! And you should SEE what—"

"Worry about yourself, Jeb."

Fuck. The sprites are already looking restless. Scary face. Scary aura. He's always been cloaked in that stratum of rage.

"What do you want?" I carry on. "I'm trying to sleep."

"Hold on, are you back at the MANOR?! Is that your room?! Is *she* there with you?"

"You keep notecards for all the questions they told you to ask me?"

"Oh, stop. I was just trying to save you from your reckless, lecherous self like I failed to do six years ago. You're going to be completely disinherited if you keep this up. Or worse."

"*If* Beckham takes over," I'm sure to clarify. "And I don't appreciate being reamed out in the middle of the night. I'm hanging up."

"NO. Wait." Jeb's quiet, swallowing that temper that so easily flares in him. Sucks for him. Beck took his share. I mostly passed it up. And Jeb got stuck with the rest. "I need a favor," he says.

"I owe you no favors."

"A new one. I need your—I need Dolly Jones."

The tanks oxygenate.

"Goodbye, Jeb."

"Wait! This is personal. Not related to Beck or Mother. I need her, Arrik."

He still looks scary. But that's his version of desperate. Desperately asking his big brother to step in and save him from the dark. *Again.* "What the fuck for?" I ask.

He checks the space behind his shoulder before returning to his Ray. "I need her to convince my master to start using his wishes."

"Ha!" My head falls backward. "After all the shit you gave the kid. Must be something in the water. You know, *I've* never failed to deliver."

"*Shut up.* This is your fault. He was already having issues building trust, but after seeing the way you were with her in that alley, he's convinced you're a demon and that I am too. He said he's prepared to hold out until I *give up.*" Jeb emits a grunt of frustration. "I contracted him through my vessel. There is no *giving* up."

I shrug. "Not my problem. You're a shit wish granter. Stay there and rot."

"*Arrik.* Enough. I want my life back, and I know you do too. Even if I hadn't called them, they would have found out. Better that one of us stay in their good graces if you're going to do whatever it is you're doing. You missed *multiple* check-ins. I knew there was no turning back for you. Get me Dolly Jones. I'll make this worth your while."

There's nothing he could give me that would make me betray my mast—

"Sarah. I'll tell you where they put her."

The sprites list.

"Did you hear me? Her body. I can say it out loud now that Beck's given up her soul."

The ceiling eddies.

"It almost seems like you actually like this one, which is comically stupid, even for you. She's Velis's *mate*, Arrik. Even if she makes it through this alive, there's no way you'll be able to keep her. Why must you always *lust* for things you can't have?" Jeb tosses another glance over his shoulder. "Think about my offer and call me back."

Ping!

My younger brother's scary mug ripples away.

I throw my Ray across the room and watch its light fade into the dark before I return my attention to the ceiling.

Where they put her.

That is tempting.

I pull my fingers through the layers of Maka in the air to manifest the soul I recently re-acquired. Cold and withered, it's nothing like the soul I tasted today.

But it smells like her, faintly.

'Her.'

I wish you wouldn't ever speak my name again!

I crumple it into my fist to send it back into the abyss.

That soul is barely a soul anymore. Especially after being around one so—

Mm.

Velis is a goddamned saint for leaving Master's soul intact. I've only felt whispers of affection from her, but to have the real thing?

"We don't really devour souls, but I would devour yours, Dolly Jones. And then I would do things to you that would make you *beg* me not to stop."

I close my eyes and listen to the speed of her heart far across the manor. She's sleeping. She feels warm. I focus on the feel of her fatigue. Make it my own, the way I did back at her mother's. Now that she's mine, it's closer. Like she's under these covers with me. Like my mouth is in her neck.

Breathe with her.
Breathe.
Master.

Acknowledgments

Listen, okay, when I wrote Come True, I NEVER expected the kind of sparkling feedback you guys would give me. I am a sufferer of perpetual self-doubt, and let me tell you, the things you had to say about that book made me really start to look at myself in a different light. To everyone that took the time to read and review Book 1, thank you. You are the reason Book 2 exists. I love this series. I love the genies, the magic, the steam. There's so much of me in Dolly, so many of her struggles a reflection of my own journey. I love Velis. He's the best parts of the people I've dated, and Arrik, well, I love him too. Whatever else happens in this series, I promise you, I'll take care of these characters you've come to know and cheer on. I'll write a million books in this series if you'll let me, so please, help me spread the word, leave a review, get others on this genie train, and consequently allow me the time and resources I need to do this thing right. I can't do it alone.

To my MTP tribe, you guys are fucking amazing. When I joined this publishing company, I expected resources, some exposure, but I never expected to make so many incredible friends, friends that I have so much in common with and jive with on such a kooky, wonderful level. The struggles we all face as people creating art and trying to get that art noticed, it's such a bonding thing, and I'm honored to be alongside you witty emmer-effers on this journey.

To my editor, Meg, you wonderful, magical creature, I don't think I could release a book without you now. Didn't you know that editing is supposed to be painful? Stop making it so fun. (Kidding! Don't change!)

To my cover artist, Em, I don't really think it needs to be said, but you continue to KILL it. I'm certain I'll pull new readers just based on how sexy Arrik looks on that cover. Who cares what the book is about, right? Haha, thank you for putting so much care into every cover you create. I ADORE it!

To my IRL friends and family, thanks for bearing with me this summer while I disappeared off the face of the planet (seriously—I was in Makaya) to write this book. Your texts of encouragement and catering to my chaotic schedule to show your support mean so, so much to me. To 'the nurse,' Kent, thank you for dealing with my batshit neurosis while I obsessively checked reviews, reread the same passages out loud while editing over and over, and asked for constant reassurance all while you were dealing with your own career and education. I'm so proud of what you accomplished this year while I was low-key stealing the spotlight. And to my mom, thanks for reading every single review right along with me, liking all my cringy TikToks, and being a soundboard throughout this entire process. I love you to the moons and back.

Last but not least—thank you, Kara (@ecce.libri) for that 'OMGenie!' line from your review that I totally, shamelessly stole for the book. I told you I would!

I hope you guys loved this book. I hope I did Arrik justice. I hope you'll stick around to see what's in store for Book 3. Didja . . . didja sneak a peek of the title yet? *Side-eye emoji* Stay fabulous, weirdos!

Xoxo,
Brindi

About Brindi Quinn

Brindi Quinn is a Minnesota-based author known for swoony romances and sparkly worldbuilding. Since 2011, she has penned over a dozen young adult and new adult novels, often blurring genre conventions to bring readers a unique blend of fantasy, paranormal romance, science fiction, and comedy. Brindi adores quirky yet relatable characters and loves playing with reluctant or forbidden attraction, adding in a healthy dose of forced proximity and banter wherever she can.

When not headfirst in her work, Brindi enjoys biking with her soulmate, playing video games with her dog, and engaging with the book community. She is also one of the founders of Never and Ever Publishing.

Find out more at: www.brindiful.com

- facebook.com/brindiful
- instagram.com/brindiful
- tiktok.com/@brindiful
- goodreads.com/brindiful
- bookbub.com/authors/brindi-quinn
- youtube.com/@brindiquinn

Paranormal & Dystopian Romance Books by Brindi Quinn

Evermore

The Come True Series

Come True (2022)

Granted (2022)

Dreams Really Do (2023)

Bottle Service (2024)

The Lightborne Duet

Lightborne (2016)

Nightborne (2018)

Standalones

The World Remains (2013)

The Pursuit of Zillow Stone (2017)

Epic Fantasy Romance Books by Brindi Quinn

N & E

The Crown Saga

A Crown of Echoes (2020)

A Crown of Reveries (2020)

A Crown of Felling (2021)

A Crown of Dawn (2021)

The Crown Saga (Omnibus, 2021)

The Farellah Series

Heart of Farellah (2011)

Moon of Farellah (2011)

Fate of Farellah (2011)

Atto's Tale (2013)

Young Adult Romance Books by Brindi Quinn

Forever Young

The Eternity Duet

EverDare (2013)

NeverSleep (2014)

The Eternity Duet (Omnibus, 2016)

Standalones

Seconds: The Shared Soul Chronicles (2012)

Sil in a Dark World (2012)

The Death and Romancing of Marley Craw (2014)